James Russell Lowell

Lowell's Prose Works

Vol. 1

James Russell Lowell

Lowell's Prose Works
Vol. 1

ISBN/EAN: 9783337371777

Printed in Europe, USA, Canada, Australia, Japan

Cover: Foto ©Andreas Hilbeck / pixelio.de

More available books at **www.hansebooks.com**

LITERARY ESSAYS

I.

BY

JAMES RUSSELL LOWELL

BOSTON AND NEW YORK

HOUGHTON, MIFFLIN AND COMPANY

The Riverside Press, Cambridge

M DCCCC

CONTENTS

PREFATORY NOTE TO THE ESSAYS

THE greater part of the literary and critical essays here collected was originally written as lectures for an audience consisting not only of my own classes but also of such other members of the University as might choose to attend them. This will account for, if it do not excuse, a more rhetorical tone in them here and there than I should have allowed myself had I been writing for the eye and not for the ear. They were meant to be suggestive of certain broader principles of criticism based on the comparative study of literature in its large meaning, rather than methodically pedagogic, to stimulate rather than to supply the place of individual study. This was my deliberate intention, but I am sensible that it may have been in a manner forced upon me by my own limitations; for, though capable of whatever drudgery in acquisition, I am by temperament impatient of detail in communicating what I have acquired, and too often put into a parenthesis or a note conclusions arrived at by long study and reflection when perhaps it had been wiser to expand them, not to mention that much of my illustration was extemporaneous and is now lost to me. I am apt also to fancy that what has long been familiar to my own mind must be equally so to the minds of others, and this uncomfortable suspicion makes one shy of insisting on what may be already only too little in need of it. But Sir Kenelm Digby, in the dedication of what Sir Thomas Browne calls his "excellent Treaty of Bodies," has said better than I could what I wish to say. "For besides what faylings may be in the matter, I cannot doubt but that even in the expressions of it, there must often be great obscurity and shortnesse; which I, who have my thoughts filled with the things themselves, am not aware of. So that, what peradventure may seeme very full to me, because every imperfect touch bringeth into my mind the entire notion and whole chain of circumstances belonging to that thing I have so often beaten upon, may appeare very crude and maymed to a stranger, that cannot guesse what I would be at, otherwise than as my direct words do lead him."

Let me add that in preparing these papers for the press I omitted much illustrative and subsidiary matter, and this I regret when it is too late. Five or six lectures, for instance, were condensed into the essay on Rousseau. The dates attached were those of publication, but the bulk of the material was written many years earlier, some of it so long ago as 1854. I have refrained from modify-

ing what was written by one — I know not whether
to say so much older or so much younger than I —
but at any rate different in some important respects, and this partly from deference to him,
partly from distrust of myself.

J. R. L.

25th *April*, 1890.

LITERARY ESSAYS

A MOOSEHEAD JOURNAL

1853

ADDRESSED TO THE EDELMANN STORG AT THE BAGNI DI LUCCA.

THURSDAY, 11*th August*. — I knew as little yesterday of the interior of Maine as the least penetrating person knows of the inside of that great social millstone which, driven by the river Time, sets imperatively agoing the several wheels of our individual activities. Born while Maine was still a province of native Massachusetts, I was as much a foreigner to it as yourself, my dear Storg. I had seen many lakes, ranging from that of Virgil's Cumæan to that of Scott's Caledonian Lady; but Moosehead, within two days of me, had never enjoyed the profit of being mirrored in my retina. At the sound of the name, no reminiscential atoms (according to Kenelm Digby's Theory of Association, — as good as any) stirred and marshalled themselves in my brain. The truth is, we think lightly of Nature's penny shows, and estimate what we see by the cost of the ticket. Empedocles gave

his life for a pit-entrance to Ætna, and no doubt
found his account in it. Accordingly, the clean
face of Cousin Bull is imaged patronizingly in
Lake George, and Loch Lomond glasses the hurried countenance of Jonathan, diving deeper in the
streams of European association (and coming up
drier) than any other man. Or is the cause of our
not caring to see what is equally within the reach
of all our neighbors to be sought in that aristo-
cratic principle so deeply implanted in human
nature? I knew a pauper graduate who always
borrowed a black coat, and came to eat the Commencement dinner, — not that it was better than
the one which daily graced the board of the public institution in which he hibernated (so to speak)
during the other three hundred and sixty-four
days of the year, save in this one particular, that
none of his eleemosynary fellow-commoners could
eat it. If there are unhappy men who wish that
they were as the Babe Unborn, there are more who
would aspire to the lonely distinction of being that
other figurative personage, the Oldest Inhabitant.
You remember the charming irresolution of our
dear Esthwaite, (like Macheath between his two
doxies,) divided between his theory that he is under thirty, and his pride at being the only one of
us who witnessed the September gale and the re-
joicings at the Peace? Nineteen years ago I was
walking through the Franconia Notch, and stopped
to chat with a hermit, who fed with gradual logs the
unwearied teeth of a saw-mill. As the strident steel
slit off the *slabs* of the log, so did the less willing

machine of talk, acquiring a steadier up-and-down motion, pare away that outward bark of conversation which protects the core, and which, like other bark, has naturally most to do with the weather, the season, and the heat of the day. At length I asked him the best point of view for the Old Man of the Mountain.

" Dunno, — never see it."

Too young and too happy either to feel or affect the Horatian indifference, I was sincerely astonished, and I expressed it.

The log-compelling man attempted no justification, but after a little asked, " Come from Baws'n ? "

" Yes " (with peninsular pride).

" Goodle to see in the vycinity o' Baws'n."

" Oh, yes ! " I said ; and I thought, — see Boston and die ! see the State-Houses, old and new, the caterpillar wooden bridges crawling with innumerable legs across the flats of Charles ; see the Common, — largest park, doubtless, in the world, — with its files of trees planted as if by a drill-sergeant, and then for your *nunc dimittis !*

"·I should like, 'awl, I *should* like to stan' on Bunker Hill. You 've ben there offen, likely ? "

" N-o-o," unwillingly, seeing the little end of the horn in clear vision at the terminus of this Socratic perspective.

" 'Awl, my young frien', you 've larned neow thet wut a man *kin* see any day for nawthin', childern half price, he never *doos* see. Nawthin' pay, nawthin' vally."

With this modern instance of a wise saw, I departed, deeply revolving these things with myself, and convinced that, whatever the ratio of population, the average amount of human nature to the square mile differs little the world over. I thought of it when I saw people upon the Pincian wondering at the alchemist sun, as if he never burned the leaden clouds to gold in sight of Charles Street. I thought of it when I found eyes first discovering at Mont Blanc how beautiful snow was. As I walked on, I said to myself, There is one exception, wise hermit, — it is just these *gratis* pictures which the poet puts in his show-box, and which we all gladly pay Wordsworth and the rest for a peep at. The divine faculty is to see what everybody can look at.

While every well-informed man in Europe, from the barber down to the diplomatist, has his view of the Eastern Question, why should I not go personally down East and see for myself? Why not, like Tancred, attempt my own solution of the Mystery of the Orient, — doubly mysterious when you begin the two words with capitals? You know my way of doing things, to let them simmer in my mind gently for months, and at last do them *impromptu* in a kind of desperation, driven by the Eumenides of unfulfilled purpose. So, after talking about Moosehead till nobody believed me capable of going thither, I found myself at the Eastern Railway station. The only event of the journey hither (I am now at Waterville) was a boy hawking exhilaratingly the last great railroad smash, —

thirteen lives lost, — and no doubt devoutly wishing there had been fifty. This having a mercantile interest in horrors, holding stock, as it were, in murder, misfortune, and pestilence, must have an odd effect on the human mind. The birds of ill-omen, at whose sombre flight the rest of the world turn pale, are the ravens which bring food to this little outcast in the wilderness. If this lad give thanks for daily bread, it would be curious to inquire what that phrase represents to his understanding. If there ever be a plum in it, it is Sin or Death that puts it in. Other details of my dreadful ride I will spare you. Suffice it that I arrived here in safety, — in complexion like an Ethiopian serenader half got-up, and so broiled and peppered that I was more like a devilled kidney than anything else I can think of.

10 P. M. — The civil landlord and neat chamber at the "Elmwood House" were very grateful, and after tea I set forth to explore the town. It has a good chance of being pretty; but, like most American towns, it is in a hobbledehoy age, growing yet, and one cannot tell what may happen. A child with great promise of beauty is often spoiled by its second teeth. There is something agreeable in the sense of completeness which a walled town gives one. It is entire, like a crystal, — a work which man has succeeded in finishing. I think the human mind pines more or less where everything is new, and is better for a diet of stale bread. The number of Americans who visit the Old World, and the deep inspirations with which they breathe

the air of antiquity, as if their mental lungs had
been starved with too thin an atmosphere, is beginning to afford matter of speculation to obser-
vant Europeans. For my own part, I never saw a
house which I thought old enough to be torn down.
It is too like that Scythian fashion of knocking old
people on the head. I cannot help thinking that
the indefinable something which we call *character*
is cumulative, — that the influence of the same
climate, scenery, and associations for several generations is necessary to its gathering head, and that
the process is disturbed by continual change of
place. The American is nomadic in religion, in
ideas, in morals, and leaves his faith and opinions
with as much indifference as the house in which he
was born. However, we need not bother: Nature
takes care not to leave out of the great heart of
society either of its two ventricles of hold-back and
go-ahead.

It seems as if every considerable American town
must have its one specimen of everything, and so
there is a college in Waterville, the buildings of
which are three in number, of brick, and quite up
to the average ugliness which seems essential in
edifices of this description. Unhappily, they do
not reach that extreme of ugliness where it and
beauty come together in the clasp of fascination.
We erect handsomer factories for cottons, woollens,
and steam-engines, than for doctors, lawyers, and
parsons. The truth is, that, till our struggle with
nature is over, till this shaggy hemisphere is tamed
and subjugated, the workshop will be the college

whose degrees will be most valued. Moreover, steam has made travel so easy that the great university of the world is open to all comers, and the old cloister system is falling astern. Perhaps it is only the more needed, and, were I rich, I should like to found a few lazyships in my Alma Mater as a kind of counterpoise. The Anglo-Saxon race has accepted the primal curse as a blessing, has deified work, and would not have thanked Adam for abstaining from the apple. They would have dammed the four rivers of Paradise, substituted cotton for fig-leaves among the antediluvian populations, and commended man's first disobedience as a wise measure of political economy. But to return to our college. We cannot have fine buildings till we are less in a hurry. We snatch an education like a meal at a railroad-station. Just in time to make us dyspeptic, the whistle shrieks, and we must rush, or lose our places in the great train of life. Yet noble architecture is one element of patriotism, and an eminent one of culture, the finer portions of which are taken in by unconscious absorption through the pores of the mind from the surrounding atmosphere. I suppose we must wait, for we are a great bivouac as yet, rather than a nation on the march from the Atlantic to the Pacific, and pitch tents instead of building houses. Our very villages seem to be in motion, following westward the bewitching music of some Pied Piper of Hamelin. We still feel the great push toward sundown given to the peoples somewhere in the gray dawn of history. The cliff-swallow alone of all animated nature emigrates eastward.

Friday, 12th. — The coach leaves Waterville at five o'clock in the morning, and one must breakfast in the dark at a quarter past four, because a train starts at twenty minutes before five, — the passengers by both conveyances being pastured gregariously. So one must be up at half past three. The primary geological formations contain no trace of man, and it seems to me that these eocene periods of the day are not fitted for sustaining the human forms of life. One of the Fathers held that the sun was created to be worshipped at his rising by the Gentiles. The more reason that Christians (except, perhaps, early Christians) should abstain from these heathenish ceremonials. As one arriving by an early train is welcomed by a drowsy maid with the sleep scarce brushed out of her hair, and finds empty grates and polished mahogany, on whose arid plains the pioneers of breakfast have not yet encamped, so a person waked thus unseasonably is sent into the world before his faculties are up and dressed to serve him. It might have been for this reason that my stomach resented for several hours a piece of fried beefsteak which I forced upon it, or, more properly speaking, a piece of that leathern conveniency which in these regions assumes the name. You will find it as hard to believe, my dear Storg, as that quarrel of the Sorbonists, whether one should say *ego amat* or no, that the use of the gridiron is unknown hereabout, and so near a river named after St. Lawrence, too!

To-day has been the hottest day of the season,

yet our drive has not been unpleasant. For a considerable distance we followed the course of the Sebasticook River, a pretty stream with alternations of dark brown pools and wine-colored rapids. On each side of the road the land had been cleared, and little one-story farm-houses were scattered at intervals. But the stumps still held out in most of the fields, and the tangled wilderness closed in behind, striped here and there with the slim white trunks of the elm. As yet only the edges of the great forest have been nibbled away. Sometimes a root-fence stretched up its bleaching antlers, like the trophies of a giant hunter. Now and then the houses thickened into an unsocial-looking village, and we drove up to the grocery to leave and take a mail-bag, stopping again presently to water the horses at some pallid little tavern, whose one red-curtained eye (the bar-room) had been put out by the inexorable thrust of Maine Law. Had Shenstone travelled this road, he would never have written that famous stanza of his; had Johnson, he would never have quoted it. They are to real inns as the skull of Yorick to his face. Where these villages occurred at a distance from the river, it was difficult to account for them. On the river-bank, a saw-mill or a tannery served as a logical premise, and saved them from total inconsequentiality. As we trailed along, at the rate of about four miles an hour, it was discovered that one of our mail-bags was missing. "Guess somebody 'll pick it up," said the driver coolly; "'t any rate, likely there's nothin' in it." Who knows how long it took some Elam D. or Zebulon K. to compose the missive intrusted to that vagrant bag, and how much longer to persuade Pamela Grace or Sophronia Melissa that it had really and truly been written? The discovery of our loss was made by a tall man who sat next to me on the top of the coach, every one of whose senses seemed to be prosecuting its several investigation as we went along. Presently, sniffing gently, he remarked: "'Pears to me 's though I smelt sunthin'. Ain't the aix het, think?" The driver pulled up, and, sure enough, the off fore-wheel was found to be smoking. In three minutes he had snatched a rail from the fence, made a lever, raised the coach, and taken off the wheel, bathing the hot axle and box with water from the river. It was a pretty spot, and I was not sorry to lie under a beech-tree (Tityrus-like, meditating over my pipe) and watch the operations of the fire-annihilator. I could not help contrasting the ready helpfulness of our driver, all of whose wits were about him, current, and redeemable in the specie of action on emergency, with an incident of travel in Italy, where, under a somewhat similar stress of circumstances, our *vetturino* had nothing for it but to dash his hat on the ground and call on Sant' Antonio, the Italian Hercules.

There being four passengers for the Lake, a vehicle called a mud-wagon was detailed at Newport for our accommodation. In this we jolted and rattled along at a livelier pace than in the coach. As we got farther north, the country (especially

the hills) gave evidence of longer cultivation.
About the thriving town of Dexter we saw fine
farms and crops. The houses, too, became pret-
tier; hop-vines were trained about the doors, and
hung their clustering thyrsi over the open windows. A kind of wild rose (called by the country
folk the primrose) and asters were planted about
the door-yards, and orchards, commonly of natural
fruit, added to the pleasant home-look. But everywhere we could see that the war between the white
man and the forest was still fierce, and that it
would be a long while yet before the axe was
buried. The haying being over, fires blazed or
smouldered against the stumps in the fields, and
the blue smoke widened slowly upward through the
quiet August atmosphere. It seemed to me that I
could hear a sigh now and then from the immemorial pines, as they stood watching these camp-
fires of the inexorable invader. Evening set in,
and, as we crunched and crawled up the long
gravelly hills, I sometimes began to fancy that
Nature had forgotten to make the corresponding
descent on the other side. But erelong we were
rushing down at full speed; and, inspired by the
dactylic beat of the horses' hoofs, I essayed to repeat the opening lines of Evangeline. At the moment I was beginning, we plunged into a hollow,
where the soft clay had been overcome by a road of
unhewn logs. I got through one line to this cor-
duroy accompaniment, somewhat as a country choir
stretches a short metre on the Procrustean rack of
a long-drawn tune. The result was like this: —

"Thihis ihis thehe fohorest prihihimeheval; thehe murhurmuring pihines hahand thehe hehemlohocks!"

At a quarter past eleven, P. M., we reached Greenville, (a little village which looks as if it had dripped down from the hills, and settled in the hollow at the foot of the lake,) having accomplished seventy-two miles in eighteen hours. The tavern was totally extinguished. The driver rapped upon the bar-room window, and after a while we saw heat-lightnings of unsuccessful matches followed by a low grumble of vocal thunder, which I am afraid took the form of imprecation. Presently there was a great success, and the steady blur of lighted tallow succeeded the fugitive brilliance of the pine. A hostler fumbled the door open, and stood staring at but not seeing us, with the sleep sticking out all over him. We at last contrived to launch him, more like an insensible missile than an intelligent or intelligible being, at the slumbering landlord, who came out wide-awake, and welcomed us as so many half-dollars, — twenty-five cents each for bed, *ditto* breakfast. O Shenstone, Shenstone! The only roost was in the garret, which had been made into a single room, and contained eleven double-beds, ranged along the walls. It was like sleeping in a hospital. However, nice customs curtsy to eighteen-hour rides, and we slept.

Saturday, 13th. — This morning I performed my toilet in the bar-room, where there was an abundant supply of water, and a halo of interested spectators. After a sufficient breakfast, we embarked on the little steamer Moosehead, and were soon throbbing up the lake. The boat, it appeared, had been chartered by a party, this not being one of her regular trips. Accordingly we were mulcted in twice the usual fee, the philosophy of which I could not understand. However, it always comes easier to us to comprehend why we receive than why we pay. I dare say it was quite clear to the captain. There were three or four clearings on the western shore ; but after passing these, the lake became wholly primeval, and looked to us as it did to the first adventurous Frenchman who paddled across it. Sometimes a cleared point would be pink with the blossoming willow-herb, "a cheap and excellent substitute " for heather, and, like all such, not *quite* so good as the real thing. On all sides rose deep-blue mountains, of remarkably graceful outline, and more fortunate than common in their names. There were the Big and Little Squaw, the Spencer and Lily-bay Mountains. It was debated whether we saw Katahdin or not, (perhaps more useful as an intellectual exercise than the assured vision would have been), and presently Mount Kineo rose abruptly before us, in shape not unlike the island of Capri. Mountains are called great natural features, and why they should not retain their names long enough for these also to become naturalized, it is hard to say. Why should every new surveyor rechristen them with the gubernatorial patronymics of the current year? They are geological noses, and as they are aquiline or pug, indicate terrestrial idiosyncrasies. A cosmical physiognomist, after a glance at them, will draw no vague inference as to the character of the country. The word *nose* is no better than any other word ; but since the organ has got that name, it is convenient to keep it. Suppose we had to label our facial prominences every season with the name of our provincial governor, how should *we* like it? If the old names have no other meaning, they have that of age ; and, after all, meaning is a plant of slow growth, as every reader of Shakespeare knows. It is well enough to call mountains after their discoverers, for Nature has a knack of throwing doublets, and somehow contrives it that discoverers have good names. Pike's Peak is a curious hit in this way. But these surveyors' names have no natural *stick* in them. They remind one of the epithets of poetasters, which peel off like a badly gummed postage-stamp. The early settlers did better, and there is something pleasant in the sound of Graylock, Saddleback, and Great Haystack.

> "I love those names
> Wherewith the exiled farmer tames
> Nature down to companionship
>   With his old world's more homely mood,
> And strives the shaggy wild to clip
>   In the arms of familiar habitude."

It is possible that Mount Marcy and Mount Hitchcock may sound as well hereafter as Hellespont and Peloponnesus, when the heroes, their namesakes, have become mythic with antiquity. But that is to look forward a great way. I am no fanatic for Indian nomenclature, — the name of my native district having been Pigsgusset, — but let us at least agree on names for ten years.

There were a couple of loggers on board, in red flannel shirts, and with rifles. They were the first I had seen, and I was interested in their appearance. They were tall, well-knit men, straight as Robin Hood, and with a quiet, self-contained look that pleased me. I fell into talk with one of them.

"Is there a good market for the farmers here in the woods?" I asked.

"None better. They can sell what they raise at their doors, and for the best of prices. The lumberers want it all, and more."

"It must be a lonely life. But then we all have to pay more or less life for a living."

"Well, it *is* lonesome. Should n't like it. After all, the best crop a man can raise is a good crop of society. We don't live none too long, anyhow; and without society a fellow could n't tell more 'n half the time whether he was alive or not."

This speech gave me a glimpse into the life of the lumberers' camp. It was plain that there a man would soon find out how much alive he was, — there he could learn to estimate his quality, weighed in the nicest self-adjusting balance. The best arm at the axe or the paddle, the surest eye for a road or for the weak point of a *jam*, the steadiest foot upon the squirming log, the most persuasive voice to the tugging oxen, — all these things are rapidly settled, and so an aristocracy is evolved from this democracy of the woods, for good old mother Nature speaks Saxon still, and with her either Canning or Kenning means King.

A string of five loons was flying back and forth in long, irregular zigzags, uttering at intervals their wild, tremulous cry, which always seems far away, like the last faint pulse of echo dying among the hills, and which is one of those few sounds that, instead of disturbing solitude, only deepen and confirm it. On our inland ponds they are usually seen in pairs, and I asked if it were common to meet five together. My question was answered by a queer-looking old man, chiefly remarkable for a pair of enormous cowhide boots, over which large blue trousers of frocking strove in vain to crowd themselves.

"Wahl, 't ain't ushil," said he, "and it 's called a sign o' rain comin', that is."

"Do you think it will rain?"

With the caution of a veteran *auspex*, he evaded a direct reply. "Wahl, they *du* say it 's a sign o' rain comin'," said he.

I discovered afterward that my interlocutor was Uncle Zeb. Formerly, every New England town had its representative uncle. He was not a pawn-broker, but some elderly man who, for want of more defined family ties, had gradually assumed this avuncular relation to the community, inhabiting the border-land between respectability and the alms-house, with no regular calling, but ready for odd jobs at haying, wood-sawing, whitewashing, associated with the demise of pigs and the ailments of cattle, and possessing as much patriotism as might be implied in a devoted attachment to "New England" — with a good deal of sugar and very little

water in it.   Uncle Zeb was a good specimen of this
palæozoic class, extinct among us for the most part,
or surviving, like the Dodo, in the Botany Bays of
society.   He was ready to contribute (somewhat
muddily) to all general conversation; but his chief
topics were his boots and the 'Roostick war.   Upon
the lowlands and levels of ordinary palaver he
would make rapid and unlooked-for incursions;
but, provision failing, he would retreat to these
two fastnesses, whence it was impossible to dislodge
him, and to which he knew innumerable passes
and short cuts quite beyond the conjecture of common woodcraft.   His mind opened naturally to
these two subjects, like a book to some favorite
passage.   As the ear accustoms itself to any sound
recurring regularly, such as the ticking of a clock,
and, without a conscious effort of attention, takes
no impression from it whatever, so does the mind
find a natural safeguard against this pendulum
species of discourse, and performs its duties in the
parliament by an unconscious reflex action, like
the beating of the heart or the movement of the
lungs.   If talk seemed to be flagging, our Uncle
would put the heel of one boot upon the toe of the
other, to bring it within point-blank range, and
say, " Wahl, I stump the Devil himself to make
that 'ere boot hurt *my* foot," leaving us in doubt
whether it were the virtue of the foot or its case
which set at naught the wiles of the adversary; or,
looking up suddenly, he would exclaim, " Wahl,
we eat *some* beans to the 'Roostick war, I tell
you!"   When his poor old clay was wet with gin,

his thoughts and words acquired a rank flavor from it, as from too strong a fertilizer. At such times, too, his fancy commonly reverted to a prehistoric period of his life, when he singly had settled all the surrounding country, subdued the Injuns and other wild animals, and named all the towns.

We talked of the winter-camps and the life there. "The best thing is," said our Uncle, "to hear a log squeal thru the snow. Git a good, col', frosty mornin', in Febuary say, an' take an' hitch the critters on to a log that 'll scale seven thousan', an' it 'll squeal as pooty as an'thin' *you* ever hearn, I tell *you*."

A pause.

"Lessee,—seen Cal Hutchins lately?"

"No."

"Seems to me 's though I hed n't seen Cal sence the 'Roostick war. Wahl," &c., &c.

Another pause.

"To look at them boots you 'd think they was too large; but kind o' git your foot into 'em, and they 're as easy 's a glove." (I observed that he never seemed really to get his foot in,—there was always a qualifying *kind o'*.) "Wahl, my foot can play in 'em like a young hedgehog."

By this time we had arrived at Kineo,—a flourishing village of one house, the tavern kept by 'Squire Barrows. The 'Squire is a large, hearty man, with a voice as clear and strong as a northwest wind, and a great laugh suitable to it. His table is neat and well supplied, and he waits upon it himself in the good old landlordly fashion. One may be much better off here, to my thinking, than in one of those gigantic Columbaria which are foisted upon us patient Americans for hotels, and where one is packed away in a pigeon-hole so near the heavens that, if the comet should flirt its tail, (no unlikely thing in the month of flies,) one would run some risk of being brushed away. Here one does not pay his diurnal three dollars for an undivided five-hundredth part of the pleasure of looking at gilt gingerbread. Here one's relations are with the monarch himself, and one is not obliged to wait the slow leisure of those "attentive clerks" whose praises are sung by thankful deadheads, and to whom the slave who pays may feel as much gratitude as might thrill the heart of a brown-paper parcel toward the express-man who labels it and chucks it under his counter.

Sunday, 14*th*. — The loons were right. About midnight it began to rain in earnest, and did not hold up till about ten o'clock this morning. "This is a Maine dew," said a shaggy woodman cheerily, as he shook the water out of his wide-awake, "if it don't look out sharp, it 'll begin to rain afore it thinks on 't." The day was mostly spent within doors ; but I found good and intelligent society. We should have to be shipwrecked on Juan Fernandez not to find men who knew more than we. In these travelling encounters one is thrown upon his own resources, and is worth just what he carries about him. The social currency of home, the smooth-worn coin which passes freely among friends and neighbors, is of no account. We are thrown back upon the old system of barter; and, even with savages, we bring away only as much of the wild wealth of the woods as we carry beads of thought and experience, strung one by one in painful years, to pay for them with. A useful old jackknife will buy more than the daintiest Louis Quinze paper-folder fresh from Paris. Perhaps the kind of intelligence one gets in these out-of-the-way places is the best, — where one takes a fresh man after breakfast instead of the damp morning paper, and where the magnetic telegraph of human sympathy flashes swift news from brain to brain.

Meanwhile, at a pinch, to-morrow's weather can be discussed. The augury from the flight of birds is favorable, — the loons no longer prophesying rain. The wind also is hauling round to the right quarter, according to some, — to the wrong, if we are to believe others. Each man has his private barometer of hope, the mercury in which is more or less sensitive, and the opinion vibrant with its rise or fall. Mine has an index which can be moved mechanically. I fixed it at *set fair*, and resigned myself. I read an old volume of the Patent-Office Report on Agriculture, and stored away a beautiful pile of facts and observations for future use, which the current of occupation, at its first freshet, would sweep quietly off to blank oblivion. Practical application is the only mordant which will set things in the memory. Study, without it, is gymnastics, and not work, which alone will get intellectual bread. One learns more metaphysics from a single temptation than from all the philosophers. It is curious, though, how tyrannical the habit of reading is, and what shifts we make to escape thinking. There is no bore we dread being left alone with so much as our own minds. I have seen a sensible man study a stale newspaper in a country tavern, and husband it as he would an old shoe on a raft after shipwreck. Why not try a bit of hibernation? There are few brains that would not be better for living on their own fat a little while. With these reflections, I, notwithstanding, spent the afternoon over my Report. If our own experience is of so little use to us, what a dolt is he who recommends to man or nation the experience of others! Like the mantle in the old ballad, it is always too short or too long, and exposes or trips us up. "Keep out of that candle," says old Father Miller, "or you 'll get a singeing." "Pooh, pooh, father, I 've been dipped in the new asbestos preparation," and *frozz!* it is all over with young Hopeful. How many warnings have been drawn from Pretorian bands, and Janizaries, and Mamelukes, to make Napoleon III. impossible in 1851! I found myself thinking the same thoughts over again, when we walked later on the beach and picked up pebbles. The old time-ocean throws upon its shores just such rounded and polished results of the eternal turmoil, but we only see the beauty of those we have got the headache in stooping for ourselves, and wonder at the dull brown bits of common stone with which our comrades have stuffed their pockets. Afterwards this little fable came of it.

DOCTOR LOBSTER.

A PERCH, who had the toothache, once
Thus moaned, like any human dunce:
" Why must great souls exhaust so soon
Life's thin and unsubstantial boon ?
Existence on such sculpin terms,
Their vulgar loves and hard-won worms,
What is it all but dross to me,
Whose nature craves a larger sea ;
Whose inches, six from head to tail,
Enclose the spirit of a whale ;
Who, if great baits were still to win,
By watchful eye and fearless fin
Might with the Zodiac's awful twain
Room for a third immortal gain ?
Better the crowd's unthinking plan,
The hook, the jerk, the frying-pan !
O Death, thou ever roaming shark,
Ingulf me in eternal dark ! "

The speech was cut in two by flight:
A real shark had come in sight ;
No metaphoric monster, one
It soothes despair to call upon,
But stealthy, sidelong, grim, i-wis,
A bit of downright Nemesis ;
While it recovered from the shock,
Our fish took shelter 'neath a rock :
This was an ancient lobster's house,
A lobster of prodigious *nous*,
So old that barnacles had spread
Their white encampments o'er his head,
And of experience so stupend,
His claws were blunted at the end,
Turning life's iron pages o'er,
That shut and can be oped no more.

Stretching a hospitable claw,
" At once," said he, " the point I saw ;

My dear young friend, your case I rue,
Your great-great-grandfather I knew;
He was a tried and tender friend
I know, — I ate him in the end:
In this vile sea a pilgrim long,
Still my sight 's good, my memory strong;
The only sign that age is near
Is a slight deafness in this ear;
I understand your case as well
As this my old familiar shell;
This Welt-schmerz is a brand-new notion,
Come in since first I knew the ocean;
We had no radicals, nor crimes,
Nor lobster-pots, in good old times;
Your traps and nets and hooks we owe
To Messieurs Louis Blanc and Co.;
I say to all my sons and daughters,
Shun Red Republican hot waters;
No lobster ever cast his lot
Among the reds, but went to pot:
Your trouble 's in the jaw, you said?
Come, let me just nip off your head,
And, when a new one comes, the pain
Will never trouble you again:
Nay, nay, fear naught: 't is nature's law.
Four times I 've lost this starboard claw;
And still, erelong, another grew,
Good as the old, — and better too! "

The perch consented, and next day
An osprey, marketing that way,
Picked up a fish without a head,
Floating with belly up, stone dead.

MORAL.

Sharp are the teeth of ancient saws,
And sauce for goose is gander's sauce;
But perch's heads are n't lobster's claws.

Monday, 15th. — The morning was fine, and we
were called at four o'clock. At the moment my

door was knocked at, I was mounting a giraffe with
that charming *nil admirari* which characterizes
dreams, to visit Prester John. *Rat-tat-tat-tat!*
upon my door and upon the horn gate of dreams
also. I remarked to my skowhegan (the Tâtar for
giraffe-driver) that I was quite sure the animal had
the *raps*, a common disease among them, for I heard
a queer knocking noise inside him. It is the sound
of his joints, O Tambourgi! (an Oriental term
of reverence,) and proves him to be of the race of
El Keirat. *Rat-tat-tat-too!* and I lost my dinner
at the Prester's, embarking for a voyage to the
Northwest Carry instead. Never use the word
canoe, my dear Storg, if you wish to retain your
self-respect. *Birch* is the term among us back-
woodsmen. I never knew it till yesterday; but,
like a true philosopher, I made it appear as if I
had been intimate with it from childhood. The
rapidity with which the human mind levels itself
to the standard around it gives us the most pertinent warning as to the company we keep. It is
as hard for most characters to stay at their own
average point in all companies, as for a thermometer to say 65° for twenty-four hours together. I
like this in our friend Johannes Taurus, that he
carries everywhere and maintains his insular tem-
perature, and will have everything accommodate
itself to that. Shall I confess that this morning I
would rather have broken the moral law, than have
endangered the equipoise of the birch by my awk-
wardness? that I should have been prouder of a
compliment to my paddling, than to have had both

my guides suppose me the author of Hamlet?
Well, Cardinal Richelieu used to jump over chairs.

We were to paddle about twenty miles ; but we
made it rather more by crossing and recrossing the
lake. Twice we landed, — once at a camp, where
we found the cook alone, baking bread and gingerbread. Monsieur Soyer would have been startled
a little by this shaggy professor, — this Pre-Raphaelite of cookery. He represented the *salœratus*
period of the art, and his bread was of a brilliant
yellow, like those cakes tinged with saffron, which
hold out so long against time and the flies in little
water-side shops of seaport towns, — dingy extremities of trade fit to moulder on Lethe wharf. His
water was better, squeezed out of ice-cold granite
in the neighboring mountains, and sent through
subterranean ducts to sparkle up by the door of
the camp.

" There 's nothin' so sweet an' hulsome as your
real spring water," said Uncle Zeb, " git it pure.
But it 's dreffle hard to git it that ain't got sunthin'
the matter of it. Snow-water 'll burn a man's inside out, — I larned that to the 'Roostick war, —
and the snow lays terrible long on some o' thes'ere
hills. Me an' Eb Stiles was up old Ktahdn onct
jest about this time o' year, an' we come acrost a
kind o' holler like, as full o' snow as your stockin 's
full o' your foot. *I* see it fust, an' took an'
rammed a settin'-pole — wahl, it was all o' twenty
foot into 't, an' could n't fin' no bottom. I dunno
as there 's snow-water enough in this to do no hurt.
I don't somehow seem to think that *real* spring-

water's so plenty as it used to be." And Uncle
Zeb, with perhaps a little over-refinement of scru-
pulosity, applied his lips to the Ethiop ones of a
bottle of raw gin, with a kiss that drew out its very
soul, — a *basia* that Secundus might have sung.
He must have been a wonderful judge of water, for
he analyzed this, and detected its latent snow simply by his eye, and without the clumsy process of
tasting. I could not help thinking that he had
made the desert his dwelling-place chiefly in order
to enjoy the ministrations of this one fair spirit
unmolested.

We pushed on. Little islands loomed trembling
between sky and water, like hanging gardens.
Gradually the filmy trees defined themselves, the
aerial enchantment lost its potency, and we came
up with common prose islands that had so late been
magical and poetic. The old story of the attained
and unattained. About noon we reached the head
of the lake, and took possession of a deserted *wongen*, in which to cook and eat our dinner. No Jew,
I am sure, can have a more thorough dislike of salt
pork than I have in a normal state, yet I had
already eaten it raw with hard bread for lunch, and
relished it keenly. We soon had our tea-kettle
over the fire, and before long the cover was chattering with the escaping steam, which had thus vainly
begged of all men to be saddled and bridled, till
James Watt one day happened to overhear it.
One of our guides shot three Canada grouse, and
these were turned slowly between the fire and a bit
of salt pork, which dropped fatness upon them as

it fried. Although *my* fingers were certainly not made before knives and forks, yet they served as a convenient substitute for those more ancient inventions. We sat round, Turk-fashion, and ate thankfully, while a party of aborigines of the Mosquito tribe, who had camped in the *wongen* before we arrived, dined upon us. I do not know what the British Protectorate of the Mosquitoes amounts to; but, as I squatted there at the mercy of these bloodthirsty savages, I no longer wondered that the classic Everett had been stung into a willingness for war on the question.

"This 'ere 'd be about a complete place for a camp, ef there was on'y a spring o' sweet water handy. Frizzled pork goes wal, don't it? Yes, an' sets wal, too," said Uncle Zeb, and he again tilted his bottle, which rose nearer and nearer to an angle of forty-five at every gurgle. He then broached a curious dietetic theory: "The reason we take salt pork along is cos it packs handy: you git the greatest amount o' board in the smallest compass, — let alone that it 's more nourishin' than an'thin' else. It kind o' don't disgest so quick, but stays by ye, anourishin' ye all the while.

"A feller can live wal on frizzled pork an' good spring-water, git it *good*. To the 'Roostick war we did n't ask for nothin' better, — on'y beans." (*Tilt, tilt, gurgle, gurgle.*) Then, with an apparent feeling of inconsistency, "But then, come to git used to a particular *kind* o' spring-water, an' it makes a feller hard to suit. Most all sorts o' water taste kind o' *insipid* away from home. Now,

I 've gut a spring to my place that 's as sweet — wahl, it 's as sweet as maple sap. A feller acts about water jest as he doos about a pair o' boots. It 's all on it in gittin' wonted. Now, *them* boots," &c., &c. (*Gurgle, gurgle, gurgle, smack!*)

All this while he was packing away the remains of the pork and hard bread in two large firkins. This accomplished, we reëmbarked, our uncle on his way to the birch essaying a kind of song in four or five parts, of which the words were hilarious and the tune profoundly melancholy, and which was finished, and the rest of his voice apparently jerked out of him in one sharp falsetto note, by his tripping over the root of a tree. We paddled a short distance up a brook which came into the lake smoothly through a little meadow not far off. We soon reached the Northwest Carry, and our guide, pointing through the woods, said: "That 's the Cannydy road. You can travel that clearn to Kebeck, a hunderd an' twenty mile," — a privilege of which I respectfully declined to avail myself. The offer, however, remains open to the public. The Carry is called two miles; but this is the estimate of somebody who had nothing to lug. I had a headache and all my baggage, which, with a traveller's instinct, I had brought with me. (P. S. — I did not even take the keys out of my pocket, and both my bags were wet through before I came back.) *My* estimate of the distance is eighteen thousand six hundred and seventy-four miles and three quarters, — the fraction being the part left to be travelled after one of my com-

panions most kindly insisted on relieving me of
my heaviest bag. I know very well that the ancient Roman soldiers used to carry sixty pounds'
weight, and all that; but I am not, and never shall
be, an ancient Roman soldier, — no, not even in
the miraculous Thundering Legion. Uncle Zeb
slung the two provender firkins across his shoulder,
and trudged along, grumbling that " he never see
sech a contrairy pair as them." He had begun
upon a second bottle of his "particular kind o'
spring-water," and, at every rest, the gurgle of this
peripatetic fountain might be heard, followed by a
smack, a fragment of mosaic song, or a confused
clatter with the cowhide boots, being an arbitrary
symbol, intended to represent the festive dance.
Christian's pack gave him not half so much trouble
as the firkins gave Uncle Zeb. It grew harder
and harder to sling them, and with every fresh
gulp of the Batavian elixir, they got heavier. Or
rather, the truth was, that his hat grew heavier,
in which he was carrying on an extensive manu-
facture of bricks without straw. At last affairs
reached a crisis, and a particularly favorable pitch
offering, with a puddle at the foot of it, even *the*
boots afforded no sufficient ballast, and away went
our uncle, the satellite firkins accompanying faithfully his headlong flight. Did ever exiled monarch
or disgraced minister find the cause of his fall in
himself? Is there not always a strawberry at the
bottom of our cup of life, on which we can lay all
the blame of our deviations from the straight path?
Till now Uncle Zeb had contrived to give a gloss

of volition to smaller stumblings and gyrations, by exaggerating them into an appearance of playful burlesque. But the present case was beyond any such subterfuges. He held a bed of justice where he sat, and then arose slowly, with a stern determination of vengeance stiffening every muscle of his face. But what would he select as the culprit? " It 's that cussed firkin," he mumbled to himself. " I never knowed a firkin cair on so, — no, not in the 'Roostehicick war. There, go long, will ye? and don't come back till you 've larned how to walk with a genelman ! " And, seizing the unhappy scapegoat by the" bail, he hurled it into the forest. It is a curious circumstance, that it was not the firkin containing the bottle which was thus condemned to exile.

The end of the Carry was reached at last, and, as we drew near it, we heard a sound of shouting and laughter. It came from a party of men making hay of the wild grass in Seboomok meadows, which lie around Seboomok pond, into which the Carry empties itself. Their camp was near, and our two hunters set out for it, leaving us seated in the birch on the plashy border of the pond. The repose was perfect. Another heaven hallowed and deepened the polished lake, and through that nether world the fish-hawk's double floated with balanced wings, or, wheeling suddenly, flashed his whitened breast against the sun. As the clattering kingfisher flew unsteadily across, and seemed to push his heavy head along with ever-renewing effort, a visionary mate flitted from downward tree to tree below. Some tall alders shaded us from the sun. in whose yellow afternoon light the drowsy forest was steeped, giving out that wholesome resinous perfume, almost the only warm odor which it is refreshing to breathe. The tame hay-cocks in the midst of the wildness gave one a pleasant reminiscence of home, like hearing one's native tongue in a strange country.

Presently our hunters came back, bringing with them a tall, thin, active-looking man, with black eyes, that glanced unconsciously on all sides, like one of those spots of sunlight which a child dances up and down the street with a bit of looking-glass. This was M., the captain of the hay-makers, a famous river-driver, and who was to have fifty men under him next winter. I could now understand that sleepless vigilance of eye. He had consented to take two of our party in his birch to seek for moose. A quick, nervous, decided man, he got them into the birch, and was off instantly, without a superfluous word. He evidently looked upon them as he would upon a couple of logs which he was to deliver at a certain place. Indeed, I doubt if life and the world presented themselves to Napier himself in a more logarithmic way. His only thought was to do the immediate duty well, and to pilot his particular raft down the crooked stream of life to the ocean beyond. The birch seemed to feel him as an inspiring soul, and slid away straight and swift for the outlet of the pond. As he disappeared under the over-arching alders of the brook, our two hunters could ·not repress a grave and measured applause. There is never any extravagance among these woodmen; their eye, accustomed to reckoning the number of feet which a tree will *scale*, is rapid and close in its guess of the amount of stuff in a man. It was *laudari a laudato*, however, for they themselves were accounted good men in a birch. I was amused, in talking with them about him, to meet with an instance of that tendency of the human mind to assign some utterly improbable reason for gifts which seem unaccountable. After due praise, one of them said, "I guess he 's got some Injun in him," although I knew very well that the speaker had a thorough contempt for the red-man, mentally and physically. Here was mythology in a small way, — the same that under more favorable auspices hatched Helen out of an egg and gave Merlin an Incubus for his father. I was pleased with all I saw of M. He was in his narrow sphere a true ἄναξ ἀνδρῶν, and the ragged edges of his old hat seemed to become coronated as I looked at him. He impressed me as a man really educated, — that is, with his aptitudes *drawn out* and ready for use. He was A. M. and LL. D. in Woods College, — Axe-master and Doctor of Logs. Are not *our* educations commonly like a pile of books laid over a plant in a pot? The compressed nature struggles through at every crevice, but can never get the cramp and stunt out of it. We spend all our youth in building a vessel for our voyage of life, and set forth with streamers flying; but the moment we come nigh the great loadstone mountain of our proper destiny, out leap all our carefully-driven bolts and nails, and we get many a mouthful of good salt brine, and many a buffet of the rough water of experience, before we secure the bare right to live.

We now entered the outlet, a long-drawn aisle of alder, on each side of which spired tall firs, spruces, and white cedars. The motion of the birch reminded me of the gondola, and they represent among water-craft the *felidæ*, the cat tribe, stealthy, silent, treacherous, and preying by night. I closed my eyes, and strove to fancy myself in the dumb city, whose only horses are the bronze ones of St. Mark and that of Colleoni. But Nature would allow no rival, and bent down an alder-bough to brush my cheek and recall me. Only the robin sings in the emerald chambers of these tall sylvan palaces, and the squirrel leaps from hanging balcony to balcony.

The rain which the loons foreboded had raised the west branch of the Penobscot so much, that a strong current was setting back into the pond; and, when at last we brushed through into the river, it was full to the brim, — too full for moose, the hunters said. Rivers with low banks have always the compensation of giving a sense of entire fulness. The sun sank behind its horizon of pines, whose pointed summits notched the rosy west in an endless black *sierra*. At the same moment the golden moon swung slowly up in the east, like the other scale of that Homeric balance in which Zeus weighed the deeds of men. Sunset and moonrise at once! Adam had no more in Eden -- except the head of Eve upon his shoulder. The stream was so smooth, that the floating logs we met seemed to hang in a glowing atmosphere, the shadow-half being as real as the solid. And gradually the mind was etherized to a like dreamy placidity, till fact and fancy, the substance and the image, floating on the current of reverie, became but as the upper and under halves of one unreal reality.

In the west still lingered a pale-green light. I do not know whether it be from lifelong familiarity, but it always seems to me that the pinnacles of pine-trees make an edge to the landscape which tells better against the twilight, or the fainter dawn before the rising moon, than the rounded and cloud-cumulus outline of hard-wood trees.

After paddling a couple of miles, we found the arbored mouth of the little Malahoodus River, famous for moose. We had been on the lookout for it, and I was amused to hear one of the hunters say to the other, to assure himself of his familiarity with the spot, "You *drove* the West Branch last spring, did n't you?" as one of us might ask about a horse. We did not explore the Malahoodus far, but left the other birch to thread its cedared solitudes, while we turned back to try our fortunes in the larger stream. We paddled on about four miles farther, lingering now and then opposite the black mouth of a moose-path. The incidents of our voyage were few, but quite as exciting and profitable as the *items* of the newspapers. A stray log compensated very well for the ordinary run of accidents, and the floating *carkiss* of a moose which we met could pass muster instead of a singular discovery of human remains by workmen in digging a cellar. Once or twice we saw what seemed ghosts of trees; but they turned out to be dead cedars, in winding-sheets of long gray moss, made spectral by the moonlight. Just as we were turning to drift back down-stream, we heard a loud gnawing sound close by us on the bank. One of our guides thought it a hedgehog, the other a bear. I inclined to the bear, as making the adventure more imposing. A rifle was fired at the sound, which began again with the most provoking indifference, ere the echo, flaring madly at first from shore to shore, died far away in a hoarse sigh.

Half past Eleven, P. M. — No sign of a moose yet. The birch, it seems, was strained at the Carry, or the pitch was softened as she lay on the shore during dinner, and she leaks a little. If there be any virtue in the *sitzbad*, I shall discover it. If I cannot extract green cucumbers from the moon's rays, I get something quite as cool. One of the guides shivers so as to shake the birch.

Quarter to Twelve. — *Later from the Freshet!* — The water in the birch is about three inches deep, but the dampness reaches already nearly to the waist. I am obliged to remove the matches from the ground-floor of my trousers into the upper story of a breast-pocket. Meanwhile, we are to sit immovable, — for fear of frightening the moose, — which induces cramps.

Half past Twelve. — A crashing is heard on the left bank. This is a moose in good earnest. We are besought to hold our breaths, if possible. My fingers so numb, I could not, if I tried. *Crash! crash!* again, and then a plunge, followed by dead stillness. "Swimmin' crik," whispers guide, suppressing all unnecessary parts of speech, — "don't stir." I, for one, am not likely to. A cold fog which has been gathering for the last hour has finished me. I fancy myself one of those naked pigs that seem rushing out of market-doors in winter, frozen in a ghastly attitude of gallop. If I were to be shot myself, I should feel no interest in it. As it is, I am only a spectator, having declined a gun. *Splash!* again; this time the moose is in sight, and *click! click!* one rifle misses fire after the other. The fog has quietly spiked our batteries. The moose goes crashing up the bank, and presently we can hear it chawing its cud close by. So we lie in wait, freezing.

At one o'clock, I propose to land at a deserted *wongen* I had noticed on the way up, where I will make a fire, and leave them to refrigerate as much longer as they please. Axe in hand, I go plunging through waist-deep weeds dripping with dew, haunted by an intense conviction that the gnawing sound we had heard *was* a bear, and a bear at least eighteen hands high. There is something pokerish about a deserted dwelling, even in broad daylight; but here in the obscure wood, and the moon filtering unwillingly through the trees! Well, I made the door at last, and found the place packed fuller with darkness than it ever had been with hay. Gradually I was able to make things out a little,

· and began to hack frozenly at a log which I groped
out. I was relieved presently by one of the guides.
He cut at once into one of the uprights of the building till he got some dry splinters, and we soon had
a fire like the burning of a whole wood-wharf in our
part of the country. My companion went back to
the birch, and left me to keep house. First I
knocked a hole in the roof (which the fire began
to lick in a relishing way) for a chimney, and then
cleared away a damp growth of " pison-elder," to
make a sleeping place. When the unsuccessful
hunters returned, I had everything quite comfortable, and was steaming at the rate of about ten
horse-power a minute. Young Telemachus [1] was
sorry to give up the moose so soon, and, with the
teeth chattering almost out of his head, he declared
that he would like to stick it out all night. However, he reconciled himself to the fire, and, making
our beds of some " splits " which we poked from
the roof, we lay down at half past two. I, who
have inherited a habit of looking into every closet
before I go to bed, for fear of fire, had become in
two days such a stoic of the woods, that I went to
sleep tranquilly, certain that my bedroom would be
in a blaze before morning. And so, indeed, it was ;
and the withes that bound it together being burned
off, one of the sides fell in without waking me.

Tuesday, 16th. — After a sleep of two hours and
a half, so sound that it was as good as eight, we
started at half past four for the hay-makers' camp

---

[1] This was my nephew, Charles Russell Lowell, who fell at the
head of his brigade in the battle of Cedar Creek.

again. We found them just getting breakfast.
We sat down upon the *deacon-seat* before the fire
blazing between the bedroom and the *salle à man-
ger*, which were simply two roofs of spruce-bark,
sloping to the ground on one side, the other three
being left open. We found that we had, at least,
been luckier than the other party, for M. had
brought back his convoy without even seeing a
moose. As there was not room at the table for all of
us to breakfast together, these hospitable woodmen
forced us to sit down first, although we resisted
stoutly. Our breakfast consisted of fresh bread,
fried salt pork, stewed whortleberries, and tea. Our
kind hosts refused to take money for it, nor would
M. accept anything for his trouble. This seemed
even more open-handed when I remembered that
they had brought all their stores over the Carry
upon their shoulders, paying an ache *extra* for
every pound. If their hospitality lacked anything
of hard external polish, it had all the deeper grace
which springs only from sincere manliness. I have
rarely sat at a *table d'hôte* which might not have
taken a lesson from them in essential courtesy. I
have never seen a finer race of men. They have
all the virtues of the sailor, without that unsteady
roll in the gait with which the ocean proclaims itself quite as much in the moral as in the physical
habit of a man. They appeared to me to have hewn
out a short northwest passage through wintry woods
to those spice-lands of character which we dwellers
in cities must reach, if at all, by weary voyages in
the monotonous track of the trades.

By the way, as we were embirching last evening for our moose-chase, I asked what I was to do with my baggage. " Leave it here," said our guide, and he laid the bags upon a platform of alders, which he bent down to keep them beyond reach of the rising water.

" Will they be safe here ? "

" As safe as they would be locked up in your house at home."

And so I found them at my return; only the hay-makers had carried them to their camp for greater security against the chances of the weather.

We got back to Kineo in time for dinner; and in the afternoon, the weather being fine, went up the mountain. As we landed at the foot, our guide pointed to the remains of a red shirt and a pair of blanket trousers. " That," said he, " is the reason there 's such a trade in ready-made clo'es. A suit gits pooty well wore out by the time a camp breaks up in the spring, and the lumberers want to look about right when they come back into the settlements, so they buy somethin' ready-made, and heave ole bust-up into the bush." True enough, thought I, this is the Ready-made Age. It is quicker being covered than fitted. So we all go to the slop-shop and come out uniformed, every mother's son with habits of thinking and doing cut on one pattern, with no special reference to his peculiar build.

Kineo rises 1750 feet above the sea, and 750 above the lake. The climb is very easy, with fine outlooks at every turn over lake and forest. Near the top is a spring of water, which even Uncle Zeb might have allowed to be wholesome. The little tin dipper was scratched all over with names, showing that vanity, at least, is not put out of breath by the ascent. O Ozymandias, King of kings! We are all scrawling on something of the kind. "My name is engraved on the institutions of my country," thinks the statesman. But, alas! institutions are as changeable as tin-dippers; men are content to drink the same old water, if the shape of the cup only be new, and our friend gets two lines in the Biographical Dictionaries. After all, these inscriptions, which make us smile up here, are about as valuable as the Assyrian ones which Hincks and Rawlinson read at cross-purposes. Have we not Smiths and Browns enough, that we must ransack the ruins of Nimroud for more? Near the spring we met a Bloomer! It was the first chronic one I had ever seen. It struck me as a sensible costume for the occasion, and it will be the only wear in the Greek Kalends, when women believe that sense is an equivalent for grace.

The forest primeval is best seen from the top of a mountain. It then impresses one by its extent, like an Oriental epic. To be in it is nothing, for then an acre is as good as a thousand square miles. You cannot see five rods in any direction, and the ferns, mosses, and tree-trunks just around you are the best of it. As for solitude, night will make a better one with ten feet square of pitch dark; and mere size is hardly an element of grandeur, except in works of man, — as the Colosseum. It is through one or the other pole of vanity that men feel the sublime in mountains. It is either, How small great I am beside it! or, Big as you are, little I's soul will hold a dozen of you. The true idea of a forest is not a *selva selvaggia*, but something humanized a little, as we imagine the forest of Arden, with trees standing at royal intervals, — a commonwealth, and not a communism. To some moods, it is congenial to look over endless leagues of unbroken savagery without a hint of man.

Wednesday. — This morning fished. Telemachus caught a *laker* of thirteen pounds and a half, and I an overgrown cusk, which we threw away, but which I found afterwards Agassiz would have been glad of, for all is fish that comes to his net, from the fossil down. The fish, when caught, are straightway knocked on the head. A lad who went with us seeming to show an over-zeal in this operation, we remonstrated. But he gave a good, human reason for it, — "He no need to ha' gone and been a fish if he did n't like it," — an excuse which superior strength or cunning has always found sufficient. It was some comfort, in this case, to think that St. Jerome believed in a limitation of God's providence, and that it did not extend to inanimate things or creatures devoid of reason.

Thus, my dear Storg, I have finished my Oriental adventures, and somewhat, it must be owned, in the diffuse Oriental manner. There is very little about Moosehead Lake in it, and not even the Latin name for moose, which I might have obtained by sufficient research. If I had killed one, I would

have given you his name in that dead language.   I
did not profess to give you an account of the lake;
but a journal, and, moreover, *my* journal, with a
little nature, a little human nature, and a great
deal of I in it, which last ingredient I take to
be the true spirit of this species of writing; all the
rest being so much water for tender throats which
cannot take it neat.

CAMBRIDGE THIRTY YEARS AGO

1854

A MEMOIR ADDRESSED TO THE EDELMANN STORG IN ROME.

IN those quiet old winter evenings, around our Roman fireside, it was not seldom, my dear Storg, that we talked of the advantages of travel, and in speeches not so long that our cigars would forget their fire (the measure of just conversation) debated the comparative advantages of the Old and New Worlds. You will remember how serenely I bore the imputation of provincialism, while I asserted that those advantages were reciprocal; that an orbed and balanced life would revolve between the Old and the New as opposite, but not antagonistic poles, the true equator lying somewhere midway between them. I asserted also, that there were two epochs at which a man might travel, — before twenty, for pure enjoyment, and after thirty, for instruction. At twenty, the eye is sufficiently delighted with merely seeing; new things are pleasant only because they are not old; and we take everything heartily and naturally in the right way, — for even mishaps are like knives, that either serve us or cut us, as we grasp them by the blade or the handle. After thirty, we carry along our

scales, with lawful weights stamped by experience,
and our chemical tests acquired by study, with
which to ponder and assay all arts, institutions,
and manners, and to ascertain either their absolute
worth or their merely relative value to ourselves.
On the whole, I declared myself in favor of the
after thirty method, — was it partly (so difficult is
it to distinguish between opinions and personalities)
because I had tried it myself, though with scales so
imperfect and tests so inadequate? Perhaps so,
but more because I held that a man should have
travelled thoroughly round himself and the great
terra incognita just outside and inside his own
threshold, before he undertook voyages of discovery
to other worlds. "Far countries he can safest
visit who himself is doughty," says Beowulf. Let
him first thoroughly explore that strange country
laid down on the maps as SEAUTON; let him look
down into its craters, and find whether they be
burnt-out or only smouldering; let him know between the good and evil fruits of its passionate
tropics; let him experience how healthful are its
serene and high-lying table-lands; let him be many
times driven back (till he wisely consent to be baffled) from its speculatively inquisitive northwest
passages that lead mostly to the dreary solitudes
of a sunless world, before he think himself morally
equipped for travels to more distant regions. So
thought pithy Thomas Fuller. "Who," he says,
"hath sailed about the world of his own heart,
sounded each creek, surveyed each corner, but that
still there remains therein much 'terra incognita'

to himself?"[1]   But does he commonly even so
much as think of this, or, while buying amplest
trunks for his corporeal apparel, does it once occur
to him how very small a portmanteau will contain
all his mental and spiritual outfit?   It is more
often true that a man who could scarce be induced
to expose his unclothed body even to a village of
prairie-dogs, will complacently display a mind as
naked as the day it was born, without so much as
a fig-leaf of acquirement on it, in every gallery of
Europe, —

> "Not caring, so that sumpter-horse, the back,
>   Be hung with gaudy trappings, in what coarse,
>   Yea, rags most beggarly, they clothe the soul."

If not with a robe dyed in the Tyrian purple of
imaginative culture, if not with the close-fitting,
work-day dress of social or business training, — at
least, my dear Storg, one might provide himself
with the merest waist-clout of modesty!

But if it be too much to expect men to traverse
and survey themselves before they go abroad, we
might certainly ask that they should be familiar
with their own villages.   If not even that, then it
is of little import whither they go; and let us hope
that, by seeing how calmly their own narrow neighborhood bears their departure, they may be led to
think that the circles of disturbance set in motion
by the fall of their tiny ·drop into the ocean of
eternity will not have a radius of more than a
week in any direction; and that the world can
endure the subtraction of even a justice of the

----

[1] *Holy State: The Constant Virgin.*

peace with provoking equanimity.   In this way, at least, foreign travel may do them good, — may make them, if not wiser, at any rate less fussy.   Is it a great way to go to school, and a great fee to pay for the lesson?   We cannot give too much for the genial stoicism which, when life flouts us, and says, *Put that in your pipe and smoke it!* can puff away with as sincere a relish as if it were tobacco of Mount Lebanon in a *narghileh* of Damascus.

It has passed into a scornful proverb, that it needs good optics to see what is not to be seen; and yet I should be inclined to say that the first essential of a good traveller was to be gifted with eyesight of precisely that kind.   All his senses should be as delicate as eyes; and, above all, he should be able to see with the fine eye of imagination, compared with which all the other organs with which the mind grasps and the memory holds are as clumsy as thumbs.   The demand for this kind of traveller and the opportunity for him increase as we learn more and more minutely the dry facts and figures of the most inaccessible corners of the earth's surface.   There is no hope of another Ferdinand Mendez Pinto, with his statistics of Dreamland, who makes no difficulty of impressing "fourscore thousand rhinocerots" to draw the wagons of the King of Tartary's army, or of killing eight hundred and fifty thousand men with a flourish of his quill, — for what were a few ciphers to him, when his inkhorn was full and all Christendom to be astonished? — but there is all the more need of voyagers who give us something better than a census of population, and who know of other exports from strange countries than can be expressed by $——. Give me the traveller who makes me feel the mystery of the Figure at Saïs, whose veil hides a new meaning for every beholder, rather than him who brings back a photograph of the uncovered countenance, with its one unvarying granite story for all. There is one glory of the Gazetteer with his fixed facts, and another of the Poet with his variable quantities of fancy.

After all, my dear Storg, it is to know *things* that one has need to travel, and not *men*. Those force us to come to them, but these come to us, — sometimes whether we will or no. These exist for us in every variety in our own town. You may find your antipodes without a voyage to China; he lives there, just round the next corner, precise, formal, the slave of precedent, making all his teacups with a break in the edge, because his model had one, and your fancy decorates him with an endlessness of airy pigtail. There, too, are John Bull, Jean Crapaud, Hans Sauerkraut, Pat Murphy, and the rest.

It has been written:

> " He needs no ship to cross the tide,
>   Who, in the lives around him, sees
>   Fair window-prospects opening wide
>   O'er history's fields on every side,
>   Rome, Egypt. England, Ind, and Greece.
>
> " Whatever moulds of various brain
>   E'er shaped the world to weal or woe,
>   Whatever empires' wax and wane,

> To him who hath not eyes in vain,
> His village-microcosm can show."

But every thing is not a Thing, and all *things* are good for nothing out of their natural *habitat*. If the heroic Barnum had succeeded in transplanting Shakespeare's house to America, what interest would it have had for us, torn out of its appropriate setting in softly-hilled Warwickshire, which showed us that the most English of poets must be born in the most English of counties? I mean by a *Thing* that which is not a mere spectacle, that which some virtue of the mind leaps forth to, as it also sends forth its sympathetic flash to the mind, as soon as they come within each other's sphere of attraction, and, with instantaneous coalition, form a new product, — knowledge.

Such, in the understanding it gives us of early Roman history, is the little territory around Rome, the *gentis cunabula*, without a sight of which Livy and Niebuhr and the maps are vain. So, too, one must go to Pompeii and the *Museo Borbonico*, to get a true conception of that wondrous artistic nature of the Greeks, strong enough, even in that petty colony, to survive foreign conquest and to assimilate barbarian blood, showing a grace and fertility of invention whose Roman copies Rafaello himself could only copy, and enchanting even the base utensils of the kitchen with an inevitable sense of beauty to which we subterranean Northmen have not yet so much as dreamed of climbing. Mere sights one can see quite as well at home. Mont Blanc does not tower more grandly in the

memory than did the dream-peak which loomed
afar on the morning horizon of hope, nor did the
smoke-palm of Vesuvius stand more erect and fair,
with tapering stem and spreading top, in that Par-
thenopean air, than under the diviner sky of imagination. I know what Shakespeare says about
homekeeping youths, and I can fancy what you
will add about America being interesting only as a
phenomenon, and uncomfortable to live in, because
we have not yet done with getting ready to live.
But is not your Europe, on the other hand, a place
where men have done living for the present, and
of value chiefly because of the men who had done
living in it long ago? And if, in our rapidly
moving country, one feel sometimes as if he had
his home on a railroad-train, is there not also a
satisfaction in knowing that one *is* going *somewhere*? To what end visit Europe, if people carry
with them, as most do, their old parochial horizon,
going hardly as Americans even, much less as
men? Have we not both seen persons abroad who
put us in mind of parlor gold-fish in their vase,
isolated in that little globe of their own element,
incapable of communication with the strange world
around them, a show themselves, while it was always doubtful if they could see at all beyond the
limits of their portable prison? The wise man
travels to discover himself; it is to find himself out
that he goes out of himself and his habitual associations, trying everything in turn till he find that
one activity, that royal standard, sovran over him
by divine right, toward which all the disbanded

powers of his nature and the irregular tendencies
of his life gather joyfully, as to the common rally-
ing-point of their loyalty.

All these things we debated while the ilex logs
upon the hearth burned down to tinkling coals,
over which a gray, soft moss of ashes grew betimes,
mocking the poor wood with a pale travesty of that
green and gradual decay on forest-floors, its natural
end. Already the clock at the *Cappuccini* told
the morning quarters, and on the pauses of our
talk no sound intervened but the muffled hoot of
an owl in the near convent-garden, or the rattling
tramp of a patrol of that French army which keeps
him a prisoner in his own city who claims to lock
and unlock the doors of heaven. But still the discourse would eddy round one obstinate rocky tenet
of mine, for I maintained, you remember, that the
wisest man was he who stayed at home; that to see
the antiquities of the Old World was nothing,
since the youth of the world was really no farther
away from us than our own youth; and that, moreover, we had also in America things amazingly old,
as our boys, for example. Add, that in the end
this antiquity is a matter of comparison, which
skips from place to place as nimbly as Emerson's
Sphinx, and that one old thing is good only till we
have seen an older. England is ancient till we go
to Rome; Etruria dethrones Rome, but only to
pass this sceptre of antiquity which so lords it over
our fancies to the Pelasgi, from whom Egypt
straightway wrenches it, to give it up in turn to
older India. And whither then? As well rest

upon the first step, since the effect of what is old upon the mind is single and positive, not cumulative. As soon as a thing is past, it is as infinitely far away from us as if it had happened millions of years ago. And if the learned Huet be correct, who reckoned that all human thoughts and records could be included in ten folios, what so frightfully old as we ourselves, who can, if we choose, hold in our memories every syllable of recorded time, from the first crunch of Eve's teeth in the apple downward, being thus ideally contemporary with hoariest Eld ?

> "Thy pyramids built up with newer might
> To us are nothing novel, nothing strange."

Now, my dear Storg, you know my (what the phrenologists call) inhabitiveness and adhesiveness, — how I stand by the old thought, the old thing, the old place, and the old friend, till I am very sure I have got a better, and even then migrate painfully. Remember the old Arabian story, and think how hard it is to pick up all the pomegranate-seeds of an opponent's argument, and how, so long as one remains, you are as far from the end as ever. Since I have you entirely at my mercy, (for you cannot answer me under five weeks,) you will not be surprised at the advent of this letter. I had always one impregnable position, which was, that, however good other places might be, there was only one in which we could be born, and which therefore possessed a quite peculiar and inalienable virtue. We had the fortune, which neither of us have had reason to call other than good, to journey

together through the green, secluded valley of boyhood; together we climbed the mountain wall which
shut in, and looked down upon, those Italian plains
of early manhood; and, since then, we have met
sometimes by a well, or broken bread together at
an oasis in the arid desert of life, as it truly is.
With this letter I propose to make you my fellow-
traveller in one of those fireside voyages which,
as we grow older, we make oftener and oftener
through our own past. Without leaving your elbow-
chair, you shall go back with me thirty years, which
will bring you among things and persons as thoroughly preterite as Romulus or Numa. For so
rapid are our changes in America that the transition from old to new, the shifting from habits and
associations to others entirely different, is as rapid
almost as the passing in of one scene and the drawing out of another on the stage. And it is this
which makes America so interesting to the philo-
sophic student of history and man. Here, as in
a theatre, the great problems of anthropology —
which in the Old World were ages in solving, but
which are solved, leaving only a dry net result —
are compressed, as it were, into the entertainment
of a few hours. Here we have I know not how
many epochs of history and phases of civilization
contemporary with each other, nay, within five
minutes of each other, by the electric telegraph.
In two centuries we have seen rehearsed the dis-
persion of man from a small point over a whole
continent; we witness with our own eyes the action
of those forces which govern the great migration of

the peoples now historical in Europe; we can watch the action and reaction of different races, forms of government, and higher or lower civilizations. Over there, you have only the dead precipitate, demanding tedious analysis ; but here the elements are all in solution, and we have only to look to see how they will combine. History, which every day makes less account of governors and more of man, must find here the compendious key to all that picture-writing of the Past. Therefore it is, my dear Storg, that we Yankees may still esteem our America a place worth living in. But calm your apprehensions ; I do not propose to drag you with me on such an historical circumnavigation of the globe, but only to show you that (however needful it may be to go abroad for the study of æsthetics) a man who uses the eyes of his heart may find here also pretty bits of what may be called the social picturesque, and little landscapes over which that Indian-summer atmosphere of the Past broods as sweetly and tenderly as over a Roman ruin. Let us look at the Cambridge of thirty years since.

The seat of the oldest college in America, it had, of course, some of that cloistered quiet which characterizes all university towns. Even now delicately-thoughtful A. H. C. tells me that he finds in its intellectual atmosphere a repose which recalls that of grand old Oxford. But, underlying this, it had an idiosyncrasy of its own. Boston was not yet a city, and Cambridge was still a country village, with its own habits and traditions, not yet feeling too strongly the force of suburban gravitation.

Approaching it from the west by what was then called the New Road (so called no longer, for we change our names as readily as thieves, to the great detriment of all historical association), you would pause on the brow of Symonds' Hill to enjoy a view singularly soothing and placid.   In front of you lay the town, tufted with elms, lindens, and horse-chestnuts, which had seen Massachusetts a colony, and were fortunately unable to emigrate with the Tories by whom, or by whose fathers, they were planted.   Over it rose the noisy belfry of the College, the square, brown tower of the church, and the slim, yellow spire of the parish meeting-house, by no means ungraceful, and then an invariable characteristic of New England religious architecture.   On your right, the Charles slipped smoothly through green and purple salt-meadows, darkened, here and there, with the blossoming black-grass as with a stranded cloud-shadow.   Over these marshes, level as water, but without its glare, and with softer and more soothing gradations of perspective, the eye was carried to a horizon of softly-rounded hills. To your left hand, upon the Old Road, you saw some half-dozen dignified old houses of the colonial time, all comfortably fronting southward.   If it were early June, the rows of horse-chestnuts along the fronts of these houses showed, through every crevice of their dark heap of foliage, and on the end of every drooping limb, a cone of pearly flowers, while the hill behind was white or rosy with the crowding blooms of various fruit-trees.   There is no sound, unless a horseman clatters over the

loose planks of the bridge, while his antipodal
shadow glides silently over the mirrored bridge below, or unless,

> " O wingëd rapture, feathered soul of spring,
> Blithe voice of woods, fields, waters, all in one,
> Pipe blown through by the warm, mild breath of June
> Shepherding her white flocks of woolly clouds,
> The bobolink has come, and climbs the wind
> With rippling wings that quiver not for flight,
> But only joy, or, yielding to its will,
> Runs down, a brook of laughter, through the air."

Such was the charmingly rural picture which he
who, thirty years ago, went eastward over Symonds'
Hill had given him for nothing, to hang in the
Gallery of Memory. But we are a city now, and
Common Councils have as yet no notion of the truth
(learned long ago by many a European hamlet)
that picturesqueness adds to the actual money value
of a town. To save a few dollars in gravel, they
have cut a kind of dry ditch through the hill, where
you suffocate with dust in summer, or flounder
through waist-deep snow-drifts in winter, with no
prospect but the crumbling earth-walls on either
side. The landscape was carried away cart-load by
cart-load, and, dumped down on the roads, forms a
part of that unfathomable pudding, which has, I
fear, driven many a teamster and pedestrian to the
use of phrases not commonly found in English dictionaries.

We called it "the Village" then (I speak of
Old Cambridge), and it was essentially an English
village, quiet, unspeculative, without enterprise, suf-
ficing to itself, and only showing such differences

from the original type as the public school and the system of town government might superinduce. A few houses, chiefly old, stood around the bare Common, with ample elbow-room, and old women, capped and spectacled, still peered through the same windows from which they had watched Lord Percy's artillery rumble by to Lexington, or caught a glimpse of the handsome Virginia General who had come to wield our homespun Saxon chivalry. People were still living who regretted the late unhappy separation from the mother island, who had seen no gentry since the Vassalls went, and who thought that Boston had ill kept the day of her patron saint, Botolph, on the 17th of June, 1775. The hooks were to be seen in Massachusetts Hall from which had swung the hammocks of Burgoyne's captive redcoats. If memory does not deceive me, women still washed clothes in the town spring, clear as that of Bandusia. One coach sufficed for all the travel to the metropolis. Commencement had not ceased to be the great holiday of the Puritan Commonwealth, and a fitting one it was,—the festival of Santa Scholastica, whose triumphal path one may conceive strewn with leaves of spelling-book instead of bay. The students (scholars they were called then) wore their sober uniform, not ostentatiously distinctive or capable of rousing democratic envy, and the old lines of caste were blurred rather than rubbed out, as servitor was softened into beneficiary. The Spanish king felt sure that the gesticulating student was either mad or reading Don Quixote, and if, in those days, you met a youth

swinging his arms and talking to himself, you might
conclude that he was either a lunatic or one who
was to appear in a "part" at the next Exhibition
or Commencement. A favorite place for the rehearsal of these orations was the retired amphi-
theatre of the Gravel-pit, perched unregarded on
whose dizzy edge, I have heard many a burst of
plusquam Ciceronian eloquence, and (often repeated) the regular *saluto vos, præstantissimæ*
&c., which every year (with a glance at the gallery) causes a flutter among the fans innocent
of Latin, and delights to applauses of conscious
superiority the youth almost as innocent as they.
It is curious, by the way, to note how plainly one
can feel the pulse of self in the plaudits of an audience. At a political meeting, if the enthusiasm
of the lieges hang fire, it may be exploded at once
by an allusion to their intelligence or patriotism;
and at a literary festival, the first Latin quotation
draws the first applause, the clapping of hands
being intended as a tribute to our own familiarity
with that sonorous tongue, and not at all as an
approval of the particular sentiment conveyed in it.
For if the orator should say, " Well has Tacitus
remarked, *Americani omnes quâdam vi naturæ
furcâ dignissimi,*" it would be all the same. But
the Gravel-pit was patient, if irresponsive; nor did
the declaimer always fail to bring down the house,
bits of loosened earth falling now and then from
the precipitous walls, their cohesion perhaps overcome by the vibrations of the voice, and happily
satirizing the effect of most popular discourses,

which prevail rather with the earthy than the spiritual part of the hearer. Was it possible for us in
those days to conceive of a greater potentate than
the President of the University, in his square doctor's cap, that still filially recalled Oxford and
Cambridge? If there was a doubt, it was suggested only by the Governor, and even by him on
artillery-election days alone, superbly martial with
epaulets and buckskin breeches, and bestriding the
war-horse, promoted to that solemn duty for his
tameness and steady habits.

Thirty years ago, the town had indeed a character. Railways and omnibuses had not rolled
flat all little social prominences and peculiarities,
making every man as much a citizen everywhere as
at home. No Charlestown boy could come to our
annual festival without fighting to avenge a certain
traditional porcine imputation against the inhabitants of that historic spot, to which our youth gave
vent in fanciful imitations of the dialect of the sty,
or derisive shouts of "Charlestown hogs!" The
penny newspaper had not yet silenced the tripod
of the barber, oracle of news. Everybody knew
everybody, and all about everybody, and village
wit, whose high 'change was around the little mar-
ket-house in the town square, had labelled every
more marked individuality with nicknames that
clung like burs. Things were established then, and
men did not run through all the figures on the dial
of society so swiftly as now, when hurry and competition seem to have quite unhung the modulating
pendulum of steady thrift and competent train-

ing. Some slow-minded persons even followed their father's trade, — a humiliating spectacle, rarer every day. We had our established loafers, topers, proverb-mongers, barber, parson, nay, postmaster, whose tenure was for life. The great political engine did not then come down at regular quadrennial intervals, like a nail-cutting machine, to make all official lives of a standard length, and to generate lazy and intriguing expectancy. Life flowed in recognized channels, narrower perhaps, but with all the more individuality and force.

There was but one white-and-yellow-washer, whose own cottage, fresh-gleaming every June through grape-vine and creeper, was his only sign and advertisement. He was said to possess a secret, which died with him like that of Luca della Robbia, and certainly conceived all colors but white and yellow to savor of savagery, civilizing the stems of his trees annually with liquid lime, and meditating how to extend that candent baptism even to the leaves. His *pie-plants* (the best in town), compulsory monastics, blanched under barrels, each in his little hermitage, a vegetable Certosa. His fowls, his ducks, his geese, could not show so much as a gray feather among them, and he would have given a year's earnings for a white peacock. The flowers which decked his little *door-yard* were whitest China-asters and goldenest sunflowers, which last, backsliding from their traditional Parsee faith, used to puzzle us urchins not a little by staring brazenly every way except towards the sun. Celery, too, he raised, whose virtue is its paleness, and the silvery onion, and turnip, which, though outwardly conforming to the green heresies of summer, nourish a purer faith subterraneously, like early Christians in the catacombs. In an obscure corner grew the sanguine beet, tolerated only for its usefulness in allaying the asperities of Saturday's salt-fish. He loved winter better than summer, because Nature then played the whitewasher, and challenged with her snows the scarce inferior purity of his overalls and neck-cloth. I fancy that he never rightly liked Commencement, for bringing so many black coats together. He founded no school. Others might essay his art, and were allowed to try their prentice hands on fences and the like coarse subjects, but the ceiling of every housewife waited on the leisure of Newman (*ichneumon* the students called him for his diminutiveness), nor would consent to other brush than his. There was also but one brewer, — Lewis, who made the village beer, both spruce and ginger, a grave and amiable Ethiopian, making a discount always to the boys, and wisely, for they were his chiefest patrons. He wheeled his whole stock in a white-roofed handcart, on whose front a signboard presented at either end an insurrectionary bottle ; yet insurgent after no mad Gallic fashion, but soberly and Saxonly discharging itself into the restraining formulary of a tumbler, symbolic of orderly prescription. The artist had struggled manfully with the difficulties of his subject, but had not succeeded so well that we did not often debate in which of the twin bottles Spruce was typified, and in which

Ginger.   We always believed that Lewis mentally distinguished between them, but by some peculiarity occult to exoteric eyes.   This ambulatory chapel of the Bacchus that gives the colic, but not inebriates, only appeared at the Commencement holidays, and the lad who bought of Lewis laid out his money well, getting respect as well as beer, three *sirs* to every glass, — " Beer, sir? yes, sir : spruce or ginger, sir?"   I can yet recall the innocent pride with which I walked away after that somewhat risky ceremony, (for a bottle sometimes blew up,) dilated not alone with carbonic acid gas, but with the more ethereal fixed air of that titular flattery.   Nor was Lewis proud.   When he tried his fortunes in the capital on Election-days, and stood amid a row of rival venders in the very flood of custom, he never forgot his small fellow-citizens, but welcomed them with an assuring smile, and served them with the first.

The barber's shop was a museum, scarce second to the larger one of Greenwood in the metropolis. The boy who was to be clipped there was always accompanied to the sacrifice by troops of friends, who thus inspected the curiosities *gratis*.   While the watchful eye of R. wandered to keep in check these rather unscrupulous explorers, the unpausing shears would sometimes overstep the boundaries of strict tonsorial prescription, and make a notch through which the phrenological developments could be distinctly seen.   As Michael Angelo's design was modified by the shape of his block, so R., rigid in artistic proprieties, would con-

trive to give an appearance of design to this aber-
ration, by making it the key-note to his work,
and reducing the whole head to an appearance of
premature baldness. What a charming place it
was, — how full of wonder and delight! The sunny little room, fronting southwest upon the Common, rang with canaries and Java sparrows, nor
were the familiar notes of robin, thrush, and bobo-
link wanting. A large white cockatoo harangued
vaguely, at intervals, in what we believed (on R.'s
authority) to be the Hottentot language. He had
an unveracious air, but in what inventions of former grandeur he was indulging, what sweet South-
African Argos he was remembering, what tropical heats and giant trees by unconjectured rivers,
known only to the wallowing hippopotamus, we
could only guess at. The walls were covered with
curious old Dutch prints, beaks of albatross and
penguin, and whales' teeth fantastically engraved.
There was Frederick the Great, with head drooped
plottingly, and keen sidelong glance from under
the three-cornered hat. There hung Bonaparte,
too, the long-haired, haggard general of Italy, his
eyes sombre with prefigured destiny; and there
was his island grave; — the dream and the fulfilment. Good store of sea-fights there was also;
above all, Paul Jones in the Bonhomme Richard:
the smoke rolling courteously to leeward, that we
might see him dealing thunderous wreck to the two
hostile vessels, each twice as large as his own, and
the reality of the scene corroborated by streaks of
red paint leaping from the mouth of every gun.

Suspended over the fireplace, with the curling-tongs, were an Indian bow and arrows, and in the corners of the room stood New Zealand paddles and war-clubs, quaintly carved. The model of a ship in glass we variously estimated to be worth from a hundred to a thousand dollars, R. rather favoring the higher valuation, though never distinctly committing himself. Among these wonders, the only suspicious one was an Indian tomahawk, which had too much the peaceful look of a shingling-hatchet. Did any rarity enter the town, it gravitated naturally to these walls, to the very nail that waited to receive it, and where, the day after its accession, it seemed to have hung a lifetime. We always had a theory that R. was immensely rich, (how could he possess so much and be otherwise?) and that he pursued his calling from an amiable eccentricity. He was a conscientious artist, and never submitted it to the choice of his victim whether he would be perfumed or not. Faithfully was the bottle shaken and the odoriferous mixture rubbed in, a fact redolent to the whole school-room in the afternoon. Sometimes the persuasive tonsor would impress one of the attendant volunteers, and reduce his poll to shoe-brush crispness, at cost of the reluctant ninepence hoarded for Fresh Pond and the next half-holiday. So purely indigenous was our population then, that R. had a certain exotic charm, a kind of game flavor, by being a Dutchman.

Shall the two groceries want their *vates sacer,* where E. & W. I. goods and country prodooce were sold with an energy mitigated by the quiet genius of the place, and where strings of urchins waited, each with cent in hand, for the unweighed dates (thus giving an ordinary business transaction all the excitement of a lottery), and buying, not only that cloying sweetness, but a dream also of Egypt, and palm-trees, and Arabs, in which vision a print of the Pyramids in our geography tyrannized like that taller thought of Cowper's?

At one of these the unwearied students used to ply a joke handed down from class to class. *Enter A*, and asks gravely, " Have you any sour apples, Deacon ? "

" Well, no, I have n't any just now that are exactly sour; but there 's the bell-flower apple, and folks that like a sour apple generally like that." (*Exit A.*)

Enter B. " Have you any sweet apples, Deacon ? "

" Well, no, I have n't any just now that are exactly sweet; but there 's the bell-flower apple, and folks that like a sweet apple generally like that." (*Exit B.*)

There is not even a tradition of any one's ever having turned the wary Deacon's flank, and his Laodicean apples persisted to the end, neither one thing nor another. Or shall the two town-constables be forgotten, in whom the law stood worthily and amply embodied, fit either of them to fill the uniform of an English beadle? Grim and silent as Ninevite statues they stood on each side of the meeting-house door at Commencement, propped by long staves of blue and red, on which the Indian

with bow and arrow, and the mailed arm with the
sword, hinted at the invisible sovereignty of the
state ready to reinforce them, as

> " For Achilles' portrait stood a spear
>   Grasped in an arméd hand."

Stalwart and rubicund men they were, second only,
if second, to S., champion of the county, and not
incapable of genial unbendings when the fasces
were laid aside.   One of them still survives in
octogenarian vigor, the Herodotus of village and
college legend, and may it be long ere he depart,
to carry with him the pattern of a courtesy, now,
alas! old-fashioned, but which might profitably
make part of the instruction of our youth among
the other humanities!   Long may R. M. be spared
to us, so genial, so courtly, the last man among us
who will ever know how to lift a hat with the nice
graduation of social distinctions.   Something of a
Jeremiah now, he bewails the decline of our manners.   "My children," he says, "say, ' Yes sir,'
and ' No sir '; my grandchildren, ' Yes ' and ' No ';
and I am every day expecting to hear ' D—n your
eyes! ' for an answer when I ask a service of my
great-grandchildren.   Why, sir, I can remember
when more respect was paid to Governor Hancock's
lackey at Commencement, than the Governor and
all his suite get now."   M. is one of those invalu-
able men who remember your grandfather, and
value you accordingly.

In those days the population was almost wholly
without foreign admixture.   Two Scotch gardeners
there were, — Rule, whose daughter (glimpsed per-

haps at church, or possibly the mere Mrs. Harris of fancy) the students nicknamed Anarchy or Miss Rule, — and later Fraser, whom whiskey sublimed into a poet, full of bloody histories of the Forty-twa, and showing an imaginary French bullet, sometimes in one leg, sometimes in the other, and sometimes, toward nightfall, in both. He asserted that he had been at Coruña, calling it by its archaic name of the Groyne, and thus raising doubts in the mind of the young listener who could find no such place on his map. With this claim to a military distinction he adroitly contrived to mingle another to a natural one, asserting double teeth all round his jaws, and, having thus created two sets of doubts, silenced both at once by a single demonstration, displaying the grinders to the confusion of the infidel.

The old court-house stood then upon the square. It has shrunk back out of sight now, and students box and fence where Parsons once laid down the law, and Ames and Dexter showed their skill in the fence of argument. Times have changed, and manners, since Chief Justice Dana (father of Richard the First, and grandfather of Richard the Second) caused to be arrested for contempt of court a butcher who had come in without a coat to witness the administration of his country's laws, and who thus had his curiosity exemplarily gratified. Times have changed also since the cellar beneath it was tenanted by the twin-brothers Snow. Oyster men were they indeed, silent in their subterranean burrow, and taking the ebbs and flows

of custom with bivalvian serenity. Careless of the
months with an R in them, the maxim of Snow
(for we knew them but as a unit) was, " When
'ysters are good, they *air* good; and when they
ain't, they *is n't.*" Grecian F. (may his shadow
never be less!) tells this, his great laugh expected
all the while from deep vaults of chest, and then
coming in at the close, hearty, contagious, mounting with the measured tread of a jovial but stately
butler who brings ancientest goodfellowship from
exhaustless bins, and enough, without other sauce,
to give a flavor of stalled ox to a dinner of herbs.
Let me preserve here an anticipatory elegy upon
the Snows, written years ago by some nameless
college rhymer.

DIFFUGERE NIVES.

Here lies, or lie, — decide the question, you,
If they were two in one or one in two. —
P. & S. Snow, whose memory shall not fade,
Castor and Pollux of the oyster-trade:
Hatched from one egg, at once the shell they burst,
(The last, perhaps, a P. S. to the first,)
So homoöusian both in look and soul,
So undiscernibly a single whole,
That whether P. was S., or S. was P.,
Surpassed all skill in etymology;
One kept the shop at once, and all we know
Is that together they were *the* Great Snow,
A snow not deep, yet with a crust so thick
It never melted to the son of Tick;
Perpetual ? nay, our region was too low,
Too warm, too southern, for perpetual Snow;
Still, like fair Leda's sons, to whom 't was given
To take their turns in Hades and in Heaven,
Our Dioscuri new would bravely share
The cellar's darkness and the upper air;

Twice every year would each the shades escape,
And, like a sea-bird, seek the wave-washed Cape,
Where (Rumor voiced) one spouse sufficed for both;
No bigamist, for she upon her oath,
Unskilled in letters, could not make a guess
At any difference twixt P. and S. —
A thing not marvellous, since Fame agrees
They were as little different as two peas,
And she, like Paris, when his Helen laid
Her hand 'mid snows from Ida's top conveyed
To cool their wine of Chios, could not know,
Between those rival candors, which was Snow.
Whiche'er behind the counter chanced to be
Oped oysters oft, his clam-shells seldom he;
If e'er he laughed, 't was with no loud guffaw,
The fun warmed through him with a gradual thaw:
The nicer shades of wit were not his gift,
Nor was it hard to sound Snow's simple drift;
His were plain jokes, that many a time before
Had set his tarry messmates in a roar,
When floundering cod beslimed the deck's wet planks, —
The humorous specie of Newfoundland Banks.

But Snow is gone, and, let us hope, sleeps well,
Buried (his last breath asked it) in a shell;
Fate with an oyster-knife sawed off his thread.
And planted him upon his latest bed.

Him on the Stygian shore my fancy sees
Noting choice shoals for oyster colonies,
Or, at a board stuck full of ghostly forks,
Opening for practice visionary Yorks.
And whither he has gone, may we too go, —
Since no hot place were fit for keeping Snow!

Jam satis nivis.

Cambridge has long had its port, but the greater
part of its maritime trade was, thirty years ago,
intrusted to a single Argo, the sloop Harvard,
which belonged to the College, and made annual

voyages to that vague Orient known as Down East, bringing back the wood that, in those days, gave to winter life at Harvard a crackle and a cheerfulness, for the loss of which the greater warmth of anthracite hardly compensates. New England life, to be genuine, must have in it some sentiment of the sea, — it was this instinct that printed the device of the pine-tree on the old money and the old flag, — and these periodic ventures of the sloop Harvard made the old Viking fibre vibrate in the hearts of all the village boys. What a perspective of mystery and adventure did her sailing open to us! With what pride did we hail her return! She was our scholiast upon Robinson Crusoe and the mutiny of the Bounty. Her captain still lords it over our memories, the greatest sailor that ever sailed the seas, and we should not look at Sir John Franklin himself with such admiring interest as that with which we enhaloed some larger boy who had made a voyage in her, and had come back without braces (*gallowses* we called them) to his trousers, and squirting ostentatiously the juice of that weed which still gave him little private returns of something very like sea-sickness. All our shingle vessels were shaped and rigged by her, who was our glass of naval fashion and our mould of aquatic form. We had a secret and wild delight in believing that she carried a gun, and imagined her sending grape and canister among the treacherous savages of Oldtown. Inspired by her were those first essays at navigation on the Winthrop duck-pond, of the plucky boy who was afterwards to serve two famous years before the mast.

The greater part of what is now Cambridgeport was then (in the native dialect) a *huckleberry pastur.* Woods were not wanting on its outskirts, of pine, and oak, and maple, and the rarer tupelo with downward limbs. Its veins did not draw their blood from the quiet old heart of the village, but it had a distinct being of its own, and was rather a great caravansary than a suburb. The chief feature of the place was its inns, of which there were five, with vast barns and court-yards, which the railroad was to make as silent and deserted as the palaces of Nimroud. Great white-topped wagons, each drawn by double files of six or eight horses, with its dusty bucket swinging from the hinder axle, and its grim bull-dog trotting silent underneath, or in midsummer panting on the lofty perch beside the driver, (how elevated thither baffled conjecture,) brought all the wares and products of the country to their mart and seaport in Boston. These filled the inn-yards, or were ranged side by side under broad-roofed sheds, and far into the night the mirth of their lusty drivers clamored from the red-curtained bar-room, while the single lantern, swaying to and fro in the black cavern of the stables, made a Rembrandt of the group of ostlers and horses below. There were, beside the taverns, some huge square stores where groceries were sold, some houses, by whom or why inhabited was to us boys a problem, and, on the edge of the marsh, a currier's shop, where, at high tide, on a floating platform, men were always beating skins in a way to remind one of Don Quixote's fulling-mills. Nor did these make all the Port. As there is always a Coming Man who never comes, so there is a man who always comes (it may be only a quarter of an hour) too early. This man, so far as the Port is concerned, was Rufus Davenport. Looking at the marshy flats of Cambridge, and considering their nearness to Boston, he resolved that there should grow up a suburban Venice. Accordingly, the marshes were bought, canals were dug, ample for the commerce of both Indies, and four or five rows of brick houses were built to meet the first wants of the wading settlers who were expected to rush in — WHENCE? This singular question had never occurred to the enthusiastic projector. There are laws which govern human migrations quite beyond the control of the speculator, as many a man with desirable building-lots has discovered to his cost. Why mortal men will pay more for a chess-board square in that swamp, than for an acre on the breezy upland close by, who shall say? And again, why, having shown such a passion for *your* swamp, they are so coy of *mine*, who shall say? Not certainly any one who, like Davenport, had got up too early for his generation. If we could only carry that slow, imperturbable old clock of Opportunity, that never strikes a second too soon or too late, in our fobs, and push the hands forward as we can those of our watches! With a foreseeing economy of space which now seems ludicrous, the roofs of this forlorn-hope of houses were made flat, that the swarming population might have where to dry their clothes. But A. U. C. 30 showed the

same view as A. U. C. 1, — only that the brick
blocks looked as if they had been struck by a
malaria. The dull weed upholstered the decaying
wharves, and the only freight that heaped them
was the kelp and eel-grass left by higher floods.
Instead of a Venice, behold a Torzelo! The unfortunate projector took to the last refuge of the
unhappy — book-making, and bored the reluctant
public with what he called a right-aim Testament,
prefaced by a recommendation from General Jack-
son, who perhaps, from its title, took it for some
treatise on ball-practice.

But even Cambridgeport, my dear Storg, did
not want associations poetic and venerable. The
stranger who took the "Hourly" at Old Cambridge, if he were a physiognomist and student of
character, might perhaps have had his curiosity excited by a person who mounted the coach at the
Port. So refined was his whole appearance, so
fastidiously neat his apparel, — but with a neatness
that seemed less the result of care and plan than a
something as proper to the man as whiteness to the
lily, — that you would have at once classed him
with those individuals, rarer than great captains
and almost as rare as great poets, whom Nature
sends into the world to fill the arduous office of
Gentleman. Were you ever emperor of that Bara-
taria which under your peaceful sceptre would
present, of course, a model of government, this
remarkable person should be Duke of Bienséance
and Master of Ceremonies. There are some men
whom destiny has endowed with the faculty of

external neatness, whose clothes are repellent of dust and mud, whose unwithering white neck-cloths persevere to the day's end, unappeasably seeing the sun go down upon their starch, and whose linen makes you fancy them heirs in the maternal line to the instincts of all the washerwomen from Eve downward. There are others whose inward natures possess this fatal cleanness, incapable of moral dirt-spot. You are not long in discovering that the stranger combines in himself both these properties. A *nimbus* of hair, fine as an infant's, and early white, showing refinement of organization and the predominance of the spiritual over the physical, undulated and floated around a face that seemed like pale flame, and over which the flitting shades of expression chased each other, fugitive and gleaming as waves upon a field of rye. It was a countenance that, without any beauty of feature, was very beautiful. I have said that it looked like pale flame, and can find no other words for the impression it gave. Here was a man all soul, his body seeming a lamp of finest clay, whose service was to feed with magic oils, rare and fragrant, that wavering fire which hovered over it. You, who are an adept in such matters, would have detected in the eyes that artist-look which seems to see pictures ever in the air, and which, if it fall on you, makes you feel as if all the world were a gallery, and yourself the rather indifferent Portrait of a Gentleman hung therein. As the stranger brushes by you in alighting, you detect a single incongruity, — a smell of dead tobacco-smoke. You ask his name, and the answer is, " Mr. Allston."

"Mr. Allston!" and you resolve to note down at once in your diary every look, every gesture, every word of the great painter? Not in the least. You have the true Anglo-Norman indifference, and most likely never think of him again till you hear that one of his pictures has sold for a great price, and then contrive to let your grandchildren know twice a week that you met him once in a coach, and that he said, "Excuse me, sir," in a very Titianesque manner, when he stumbled over your toes in getting out. Hitherto Boswell is quite as unique as Shakespeare. The country-gentleman, journeying up to London, inquires of Mistress Davenant at the Oxford inn the name of his pleasant companion of the night before. "Master Shakespeare, an't please your worship." And the Justice, not without a sense of the unbending, says, "Truly, a merry and conceited gentleman!" It is lucky for the peace of great men that the world seldom finds out contemporaneously who its great men are, or, perhaps, that each man esteems himself the fortunate he who shall draw the lot of memory from the helmet of the future. Had the eyes of some Stratford burgess been achromatic telescopes, capable of a perspective of two hundred years! But, even then, would not his record have been fuller of *says I's* than of *says he's?* Nevertheless, it is curious to consider from what infinitely varied points of view we might form our estimate of a great man's character, when we remember that he had his points of contact with the butcher, the baker, and the candlestick-maker, as well as with

the ingenious A, the sublime B, and the Right
Honorable C. If it be true that no man ever clean
forgets everything, and that the act of drowning
(as is asserted) forthwith brightens up all those
o'er-rusted impressions, would it not be a curious
experiment, if, after a remarkable person's death,
the public, eager for minutest particulars, should
gather together all who had ever been brought into
relations with him, and, submerging them to the
hair's-breadth hitherward of the drowning-point,
subject them to strict cross-examination by the
Humane Society, as soon as they become conscious
between the resuscitating blankets? All of us
probably have brushed against destiny in the street,
have shaken hands with it, fallen asleep with it in
railway carriages, and knocked heads with it in
some one or other of its yet unrecognized incarna-
tions.

Will it seem like presenting a tract to a *colpor-
teur*, my dear Storg, if I say a word or two about
an artist to you over there in Italy? Be patient,
and leave your button in my grasp yet a little
longer. T. G. A., a person whose opinion is worth
having, once said to me, that, however one's notions
might be modified by going to Europe, one always
came back with a higher esteem for Allston. Certainly he is thus far the greatest English painter of
historical subjects. And only consider how strong
must have been the artistic bias in him, to have
made him a painter at all under the circumstances.
There were no traditions of art, so necessary for
guidance and inspiration. Blackburn, Smibert,

Copley, Trumbull, Stuart, — it was, after all, but
a Brentford sceptre which their heirs could aspire
to, and theirs were not names to conjure with, like
those from which Fame, as through a silver trumpet, had blown for three centuries. Copley and
Stuart were both remarkable men ; but the one
painted like an inspired silk-mercer, and the other,
though at his best one of the greatest of por-
trait-painters, seems sometimes to have mixed his
colors with the claret of which he and his generation were so fond. And what could a successful
artist hope for, at that time, beyond the mere
wages of his work ? His picture would hang in
cramped back-parlors, between deadly cross-fires
of lights, sure of the garret or the auction-room erelong, in a country where the nomad population
carry no household gods with them but their five
wits and their ten fingers. As a race, we care nothing about Art ; but the Puritan and the Quaker are
the only Englishmen who have had pluck enough
to confess it. If it were surprising that Allston
should have become a painter at all, how almost
miraculous that he should have been a great and
original one ! I call him original deliberately,
because, though his school be essentially Italian, it
is of less consequence where a man buys his tools,
than what use he makes of them. Enough English artists went to Italy and came back painting
history in a very Anglo-Saxon manner, and creat-
ing a school as melodramatic as the French, without its perfection in technicalities. But Allston
carried thither a nature open on the southern side,

and brought it back so steeped in rich Italian sunshine that the east winds (whether physical or intellectual) of Boston and the dusts of Cambridgeport assailed it in vain. To that bare wooden studio one might go to breathe Venetian air, and, better yet, the very spirit wherein the elder brothers of Art labored, etherealized by metaphysical speculation, and sublimed by religious fervor. The beautiful old man! Here was genius with no volcanic explosions (the mechanic result of vulgar gunpowder often), but lovely as a Lapland night; here was fame, not sought after nor worn in any cheap French fashion as a ribbon at the buttonhole, but so gentle, so retiring, that it seemed no more than an assured and emboldened modesty; here was ambition, undebased by rivalry and incapable of the sidelong look; and all these massed and harmonized together into a purity and depth of character, into a *tone*, which made the daily life of the man the greatest masterpiece of the artist.

But let us go back to the Old Town. Thirty years since, the Muster and the Cornwallis allowed some vent to those natural instincts which Puritanism scotched, but not killed. The Cornwallis had entered upon the estates of the old Guy-Fawkes procession, confiscated by the Revolution. It was a masquerade, in which that grave and suppressed humor, of which the Yankees are fuller than other people, burst through all restraints, and disported itself in all the wildest vagaries of fun. Commonly the Yankee in his pleasures suspects the presence of Public Opinion as a detective, and accordingly

is apt to pinion himself in his Sunday suit. It is a
curious commentary on the artificiality of our lives,
that men must be disguised and masked before they
will venture into the obscurer corners of their individuality, and display the true features of their
nature. One remarked it in the Carnival, and one
especially noted it here among a race naturally
self-restrained ; for Silas and Ezra and Jonas were
not only disguised as Redcoats, Continentals, and
Indians, but not unfrequently disguised in drink
also. It is a question whether the Lyceum, where
the public is obliged to comprehend all vagrom
men, supplies the place of the old popular amuse-
ments. A hundred and fifty years ago, Cotton
Mather bewails the carnal attractions of the tavern
and the training-field, and tells of an old Indian
who imperfectly understood the English tongue,
but desperately mastered enough of it (when under
sentence of death) to express a desire for instant
hemp rather than listen to any more ghostly conso-
lations. Puritanism — I am perfectly aware how
great a debt we owe it — tried over again the old
experiment of driving out nature with a pitchfork,
and had the usual success. It was like a ship inwardly on fire, whose hatches must be kept hermet-
ically battened down ; for the admittance of an
ounce of Heaven's own natural air would explode
it utterly. Morals can never be safely embodied
in the constable. Polished, cultivated, fascinating
Mephistopheles ! it is for the ungovernable break-
ings-away of the soul from unnatural compressions
that thou waitest with a deprecatory smile. Then

it is that thou offerest thy gentlemanly arm to unguarded youth for a pleasant stroll through the City of Destruction, and, as a special favor, introducest him to the bewitching Miss Circe, and to that model of the hospitable old English gentleman, Mr. Comus.

But the Muster and the Cornwallis were not peculiar to Cambridge. Commencement-day was. Saint Pedagogus was a worthy whose feast could be celebrated by men who quarrelled with mincedpies, and blasphemed custard through the nose. The holiday preserved all the features of an English fair. Stations were marked out beforehand by the town constables, and distinguished by numbered stakes. These were assigned to the different venders of small wares and exhibitors of rarities, whose canvas booths, beginning at the marketplace, sometimes half encircled the Common with their jovial embrace. Now all the Jehoiada-boxes in town were forced to give up their rattling deposits of specie, if not through the legitimate orifice, then to the brute force of the hammer. For hither were come all the wonders of the world, making the Arabian Nights seem possible, and these we beheld for half price; not without mingled emotions, — pleasure at the economy, and shame at not paying the more manly fee. Here the mummy unveiled her withered charms, — a more marvellous Ninon, still attractive in her three-thousandth year. Here were the Siamese twins; ah! if all such forced and unnatural unions were made a show of! Here were the flying horses (their supernatural effect injured — like that of some poems — by the visibility of the man who turned the crank), on which, as we tilted at the ring, we felt our shoulders tingle with the *accolade*, and heard the clink of golden spurs at our heels.   Are the realities of life ever worth half so much as its cheats?   And are there any feasts half so filling at the price as those Barmecide ones spread for us by Imagination?   Hither came the Canadian giant, surreptitiously seen, without price, as he alighted, in broad day, (giants were always foolish,) at the tavern.   Hither came the great horse Columbus, with shoes two inches thick, and more wisely introduced by night.   In the trough of the town-pump might be seen the mermaid, its poor monkey's head carefully sustained above water, to keep it from drowning.   There were dwarfs, also, who danced and sang, and many a proprietor regretted the transaudient properties of canvas, which allowed the frugal public to share in the melody without entering the booth.   Is it a slander of J. H., who reports that he once saw a deacon, eminent for psalmody, lingering near one of those vocal tents, and, with an assumed air of abstraction, furtively drinking in, with unhabitual ears, a song, not secular merely, but with a dash of libertinism? The New England proverb says, " All deacons are good, but — there 's odds in deacons."   On these days Snow became superterranean, and had a stand in the square, and Lewis temperately contended with the stronger fascinations of egg-pop.   But space would fail me to make a catalogue of everything. No doubt, Wisdom also, as usual, had her quiet booth at the corner of some street, without entrance-fee, and, even at that rate, got never a customer the whole day long. For the bankrupt afternoon there were peep-shows, at a cent each.

But all these shows and their showmen are as clean gone now as those of Cæsar and Timour and Napoleon, for which the world paid dearer. They are utterly gone out, not leaving so much as a snuff behind, — as little thought of now as that John Robins, who was once so considerable a phenomenon as to be esteemed the last great Antichrist and son of perdition by the entire sect of Muggletonians. Were Commencement what it used to be, I should be tempted to take a booth myself, and try an experiment recommended by a satirist of some merit, whose works were long ago dead and (I fear) deedeed to boot.

"Menenius, thou who fain wouldst know how calmly men can
     pass
  Those biting portraits of themselves, disguised as fox or ass,
  Go borrow coin enough to buy a full-length psyche-glass,
  Engage a rather darkish room in some well-sought position,
  And let the town break out with bills, so much per head admis-
     sion,
  GREAT NATURAL CURIOSITY!! THE BIGGEST LIVING FOOL!!
  Arrange your mirror cleverly, before it set a stool,
  Admit the public one by one, place each upon the seat,
  Draw up the curtain, let him look his fill, and then retreat.
  Smith mounts and takes a thorough view, then comes serenely
     down,
  Goes home and tells his wife the thing is curiously like Brown;
  Brown goes and stares, and tells his wife the wonder's core and
     pith
  Is that 't is just the counterpart of that conceited Smith.

> Life calls us all to such a show: Menenius, trust in me,
> While thou to see thy neighbor smil'st, he does the same for
>   thee."

My dear Storg, would you come to my show, and, instead of looking in my glass, insist on taking your money's worth in staring at the exhibiter?

Not least among the curiosities which the day brought together were some of the graduates, posthumous men, as it were, disentombed from country parishes and district-schools, but perennial also, in whom freshly survived all the college jokes, and who had no intelligence later than their Senior year. These had gathered to eat the College dinner, and to get the Triennial Catalogue (their *libro d'oro*), referred to oftener than any volume but the Concordance. Aspiring men they were certainly, but in a right unworldly way; this scholastic festival opening a peaceful path to the ambition which might else have devastated mankind with Prolusions on the Pentateuch, or Genealogies of the Dormouse Family. For since in the academic processions the classes are ranked in the order of their graduation, and he has the best chance at the dinner who has the fewest teeth to eat it with, so, by degrees, there springs up a competition in longevity,— the prize contended for being the oldest surviving graduateship. This is an office, it is true, without emolument, but having certain advantages, nevertheless. The incumbent, if he come to Commencement, is a prodigious lion, and commonly gets a paragraph in the newspapers once a year with the (fiftieth) last survivor of Washington's Life-Guard. If a clergyman, he is expected to ask a blessing and return thanks at the dinner, a function which he performs with centenarian longanimity, as if he reckoned the ordinary life of man to be fivescore years, and that a grace must be long to reach so far away as heaven. Accordingly, this silent race is watched, on the course of the Catalogue, with an interest worthy of Newmarket; and as star after star rises in the galaxy of death, till one name is left alone, an oasis of life in the stellar desert, it grows solemn. The natural feeling is reversed, and it is the solitary life that becomes sad and monitory, the Stylites there on the lonely top of his century-pillar, who has heard the passing-bell of youth, love, friendship, hope, — of everything but immitigable eld.

Dr. K. was President of the University then, a man of genius, but of genius that evaded utilization, — a great water-power, but without rapids, and flowing with too smooth and gentle a current to be set turning wheels and whirling spindles. His was not that restless genius of which the man seems to be merely the representative, and which wreaks itself in literature or politics, but of that milder sort, quite as genuine, and perhaps of more contemporaneous value, which *is* the man, permeating the whole life with placid force, and giving to word, look, and gesture a meaning only justifiable by our belief in a reserved power of latent reinforcement. The man of talents possesses them like so many

tools, does his job with them, and there an end;
but the man of genius is possessed by it, and it
makes him into a book or a life according to its
whim.   Talent takes the existing moulds, and
makes its castings, better or worse, of richer or
baser metal, according to knack and opportunity;
but genius is always shaping new ones, and runs
the man in them, so that there is always that human feel in its results which gives us a kindred
thrill.   *What* it will make, we can only conjecture,
contented always with knowing the infinite balance
of possibility against which it can draw at pleasure.
Have you ever seen a man whose cheque would be
honored for a million pay his toll of one cent? and
has not that bit of copper, no bigger than your
own, and piled with it by the careless toll-man,
given you a tingling vision of what golden bridges
he could pass, — into what Elysian regions of taste
and enjoyment and culture, barred to the rest of us?
Something like it is the impression made by such
characters as K.'s on those who come in contact
with them.

There was that in the soft and rounded (I had
almost said melting) outlines of his face which
reminded one of Chaucer.   The head had a placid
yet dignified droop like his.   He was an anachronism, fitter to have been Abbot of Fountains or
Bishop Golias, courtier and priest, humorist and
lord spiritual, all in one, than for the mastership
of a provincial college, which combined, with its
purely scholastic functions, those of accountant and
chief of police.   For keeping books he was incom-

petent (unless it were those he borrowed), and the only discipline he exercised was by the unobtrusive pressure of a gentlemanliness which rendered insubordination to *him* impossible. But the world always judges a man (and rightly enough, too) by his little faults, which he shows a hundred times a day, rather than by his great virtues, which he discloses perhaps but once in a lifetime, and to a single person, — nay, in proportion as they are rarer, and he is nobler, is shyer of letting their existence be known at all. He was one of those misplaced persons whose misfortune it is that their lives overlap two distinct eras, and are already so impregnated with one that they can never be in healthy sympathy with the other. Born when the New England clergy were still an establishment and an aristocracy, and when office was almost always for life, and often hereditary, he lived to be thrown upon a time when avocations of all colors might be shuffled together in the life of one man, like a pack of cards, so that you could not prophesy that he who was ordained to-day might not accept a colonelcy of filibusters to-morrow. Such temperaments as his attach themselves, like barnacles, to what seems permanent; but presently the good ship Progress weighs anchor, and whirls them away from drowsy tropic inlets to arctic waters of unnatural ice. To such crustaceous natures, created to cling upon the immemorial rock amid softest mosses, comes the bustling Nineteenth Century and says, " Come, come, bestir yourself and be practical! get out of that old shell of yours forthwith ! "   Alas ! to get out of the shell is to die !

One of the old travellers in South America tells of fishes that built their nests in trees, (*piscium et summa hæsit genus ulmo,*) and gives a print of the mother fish upon her nest, while her mate mounts perpendicularly to her without aid of legs or wings.   Life shows plenty of such incongruities between a man's place and his nature, (not so easily got over as by the traveller's undoubting engraver,) and one cannot help fancying that K. was an instance in point.   He never encountered, one would say, the attraction proper to draw out his native force.   Certainly, few men who impressed others so strongly, and of whom so many good things are remembered, left less behind them to justify contemporary estimates.   He printed nothing, and was, perhaps, one of those the electric sparkles of whose brains, discharged naturally and healthily in conversation, refuse to pass through the non-conducting medium of the inkstand.   His *ana* would make a delightful collection.   One or two of his official ones will be in place here. Hearing that Porter's flip (which was exemplary) had too great an attraction for the collegians, he resolved to investigate the matter himself.   Accordingly, entering the old inn one day, he called for a mug of it, and, having drunk it, said, " And so, Mr. Porter, the young gentlemen come to drink your flip, do they ? "   " Yes, sir, — sometimes." " Ah, well, I should think they would.   Good day, Mr. Porter," and departed, saying nothing more ;

for he always wisely allowed for the existence of a
certain amount of human nature in ingenuous youth.
At another time the " Harvard Washington " asked
leave to go into Boston to a collation which had
been offered them. " Certainly, young gentlemen,"
said the President, " but have you engaged any one
to bring home your muskets ? " — the College being responsible for these weapons, which belonged
to the State.   Again, when a student came with a
physician's certificate, and asked leave of absence,
K. granted it at once, and then added, " By the way,
Mr. ——, persons interested in the relation which
exists between states of the atmosphere and health
have noticed a curious fact in regard to the climate
of Cambridge, especially within the College limits,
— the very small number of deaths in proportion
to the cases of dangerous illness."   This is told of
Judge W., himself a wit, and capable of enjoying
the humorous delicacy of the reproof.

Shall I take Brahmin Alcott's favorite word,
and call him a dæmonic man ?   No, the Latin *genius* is quite old-fashioned enough for me, means the
same thing, and its derivative *geniality* expresses,
moreover, the base of K.'s being.   How he suggested cloistered repose, and quadrangles mossy with
centurial associations !   How easy he was, and how
without creak was every movement of his mind !
This life was good enough for him, and the next
not too good.   The gentleman-like pervaded even
his prayers.   His were not the manners of a man
of the world, nor of a man of the other world
either ; but both met in him to balance each other

in a beautiful equilibrium. Praying, he leaned
forward upon the pulpit-cushion as for conversation, and seemed to feel himself (without irrever-
ence) on terms of friendly, but courteous, familiarity with Heaven. The expression of his face was
that of tranquil contentment, and he appeared less
to be supplicating expected mercies than thankful
for those already found, — as if he were saying the
gratias in the refectory of the Abbey of Theleme.
Under him flourished the Harvard Washington
Corps, whose gyrating banner, inscribed *Tam
Marti quam Mercurio (atqui magis Lyæo* should
have been added,) on the evening of training-days,
was an accurate dynamometer of Willard's punch
or Porter's flip. It was they who, after being roy-
ally entertained by a maiden lady of the town, entered in their orderly book a vote that Miss Blank
was a gentleman. I see them now, returning from
the imminent deadly breach of the law of Rechab,
unable to form other than the serpentine line of
beauty, while their officers, brotherly rather than
imperious, instead of reprimanding, tearfully em-
braced the more eccentric wanderers from military
precision. Under him the Med. Facs. took their
equal place among the learned societies of Europe,
numbering among their grateful honorary members Alexander, Emperor of all the Russias, who
(if College legends may be trusted) sent them in
return for their diploma a gift of medals confiscated by the authorities. Under him the College
fire-engine was vigilant and active in suppressing
any tendency to spontaneous combustion among the

Freshmen, or rushed wildly to imaginary conflagrations, generally in a direction where punch was to be had. All these useful conductors for the natural electricity of youth, dispersing it or turning it harmlessly into the earth, are taken away now, — wisely or not, is questionable.

An academic town, in whose atmosphere there is always something antiseptic, seems naturally to draw to itself certain varieties and to preserve certain humors (in the Ben Jonsonian sense) of character, — men who come not to study so much as to be studied. At the headquarters of Washington once, and now of the Muses, lived C——, but before the date of these recollections. Here for seven years (as the law was then) he made his house his castle, sunning himself in his elbow-chair at the front-door, on that seventh day, secure from every arrest but Death's. Here long survived him his turbaned widow, studious only of Spinoza, and refusing to molest the canker-worms that annually disleaved her elms, because we were all vermicular alike. She had been a famous beauty once, but the canker years had left her leafless, too; and I used to wonder, as I saw her sitting always turbaned and always alone at her accustomed window, whether she were ever visited by the reproachful shade of him who (in spite of Rosalind) died broken-hearted for her in her radiant youth.

And this reminds me of J. F., who, also crossed in love, allowed no mortal eye to behold his face for many years. The eremitic instinct is not peculiar to the Thebais, as many a New England village can testify; and it is worthy of consideration that the Romish Church has not forgotten this among her other points of intimate contact with human nature. F. became purely vespertinal, never stirring abroad till after dark. He occupied two rooms, migrating from one to the other, as the necessities of housewifery demanded, thus shunning all sight of womankind, and being practically more solitary in his dual apartment than Montaigne's Dean of St. Hilaire in his single one. When it was requisite that he should put his signature to any legal instrument, (for he was an anchorite of ample means,) he wrapped himself in a blanket, allowing nothing to be seen but the hand which acted as scribe. What impressed us boys more than anything else was the rumor that he had suffered his beard to grow, — such an anti-Sheffieldism being almost unheard of in those days, and the peculiar ornament of man being associated in our minds with nothing more recent than the patriarchs and apostles, whose effigies we were obliged to solace ourselves with weekly in the Family Bible. He came out of his oysterhood at last, and I knew him well, a kind-hearted man, who gave annual sleigh-rides to the town-paupers, and supplied the poorer children with school-books. His favorite topic of conversation was Eternity, and, like many other worthy persons, he used to fancy that meaning was an affair of aggregation, and that he doubled the intensity of what he said by the sole aid of the multiplication-table. "Eternity!" he used to say, "it is not a day; it is not a year; it is not a hundred years; it is not a thousand years; it is not a million years; no, sir," (the *sir* being thrown in to recall wandering attention,) " it is not ten million years!" and so on, his enthusiasm becoming a mere frenzy when he got among his sextillions, till I sometimes wished he had continued in retirement. He used to sit at the open window during thunder-storms, and had a Grecian feeling about death by lightning. In a certain sense he had his desire, for he died suddenly, — not by fire from heaven, but by the red flash of apoplexy, leaving his whole estate to charitable uses.

If K. were out of place as President, that was not P. as Greek Professor. Who that ever saw him can forget him, in his old age, like a lusty winter, frosty but kindly, with great silver spectacles of the heroic period, such as scarce twelve noses of these degenerate days could bear? He was a natural celibate, not dwelling " like the fly in the heart of the apple," but like a lonely bee rather, absconding himself in Hymettian flowers, incapable of matrimony as a solitary palm-tree. There was, to be sure, a tradition of youthful disappointment, and a touching story which L. told me perhaps confirms it. When Mrs. —— died, a carriage with blinds drawn followed the funeral train at some distance, and, when the coffin had been lowered into the grave, drove hastily away to escape that saddest of earthly sounds, the first rattle of earth upon the lid. It was afterward known that the carriage held a single mourner, — our grim and undemonstrative Professor. Yet I cannot bring myself to suppose him susceptible to any tender passion after that single lapse in the immaturity of reason. He might have joined the Abderites in singing their mad chorus from the Andromeda; but it would have been in deference to the language merely, and with a silent protest against the sentiment. I fancy him arranging his scrupulous toilet, not for Amaryllis or Neæra, but, like Machiavelli, for the society of his beloved classics. His ears had needed no prophylactic wax to pass the Sirens' isle; nay, he would have kept them the wider open, studious of the dialect in.which they sang, and perhaps triumphantly detecting the Æolic digamma in their lay. A thoroughly single man, single-minded, single-hearted, buttoning over his single heart a single - breasted surtout, and wearing always a hat of a single fashion, — did he in secret regard the dual number of his favorite language as a weakness? The son of an officer of distinction in the Revolutionary War, he mounted the pulpit' with the erect port of a soldier, and carried his cane more in the fashion of a weapon than a staff, but with the point lowered, in token of surrender to the peaceful proprieties of his calling. Yet sometimes the martial instincts would burst the cerements of black coat and clerical neckcloth, as once, when the students had got into a fight upon the training-field, and the licentious soldiery, furious with rum, had driven them at point of bayonet to the College gates, and even threatened to lift their arms against the Muses' bower. Then, like Major Goffe at Deerfield, suddenly appeared the gray-haired P., all his father resurgent in him, and shouted: "Now, my lads, stand your ground, you're in the right now! Don't let one of them set foot within the College grounds!" Thus he allowed arms to get the better of the *toga;* but raised it, like the Prophet's breeches, into a banner, and carefully ushered resistance with a preamble of infringed right. Fidelity was his strong characteristic, and burned equally in him through a life of eighty-three years. He drilled himself till inflexible habit stood sentinel before all those postern-weaknesses which temperament leaves unbolted to temptation. A lover of the scholar's herb, yet loving freedom more, and knowing that the animal appetites ever hold one hand behind them for Satan to drop a bribe in, he would never have two cigars in his house at once, but walked every day to the shop to fetch his single diurnal solace. Nor would he trust himself with two on Saturdays, preferring (since he could not violate the Sabbath even by that infinitesimal traffic) to depend on Providential ravens, which were seldom wanting in the shape of some black-coated friend who knew his need, and honored the scruple that occasioned it. He was faithful, also, to his old hats, in which appeared the constant service of the antique world, and which he preserved forever, piled like a black pagoda under his dressing-table. No scarecrow was ever the residuary legatee of *his* beavers, though one of them in any of the neighboring peach-orchards would have been sovereign against an attack of Freshmen.   He wore them all in turn, getting through all in the course of the year, like the sun through the signs of the zodiac, modulating them according to seasons and celestial phenomena, so that never was spider-web or chickweed so sensitive a weather-gauge as they.   Nor did his political party find him less loyal.   Taking all the tickets, he would seat himself apart, and carefully compare them with the list of regular nominations as printed in his Daily Advertiser, before he dropped his ballot in the box.   In less ambitious moments, it almost seems to me that I would rather have had that slow, conscientious vote of P.'s alone, than to have been chosen Alderman of the Ward!

If you had walked to what was then Sweet Auburn by the pleasant Old Road, on some June morning thirty years ago, you would very likely have met two other characteristic persons, both phantasmagoric now, and belonging to the past. Fifty years earlier, the scarlet-coated, rapiered figures of Vassall, Lechmere, Oliver, and Brattle creaked up and down there on red-heeled shoes, lifting the ceremonious three-cornered hat, and offering the fugacious hospitalities of the snuff-box. They are all shadowy alike now, not one of your Etruscan Lucumos or Roman Consuls more so, my dear Storg.   First is W., his *queue* slender and tapering, like the tail of a violet crab, held out horizontally by the high collar of his shepherd's-gray overcoat, whose style was of the latest when he studied at Leyden in his hot youth.   The ago of cheap clothes sees no more of those faithful old garments, as proper to their wearers and as distinctive as the barks of trees, and by long use interpenetrated with their very nature. Nor do we see so many Humors (still in the old sense) now that every man's soul belongs to the Public, as when social distinctions were more marked, and men felt that their personalities were their castles, in which they could intrench themselves against the world. Nowadays men are shy of letting their true selves be seen, as if in some former life they had committed a crime, and were all the time afraid of discovery and arrest in this. Formerly they used to insist on your giving the wall to their peculiarities, and you may still find examples of it in the parson or the doctor of retired villages. One of W.'s oddities was touching. A little brook used to run across the street, and the sidewalk was carried over it by a broad stone. Of course there is no brook now. What use did that little glimpse of a ripple serve, where the children used to launch their chip fleets? W., in going over this stone, which gave a hollow resonance to the tread, had a trick of striking upon it three times with his cane, and muttering, "Tom, Tom, Tom!" I used to think he was only mimicking with his voice the sound of the blows, and possibly it was that sound which suggested his thought, for he was remembering a favorite nephew, prematurely dead. Perhaps Tom had sailed his boats there; perhaps the reverberation under the old man's foot hinted at the hollowness of life; perhaps the fleeting eddies of

the water brought to mind the *fugaces annos.*
W., like P., wore amazing spectacles, fit to transmit no smaller image than the page of mightiest folios of Dioscorides or Hercules de Saxonia, and rising full-disked upon the beholder like those prodigies of two moons at once, portending change to monarchs. The great collar disallowing any independent rotation of the head, I remember he used to turn his whole person in order to bring their *foci* to bear upon an object. One can fancy that terrified Nature would have yielded up her secrets at once, without cross-examination, at their first glare. Through them he had gazed fondly into the great mare's-nest of Junius, publishing his observations upon the eggs found therein in a tall octavo. It was he who introduced vaccination to this Western World. Malicious persons disputing his claim to this distinction, he published this advertisement: "Lost, a gold snuff-box, with the inscription, 'The Jenner of the Old World to the Jenner of the New.' Whoever shall return the same to Dr. —— shall be suitably rewarded." It was never returned. Would the search after it have been as fruitless as that of the alchemist after his equally imaginary gold? Malicious persons persisted in believing the box as visionary as the claim it was meant to buttress with a semblance of reality. He used to stop and say good-morning kindly, and pat the shoulder of the blushing school-boy who now, with the fierce snow-storm wildering without, sits and remembers sadly those old meetings and partings in the June sunshine.

Then there was S., whose resounding "Haw, haw, haw! by Shorge!" positively enlarged the income of every dweller in Cambridge. In downright, honest good cheer and good neighborhood, it was worth five hundred a year to every one of us. Its jovial thunders cleared the mental air of every sulky cloud. Perpetual childhood dwelt in him, the childhood of his native Southern France, and its fixed air was all the time bubbling up and sparkling and winking in his eyes. It seemed as if his placid old face were only a mask behind which a merry Cupid had ambushed himself, peeping out all the while, and ready to drop it when the play grew tiresome. Every word he uttered seemed to be hilarious, no matter what the occasion. If he were sick, and you visited him, if he had met with a misfortune, (and there are few men so wise that they can look even at the back of a retiring sorrow with composure,) it was all one; his great laugh went off as if it were set like an alarm-clock, to run down, whether he would or no, at a certain nick. Even after an ordinary *Good morning!* (especially if to an old pupil, and in French,) the wonderful *Haw, haw, haw! by Shorge!* would burst upon you unexpectedly, like a salute of artillery on some holiday which you had forgotten. Everything was a joke to him, — that the oath of allegiance had been administered to him by your grandfather, — that he had taught Prescott his first Spanish (of which he was proud),—no matter what. Everything came to him marked by Nature *Right side up, with care*, and he kept it so. The world

to him, as to all of us, was like a medal, on the
obverse of which is stamped the image of Joy, and
on the reverse that of Care. S. never took the
foolish pains to look at that other side, even if
he knew its existence; much less would it have occurred to him to turn it into view, and insist that
his friends should look at it with him. Nor was
this a mere outside good-humor; its source was
deeper, in a true Christian kindliness and amenity.
Once, when he had been knocked down by a tip-
sily-driven sleigh, and was urged to prosecute the
offenders, "No, no," he said, his wounds still fresh,
"young blood! young blood! it must have its way;
I was young myself." *Was!* few men come into
life so young as S. went out. He landed in Boston
(then the front door of America) in '93, and, in
honor of the ceremony, had his head powdered
afresh, and put on a suit of court-mourning for
Louis XVI. before he set foot on the wharf. My
fancy always dressed him in that violet silk, and
his soul certainly wore a full court-suit. What
was there ever like his bow? It was as if you
had received a decoration, and could write yourself
gentleman from that day forth. His hat rose, re-
greeting your own, and, having sailed through the
stately curve of the old *régime*, sank gently back
over that placid brain, which harbored no thought
less white than the powder which covered it. I
have sometimes imagined that there was a graduated arc over his head, invisible to other eyes than
his, by which he meted out to each his rightful
share of castorial consideration. I carry in my

memory three exemplary bows. The first is that of an old beggar, who, already carrying in his hand a white hat, the gift of benevolence, took off the black one from his head also, and profoundly saluted me with both at once, giving me, in return for my alms, a dual benediction, puzzling as a nod from Janus Bifrons. The second I received from an old Cardinal, who was taking his walk just outside the Porta San Giovanni at Rome. I paid him the courtesy due to his age and rank. Forthwith rose, first, *the* Hat; second, the hat of his confessor; third, that of another priest who attended him; fourth, the fringed cocked-hat of his coachman; fifth and sixth, the ditto, ditto, of his two footmen. Here was an investment, indeed; six hundred per cent. interest on a single bow! The third bow, worthy to be noted in one's almanac among the other *mirabilia*, was that of S., in which courtesy had mounted to the last round of her ladder, — and tried to draw it up after her.

But the genial veteran is gone even while I am writing this, and I will play Old Mortality no longer. Wandering among these recent graves, my dear friend, we may chance upon ———; but no, I will not end my sentence. I bid you heartily farewell!

LEAVES FROM MY JOURNAL IN ITALY AND ELSEWHERE

1854

I

AT SEA

THE sea was meant to be looked at from shore, as mountains are from the plain. Lucretius made this discovery long ago, and was blunt enough to blurt it forth, romance and sentiment — in other words, the pretence of feeling what we do not feel — being inventions of a later day. To be sure, Cicero used to twaddle about Greek literature and philosophy, much as people do about ancient art nowadays; but I rather sympathize with those stout old Romans who despised both, and believed that to found an empire was as grand an achievement as to build an epic or to carve a statue. But though there might have been twaddle, (as why not, since there was a Senate?) I rather think Petrarch was the first choragus of that sentimental dance which so long led young folks away from the realities of life like the piper of Hamelin, and whose succession ended, let us hope, with Chateaubriand. But for them, Byron, whose real strength lay in his sincerity, would never have talked about the " sea bounding beneath him like a steed that knows his rider," and all that sort of thing. Even if it had been true, steam has been as fatal to that part of the romance of the sea as to hand-loom weaving. But what say you to a twelve days' calm such as we dozed through in mid-Atlantic and in mid-August? I know nothing so tedious at once and exasperating as that regular slap of the wilted sails when the ship rises and falls with the slow breathing of the sleeping sea, one greasy, brassy swell following another, slow, smooth, immitigable as the series of Wordsworth's Ecclesiastical Sonnets. Even at his best, Neptune, in a *tête-à-tête*, has a way of repeating himself, an obtuseness to the *ne quid nimis*, that is stupefying. It reminds me of organ-music and my good friend Sebastian Bach. A fugue or two will do very well; but a concert made up of nothing else is altogether too epic for me. There is nothing so desperately monotonous as the sea, and I no longer wonder at the cruelty of pirates. Fancy an existence in which the coming up of a clumsy finback whale, who says *Pooh !* to you solemnly as you lean over the taff-rail, is an event as exciting as an election on shore ! The dampness seems to strike into the wits as into the lucifer-matches, so that one may scratch a thought half a dozen times and get nothing at last but a faint sputter, the forlorn hope of fire, which only goes far enough to leave a sense of suffocation behind it. Even smoking becomes an employment instead of a solace. Who less likely to come to their wit's end than W. M. T. and

A. H. C. ? Yet I have seen them driven to five meals a day for mental occupation. I sometimes sit and pity Noah; but even he had this advantage over all succeeding navigators, that, wherever he landed, he was sure to get no ill news from home. He should be canonized as the patron-saint of newspaper correspondents, being the only man who ever had the very last authentic intelligence from everywhere.

The finback whale recorded just above has much the look of a brown-paper parcel, — the whitish stripes that run across him answering for the pack-thread. He has a kind of accidental hole in the top of his head, through which he *pooh-poohs* the rest of creation, and which looks as if it had been made by the chance thrust of a chestnut rail. He was our first event. Our second was harpooning a sunfish, which basked dozing on the lap of the sea, looking so much like the giant turtle of an alderman's dream, that I am persuaded he would have let himself be made into mock-turtle soup rather than acknowledge his imposture. But he broke away just as they were hauling him over the side, and sank placidly through the clear water, leaving behind him a crimson trail that wavered a moment and was gone.

The sea, though, has better sights than these. When we were up with the Azores, we began to meet flying-fish and Portuguese men-of-war beautiful as the galley of Cleopatra, tiny craft that dared these seas before Columbus. I have seen one of the former rise from the crest of a wave,

and, glancing from another some two hundred feet
beyond, take a fresh flight of perhaps as far. How
Calderon would have similized this pretty creature
had he ever seen it! How would he have run him
up and down the gamut of simile! If a fish, then
a fish with wings ; if a bird, then a bird, with fins ;
and so on, keeping up the light shuttle-cock of a
conceit as is his wont. Indeed, the poor thing is
the most killing bait for a comparison, and I assure
you I have three or four in my inkstand ; — but be
calm, they shall stay there. Moore, who looked
on all nature as a kind of *Gradus ad Parnassum*,
a *thesaurus* of similitude, and spent his life in a
game of What is my thought like? with himself,
did the flying-fish on his way to Bermuda.   So
I leave him in peace.

The most beautiful thing I have seen at sea, all
the more so that I had never heard of it, is the
trail of a shoal of fish through the phosphorescent
water. It is like a flight of silver rockets, or the
streaming of northern lights through that silent
nether heaven. I thought nothing could go beyond
that rustling star-foam which was churned up by
our ship's bows, or those eddies and disks of dreamy
flame that rose and wandered out of sight behind
us.

> 'T was fire our ship was plunging through,
> Cold fire that o'er the quarter flew ;
> And wandering moons of idle flame
> Grew full and waned, and went and came,
> Dappling with light the huge sea-snake
> That slid behind us in the wake.

But there was something even more delicately rare

in the apparition of the fish, as they turned up in
gleaming furrows the latent moonshine which the
ocean seemed to have hoarded against these vacant
interlunar nights.   In the Mediterranean one day,
as we were lying becalmed, I observed the water
freckled with dingy specks, which at last gathered
to a pinkish scum on the surface.   The sea had
been so phosphorescent for some nights, that when
the Captain gave me my bath, by dousing me with
buckets from the house on deck, the spray flew
off my head and shoulders in sparks.   It occurred
to me that this dirty-looking scum might be the
luminous matter, and I had a pailful dipped up to
keep till after dark.   When I went to look at it
after nightfall, it seemed at first perfectly dead;
but when I shook it, the whole broke out into what
I can only liken to milky flames, whose lambent
silence was strangely beautiful, and startled me almost as actual projection might an alchemist.   I
could not bear to be the death of so much beauty;
so I poured it all overboard again.

Another sight worth taking a voyage for is that
of the sails by moonlight.   Our course was " south
and by east, half south," so that we seemed bound
for the full moon as she rolled up over our wavering horizon.   Then I used to go forward to the
bowsprit and look back.   Our ship was a clipper,
with every rag set, stunsails, sky-scrapers, and all;
nor was it easy to believe that such a wonder could
be built of canvas as that white many-storied pile
of cloud that stooped over me or drew back as we
rose and fell with the waves.

These are all the wonders I can recall of my five weeks at sea, except the sun. Were you ever alone with the sun? You think it a very simple question; but I never was, in the full sense of the word, till I was held up to him one cloudless day on the broad buckler of the ocean. I suppose one might have the same feeling in the desert. I remember getting something like it years ago, when I climbed alone to the top of a mountain, and lay face up on the hot gray moss, striving to get a notion of how an Arab might feel. It was my American commentary of the Koran, and not a bad one. In a New England winter, too, when everything is gagged with snow, as if some gigantic physical geographer were taking a cast of the earth's face in plaster, the bare knob of a hill will introduce you to the sun as a comparative stranger. But at sea you may be alone with him day after day, and almost all day long. I never understood before that nothing short of full daylight can give the supremest sense of solitude. Darkness will not do so, for the imagination peoples it with more shapes than ever were poured from the frozen loins of the populous North. The sun, I sometimes think, is a little *grouty* at sea, especially at high noon, feeling that he wastes his beams on those fruitless furrows. It is otherwise with the moon. She " comforts the night," as Chapman finely says, and I always found her a companionable creature.

In the ocean-horizon I took untiring delight. It is the true magic-circle of expectation and conjecture, — almost as good as a wishing-ring. What

will rise over that edge we sail towards daily and
never overtake? A sail? an island? the new
shore of the Old World? Something rose every
day, which I need not have gone so far to see, but
at whose levee I was a much more faithful courtier
than on shore. A cloudless sunrise in mid-ocean
is beyond comparison for simple grandeur. It is
like Dante's style, bare and perfect. Naked sun
meets naked sea, the true classic of nature. There
may be more sentiment in morning on shore, — the
shivering fairy-jewelry of dew, the silver point-lace
of sparkling hoar-frost, — but there is also more
complexity, more of the romantic. The one savors
of the elder Edda, the other of the Minnesingers.

> And I thus floating, lonely elf,
> A kind of planet by myself,
> The mists draw up and furl away,
> And in the east a warming gray,
> Faint as the tint of oaken woods
> When o'er their buds May breathes and broods,
> Tells that the golden sunrise-tide
> Is lapsing up earth's thirsty side,
> Each moment purpling on the crest
> Of some stark billow farther west:
> And as the sea-moss droops and hears
> The gurgling flood that nears and nears,
> And then with tremulous content
> Floats out each thankful filament,
> So waited I until it came,
> God's daily miracle, — O shame
> That I had seen so many days
> Unthankful, without wondering praise,
> Not recking more this bliss of earth
> Than the cheap fire that lights my hearth!
> But now glad thoughts and holy pour
> Into my heart, as once a year
> To San Miniato's open door,

> In long procession, chanting clear,
> Through slopes of sun, through shadows hoar,
> The coupled monks slow-climbing sing,
> And like a golden censer swing
> From rear to front, from front to rear
> Their alternating bursts of praise,
> Till the roof's fading seraphs gaze
> Down through an odorous mist, that crawls
> Lingeringly up the darkened walls,
> And the dim arches, silent long,
> Are startled with triumphant song.

I wrote yesterday that the sea still rimmed our prosy lives with mystery and conjecture. But one is shut up on shipboard like Montaigne in his tower, with nothing to do but to review his own thoughts and contradict himself. *Dire, redire, et me contredire*, will be the staple of my journal till I see land. I say nothing of such matters as the *montagna bruna* on which Ulysses wrecked; but since the sixteenth century could any man reasonably hope to stumble on one of those wonders which were cheap as dirt in the days of St. Saga? Faustus, Don Juan, and Tannhäuser are the last ghosts of legend, that lingered almost till the Gallic cockcrow of universal enlightenment and disillusion. The Public School has done for Imagination. What shall I see in Outre-Mer, or on the way thither, but what can be seen with eyes? To be sure, I stick by the sea-serpent, and would fain believe that science has scotched, not killed him. Nor is he to be lightly given up, for, like the old Scandinavian snake, he binds together for us the two hemispheres of Past and Present, of Belief and Science. He is the link which knits us seaboard Yankees with our

Norse progenitors, interpreting between the age of
the dragon and that of the railroad-train. We
have made ducks and drakes of that large estate of
wonder and delight bequeathed to us by ancestral
vikings, and this alone remains to us unthrift Heirs
of Linn.

I feel an undefined respect for a man who has
seen the sea-serpent. He is to his brother-fishers
what the poet is to his fellow-men. Where they
have seen nothing better than a school of horse-
mackerel, or the idle coils of ocean round Half-way
Rock, he has caught authentic glimpses of the with-
drawing mantle-hem of the Edda age. I care not
for the monster himself. It is not the thing, but
the belief in the thing, that is dear to me. May
it be long before Professor Owen is comforted with
the sight of his unfleshed vertebræ, long before
they stretch many a rood behind Kimball's or Barnum's glass, reflected in the shallow orbs of Mr.
and Mrs. Public, which stare, but see not! I
speak of him in the singular number, for I insist
on believing that there is but one left, without
chance of duplicate. When we read that Captain
Spalding, of the pink-stern *Three Pollies*, has beheld him rushing through the brine like an infinite
series of bewitched mackerel-casks, we feel that the
mystery of old Ocean, at least, has not yet been
sounded, — that Faith and Awe survive there un-
evaporate. I once ventured the horse - mackerel
theory to an old fisherman, browner than a tomcod.
"Hos-mackril!" he exclaimed indignantly, "hos-
mackril be —" (here he used a phrase commonly

indicated in laical literature by the same sign which
serves for Doctorate in Divinity,) "don't yer spose
I know a hos-mackril?"   The intonation of that
"*I*" would have silenced Professor Monkbarns
Owen with his provoking *phoca* forever.   What if
one should ask *him* if he knew a trilobite?

The fault of modern travellers is, that they see
nothing out of sight.   They talk of eocene periods
and tertiary formations, and tell us how the world
looked to the plesiosaur.   They take science (or
nescience) with them, instead of that soul of generous trust their elders had.   All their senses are
sceptics and doubters, materialists reporting things
for other sceptics to doubt still further upon.   Nature becomes a reluctant witness upon the stand,
badgered with geologist hammers and phials of acid.
There have been no travellers since those included
in Hakluyt and Purchas, except Martin, perhaps,
who saw an inch or two into the invisible at the
Western Islands.   We have peripatetic lecturers,
but no more travellers.   Travellers' stories are no
longer proverbial.   We have picked nearly every
apple (wormy or otherwise) from the world's tree
of knowledge, and that without an Eve to tempt us.
Two or three have hitherto hung luckily beyond
reach on a lofty bough shadowing the interior of
Africa, but there is a German Doctor at this very
moment pelting at them with sticks and stones.   It
may be only next week, and these too, bitten by
geographers and geologists, will be thrown away.

Analysis is carried into everything.   Even Deity
is subjected to chemic tests.   We must have exact

knowledge, a cabinet stuck full of facts pressed,
dried, or preserved in spirits, instead of the large,
vague world our fathers had. With them science
was poetry ; with us, poetry is science. Our modern
Eden is a *hortus siccus*. Tourists defraud rather
than enrich us. They have not that sense of æsthetic proportion which characterized the elder traveller. Earth is no longer the fine work of art it was,
for nothing is left to the imagination. Job Hortop,
arrived at the height of the Bermudas, thinks it
full time to indulge us in a merman. Nay, there
is a story told by Webster, in his Witchcraft, of
a merman with a mitre, who, on being sent back
to his watery diocese of finland, made what advances he could toward an episcopal benediction by
bowing his head thrice. Doubtless he had been
consecrated by St. Antony of Padua. A dumb
bishop would be sometimes no unpleasant phenomenon, by the way. Sir John Hawkins is not satisfied with telling us about the merely sensual Canaries, but is generous enough to throw us in a hand-
ful of " certain flitting islands " to boot. Henry
Hawkes describes the visible Mexican cities, and
then is not so frugal but that he can give us a few
invisible ones. Thus do these generous ancient
mariners make children of us again. Their succes-
sors show us an earth effete and in a double sense
past bearing, tracing out with the eyes of indus-
trious fleas every wrinkle and crowfoot.

The journals of the elder navigators are prose
Odysseys. The geographies of our ancestors were
works of fancy and imagination. They read poems

where we yawn over items. Their world was a
huge wonder-horn, exhaustless as that which Thor
strove to drain. Ours would scarce quench the
small thirst of a bee. No modern voyager brings
back the magical foundation-stones of a Tempest.
No Marco Polo, traversing the desert beyond the
city of Lok, would tell of things able to inspire the
mind of Milton with

> " Calling shapes and beckoning shadows dire,
> And airy tongues that syllable men's names
> On sands and shores and desert wildernesses."

It was easy enough to believe the story of Dante,
when two thirds of even the upper-world were yet
untraversed and unmapped. With every step of
the recent traveller our inheritance of the wonderful is diminished. Those beautifully pictured
notes of the Possible are redeemed at a ruinous discount in the hard and cumbrous coin of the Actual.
How are we not defrauded and impoverished? Does
California vie with El Dorado? or are Bruce's
Abyssinian kings a set-off for Prester John? A
bird in the bush is worth two in the hand. And
if the philosophers have not even yet been able to
agree whether the world has any existence independent of ourselves, how do we not gain a loss in
every addition to the catalogue of Vulgar Errors?
Where are the fishes which nidificated in trees?
Where the monopodes sheltering themselves from
the sun beneath their single umbrella-like foot, —
umbrella-like in everything but the fatal necessity
of being borrowed? Where the Acephali, with
whom Herodotus, in a kind of ecstasy, wound up

his climax of men with abnormal top-pieces?
Where the Roc whose eggs are possibly boulders,
needing no far-fetched theory of glacier or iceberg
to account for them?   Where the tails of the men
of Kent?   Where the no legs of the bird of paradise?   Where the Unicorn, with that single horn
of his, sovereign against all manner of poisons?
Where that Thessalian spring, which, without cost
to the country, convicted and punished perjurers?
Where the Amazons of Orellana?   Where, in short,
the Fountain of Youth?   All these, and a thousand
other varieties, we have lost, and have got nothing
instead of them.   And those who have robbed us
of them have stolen that which not enriches themselves.   It is so much wealth cast into the sea beyond all approach of diving-bells.   We owe no
thanks to Mr. J. E. Worcester, whose Geography
we studied enforcedly at school.   Yet even he had his
relentings, and in some softer moment vouchsafed
us a fine, inspiring print of the Maelstrom, answerable to the twenty-four mile diameter of its suc-
tion.   Year by year, more and more of the world
gets disenchanted.   Even the icy privacy of the
arctic and antarctic circles is invaded.   Our youth
are no longer ingenuous, as indeed no ingenuity is
demanded of them.   Everything is accounted for,
everything cut and dried, and the world may be
put together as easily as the fragments of a dis-
sected map.   The Mysterious bounds nothing now
on the North, South, East, or West.   We have
played Jack Horner with our earth, till there is
never a plum left in it.

II

IN THE MEDITERRANEAN

The first sight of a shore so historical as that of Europe gives an American a strange thrill. What we always feel the artistic want of at home is background. It is all idle to say we are Englishmen, and that English history is ours too. It is precisely in this that we are *not* Englishmen, inasmuch as we only possess their history through our minds, and not by life-long association with a spot and an idea we call England. History without the soil it grew in is more instructive than inspiring,— an acquisition, and not an inheritance. It is laid away in our memories, and does not run in our veins. Surely, in all that concerns æsthetics, Europeans have us at an immense advantage. They start at a point which we arrive at after weary years, for literature is not shut up in books, nor art in galleries : both are taken in by unconscious absorption through the finer pores of mind and character in the atmosphere of society. We are not yet out of our Crusoe-hood, and must make our own tools as best we may. Yet I think we shall find the good of it one of these days, in being thrown back more wholly on nature ; and our literature, when we have learned to feel our own strength, and to respect our own thought because it is ours, and not because the European Mrs. Grundy agrees with it, will have a fresh flavor and a strong body that will recommend it, especially as what we import is watered more and more liberally with every vintage.

My first glimpse of Europe was the shore of Spain. One morning a cream-colored blur on the now unwavering horizon's edge was pointed out to me as Cadiz. Since we got into the Mediterranean, we have been becalmed for some days within easy view of land. All along are fine mountains, brown all day, and with a bloom on them at sunset like that of a ripe plum. Here and there at their feet little white towns are sprinkled along the edge of the water, like the grains of rice dropped by the princess in the story. Sometimes we see larger buildings on the mountain slopes, probably convents. I sit and wonder whether the farther peaks may not be the Sierra Morena (the rusty saw) of Don Quixote. I resolve that they shall be, and am content. Surely latitude and longitude never showed me any particular respect, that I should be over-scrupulous with them.

But after all, Nature, though she may be more beautiful, is nowhere so entertaining as in man, and the best thing I have seen and learned at sea is our Chief Mate. My first acquaintance with him was made over my knife, which he asked to look at, and, after a critical examination, handed back to me, saying, " I should n't wonder if that 'ere was a good piece o' stuff." Since then he has transferred a part of his regard for my knife to its owner. I like folks who like an honest bit of steel, and take no interest whatever in " your Raphaels, Correggios, and stuff." There is always more than

the average human nature in a man who has a
hearty sympathy with iron. It is a manly metal,
with no sordid associations like gold and silver.
My sailor fully came up to my expectation on
further acquaintance. He might well be called an
old salt who had been wrecked on Spitzbergen before I was born. He was not an American, but I
should never have guessed it by his speech, which
was the purest Cape Cod, and I reckon myself a
good taster of dialects. Nor was he less Ameri-
canized in all his thoughts and feelings, a singular
proof of the ease with which our omnivorous country assimilates foreign matter, provided it be Protestant, for he was a grown man ere he became an
American citizen. He used to walk the deck with
his hands in his pockets, in seeming abstraction,
but nothing escaped his eye. *How* he saw, I could
never make out, though I had a theory that it was
with his elbows. After he had taken me (or my
knife) into his confidence, he took care that I
should see whatever he deemed of interest to a
landsman. Without looking up, he would say,
suddenly, " Ther 's a whale blowin' clearn up to
win'ard," or, " Them 's porpises to leeward : that
means chänge o' wind." He is as impervious to
cold as a polar bear, and paces the deck during his
watch much as one of those yellow hummocks goes
slumping up and down his cage. On the Atlantic, if the wind blew a gale from the northeast, and
it was cold as an English summer, he was sure to
turn out in a calico shirt and trousers, his furzy
brown chest half bare, and slippers, without stock-

ings.   But lest you might fancy this to have chanced by defect of wardrobe, he comes out in a monstrous pea-jacket here in the Mediterranean, when the evening is so hot that Adam would have been glad to leave off his fig-leaves. " It's a kind o' damp and unwholesome in these 'ere waters," he says, evidently regarding the Midland Sea as a vile standing-pool, in comparison with the bluff ocean.   At meals he is superb, not only for his strengths, but his weaknesses. He has some how or other come to think me a wag, and if I ask him to pass the butter, detects an occult joke, and laughs as much as is proper for a mate.   For you must know that our social hierarchy on shipboard is precise, and the second mate, were he present, would only laugh half as much as the first.   Mr. X. always combs his hair, and works himself into a black frock-coat (on Sundays he adds a waist-coat) before he comes to meals, sacrificing himself nobly and painfully to the social proprieties.   The second mate, on the other hand, who eats after us, enjoys the privilege of shirt-sleeves, and is, I think, the happier man of the two.   We do not have seats above and below the salt, as in old time, but above and below the white sugar.   Mr. X. always takes brown sugar, and it is delightful to see how he ignores the existence of certain delicates which he considers above his grade, tipping his head on one side with an air of abstraction, so that he may seem not to deny himself, but to omit helping himself from inadvertence or absence of mind.   At such times he wrinkles his forehead in a peculiar manner, inscrutable at first as a cuneiform inscription, but as easily read after you once get the key. The sense of it is something like this : " I, X., know my place, a height of wisdom attained by few. Whatever you may think, I do *not* see that currant jelly, nor that preserved grape. Especially, a kind Providence has made me blind to bowls of white sugar, and deaf to the pop of champagne corks. It is much that a merciful compensation gives me a sense of the dingier hue of Havana, and the muddier gurgle of beer. Are there potted meats? My physician has ordered me three pounds of minced salt-junk at every meal." There is such a thing, you know, as a ship's husband : X. is the ship's poor relation.

As I have said, he takes also a below-the-white-sugar interest in the jokes, laughing by precise point of compass, just as he would lay the ship's course, all *yawing* being out of the question with his scrupulous decorum at the helm. Once or twice I have got the better of him, and touched him off into a kind of compromised explosion, like that of damp fireworks, that splutter and simmer a little, and then go out with painful slowness and occasional relapses. But his fuse is always of the unwillingest, and you must blow your match, and touch him off again and again with the same joke. Or rather, you must magnetize him many times to get him *en rapport* with a jest. This once accomplished, you have him, and one bit of fun will last the whole voyage. He prefers those of one syllable, the *a-b abs* of humor. The gradual fattening

of the steward, a benevolent mulatto with whiskers
and ear-rings, who looks as if he had been meant
for a woman, and had become a man by accident,
as in some of those stories of the elder physiolo-
gists, is an abiding topic of humorous comment
with Mr. X. "That 'ere stooard," he says, with a
brown grin like what you might fancy on the face
of a serious and aged seal, "'s agittin' as fat 's a
porpis. He was as thin 's a shingle when he come
aboord last v'yge. Them trousis 'll bust yit. He
don't darst take 'em off nights, for the whole ship's
company could n't git him into 'em agin." And
then he turns aside to enjoy the intensity of his
emotion by himself, and you hear at intervals low
rumblings, an indigestion of laughter. He tells me
of St. Elmo's fires, Marvell's *corposants*, though
with him the original *corpos santos* has suffered
a sea change, and turned to *comepleasants*, pledges
of fine weather. I shall not soon find a pleas-
anter companion. It is so delightful to meet a
man who knows just what you do *not*. Nay, I think
the tired mind finds something in plump ignorance
like what the body feels in cushiony moss. Talk
of the sympathy of kindred pursuits! It is the
sympathy of the upper and nether millstones, both
forever grinding the same grist, and wearing each
other smooth. One has not far to seek for book-
nature, artist-nature, every variety of superinduced
nature, in short, but genuine human-nature is hard
to find. And how good it is! Wholesome as a
potato, fit company for any dish. The freemasonry
of cultivated men is agreeable, but artificial, and I

like better the natural grip with which manhood recognizes manhood.

X. has one good story, and with that I leave him, wishing him with all my heart that little inland farm at last which is his calenture as he paces the windy deck. One evening, when the clouds looked wild and whirling, I asked X. if it was coming on to blow. "No," guess not," said he; " bumby the moon 'll be up, and scoff away that 'ere loose stuff." His intonation set the phrase "scoff away" in quotation-marks as plain as print. So I put a query in each eye, and he went on. "Ther' was a Dutch cappen onct, an' his mate come to him in the cabin, where he sot takin' his schnapps, an' says, 'Cappen, it's agittin' thick, an' looks kin' o' squally, hed n't we 's good 's shorten sail?' 'Gimmy my alminick,' says the cappen. So he looks at it a spell, an' says he, ' The moon 's doo in less 'n half an hour, an' she 'll scoff away ev'ythin' clare agin.' So the mate he goes, an' bumby down he comes agin, an' says, 'Cappen, this 'ere 's the allfiredest, powerfullest moon 't ever you *did* see. She 's scoffed away the maintogallants'l, an' she 's to work on the foretops'l now. Guess you 'd better look in the alminick agin, an' fin' out when *this* moon sets.' So the cappen thought 't was 'bout time to go on deck. Dreadful slow them Dutch cappens be." And X. walked away, rumbling inwardly, like the rote of the sea heard afar.

And so we arrived at Malta. Did you ever hear of one of those eating-houses, where, for a certain

fee, the guest has the right to make one thrust
with a fork into a huge pot, in which the whole
dinner is bubbling, getting perhaps a bit of boiled
meat, or a potato, or else nothing? Well, when
the great caldron of war is seething, and the nations stand round it striving to fish out something
to their purpose from the mess, Britannia always
has a great advantage in her trident. Malta is
one of the titbits she has impaled with that awful
implement. I was not sorry for it, when I reached
my clean inn, with its kindly English landlady.

III

ITALY

The father of the celebrated Mr. Jonathan Wild
was in the habit of saying, that "travelling was
travelling in one part of the world as well as another; it consisted in being such a time from
home, and in traversing so many leagues; and he
appealed to experience whether most of our travellers in France and Italy did not prove at their return that they might have been sent as profitably
to Norway and Greenland." Fielding himself, the
author of this sarcasm, was a very different kind of
traveller, as his Lisbon journal shows; but we think
he told no more than the truth in regard to the far
greater part of those idle people who powder themselves with dust from the highways and blur their
memories with a whirl through the galleries of
Europe. They go out empty, to come home unpro-

fitably full. They go abroad to escape themselves, and fail, as Goethe says they always must, in the attempt to jump away from their own shadows. And yet even the dullest man, if he went honestly about it, might bring home something worth having from the dullest place. If Ovid, instead of sentimentalizing in the Tristia, had left behind him a treatise on the language of the Getæ which he learned, we should have thanked him for something more truly valuable than all his poems. Could men only learn how comfortably the world can get along without the various information which they bring home about themselves ! Honest observation and report will long continue, we fear, to be one of the rarest of human things, so much more easily are spectacles to be had than eyes, so much cheaper is fine writing than exactness. Let any one who has sincerely endeavored to get anything like facts with regard to the battles of our civil war only consider how much more he has learned concerning the splendid emotions of the reporter than the events of the fight, (unless he has had the good luck of a peep into the correspondence of some pricelessly uncultivated private,) and he will feel that narrative, simple as it seems, can be well done by two kinds of men only, — those of the highest genius and culture, and those wholly without either.

· It gradually becomes clear to us that the easiest things can be done with ease only by the very fewest people, and those specially endowed to that end. The English language, for instance, can show but one sincere diarist, Pepys ; and yet it should seem

a simple matter enough to jot down the events of
every day for one's self without thinking of Mrs.
Posterity Grundy, who has a perverse way, as if
she were a testatrix and not an heir, of forgetting
precisely those who pay most assiduous court to
her.   One would think, too, that to travel and tell
what you have seen should be tolerably easy; but
in ninety-nine books out of a hundred does not the
tourist bore us with the sensations he thinks he
ought to have experienced, instead of letting us
know what he saw and felt? If authors would only
consider that the way to write an enlivening book
is not by seeing and saying just what would be expected of them, but precisely the reverse, the public
would be gainers. What tortures have we not seen
the worthiest people go through in endeavoring to
get up the appropriate emotion before some famous
work in a foreign gallery, when the only sincere
feeling they had was a praiseworthy desire to escape! If one does not like the Venus of Melos, let
him not fret about it, for he may be sure she never
will.

Montaigne felt obliged to separate himself from
travelling-companions whose only notion of their
function was that of putting so many leagues a
day behind them. His theory was that of Ulysses, who was not content with seeing the cities of
many men, but would learn their minds also. And
this way of taking time enough, while we think it
the best everywhere, is especially excellent in a
country so much the reverse of *fast* as Italy, where
impressions need to steep themselves in the sun

and ripen slowly as peaches, and where *carpe diem*
should be translated *take your own time.* But is
there any particular reason why everybody should
go to Italy, or, having done so, should tell everybody else what he supposes he ought to have seen
there ? Surely, there must be some adequate cause
for so constant an effect.

Boswell, in a letter to Sir Andrew Mitchell, says,
that, if he could only *see Rome,* " it would give him
talk for a lifetime." The utmost stretch of his
longing is to pass " four months on classic ground,"
after which he will come back to Auchinleck *uti
conviva satur,* — a condition in which we fear the
poor fellow returned thither only too often, though
unhappily in no metaphorical sense. We rather
think, that, apart from the pleasure of saying he
had been there, Boswell was really drawn to Italy
by the fact that it was classic ground, and this not
so much by its association with great events as with
great men, for whom, with all his weaknesses, he
had an invincible predilection. But Italy has a
magnetic virtue quite peculiar to her, which compels alike steel and straw, finding something in
men of the most diverse temperaments by which to
draw them to herself. Like the Siren, she sings
to every voyager a different song, that lays hold on
the special weakness of his nature. The German
goes thither because Winckelmann and Goethe
went, and because he can find there a sausage
stronger than his own ; the Frenchman, that he
may flavor his infidelity with a bitter dash of Ul-
tramontanism, or find fresher zest in his chattering

boulevard after the sombre loneliness of Rome ;
the Englishman, because the same Providence that
hears the young ravens when they cry is careful to
furnish prey to the courier also, and because his
money will make him a *Milor in partibus*. But
to the American, especially if he be of an imaginative temper, Italy has a deeper charm. She
gives him cheaply what gold cannot buy for him at
home, a Past at once legendary and authentic, and
in which he has an equal claim with every other
foreigner. In England he is a poor relation whose
right in the entail of home traditions has been
docked by revolution ; of France his notions are
purely English, and he can scarce help feeling
something like contempt for a people who habitu-
ally conceal their meaning in French ; but Rome
is the mother-country of every boy who has de-
voured Plutarch or taken his daily doses of Flo-
rus. Italy gives us antiquity with good roads, cheap
living, and, above all, a sense of freedom from
responsibility. For him who has escaped thither
there is no longer any tyranny of public opinion ;
its fetters drop from his limbs when he touches
that consecrated shore, and he rejoices in the recovery of his own individuality. He is no longer
met at every turn with " Under which king, bezo-
nian ? Speak, or die ! " He is not forced to take
one side or the other about table-tipping, or the
merits of General Blank, or the constitutionality
of anarchy. He has found an Eden where he need
not hide his natural self in the livery of any opinion, and may be as happy as Adam, if he be wise

enough to keep clear of the apple of High Art. This may be very weak, but it is also very agreeable to certain temperaments ; and to be weak is to be miserable only where it is a duty to be strong.

Coming from a country where everything seems shifting like a quicksand, where men shed their homes as snakes their skins, where you may meet a three-story house, or even a church, on the highway, bitten by the universal gad-fly of bettering its position, where we have known a tree to be cut down merely because " it had got to be so old," the sense of permanence, unchangeableness, and repose which Italy gives us is delightful. The oft-repeated *non é più come era prima* may be true enough of Rome politically, but it is not true of it in most other respects. To be sure, gas and railroads have got in at last ; but one may still read by a *lucerna* and travel by *vettura*, if he like, using Alberti as a guide-book, and putting up at the Bear as a certain keen-eyed Gascon did three centuries ago.

There is, perhaps, no country with which we are so intimate as with Italy, — none of which we are always so willing to hear more. Poets and prosers have alike compared her to a beautiful woman ; and while one finds nothing but loveliness in her, another shudders at her fatal fascination. She is the very Witch-Venus of the Middle Ages. Roger Ascham says, " I was once in *Italy* myself, but I thank God my abode there was but nine days ; and yet I saw in that little time, in one city, more liberty to sin than ever I heard tell of in our noble

city of London in nine years." He quotes triumphantly the proverb, — *Inglese italianato, diavolo in-
carnato.* A century later, the entertaining " Richard Lassels, Gent., who Travelled through Italy
Five times as Tutor to several of the *English* Nobility and Gentry," and who is open to new engage-
ments in that kind, declares, that, " For the Country itself, it seemed to me to be *Nature's Darling*,
and the *Eldest Sister* of all other Countries ; carrying away from them all the greatest blessings and
favours, and receiving such gracious looks from the
Sun and *Heaven*, that, if there be any fault in
Italy, it is, that her Mother *Nature* hath cockered
her too much, even to make her become Wanton."
Plainly, our Tannhäuser is but too ready to go back
to the Venus-berg !

Another word about Italy seems a dangerous experiment. Has not all been told and told and told
again ? Is it not one chief charm of the land, that
it is changeless without being Chinese ? Did not
Abbot Samson, in 1159, *Scotti habitum induens,*
(which must have shown his massive calves to
great advantage,) probably see much the same popular characteristics that Hawthorne saw seven hundred years later ? Shall a man try to be entertaining after Montaigne, æsthetic after Winckelmann,
wise after Goethe, or trenchant after Forsyth ?
Can he hope to bring back anything so useful as
the *fork*, which honest Tom Coryate made prize of
two centuries and a half ago, and put into the
greasy fingers of Northern barbarians ? Is not
the Descrittione of Leandro Alberti still a com-

petent itinerary? And can one hope to pick up a
fresh Latin quotation, when Addison and Eustace
have been before him with their scrap-baskets?

If there be anything which a person of even
moderate accomplishments may be presumed to
know, it is Italy. The only open question left
seems to be, whether Shakespeare were the only
man that could write his name who had never been
there. I have read my share of Italian travels,
both in prose and verse, but, as the nicely discriminating Dutchman found that "too moch lager-beer
was too moch, but too moch brahndee was jost
bright," so I am inclined to say that too much
Italy is just what we want. After Des Brosses, we
are ready for Henri Beyle, and Ampère, and Hil-
lard, and About, and Gallenga, and Julia Kava-
nagh; Corinne only makes us hungry for George
Sand. That no one can tell us anything new is as
undeniable as the compensating fact that no one
can tell us anything too old.

There are two kinds of travellers, — those who
tell us what they went to see, and those who tell
us what they saw. The latter class are the only
ones whose journals are worth the sifting : and the
value of their eyes depends on the amount of individual character they took with them, and of the
previous culture that had sharpened and tutored
the faculty of observation. In our conscious age
the frankness and *naïveté* of the elder voyagers is
impossible, and we are weary of those humorous
confidences on the subject of fleas with which we
are favored by some modern travellers, whose

motto should be (slightly altered) from Horace, —
Flea-bit, et toto cantabitur urbe. A naturalist self-
sacrificing enough may have this experience nearer
home.

.   .   .   .

The impulse which sent the Edelmann Storg
and me to Subiaco was given something like two
thousand years ago. Had we not seen the Ponte
Sant' Antonio, we should not have gone to Subiaco
at this particular time ; and had the Romans been
worse masons, or more ignorant of hydrodynamics
than they were, we should never have seen the
Ponte Sant' Antonio. But first we went to Tivoli,
— two carriage-loads of us, a very agreeable mixture of English, Scots, and Yankees, — on Tuesday, the 20th April. I shall not say anything
about Tivoli. A water-fall in type is likely to
be a trifle stiffish. Old association and modern
beauty ; nature and artifice ; worship that has
passed away and the religion that abides forever ;
the green gush of the deeper torrent and the white
evanescence of innumerable cascades, delicately pal-
pitant as a fall of northern lights; the descendants
of Sabine pigeons flashing up to immemorial dove-
cots, for centuries inaccessible to man, trooping
with noisy rooks and daws; the fitful roar and the
silently hovering iris, which, borne by the wind
across the face of the cliff, transmutes the travertine to momentary opal, and whose dimmer ghost
haunts the moonlight, — as well attempt to describe
to a Papuan savage that wondrous ode of Wordsworth which rouses and stirs in the soul all its dor-

mant instincts of resurrection as with a sound of the last trumpet. No, it is impossible. Even Byron's pump *sucks* sometimes, and gives an unpleasant dry wheeze, especially, it seems to me, at Terni. It is guide-book poetry, enthusiasm manufactured by the yard, which the hurried traveller (John and Jonathan are always in a hurry when they turn peripatetics) puts on when he has not a rag of private imagination to cover his nakedness withal. It must be a queer kind of love that could "watch madness with unalterable mien," when the patient, whom any competent physician would have ordered into a strait-waistcoat long ago, has shivered himself to powder down a precipice. But there is no madness in the matter. Velino goes over in his full senses, and knows perfectly well that he shall not be hurt, that his broken fragments will reunite more glibly than the head and neck of Orrilo. He leaps exultant, as to his proper doom and fulfilment, and out of the mere waste and spray of his glory the god of sunshine and song builds over the crowning moment of his destiny a triumphal arch beyond the reach of time and of decay.

The first day we made the *Giro*, coming back to a merry dinner at the Sibilla in the evening. Then we had some special tea, — for the Italians think tea-drinking the chief religious observance of the *Inglesi*, — and then we had fifteen pauls' worth of illumination, which wrought a sudden change in the scenery, like those that seem so matter-of-course in dreams, turning the Claude we had seen in the morning into a kind of Piranesi-Rembrandt. The illumination, by the way, which had been prefigured to us by the enthusiastic Italian who conducted it as something second only to the *Girandola*, turned out to be one blue-light and two armfuls of straw.

The Edelmann Storg is not fond of pedestrian locomotion, — nay, I have even sometimes thought that he looked upon the invention of legs as a private and personal wrong done to himself. I am quite sure that he inwardly believes them to have been a consequence of the fall, and that the happier Pre-Adamites were monopodes, and incapable of any but a vehicular progression. A carriage, with horses and driver complete, he takes to be as simple a production of nature as a potato. But he is fond of sketching, and after breakfast, on the beautiful morning of Wednesday, the 21st, I persuaded him to walk out a mile or two and see a fragment of aqueduct ruin. It is a single glorious arch, buttressing the mountain-side upon the edge of a sharp descent to the valley of the Anio. The old road to Subiaco passes under it, and it is crowned by a crumbling tower built in the Middle Ages (whenever that was) against the Gaetani. While Storg sketched, I clambered. Below you, where the valley widens greenly towards other mountains, which the ripe Italian air distances with a bloom like that on unplucked grapes, are more arches, ossified arteries of what was once the heart of the world. Storg's sketch was highly approved of by Leopoldo, our guide, and by three or four peasants, who,

being on their way to their morning's work in the
fields, had, of course, nothing in particular to do,
and stopped to see us see the ruin. Any one who
has remarked how grandly the Romans do nothing
will be slow to believe them an effete race. Their
style is as the colossal to all other, and the name of
Eternal City fits Rome also, because time is of no
account in it. The Roman always waits as if he
could afford it amply, and the slow centuries move
quite fast enough for him. Time is to other races
the field of a task-master, which they must painfully
till; but to the Roman it is an entailed estate,
which he enjoys and will transmit. The Neapolitan's laziness is that of a loafer; the Roman's is
that of a noble. The poor Anglo-Saxon must count
his hours, and look twice at his small change of
quarters and minutes; but the Roman spends from
a purse of Fortunatus. His *piccolo quarto d'ora*
is like his *grosso*, a huge piece of copper, big
enough for a shield, which stands only for a half-
dime of our money. We poor fools of time always
hurry as if we were the last type of man, the full
stop with which Fate was closing the colophon of
her volume, as if we had just read in our newspaper, as we do of the banks on holidays, ☞ The
world will close to-day at twelve o'clock, an hour
earlier than usual. But the Roman is still an
Ancient, with a vast future before him to tame and
occupy. He and his ox and his plough are just as
they were in Virgil's time or Ennius's. We beat
him in many things; but in the impregnable fastness of his great rich nature he defies us.

We got back to Tivoli, — Storg affirming that he had walked fifteen miles. We saw the Temple of Cough, which is *not* the Temple of Cough, though it might have been a votive structure put up by some Tiburtine Dr. Wistar. We saw the villa of Mæcenas, which is *not* the villa of Mæcenas, and other equally satisfactory antiquities. All our English friends sketched the Citadel, of course, and one enthusiast attempted a likeness of the fall, which I unhappily mistook afterward for a semblance of the tail of one of the horses on the Monte Cavallo. Then we went to the Villa d' Este, famous on Ariosto's account, — and which Ariosto never saw. But the laurels were worthy to have made a chaplet for him, and the cypresses and the views were as fine as if he had seen them every day of his life.

Perhaps something I learned in going to see one of the gates of the town is more to the purpose, and may assist one in erecting the horoscope of *Italia Unita*. When Leopoldo first proposed to drag me through the mud to view this interesting piece of architecture, I demurred. But as he was very earnest about it, and as one seldom fails getting at a bit of character by submitting to one's guide, I yielded. Arrived at the spot, he put me at the best point of view, and said, —

"Behold, Lordship!"

" I see nothing out of the common," said I.

" Lordship is kind enough here to look at a gate, the like of which exists not in all Italy, nay, in the whole world, — I speak not of England," for he thought me an *Inglese*.

" I am not blind, Leopoldo ; where is the miracle ? "

" Here we dammed up the waters of the Anio, first by artifice conducted to this spot, and letting them out upon the Romans, who stood besieging the town, drowned almost a whole army of them. (Lordship conceives ?) They suspected nothing till they found themselves all torn to pieces at the foot of the hill yonder. (Lordship conceives ?) *Eh ! per Bacco !* we watered their porridge for them."

Leopoldo used *we* as Lord Buchan did *I*, meaning any of his ancestors.

" But tell me a little, Leopoldo, how many years is it since this happened ? "

" *Non saprei, signoria ;* it was in the antiquest times, certainly ; but the Romans never come to our Fair, that we don't have blows about it, and perhaps a stab or two. Lordship understands ? "

I was quite repaid for my pilgrimage. I think I understand Italian politics better for hearing Leopoldo speak of the Romans, whose great dome is in full sight of Tivoli, as a foreign nation. But what perennial boyhood the whole story indicates !

Storg's sketch of the morning's ruin was so successful that I seduced him into a new expedition to the Ponte Sant' Antonio, another aqueduct arch about eight miles off. This was for the afternoon, and I succeeded the more easily, as we were to go on horseback. So I told Leopoldo to be at the gate of the Villa of Hadrian, at three o'clock, with three horses. Leopoldo's face, when I said three, was worth seeing ; for the poor fellow had counted on nothing more than trotting beside our horses for sixteen miles, and getting half a dollar in the evening. Between doubt and hope, his face seemed to exude a kind of oil, which made it shine externally, after having first lubricated all the muscles inwardly.

" With *three* horses, Lordship ? "

" Yes, *three*."

" Lordship is very sagacious. With *three* horses they go much quicker. It is finished, then, and they will have the kindness to find me at the gate with the beasts, at three o'clock precisely."

Leopoldo and I had compromised upon the term "Lordship." He had found me in the morning celebrating due rites before the Sibyl's Temple with strange incense of the nicotian herb, and had marked me for his prey. At the very high tide of sentiment, when the traveller lies with oyster-like openness in the soft ooze of reverie, do these parasitic crabs, the *ciceroni*, insert themselves as his inseparable bosom companions. Unhappy bivalve, lying so softly between thy two shells, of the actual and the possible, the one sustaining, the other widening above thee, till, oblivious of native mud, thou fanciest thyself a proper citizen only of the illimitable ocean which floods thee, — there is no escape ! Vain are thy poor crustaceous efforts at self-isolation. The foe henceforth is a part of thy consciousness, thy landscape, and thyself, happy only if that irritation breed in thee the pearl of patience and of voluntary abstraction.

" Excellency wants a guide, very experienced,

who has conducted with great mutual satisfaction many of his noble compatriots."

Puff, puff, and an attempt at looking as if I did not see him.

"Excellency will deign to look at my book of testimonials. When we return, Excellency will add his own."

Puff, puff.

"Excellency regards the cascade, *præceps Anio*, as the good Horatius called it."

I thought of the *dissolve frigus* of the landlord in Roderick Random, and could not help smiling. Leopoldo saw his advantage.

"Excellency will find Leopoldo, when he shall choose to be ready."

"But I will positively not be called *Excellency*. I am not an ambassador, nor a very eminent Christian, and the phrase annoys me."

"To be sure, Excell— Lordship."

"I am an American."

"Certainly, an American, Lordship," — as if that settled the matter entirely. If I had told him I was a Caffre, it would have been just as clear to him. He surrendered the "Excellency," but on general principles of human nature, I suppose, would not come a step lower than "Lordship." So we compromised on that. — P. S. It is wonderful how soon a republican ear reconciles itself with syllables of this description. I think *citizen* would find greater difficulties in the way of its naturalization, and as for *brother* — ah! well, in a Christian sense, certainly.

Three o'clock found us at the Villa of Hadrian. We had explored that incomparable ruin, and consecrated it, in the Homeric and Anglo-Saxon manner, by eating and drinking. Some of us sat in the shadow of one of the great walls, fitter for a city than a palace, over which a Nile of ivy, gushing from one narrow source, spread itself in widening inundations. A happy few listened to stories of Bagdad from Mrs. Rich, whose silver hair gleamed, a palpable anachronism, like a snowfall in May, over that ever-youthful face, where the few sadder lines seemed but the signature of Age to a deed of quitclaim and release. Dear Tito, that exemplary traveller who never lost a day, had come back from renewed explorations, convinced by the eloquent *custode* that *Serapeion* was the name of an officer in the Prætorian Guard. I was explaining, in addition, that *Naumachia*, in the Greek tongue, signified a place artificially drained, when the horses were announced.

This put me to reflection. I felt, perhaps, a little as Mazeppa must, when told that his steed was at the door. For several years I had not been on the back of a horse, and was it not more than likely that these mountains might produce a yet more refractory breed of these ferocious animals than common? Who could tell the effect of grazing on a volcanic soil like that hereabout? I had vague recollections that the saddle nullified the laws governing the impulsion of inert bodies, exacerbating the centrifugal forces into a virulent activity, and proportionably narcotizing the centripetal. The phrase *ratio proportioned to the squares of the distances* impressed me with an awe which explained to me how the laws of nature had been of old personified and worshipped. Meditating these things, I walked with a cheerful aspect to the gate, where my saddled and bridled martyrdom awaited me.

"*Eccomi quà!*" said Leopoldo, hilariously. "Gentlemen will be good enough to select from the three best beasts in Tivoli."

"Oh, this one will serve me as well as any," said I, with an air of indifference, much as I have seen a gentleman help himself inadvertently to the best peach in the dish. I am not more selfish than becomes a Christian of the nineteenth century, but I looked on this as a clear case of *tabula in naufragio*, and had noticed that the animal in question had that tremulous droop of the lower lip which indicates senility, and the abdication of the wilder propensities. Moreover, he was the only one provided with a curb bit, or rather with two huge iron levers which might almost have served Archimedes for his problem. Our saddles were flat cushions covered with leather, brought by years of friction to the highest state of polish. Instead of a pommel, a perpendicular stake, about ten inches high, rose in front, which, in case of a stumble, would save one's brains, at the risk of certain evisceration. Behind, a glary slope invited me constantly to slide over the horse's tail. The selfish prudence of my choice had well-nigh proved the death of me, for this poor old brute, with that anxiety to oblige a *forestiero* which characterizes everybody here, could never make up his mind which of his four paces (and he had the rudiments of four — walk, trot, rack, and gallop) would be most agreeable to me. The period of transition is always unpleasant, and it was all transition. He treated me to a hodge-podge of all his several gaits at once. Saint Vitus was the only patron saint I could think of. My head jerked one way, my body another, while each of my legs became a pendulum vibrating furiously, one always forward while the other was back, so that I had all the appearance and all the labor of going afoot, and at the same time was bumped within an inch of my life. Waterton's alligator was nothing to it; it was like riding a hard-trotting armadillo bare-backed. There is a species of equitation peculiar to our native land, in which a rail from the nearest fence, with no preliminary incantation of *Horse and hattock!* is converted into a steed, and this alone may stand the comparison. Storg in the mean while was triumphantly taking the lead, his trousers working up very pleasantly above his knees, an insurrectionary movement which I also was unable to suppress in my own. I could bear it no longer.

"Le-e-o-o-p-o-o-o-l-l-l-d-d-o-o-o!" jolted I.

"Command, Lordship!" and we both came to a stop.

"It is necessary that we change horses immediately, or I shall be jelly."

"Certainly, Lordship;" and I soon had the pathetic satisfaction of seeing him subjected to all the excruciating experiments that had been tried upon myself. *Fiat experimentum in corpore vili*, thought his extempore lordship, Christopher Sly, to himself.

Meanwhile all the other accessories of our ride were delicious. It was a clear, cool day, and we soon left the high road for a bridle-path along the side of the mountain, among gigantic olive-trees, said to be five hundred years old, and which had certainly employed all their time in getting into the weirdest and wonderfullest shapes. Clearly in this green commonwealth there was no heavy roller of public opinion to flatten all character to a lawn-like uniformity. Everything was individual and eccentric. And there was something fearfully human, too, in the wildest contortions. It was some such wood that gave Dante the hint of his human forest in the seventh circle, and I should have dreaded to break a twig, lest I should hear that voice complaining,

"Perchè mi scerpi?
Non hai tu spirto di pietate alcuno?"

Our path lay along a kind of terrace, and at every opening we had glimpses of the billowy Campagna, with the great dome bulging from its rim, while on our right, changing ever as we rode, the Alban mountain showed us some new grace of that sweeping outline peculiar to volcanoes. At intervals the substructions of Roman villas would crop out from the soil like masses of rock, and deserving to rank as a geological formation by themselves. Indeed, in gazing into these dark caverns, one does

not think of man more than at Staffa.   Nature has
adopted these fragments of a race who were dear to
her.   She has not suffered these bones of the great
Queen to lack due sepulchral rites, but has flung
over them the ceremonial handfuls of earth, and
every year carefully renews the garlands of memo-
rial flowers.   Nay, if what they say in Rome be
true, she has even made a new continent of the
Colosseum, and given it a *flora* of its own.

At length, descending a little, we passed through
farm-yards and cultivated fields, where, from Leopoldo's conversations with the laborers, we discovered that he himself did not know the way for
which he had undertaken to be guide.   However,
we presently came to our ruin, and very noble it
was.   The aqueduct had here been carried across a
deep gorge, and over the little brook which wim-
pled along below towered an arch, as a bit of
Shakespeare bestrides the exiguous rill of a discourse which it was intended to ornament.   The
only human habitation in sight was a little casetta
on the top of a neighboring hill.   What else of
man's work could be seen was a ruined castle of
the Middle Ages, and, far away upon the horizon,
the eternal dome.   A valley in the moon could
scarce have been lonelier, could scarce have suggested more strongly the feeling of preteriteness
and extinction.   The stream below did not seem so
much to sing as to murmur sadly, *Conclusum est;
periisti!* and the wind, sighing through the arch,
answered, *Periisti!*   Nor was the silence of Monte
Cavi without meaning.   That cup, once full of

fiery wine, in which it pledged Vesuvius and Ætna
later born, was brimmed with innocent water now.
Adam came upon the earth too late to see the glare
of its last orgy, lighting the eyes of saurians in the
reedy Campagna below. I almost fancied I could
hear a voice like that which cried to the Egyptian
pilot, *Great Pan is dead!* I was looking into
the dreary socket where once glowed the eye that
saw the whole earth vassal. Surely, this was the
world's autumn, and I could hear the feet of Time
rustling through the wreck of races and dynasties,
cheap and inconsiderable as fallen leaves.

But a guide is not engaged to lead one into the
world of imagination. He is as deadly to sentiment as a sniff of hartshorn. His position is a
false one, like that of the critic, who is supposed to
know everything, and expends himself in showing
that he does not. If you should ever have the luck
to attend a concert of the spheres, under the pro-
tection of an Italian *cicerone*, he will expect you
to listen to him rather than to it. He will say:
" *Ecco, Signoria*, that one in the red mantle is
Signor Mars, eh! what a noblest *basso* is Signor
Mars! but nothing (Lordship understands?) to
what Signor Saturn used to be, (he with the golden
belt, *Signoria*,) only his voice is in ruins now, —
scarce one note left upon another; but Lordship
can see what it was by the remains, Roman remains, *Signoria*, Roman remains, the work of
giants. (Lordship understands?) They make no
such voices now. Certainly, Signor Jupiter (with
the yellow tunic, there) is a brave artist and a

most sincere tenor; but since the time of the Republic " (if he think you an *oscurante*, or since the
French, if he suspect you of being the least *red*)
"we have no more good singing."   And so on.

It is a well-known fact to all persons who are in
the habit of climbing Jacob's-ladders, that, if any
one speak to you during the operation, the fabric
collapses, and you come somewhat uncomfortably
to the ground.   One can be hit with a remark,
when he is beyond the reach of more material mis-
siles.   Leopoldo saw by my abstracted manner that
I was getting away from him, and I was the only
victim he had left, for Storg was making a sketch
below.   So he hastened to fetch me down again.

"Nero built this arch, Lordship."   (He did n't,
but Nero was Leopoldo's historical scapegoat.)
"Lordship sees the dome? he will deign to look
the least little to the left hand.   Lordship has
much intelligence.   Well, Nero always did thus.
His works always, always, had Rome in view."

He had already shown me two ruins, which
he ascribed equally to Nero, and which could only
have seen Rome by looking through a mountain.
However, such trifles are nothing to an accomplished guide.

I remembered his quoting Horace in the morning.

"Do you understand Latin, Leopoldo?"

"I did a little once, Lordship.   I went to the
Jesuits' school at Tivoli.   But what use of Latin
to a *poverino* like me?"

"Were you intended for the church?   Why did
you leave the school?"

"Eh, Lordship!" and one of those shrugs which might mean that he left it of his own free will, or that he was expelled at point of toe. He added some contemptuous phrase about the priests.

"But, Leopoldo, you are a good Catholic?"

"Eh, Lordship, who knows? A man is no blinder for being poor, — nay, hunger sharpens the eyesight sometimes. The cardinals (their Eminences!) tell us that it is good to be poor, and that, in proportion as we lack on earth, it shall be made up to us in Paradise. Now, if the cardinals (their Eminences!) believe what they preach, why do they want to ride in such handsome carriages?"

"But are there many who think as you do?"

"Everybody, Lordship, but a few women and fools. What imports it what the fools think?"

An immense deal, I thought, an immense deal; for of what material is public opinion manufactured?

"Do you ever go to church?"

"Once a year, Lordship, at Easter, to mass and confession."

"Why once a year?"

"Because, Lordship, one must have a certificate from the priest. One might be sent to prison else, and one had rather go to confession than to jail. Eh, Lordship, it is a *porcheria*."

It is proper to add, that in what Leopoldo said of the priests he was not speaking of his old masters, the Jesuits. One never hears anything in Italy against the purity of their lives, or their learning and ability, though much against their unscrupulousness. Nor will any one who has ever enjoyed the gentle and dignified hospitality of the Benedictines be ready to believe any evil report of them.

By this time Storg had finished his sketch, and we remounted our grazing steeds. They were brisker as soon as their noses were turned homeward, and we did the eight miles back in an hour. The setting sun streamed through and among the Michael Angelesque olive-trunks, and, through the long colonnade of the bridle-path, fired the scarlet waistcoats and bodices of homeward villagers, or was sullenly absorbed in the long black cassock and flapped hat of a priest, who courteously saluted the strangers. Sometimes a mingled flock of sheep and goats (as if they had walked out of one of Claude's pictures) followed the shepherd, who, satyr-like, in goat-skin breeches, sang such songs as were acceptable before Tubal Cain struck out the laws of musical time from his anvil. The peasant, in his ragged brown cloak, or with blue jacket hanging from the left shoulder, still strides Romanly, — *incedit rex,* — and his eyes have a placid grandeur, inherited from those which watched the glittering snake of the Triumph, as it undulated along the Via Sacra. By his side moves with equal pace his woman-porter, the caryatid of a vast entablature of household-stuff, and learning in that harsh school a sinuous poise of body and a security of step beyond the highest snatch of the posture-master.

As we drew near Tivoli the earth was fast

swinging into shadow. The darkening Campagna, climbing the sides of the nearer Monticelli in a gray belt of olive-spray, rolled on towards the blue island of Soracte, behind which we lost the sun. Yes, we had lost the sun; but in the wide chimney of the largest room at the Sibilla there danced madly, crackling with ilex and laurel, a bright ambassador from Sunland, Monsieur Le Feu, no pinchbeck substitute for his royal master. As we drew our chairs up, after the dinner due to Leopoldo's forethought, "Behold," said I, "the Resident of the great king near the court of our (this-day-created) Hogan Moganships."

We sat looking into the fire, as it wavered from shining shape to shape of unearthliest fantasy, and both of us, no doubt, making out old faces among the embers, for we both said together, "Let us talk of old times."

"To the small hours," said the Edelmann; "and instead of blundering off to Torneo to intrude chatteringly upon the midnight privacy of Apollo, let us promote the fire, there, to the rank of sun by brevet, and have a kind of undress rehearsal of those night wanderings of his here upon the ample stage of the hearth."

So we went through the whole catalogue of *Do you remembers?* and laughed at all the old stories, so dreary to an outsider. Then we grew pensive, and talked of the empty sockets in that golden band of our young friendship,—of S., with Grecian front, but unsevere, and Saxon M., to whom laughter was as natural as for a brook to ripple.

But Leopoldo had not done with us. We were to get back to Rome in the morning, and to that end must make a treaty with the company which ran the Tivoli diligence, the next day not being the regular period of departure for that prodigious structure. We had given Leopoldo twice his fee, and, setting a mean value upon our capacities in proportion, he expected to bag a neat percentage on our bargain. Alas! he had made a false estimate of the Anglo-Norman mind, which, capable of generosity as a compliment to itself, will stickle for the dust in the balance in a matter of business, and would blush at being *done* by Mercury himself.

Accordingly, at about nine o'clock there came a knock at the door, and, answering our *Favorisca!* in stalked Leopoldo, gravely followed by the two commissioners of the company.

" Behold me returned, Lordship, and these men are the *Vetturini.*"

Why is it that men who have to do with horses are the same all over Christendom ? Is it that they acquire equine characteristics, or that this particular mystery is magnetic to certain sorts of men ? Certainly they are marked unmistakably, and these two worthies would have looked perfectly natural in Yorkshire or Vermont. They were just alike, — *fortemque Gyan, fortemque Cloanthum,*—and you could not split an epithet between them. Simultaneously they threw back their large overcoats, and displayed spheroidal figures, over which the strongly pronounced stripes of their plaided waistcoats ran like parallels of latitude and longitude over a globe. Simultaneously they took off their hats and said, " Your servant, gentlemen." In Italy it is always necessary to make a *combinazione* beforehand about even the most customary matters, for there is no fixed *highest* price for anything. For a minute or two we stood reckoning each other's forces. Then I opened the first trench with the usual, " How much do you wish for carrying us to Rome at half-past seven to-morrow morning?"

The enemy glanced one at the other, and the result of this ocular *witenagemot* was that one said, " Four scudi, gentlemen."

The Edelmann Storg took his cigar from his mouth in order to whistle, and made a rather indecorous allusion to four gentlemen in the diplomatic service of his Majesty, the Prince of the Powers of the Air.

" Whe-ew! *quattro diavoli!*" said he.

" *Macchè!*" exclaimed I, attempting a flank-movement, " I had rather go on foot!" and threw as much horror into my face as if a proposition had been made to me to commit robbery, murder, and arson all together.

" For less than three scudi and a half the diligence parts not from Tivoli at an extraordinary hour," said the stout man, with an imperturbable gravity, intended to mask his retreat, and to make it seem that he was making the same proposal as at first.

Storg saw that they wavered, and opened upon them with his flying artillery of sarcasm.

"Do you take us for *Inglesi?* We are very well here, and will stay at the Sibilla," he sniffed scornfully.

"How much will Lordship give?" (This was showing the white feather.)

"Fifteen pauls," (a scudo and a half,) "*buona-mano* included."

"It is impossible, gentlemen; for less than two scudi and a half the diligence parts not from Tivoli at an extraordinary hour."

"Fifteen pauls."

"Will Lordship give two scudi?" (with a slight flavor of mendicancy.)

"Fifteen pauls," (growing firm as we saw them waver.)

"Then, gentlemen, it is all over; it is impossible, gentlemen."

"Very good; a pleasant evening to you!" and they bowed themselves out.

As soon as the door closed behind them, Leopoldo, who had looked on in more and more anxious silence as the chance of plunder was whittled slimmer and slimmer by the sharp edges of the parley, saw instantly that it was for his interest to turn state's evidence against his accomplices.

"They will be back in a moment," he said knowingly, as if he had been of our side all along.

"Of course; we are aware of that." — It is always prudent to be aware of everything in travelling.

And, sure enough, in five minutes re-enter the stout men, as gravely as if everything had been thoroughly settled, and ask respectfully at what hour we would have the diligence.

This will serve as a specimen of Italian bargain-making. They do not feel happy if they get their first price. So easy a victory makes them sorry they had not asked twice as much, and, besides, they love the excitement of the contest. I have seen as much debate over a little earthen pot (value two cents) on the Ponte Vecchio, in Florence, as would have served for an operation of millions in the funds, the demand and the offer alternating so rapidly that the litigants might be supposed to be playing the ancient game of *morra*. It is a part of the universal fondness for gaming, and lotteries. An English gentleman once asked his Italian courier how large a percentage he made on all of his employer's money which passed through his hands. "About five per cent; sometimes more, sometimes less," was the answer. "Well, I will add that to your salary, in order that I may be rid of this uncomfortable feeling of being cheated." The courier mused a moment, and said, "But no, sir, I should not be happy; then it would not be sometimes more, sometimes less, and I should miss the excitement of the game."

22*d.* — This morning the diligence was at the door punctually, and, taking our seats in the *coupé*, we bade farewell to La Sibilla. But first we ran back for a parting glimpse at the waterfall. These last looks, like lovers' last kisses, are nouns of multitude, and presently the *povero stalliere, signori,* waited upon us, cap in hand, telling us that the *vetturino* was impatient, and begging for drink-money in the same breath.   Leopoldo hovered longingly afar, for these vultures respect times and seasons, and while one is fleshing his beak upon the foreign prey, the others forbear.   The passengers in the diligence were not very lively. The Romans are a grave people, and more so than ever since '49.   Of course, there was one priest among them   There always is; for the *mantis religiosa* is as inevitable to these public convey-ances as the curculio is to the plum, and one could almost fancy that they were bred in the same way, — that the egg was inserted when the vehicle was green, became developed as it ripened, and never left it till it dropped withered from the pole. There was nothing noticeable on the road to Rome, except the strings of pack-horses and mules which we met returning with empty lime-sacks to Tivoli, whence comes the supply of Rome.   A railroad was proposed, but the government would not allow it, because it would interfere with this carrying-trade, and wisely granted instead a charter for a road to Frascati, where there was no business whatever to be interfered with.   About a mile of this is built in a style worthy of ancient Rome; and it is possible that eventually another mile may be accomplished, for some half-dozen labor-ers are at work upon it with wheelbarrows, in the leisurely Roman fashion.   If it be ever finished, it will have nothing to carry but the conviction of its own uselessness.   A railroad has been proposed to Civita Vecchia; but that is out of the question, because it would be profitable. On the whole, one does not regret the failure of these schemes. One would not approach the solitary emotion of a life-time, such as is the first sight of Rome, at the rate of forty miles an hour. It is better, after painfully crawling up one of those long paved hills, to have the postilion turn in his saddle, and, pointing with his whip, (without looking, for he knows instinctively where it is,) say, *Ecco San Pietro!* Then you look tremblingly, and see it hovering visionary on the horizon's verge, and in a moment you are rattling and rumbling and wallowing down into the valley, and it is gone. So you play hide-and-seek with it all the rest of the way, and have time to converse with your sensations. You fancy you have got used to it at last; but from the next hill-top, lo, there it looms again, a new wonder, and you do not feel sure that it will keep its tryst till you find yourself under its shadow. The Dome is to the Eternal City what Vesuvius is to Naples; only a greater wonder, for Michael Angelo hung it there. The traveller climbs it as he would a mountain, and finds the dwellings of men high up on its sacred cliffs. It has its annual eruption, too, at Easter, when the fire trickles and palpitates down its mighty shoulders, seen from far-off Tivoli. — No, the locomotive is less impertinent at Portici, hailing the imprisoned Titan there with a kindred shriek. Let it not vex the solemn Roman ghosts, or the nobly desolate Campagna, with whose solitudes the shattered vertebræ of the aqueducts are in truer sympathy.

24*th*. — To-day our journey to Subiaco properly
begins. The jocund morning had called the beggars to their street-corners, and the women to the
windows ; the players of *morra* (a game probably
as old as the invention of fingers), of chuck-far-
thing, and of bowls, had cheerfully begun the labors
of the day ; the plaintive cries of the chair-seaters,
frog-venders, and certain other peripatetic mer-
chants, the meaning of whose vocal advertisements
I could never penetrate, quaver at regular intervals, now near and now far away ; a solitary Jew
with a sack over his shoulder, and who never is
seen to stop, slouches along, every now and then
croaking a penitential *Cenci !* as if he were somehow the embodied expiation (by some post-Ovidian
metamorphosis) of that darkest Roman tragedy ;
women are bargaining for lettuce and endive ; the
slimy Triton in the Piazza Barberina spatters himself with vanishing diamonds ; a peasant leads an
ass on which sits the mother with the babe in her
arms, — a living flight into Egypt ; in short, the
beautiful spring day had awakened all of Rome
that can awaken yet, (for the ideal Rome waits for
another morning,) when we rattled along in our *carrettella* on the way to Palestrina. A *carrettella* is
to the perfected vehicle, as the coracle to the steam-
ship ; it is the first crude conception of a wheeled
carriage. Doubtless the inventor of it was a prodigious genius in his day, and rode proudly in
it, envied by the more fortunate pedestrian, and
cushioned by his own inflated imagination. If the
chariot of Achilles were like it, then was Hector

happier at the tail than the son of Thetis on the box. It is an oblong basket upon two wheels, with a single seat rising in the middle. We had not jarred over a hundred yards of the Quattro Fontane, before we discovered that no elastic propugnaculum had been interposed between the body and the axle, so that we sat, as it were, on paving-stones, mitigated only by so much as well-seasoned ilex is less flinty-hearted than *tufo* or *breccia*. If there were any truth in the theory of developments, I am certain that we should have been furnished with a pair of rudimentary elliptical springs, at least, before half our day's journey was over. However, as one of those happy illustrations of ancient manners, which one meets with so often here, it was instructive; for I now clearly understand that it was not merely by reason of pomp that Hadrian used to be three days in getting to his villa, only twelve miles off. In spite of the author of "Vestiges," Nature, driven to extremities, can develop no more easy cushion than a blister, and no doubt treated an ancient emperor and a modern republican with severe impartiality.

It was difficult to talk without biting one's tongue; but as soon as we had got fairly beyond the gate, and out of sight of the last red-legged French soldier, and tightly-buttoned *doganiere*, our driver became loquacious.

"I am a good Catholic, — better than most," said he, suddenly.

"What do you mean by that?"

"Eh! they say Saint Peter wrought miracles,

and there are enough who don't believe it; but *I* do. There's the Barberini Palace, — behold one miracle of Saint Peter! There's the Farnese, — behold another! There's the Borghese, — behold a third! But there's no end of them. No saint, nor all the saints put together, ever worked so many wonders as he; and then, *per Bacco!* he is the *uncle* of so many folks, — why, that's a miracle in itself, and of the greatest!"

Presently he added: "Do you know how we shall treat the priests when we make our next revolution? We shall treat them as they treat us, and that is after the fashion of the buffalo. For the buffalo is not content with getting a man down, but after that he gores him and thrusts him, always, always, as if he wished to cram him to the centre of the earth. Ah, if I were only keeper of hell-gate! Not a rascal of them all should ever get out into purgatory while I stood at the door!"

We remonstrated a little, but it only exasperated him the more.

"Blood of Judas! they will eat nothing else than gold, when a poor fellow's belly is as empty as San Lorenzo yonder. They'll have enough of it one of these days — but melted! How do you think they will like it for soup?"

Perhaps, if our vehicle had been blessed with springs, our *vetturino* would have been more placable. I confess a growing moroseness in myself, and a wandering speculation or two as to the possible fate of the builder of our chariot in the next world. But I am more and more persuaded every day, that, as far as the popular mind is concerned, Romanism is a dead thing in Italy. It survives only because there is nothing else to replace it with, for men must wear their old habits (however threadbare and out at elbows) till they get better. It is literally a superstition, — a something left to *stand over* till the great commercial spirit of the nineteenth century balances his accounts again, and then it will be banished to the limbo of profit and loss. The Papacy lies dead in the Vatican, but the secret is kept for the present, and government is carried on in its name. After the fact gets abroad, perhaps its ghost will terrify men a little while longer, but only while they are in the dark, though the ghost of a creed is a hard thing to give a mortal wound to, and may be laid, after all, only in a Red Sea of blood.

So we rattled along till we came to a large *albergo* just below the village of Colonna. While our horse was taking his *rinfresco*, we climbed up to it, and found it desolate enough, — the houses never rebuilt since Consul Rienzi sacked it five hundred years ago. It was a kind of gray incrustation on the top of the hill, chiefly inhabited by pigs, chickens, and an old woman with a distaff, who looked as sacked and ruinous as everything around her. There she sat in the sun, a dreary, doting Clotho, who had outlived her sisters, and span endless destinies which none was left to cut at the appointed time. Of course she paused from her work a moment, and held out a skinny hand, with the usual, "Noblest gentlemen, give me something for charity." We gave her enough to pay Charon's ferriage across to her sisters, and departed hastily, for there was something uncanny about the place. In this climate even the finger-marks of Ruin herself are indelible, and the walls were still blackened with Rienzi's fires.

As we waited for our *carrettella*, I saw four or five of the lowest-looking peasants come up and read the handbill of a *tombola* (a kind of lottery) which was stuck up beside the inn-door. One of them read it aloud for our benefit, and with remarkable propriety of accent and emphasis. This benefit of clergy, however, is of no great consequence where there is nothing to read. In Rome, this morning, the walls were spattered with placards condemning the works of George Sand, Eugène Sue, Gioberti, and others. But in Rome one may contrive to read any book he likes; and I know Italians who are familiar with Swedenborg, and even Strauss.

Our stay at the *albergo* was illustrated by one other event, — a nightingale singing in a full-blossomed elder-bush on the edge of a brook just across the road. So liquid were the notes, and so full of spring, that the twig he tilted on seemed a conductor through which the mingled magnetism of brook and blossom flowed into him and were precipitated in music. Nature understands thoroughly the value of contrasts, and accordingly a donkey from a shed hard by, hitched and hesitated and agonized through his bray, so that we might be conscious at once of the positive and negative poles of song. It was pleasant to see with what undoubting enthusiasm he went through his solo, and vindicated Providence from the imputation of weakness in making such trifles as the nightingale yonder. "Give ear, O heaven and earth!" he seemed to say, "nor dream that good, sound common-sense is extinct or out of fashion so long as *I* live." I suppose Nature made the donkey half abstractedly, while she was feeling her way up to her ideal in the horse, and that his bray is in like manner an experimental sketch for the neigh of her finished animal.

We drove on to Palestrina, passing for some distance over an old Roman road, as carriageable as when it was built. Palestrina occupies the place of the once famous Temple of Fortune, whose ruins are perhaps a fitter monument of the fickle goddess than ever the perfect fane was.

> Come hither, weary ghosts that wail
>   O'er buried Nimroud's carven walls,
> And ye whose nightly footsteps frail
>   From the dread hush of Memphian halls
>   Lead forth the whispering funerals!
>
> Come hither, shade of ancient pain
>   That, muffled sitting, hear'st the foam
> To death-deaf Carthage shout in vain,
>   And thou that in the Sibyl's tome
>   Tear-stain'st the *never* after Rome!
>
> Come, Marius, Wolsey, all ye great
>   On whom proud Fortune stamped her heel,
> And see herself the sport of Fate,
>   Herself discrowned and made to feel
>   The treason of her slippery wheel!

One climbs through a great part of the town by
stone steps, passing fragments of Pelasgic wall,
(for history, like geology, may be studied here in
successive rocky *strata*,) and at length reaches the
inn, called the *Cappellaro*, the sign of which is a
great tin cardinal's hat, swinging from a small
building on the other side of the street, so that a
better view of it may be had from the hostelry itself.   The landlady, a stout woman of about sixty
years, welcomed us heartily, and burst forth into
an eloquent eulogy on some fresh sea-fish which
she had just received from Rome.   She promised
everything for dinner, leaving us to choose; but
as a skilful juggler flitters the cards before you,
and, while he seems to offer all, forces upon you
the one he wishes, so we found that whenever we
undertook to select from her voluble bill of fare,
we had in some unaccountable manner always ordered sea-fish.   Therefore, after a few vain efforts,
we contented ourselves, and, while our dinner was
cooking, climbed up to the top of the town.   Here
stands the deserted Palazzo Barberini, in which is
a fine Roman mosaic pavement.   It was a dreary
old place.   On the ceilings of some of the apart-
ments were fading out the sprawling apotheoses of
heroes of the family, (themselves long ago faded
utterly,) who probably went through a somewhat
different ceremony after their deaths from that
represented here.   One of the rooms on the
ground-floor was still occupied, and from its huge
grated windows there swelled and subsided at intervals a confused turmoil of voices, some talking,

some singing, some swearing, and some lamenting,
as if a page of Dante's Inferno had become sud-,
denly alive under one's eye. This was the prison,
and in front of each window a large stone block
allowed *tête-à-tête* discourses between the prisoners
and their friends outside as well as the passing in
of food. English jails were like this in Queen
Elizabeth's time and later. In Heywood's " Woman killed with Kindness," Acton says of his
enemy Mountford, in prison for debt, —

> "shall we hear
> The music of his voice cry from the grate
> *Meat, for the Lord's sake ?* "

Behind the palace rises a steep, rocky hill, with a
continuation of ruined castle, the innocent fastness
now of rooks and swallows. We walked down to a
kind of terrace, and watched the Alban Mount
(which saw the sunset for us by proxy) till the
bloom trembled nearer and nearer to its summit,
then went wholly out, we could not say when, and
day was dead. Simultaneously we thought of din-
ing, and clattered hastily down to the *Cappellaro*.
We had to wait yet half an hour for dinner, and
from where I sat I could see through the door of
the dining-room a kind of large hall into which a
door from the kitchen also opened. Presently I saw
the landlady come out with a little hanging lamp
in her hand, and seat herself amply before a row of
baskets ranged upside-down along the wall. She
carefully lifted the edge of one of these, and, after
she had groped in it a moment, I heard that hoarse
choking scream peculiar to fowls when seized by

the leg in the dark, as if their throats were in their
tibiæ after sunset.   She took out a fine young cock
and set him upon his feet before her, stupid with
sleep, and blinking helplessly at the lamp, which
he perhaps took for a sun in reduced circumstances, doubtful whether to crow or cackle.   She
looked at him admiringly, felt of him, sighed, gazed
sadly at his coral crest, and put him back again.
This ceremony she repeated with five or six of the
baskets, and then went back into the kitchen.   I
thought of Thessalian hags and Arabian enchan-
tresses, and wondered if these were transformed
travellers, — for travellers go through queer trans-
formations sometimes.   Should Storg and I be
crowing and scratching to-morrow morning, instead
of going to Subiaco ?   Should we be Plato's men,
with the feathers, instead of without them ?   I
would probe this mystery.   So, when the good
woman came in to lay the table, I asked what she
had been doing with the fowls.

"I thought to kill one for the gentlemen's soup;
but they were so beautiful my heart failed me.
Still, if the gentlemen wish it — only I thought two
pigeons would be more delicate."

Of course we declined to be accessory to such a
murder, and she went off delighted, returning in a
few minutes with our dinner.   First we had soup,
then a roasted kid, then boiled pigeons, (of which
the soup had been made,) and last the *pesci di
mare*, which were not quite so great a novelty to us
as to our good hostess.   However, hospitality, like
so many other things, is reciprocal, and the guest

must bring his half, or it is naught. The prosperity of a dinner lies in the heart of him that eats it, and an appetite twelve miles long enabled us to do as great justice to the fish as if we were crowding all Lent into one meal. The landlady came and sat by us; a large and serious cat, winding her great tail round her, settled herself comfortably on the table, licking her paws now and then, with a poor relation's look at the fish; a small dog sprang into an empty chair, and a large one, with very confidential manners, would go from one to the other of us, laying his paw upon our arms as if he had an important secret to communicate, and alternately pricking and drooping his ears in hope or despondency. The *albergatrice* forthwith began to tell us her story, — how she was a widow, how she had borne thirteen children, twelve still living, and how she received a pension of sixty scudi a year, under the old Roman law, for her meritoriousness in this respect. The portrait of the son she had lost hung over the chimney-place, and, pointing to it, she burst forth into the following droll threnody. The remarks in parenthesis were screamed through the kitchen-door, which stood ajar, or addressed personally to us.

"O my son, my son! the doctors killed him, just as truly as if they had poisoned him! O how beautiful he was! beautiful! *beautiful!!* BEAUTIFUL!!! (Are not those fish done yet?) Look, that is his likeness, — but he was handsomer. He was as big as that" (extending her arms), — "big breast, big shoulders, big sides, big legs! (Eat 'em, eat 'em, they won't hurt you, fresh sea-fish, fresh! *fresh!!* FRESH!!!) I told them the doctors had murdered him, when they carried him with torches! He had been hunting, and brought home some rabbits, I remember, for he was not one that ever came empty-handed, and got the fever, and you treated him for consumption, and killed him! (Shall I come out there, or will you bring some more fish?)" So she went on, talking to herself, to us, to the little *serva* in the kitchen, and to the medical profession in general, repeating every epithet three times, with increasing emphasis, till her voice rose to a scream, and contriving to mix up her living children with her dead one, the fish, the doctors, the *serva*, and the rabbits, till it was hard to say whether it was the fish that had large legs, whether the doctors had killed them, or the *serva* had killed the doctors, and whether the *bello!* *bello!! bello!!!* referred to her son or a particularly fine rabbit.

25th. — Having engaged our guide and horses the night before, we set out betimes this morning for Olevano. From Palestrina to Cavi the road winds along a narrow valley, following the course of a stream which rustles rather than roars below. Large chestnut-trees lean every way on the steep sides of the hills above us, and at every opening we could see great stretches of Campagna rolling away and away toward the bases of purple mountains streaked with snow. The sides of the road were drifted with heaps of wild hawthorn and honeysuckle in full bloom, and bubbling with innumerable nightingales that sang unseen. Overhead the sunny sky tinkled with larks, as if the frost in the air were breaking up and whirling away on the swollen currents of spring.

Before long we overtook a little old man hobbling toward Cavi, with a bag upon his back. This was the mail! Happy country, which Hurry and Worry have not yet subjugated! Then we clattered up and down the narrow paved streets of Cavi, through the market-place, full of men dressed all alike in blue jackets, blue breeches, and white stockings, who do not stare at the strangers, and so out at the farther gate. Now oftener and oftener we meet groups of peasants in gayest dresses, ragged pilgrims with staff and scallop, singing (horribly); then processions with bag-pipes and pipes in front, droning and squealing (horribly); then strings of two-wheeled carts, eight or nine in each, and in the first the priest, book in hand, setting the stave, and all singing (horribly). This must be inquired into. Gigantic guide, who, splendid with blue sash and silver knee-buckles, has contrived, by incessant drumming with his heels, to get his mule in front, is hailed.

"Ho, Petruccio, what is the meaning of all this press of people?"

"*Festa*, Lordship, at Genezzano."

"What *Festa?*"

"Of the Madonna, Lordship," and touches his hat, for they are all dreadfully afraid of her for some reason or other.

We are in luck, this being the great *festa* of the

year among the mountains, — a thing which people go out of Rome to see.

"Where is Genezzano?"

"Just over yonder, Lordship," and pointed to the left, where was what seemed like a monstrous crystallization of rock on the crown of a hill, with three or four taller crags of castle towering in the midst, and all gray, except the tiled roofs, whose wrinkled sides were gold-washed with a bright yellow lichen, as if ripples, turned by some spell to stone, had contrived to detain the sunshine with which they were touched at the moment of transformation.

The road, wherever it came into sight, burned with brilliant costumes, like an illuminated page of Froissart. Gigantic guide meanwhile shows an uncomfortable and fidgety reluctance to turn aside and enter fairyland, which is wholly unaccountable. Is the huge earthen creature an Afrite, under sacred pledge to Solomon, and in danger of being sealed up again, if he venture near the festival of our Blessed Lady? If so, *that* also were a ceremony worth seeing, and we insist. He wriggles and swings his great feet with an evident impulse to begin kicking the sides of his mule again and fly. The way over the hills from Genezzano to Olevano he pronounces *scomodissima*, demanding of every peasant who goes by if it be not entirely impassable. This leading question, put in all the tones of plausible entreaty he can command, meets the invariable reply, "*È scomoda, davvero ; ma per le bestie — eh !*" (it is bad, of a truth, but for the beasts — eh!) and then one of those indescrib-

able shrugs, unintelligible at first as the compass
to a savage, but in which the expert can make
twenty hair's-breadth distinctions between N. E.
and N. N. E.

Finding that destiny had written it on his forehead, the guide at last turned and went cantering
and kicking toward Genezzano, we following. Just
before you reach the town, the road turns sharply
to the right, and, crossing a little gorge, loses itself
in the dark gateway. Outside the gate is an open
space, which formicated with peasantry in every
variety of costume that was *not* Parisian. Laughing women were climbing upon their horses (which
they bestride like men); pilgrims were chanting,
and beggars (the howl of an Italian beggar in the
country is something terrible) howling in discordant rivalry. It was a scene lively enough to make
Heraclitus shed a double allowance of tears; but
our giant was still discomforted. As soon as we
had entered the gate, he dodged into a little back-
street, just as we were getting out of which the
mystery of his unwillingness was cleared up. He
had been endeavoring to avoid a creditor. But it
so chanced (as Fate can hang a man with even a
rope of sand) that the enemy was in position just
at the end of this very lane, where it debouched
into the Piazza of the town.

The disputes of Italians are very droll things,
and I will accordingly bag that which is now imminent, as a specimen. They quarrel as unac-
countably as dogs, who put their noses together,
dislike each other's kind of smell, and instantly

tumble one over the other, with noise enough to draw the eyes of a whole street. So these people burst out, without apparent preliminaries, into a noise and fury and war-dance which would imply the very utmost pitch and agony of exasperation. And the subsidence is as sudden. They explode each other on mere contact, as if by a law of nature, like two hostile gases. They do not grow warm, but leap at once from zero to some degree of white-heat, to indicate which no Anglo-Saxon thermometer of wrath is highly enough graduated. If I were asked to name one universal characteristic of an Italian town, I should say, two men clamoring and shaking themselves to pieces at each other, and a woman leaning lazily out of a window, and perhaps looking at something else. Till one gets used to this kind of thing, one expects some horrible catastrophe; but during eight months in Italy I have only seen blows exchanged thrice. In the present case the explosion was of harmless gunpowder.

" Why - haven't -you-paid-those-fifty- five-bajocchi-at-the-*pizzicarolo's ?* " began the adversary, speaking with such inconceivable rapidity that he made only one word, nay, as it seemed, one monosyllable, of the whole sentence. Our giant, with a controversial genius which I should not have suspected in him, immediately, and with great adroitness, changed the ground of dispute, and, instead of remaining an insolvent debtor, raised himself at once to the ethical position of a moralist, resisting an unjust demand from principle.

“It was only *forty*-five,” roared he.

“But I say *fifty*-five,” screamed the other, and shook his close-cropped head as a boy does an apple on the end of a switch, as if he meant presently to jerk it off at his antagonist.

“*Birbone!*” yelled the guide, gesticulating so furiously with every square inch of his ponderous body that I thought he would throw his mule over, the poor beast standing all the while with drooping head and ears while the thunders of this man-quake burst over him. So feels the tortoise that sustains the globe when earth suffers fiery convulsions.

“*Birbante!*” retorted the creditor, and the opprobrious epithet clattered from between his shaking jaws as a refractory copper is rattled out of a Jehoiada-box by a child.

“*Andate vi far friggere!*” howled giant.

“*Andate ditto, ditto!*” echoed creditor,—and behold, the thing is over! The giant promises to attend to the affair when he comes back, the creditor returns to his booth, and we ride on.

Speaking of Italian quarrels, I am tempted to parenthesize here another which I saw at Civita Vecchia. We had been five days on our way from Leghorn in a French steamer, a voyage performed usually, I think, in about thirteen hours. It was heavy weather, blowing what a sailor would call half a gale of wind, and the caution of our captain, not to call it fear, led him to put in for shelter first at Porto Ferrajo in Elba, and then at Santo Stefano on the Italian coast. Our little black water-beetle of a mail-packet *was* knocked about pretty well, and all the Italian passengers disappeared in the forward cabin before we were out of port. When we were fairly at anchor within the harbor of Civita Vecchia, they crawled out again, sluggish as winter flies, their vealy faces mezzotinted with soot. One of them presently appeared in the custom-house, his only luggage being a cage closely covered with a dirty red handkerchief, which represented his linen.

" What have you in the cage ? " asked the *doganiere.*

" Eh ! nothing other than a parrot."

" There is a duty of one scudo and one bajoccho, then."

" *Santo diavolo !* but what hoggishness ! "

Thereupon instant and simultaneous blowup, or rather a series of explosions, like those in honor of a Neapolitan saint's-day, lasting about ten minutes, and followed by as sudden quiet. In the course of it, the owner of the bird, playing irreverently on the first half of its name, (*pappa*gallo,) hinted that it would be a high duty for his Holiness himself (*Papa*). After a pause for breath, he said quietly, as if nothing had happened, " Very good, then, since I must pay, I will," and began fumbling for the money.

" Meanwhile, do me the politeness to show me the bird," said the officer.

" With all pleasure," and, lifting a corner of the handkerchief, there lay the object of dispute on his back, stone-dead, with his claws curled up helplessly on each side his breast. I believe the owner would have been pleased had it even been his grandmother who had thus evaded duty, so exquisite is the pleasure of an Italian in escaping payment of anything.

"I make a present of the poor bird," said he blandly.

The publican, however, seemed to feel that he had been somehow cheated, and I left them in high debate, as to whether the bird were dead when it entered the custom-house, and, if it had been, whether a dead parrot were dutiable. Do not blame me for being entertained and trying to entertain you with these trifles. I remember Virgil's stern

"Che per poco è che teco non mi risso,"

but Dante's journey was of more import to himself and others than mine.

I am struck by the freshness and force of the passions in Europeans, and cannot help feeling as if there were something healthy in it. When I think of the versatile and accommodating habits of America, it seems like a land without thunderstorms. In proportion as man grows commercial, does he also become dispassionate and incapable of electric emotions? The driving-wheels of all-powerful natures are in the back of the head, and, as man is the highest type of organization, so a nation is better or worse as it advances toward the highest type of man, or recedes from it. But it is ill with a nation when the cerebrum sucks the cerebellum dry, for it cannot live by intellect alone. The

broad foreheads always carry the day at last, but
only when they are based on or buttressed with
massive hind-heads. It would be easier to make a
people great in whom the animal is vigorous, than
to keep one so after it has begun to spindle into
over-intellectuality. The hands that have grasped
dominion and held it have been large and hard;
those from which it has slipped, delicate, and apt
for the lyre and the pencil. Moreover, brain is
always to be bought, but passion never comes to
market. On the whole, I am rather inclined to
like this European impatience and fire, even while
I laugh at it, and sometimes find myself surmising
whether a people who, like the Americans, put up
quietly with all sorts of petty personal impositions
and injustices, will not at length find it too great a
bore to quarrel with great public wrongs.

Meanwhile, I must remember that I am in Genezzano, and not in the lecturer's desk. We walked
about for an hour or two, admiring the beauty
and grand bearing of the women, and the picturesque vivacity and ever-renewing unassuetude of
the whole scene. Take six of the most party-colored
dreams, break them to pieces, put them into a
fantasy-kaleidoscope, and when you look through it
you will see something that for strangeness, vividness, and mutability looked like the little Piazza of
Genezzano seen from the church porch. As we
wound through the narrow streets again to the
stables where we had left our horses, a branch of
laurel or ilex would mark a wine-shop, and, looking
till our eye cooled and toned itself down to dusky

sympathy with the crypt, we could see the smoky interior sprinkled with white head-cloths and scarlet bodices, with here and there a yellow spot of lettuce or the red inward gleam of a wine-flask. The head-dress is precisely of that most ancient pattern seen on Egyptian statues, and so colossal are many of the wearers, that you might almost think you saw a party of young sphinxes carousing in the sunless core of a pyramid.

We remounted our beasts, and, for about a mile, cantered gayly along a fine road, and then turned into a by-path along the flank of a mountain. Here the guide's *strada scomodissima* began, and we were forced to dismount, and drag our horses downward for a mile or two. We crossed a small plain in the valley, and then began to climb the opposite ascent. The path was perhaps four feet broad, and was paved with irregularly shaped blocks of stone, which, having been raised and lowered, tipped, twisted, undermined, and generally capsized by the rains and frosts of centuries, presented the most diabolically ingenious traps and pitfalls. All the while the scenery was beautiful. Mountains of every shape and hue changed their slow outlines ever as we moved, now opening, now closing round us, sometimes peering down solemnly at us over each other's shoulders, and then sinking slowly out of sight, or, at some sharp turn of the path, seeming to stride into the valley and confront us with their craggy challenge, — a challenge which the little valleys accepted, if we did not, matching their rarest tints of gray and brown, and pink and purple, or that royal dye to make which all these were profusely melted together for a moment's ornament, with as many shades of various green and yellow.   Gray towns crowded and clung on the tops of peaks that seemed inaccessible.   We owe a great deal of picturesqueness to the quarrels and thieveries of the barons of the Middle Ages.   The traveller and artist should put up a prayer for their battered old souls.   It was to be out of their way and that of the Saracens that people were driven to make their homes in spots so sublime and inconvenient that the eye alone finds it pleasant to climb up to them.   Nothing else but an American landcompany ever managed to induce settlers upon territory of such uninhabitable quality.   I have seen an insect that makes a mask for himself out of the lichens of the rock over which he crawls, contriving so to deceive the birds; and the towns in this wild region would seem to have been built on the same principle.   Made of the same stone with the cliffs on which they perch, it asks good eyesight to make them out at the distance of a few miles, and every wandering mountain-mist annihilates them for the moment.

At intervals, I could hear the giant, after digging at the sides of his mule with his spurless heels, growling to himself, and imprecating an apoplexy (*accidente*) upon the path and him who made it.   This is the universal malediction here, and once it was put into rhyme for my benefit.   I was coming down the rusty steps of San Gregorio one day, and having paid no heed to a stout woman

of thirty odd who begged somewhat obtrusively,
she screamed after me,

> "Ah, vi pigli un accidente,
> Voi che non date niente!"

> Ah, may a sudden apoplexy,
> You who give not, come and vex ye!

Our guide could not long appease his mind with
this milder type of objurgation, but soon intensi-
fied it into *accidentaccio*, which means a selected
apoplexy of uncommon size and ugliness. As the
path grew worse and worse, so did the repetition
of this phrase (for he was slow of invention) become more frequent, till at last he did nothing
but kick and curse, mentally, I have no doubt, in-
cluding us in his malediction. I think it would
have gratified Longinus or Fuseli (both of whom
commended swearing) to have heard him. Before
long we turned the flank of the hill by a little
shrine of the Madonna, and there was Olevano just
above us. Like the other towns in this district, it
was the diadem of an abrupt peak of rock. From
the midst of it jutted the ruins of an old strong-
hold of the Colonna. Probably not a house has
been built in it for centuries. To enter the town,
we literally rode up a long flight of stone steps,
and soon found ourselves in the Piazza. We
stopped to buy some cigars, and the *zigararo*, as
he rolled them up, asked if we did not want dinner. We told him we should get it at the inn.
Benissimo, he would be there before us. What
he meant, we could not divine; but it turned out
that he was the landlord, and that the inn only

became such when strangers arrived, relapsing again immediately into a private dwelling. We found our host ready to receive us, and went up to a large room on the first floor. After due instructions, we seated ourselves at the open windows, — Storg to sketch, and I to take a mental calotype of the view. Among the many lovely ones of the day, this was the loveliest, — or was it only that the charm of repose was added? On our right was the silent castle, and beyond it the silent mountains. To the left we looked down over the clustering houses upon a campagna-valley of peaceful cultivation, vineyards, olive-orchards, grain-fields in their earliest green, and dark stripes of new-ploughed earth, over which the cloud-shadows melted tracklessly toward the hills which round softly upward to Monte Cavi.

When our dinner came, and with it a flask of drowsy red Aleatico, like ink with a suspicion of life-blood in it, such as one might fancy Shakespeare to have dipped his quill in, we had our table so placed that the satisfaction of our hunger might be dissensualized by the view from the windows. Many a glutton has eaten up farms and woodlands and pastures, and so did we, æsthetically, saucing our *frittata* and flavoring our Aleatico with landscape. It is a fine thing when we can accustom our animal appetites to good society, when body and soul (like master and servant in an Arab tent) sit down together at the same board. This thought is forced upon one very often in Italy, as one picnics in enchanted spots, where Imagination and

Fancy play the parts of the unseen waiters in the fairy-story, and serve us with course after course of their ethereal dishes. Sense is satisfied with less and simpler food when sense and spirit are fed together, and the feast of the loaves and fishes is spread for us anew. If it be important for a state to educate its lower classes, so is it for us personally to instruct, elevate, and refine our senses, the lower classes of our private body-politic, which, if left to their own brute instincts, will disorder or destroy the whole commonwealth with flaming insurrection.

After dinner came our guide to be paid. He, too, had had his *frittata* and his *fiasco* (or two), and came back absurdly comic, reminding one of the giant who was so taken in by the little tailor. He was not in the least tipsy; but the wine had excited his poor wits, whose destiny it was (awkward servants as they were!) to trip up and tumble over each other in proportion as they became zealous. He was very anxious to *do* us in some way or other; he only vaguely guessed how, but felt so gigantically good-natured that he could not keep his face sober long enough. It is quite clear why the Italians have no word but *recitare* to express acting, for their stage is no more theatric than their street, and to exaggerate in the least would be ridiculous. We graver-tempered and -mannered Septentrions must give the pegs a screw or two to bring our spirits up to nature's concert-pitch. Storg and I sat enjoying the exhibition of our giant, as if we had no more concern in it than as a comedy. It was nothing but a spectacle to us, at which we were present as critics, while he inveighed, expostulated, argued, and besought, in a breath. Finding all his attempts miscarry, or resulting in nothing more solid than applause, he said, " *Forse non capiscono ?* " (Perhaps you don't understand ?) " *Capiscono pur' troppo,*" (They understand only too well,) replied the landlord, upon which *terræ filius* burst into a laugh, and began begging for more *buonamano.* Failing in this, he tightened his sash, offered to kiss our lordships' hands, an act of homage which we declined, and departed, carefully avoiding Genezzano on his return, I make no doubt.

We paid our bill, and after I had written in the guest-book

Bere Aleatico
Mi è molto simpatico,

went down to the door, where we found our guides and donkeys, the host's handsome wife and handsomer daughter, with two of *her* daughters, and a crowd of women and children waiting to witness the *exit* of the foreigners. We made all the mothers and children happy by a discriminating *largesse* of copper among the little ones. They are a charming people, the natives of these out-of-the-way Italian towns, if kindness, courtesy, and good looks make people charming. Our beards and felt hats, which make us pass for artists, were our passports to the warmest welcome and the best cheer everywhere. Reluctantly we mounted our donkeys, and trotted away, our guides (a man and a boy) running by the flank (true henchmen, haunchmen, *flanquiers* or flunkeys) and inspiring the little animals with pokes in the side, or with the even more effectual *ahrrrrr !* Is there any radical affinity between this rolling fire of *r*'s and the word *arra*, which means hansel or earnest-money? The sound is the same, and has a marvellous spur-power over the donkey, who seems to understand that full payment of goad or cudgel is to follow. I have known it to move even a Sicilian mule, the least sensitive and most obstinate of creatures with ears, except a British church-warden.

We wound along under a bleak hill, more desolate than anything I had ever seen. The old gray rocks seemed not to thrust themselves out of the rusty soil, but rather to be stabbed into it, as if they had been hailed down upon it by some volcano. There was nearly as much look of design as there is in a druidical circle, and the whole looked like some graveyard in an extinguished world, the monument of mortality itself, such as Bishop Wilkins might have found in the moon, if he had ever got thither. The path grew ever wilder, and Rojate, the next town we came to, grim and grizzly under a grim and grizzly sky of low-trailing clouds which had suddenly gathered, looked drearier even than the desolations we had passed. It was easy to understand why rocks should like to live here well enough; but what could have brought men hither, and then kept them here, was beyond all reasonable surmise. Barren hills stood sullenly aloof all around, incapable of any crop but lichens.

We entered the gate, and found ourselves in the

midst of a group of wild-looking men gathered about the door of a wine-shop. Some of them were armed with long guns, and we saw (for the first time *in situ*) the tall bandit hat with ribbons wound round it, — such as one is familiar with in operas, and on the heads of those inhabitants of the *Scalinata* in Rome, who have a costume of their own, and placidly serve as models through the whole pictorial range of divine and human nature, from the *Padre Eterno* to Judas. Twenty years ago, when my notion of an Italian was divided between a monk and a bravo, the first of whom did nothing but enter at secret doors and drink your health in poison, while the other lived behind corners, supporting himself by the productive industry of digging your person all over with a stiletto, I should have looked for instant assassination from these carousing ruffians. But the only blood shed on the occasion was that of the grape. A ride over the mountains for two hours had made us thirsty, and two or three bajocchi gave a tumbler of *vino asciutto* to all four of us. "You are welcome," said one of the men, " we are all artists after a fashion ; we are all brothers." The manners here are more republican, and the title of *lordship* disappears altogether. Another came up and insisted that we should drink a second flask of wine as his guests. In vain we protested ; no artist should pass through Rojate without accepting that token of good-will, and with the liberal help of our guides we contrived to gulp it down. He was for another ; but we protested that we were entirely full, and that it was impossible. I dare say the poor fellow would have spent a week's earnings on us, if we would have let him. We proposed to return the civility, and to leave a paul for them to drink a good journey to us after we were gone; but they would not listen to it. Our entertainer followed us along to the Piazza, begging one of us to let him serve as donkey-driver to Subiaco. When this was denied, he said that there was a *festa* here also, and that we must stop long enough to see the procession of *zitelle* (young girls), which would soon begin. But evening was already gathering, the clouds grew momently darker, and fierce, damp gusts, striking us with the suddenness of a blow, promised a wild night. We had still eight miles of mountain-path before us, and we struggled away. As we crossed the next summit beyond the town, a sound of chanting drifted by us on the wind, wavered hither and thither, now heard, now lost, then a doubtful something between song and gust, and, lingering a few moments, we saw the white head-dresses, gliding two by two, across a gap between the houses. The scene and the music were both in neutral tints, a sketch, as it were, in *sepia* a little blurred.

Before long the clouds almost brushed us as they eddied silently by, and then it began to rain, first mistily, and then in thick, hard drops. Fortunately there was a moon, shining placidly in the desert heaven above all this turmoil, or we could not have found our path, which in a few moments became a roaring torrent almost knee-deep. It was a cold rain, and far above us, where the moun-

tain-peaks tore gaps in the clouds, we could see the
white silence of new-fallen snow. Sometimes we
had to dismount and wade, — a circumstance which
did not make our saddles more comfortable when
we returned to them and could hear them go *crosh*,
crosh, as the water gurgled out of them at every
jolt. There was no hope of shelter nearer than
Subiaco, no sign of man, and no sound but the
multitudinous roar of waters on every side. Rivulet whispered to rivulet, and water-fall shouted to
water-fall, as they leaped from rock to rock, all
hurrying to reinforce the main torrent below, which
hummed onward toward the Anio with dilated
heart. So gathered the hoarse Northern swarms
to descend upon sunken Italy; and so forever does
physical and intellectual force seek its fatal equilibrium, rushing in and occupying wherever it is
drawn by the attraction of a lower level.

We forded large streams that had been dry beds
an hour before ; and so sudden was the creation of
the floods, that it gave one almost as fresh a feeling of water as if one had been present in Eden
when the first rock gave birth to the first fountain.
I had a severe cold, I was wet through from the hips
downward, and yet I never enjoyed anything more
in my life, — so different is the shower-bath to
which we doom ourselves from that whose string is
pulled by the prison-warden compulsion. After
our little bearers had tottered us up and down the
dusky steeps of a few more mountain-spurs, where
a misstep would have sent us spinning down the
fathomless black nowhere below, we came out upon

the highroad, and found it a fine one, as all the great Italian roads are. The rain broke off suddenly, and on the left, seeming about half a mile away, sparkled the lights of Subiaco, flashing intermittently like a knot of fire-flies in a meadow. The town, owing to the necessary windings of the road, was still three miles off, and just as the guides had prodded and *ahrred* the donkeys into a brisk joggle, I resolved to give up my saddle to the boy, and try Tom Coryate's compasses. It was partly out of humanity to myself and partly to him, for he was tired and I was cold. The elder guide and I took the lead, and, as I looked back, I laughed to see the lolling ears of Storg's donkey thrust from under his long cloak, as if he were coming out from a black Arab tent. We soon left them behind, and paused at a bridge over the Anio till we heard the patter of little hoofs again. The bridge is a single arch, bent between the steep edges of a gorge through which the Anio huddled far below, showing a green gleam here and there in the struggling moonlight, as if a fish rolled up his burnished flank. After another mile and a half, we reached the gate, and awaited our companions. It was dreary enough, — waiting always is, — and as the snow-chilled wind whistled through the damp archway where we stood, my legs illustrated feelingly to me how they cool water in the East, by wrapping the jars with wet woollen and setting them in a draught. At last they came ; I remounted, and we went sliding through the steep, wet streets till we had fairly passed through the whole town. Be-

fore a long building of two stories, without a symptom of past or future light, we stopped. " *Ecco
la Paletta!* " said the guide, and began to pound
furiously on the door with a large stone, which he
some time before had provided for the purpose.
After a long period of sullen irresponsiveness, we
heard descending footsteps, light streamed through
the chinks of the door, and the invariable " *Chi
è?* " which precedes the unbarring of all portals
here, came from within. " *Due forestieri,*" answered the guide, and the bars rattled in hasty
welcome. "Make us," we exclaimed, as we stiffly
climbed down from our perches, " your biggest fire
in your biggest chimney, and then we will talk of
supper!" In five minutes two great laurel-fagots
were spitting and crackling in an enormous fireplace ; and Storg and I were in the costume which
Don Quixote wore on the Brown Mountain. Of
course there was nothing for supper but a *frittata ;*
but there are worse things in the world than a
frittata con prosciutto, and we discussed it like a
society just emerging from barbarism, the upper
half of our persons presenting all the essentials of
an advanced civilization, while our legs skulked
under the table as free from sartorial impertinences
as those of the noblest savage that ever ran wild in
the woods. And so *eccoci finalmente arrivati!*

27*th.* — Nothing can be more lovely than the
scenery about Subiaco. The town itself is built
on a kind of cone rising from the midst of a valley
abounding in olives and vines, with a superb
mountain horizon around it, and the green Anio

cascading at its feet. As you walk to the high-
perched convent of San Benedetto, you look across
the river on your right just after leaving the town,
to a cliff over which the ivy pours in torrents,
and in which dwellings have been hollowed out.
In the black doorway of every one sits a woman
in scarlet bodice and white head-gear, with a distaff, spinning, while overhead countless nightingales sing at once from the fringe of shrubbery.
The glorious great white clouds look over the
mountain-tops into our enchanted valley, and sometimes a lock of their vapory wool would be torn
off, to lie for a while in some inaccessible ravine
like a snow-drift; but it seemed as if no shadow
could fly over our privacy of sunshine to-day.
The approach to the monastery is delicious. You
pass out of the hot sun into the green shadows
of ancient ilexes, leaning and twisting every way
that is graceful, their branches velvety with brilliant moss, in which grow feathery ferns, fringing
them with a halo of verdure. Then comes the convent, with its pleasant old monks, who show their
sacred vessels (one by Cellini) and their relics,
among which is a finger-bone of one of the Inno-
cents. Lower down is a convent of Santa Scholastica, where the first book was printed in Italy.

But though one may have daylight till after
twenty-four o'clock in Italy, the days are no longer
than ours, and I must go back to La Paletta
to see about a *vettura* to Tivoli. I leave Storg
sketching, and walk slowly down, lingering over
the ever-changeful views, lingering opposite the

nightingale-cliff, but get back to Subiaco and the *vetturino* at last. The growl of a thunder-storm soon brought Storg home, and we leave Subiaco triumphantly, at five o'clock, in a light carriage, drawn by three gray stallions (harnessed abreast) on the full gallop. I cannot describe our drive, the mountain-towns, with their files of girls winding up from the fountain with balanced water-jars of ruddy copper, or chattering round it bright-hued as parrots, the ruined castles, the green gleams of the capricious river, the one great mountain that soaked up all the rose of sunset, and, after all else grew dim, still glowed as if with inward fires, and, later, the white spray-smoke of Tivoli that drove down the valley under a clear cold moon, contrasting strangely with the red glare of the lime-furnace on the opposite hillside. It is well that we can be happy sometimes without peeping and botanizing in the materials that make us so. It is not often that we can escape the evil genius of analysis that haunts our modern day-light of self-consciousness (*wir haben ja aufge-klärt!*) and enjoy a day of right Chaucer.

P. S. Now that I am printing this, a dear friend sends me an old letter, and says, " Slip in somewhere, by way of contrast, what you wrote me of your visit to Passawampscot." It is odd, almost painful, to be confronted with your past self and your past self's doings, when you have forgotten both. But here is my bit of American scenery, such as it is.

While we were waiting for the boat, we had time to investigate P. a little. We wandered about with no one to molest us or make us afraid. No *cicerone* was lying in wait for us, no verger expected with funeral solemnity the more than compulsory shilling. I remember the whole population of Cortona gathering round me, and beseeching me not to leave their city till I had seen the *lampadone*, whose keeper had unhappily gone out for a walk, taking the key with him. Thank Fortune, here were no antiquities, no galleries of Pre-Raphaelite art, every lank figure looking as if it had been stretched on a rack, before which the Anglo-Saxon writhes because he ought to like them and cannot for the soul of him. It is a pretty little village, cuddled down among the hills, the clay soil of which gives them, to a pilgrim from the parched gravelly inland, a look of almost fanatical green. The fields are broad, and wholly given up to the grazing of cattle and sheep, which dotted them thickly in the breezy sunshine. The open doors of a barn, through which the wind flowed rustling the loose locks of the mow, attracted us. Swallows swam in and out with level wings, or crossed each other, twittering in the dusky mouth of their hay-scented cavern. Two or three hens and a cock (none of your gawky Shanghais, long-legged as a French peasant on his stilts, but the true red cock of the ballads, full-chested, coral-combed, fountain-tailed) were inquiring for hay-seed in the background. What frame in what gallery ever enclosed such a picture as is squared within the groundsel, side - posts, and lintel of a barn-door, whether for eye or fancy ? The shining floor suggests the flail - beat of autumn, that pleasantest of monotonous sounds, and the later husking- bee, where the lads and lasses sit round laughingly busy under the swinging lantern.

Here we found a fine, stalwart fellow shearing sheep. This was something new to us, and we watched him for some time with many questions, which he answered with off-hand good-nature. Going away, I thanked him for having taught me something. He laughed, and said, " Ef you'll take off them gloves o' yourn, I 'll give ye a try at the practical part on 't." He was in the right of it. I never saw anything handsomer than those brown hands of his, on which the sinews stood out, as he handled his shears, tight as a drawn bowstring. How much more admirable is this tawny vigor, the badge of fruitful toil, than the crop of early muscle that heads out under the forcing-glass of the gymnasium ! Foreigners do not feel easy in America, because there are no peasants and underlings here to be humble to them. The truth is, that none but those who feel themselves only artificially the superiors of our sturdy yeomen see in their self-respect any uncomfortable *assumption* of equality. It is the last thing the yeoman is likely to think of. They do not like the " I say, ma good fellah " kind of style, and commonly contrive to snub it. They do not value condescension at the same rate that he does who vouchsafes it to them. If it be a good thing for an English duke that he has no social superiors, I think it can hardly be bad for a Yankee farmer. If it be a bad thing for the duke that he meets none but inferiors, it cannot harm the farmer much that he never has the chance. At any rate, there was no thought of incivility in my friend Hobbinol's jibe at my kids, only a kind of jolly superiority. But I did not like to be taken for a city *gent*, so I told him I was born and bred in the country as well as he. He laughed again, and said, " Wal, anyhow, I 've the advantage of ye, for you never see a sheep shore, and I 've be'n to the Opery and shore sheep myself into the bargain." He told me that there were two hundred sheep in the town, and that his father could remember when there were four times as many. The sea laps and mumbles the soft roots of the hills, and licks away an acre or two of good pasturage every season. The father, an old man of eighty, stood looking on, pleased with his son's wit, and brown as if the Passawampscot fogs were walnut-juice.

We dined at a little tavern, with a gilded ball hung out for sign, — a waif, I fancy, from some shipwreck. The landlady was a brisk, amusing little body, who soon informed us that her husband was own cousin to a Senator of the United States. A very elaborate sampler in the parlor, in which an obelisk was wept over by a somewhat costly willow in silver thread, recorded the virtues of the Senator's maternal grandfather and grandmother. After dinner, as we sat smoking our pipes on the piazza, our good hostess brought her little daughter, and made her repeat verses utterly unintelligible, but conjecturally moral, and certainly depressing. Once set agoing, she ran down like an alarm-clock. We awaited her subsidence as that of a shower or other inevitable natural phenomenon. More refreshing was the talk of a tall returned Californian, who told us, among other things, that "he should n't mind Panahmy's bein' sunk, ollers providin' there war n't none of *our* folks onto it when it went down!"

Our landlady's exhibition of her daughter puts me in mind of something similar, yet oddly different, which happened to Storg and me at Palestrina. We jointly praised the beauty of our stout *locandiera's* little girl. "Ah, she is nothing to her eldest sister just married," said the mother. "If you could see *her!* She is bella, *bella*, BELLA!" We thought no more of it; but after dinner, the good creature, with no warning but a tap at the door and a humble *con permesso*, brought her in all her bravery, and showed her off to us as simply and naturally as if she had been a picture. The girl, who was both beautiful and modest, bore it with the dignified *aplomb* of a statue. She knew we admired her, and liked it, but with the indifference of a rose. There is something very charming, I think, in this wholly unsophisticated consciousness, with no alloy of vanity or coquetry.

IV.

A FEW BITS OF ROMAN MOSAIC.

Byron hit the white, which he often shot very wide of in his Italian Guide-Book, when he called Rome "my country." But it is a feeling which comes to one slowly, and is absorbed into one's system during a long residence. Perhaps one does not feel it till one has gone away, as things always seem fairer when we look back at them, and it is out of that inaccessible tower of the past that Longing leans and beckons. However it be, Fancy gets a rude shock at entering Rome, which it takes her a great while to get over. She has gradually made herself believe that she is approaching a city of the dead, and has seen nothing on the road from Civita Vecchia to disturb that theory. Milestones, with "Via Aurelia" carved upon them, have confirmed it. It is eighteen hundred years ago with her, and on the dial of time the shadow has not yet trembled over the line that marks the beginning of the first century. She arrives at the gate, and a dirty, blue man, with a cocked hat and a white sword-belt, asks for her passport. Then another man, as like the first as one spoon is like its fellow, and having, like him, the look of being run in a mould, tells her that she must go to the custom-house. It is as if a ghost, who had scarcely recovered from the jar of hearing Charon say, "I'll trouble you for your obolus, if you please," should have his

portmanteau seized by the Stygian tide-waiters to
be searched.   Is there anything, then, contraband
of death? asks poor Fancy of herself.

But it is the misfortune (or the safeguard) of
the English mind that Fancy is always an outlaw,
liable to be laid by the heels wherever Constable
Common Sense can catch her.   She submits quietly
as the postilion cries, " *Yee-ip!* " cracks his whip,
and the rattle over the pavement begins, struggles a moment when the pillars of the colonnade
stalk ghostly by in the moonlight, and finally gives
up all for lost when she sees Bernini's angels polk-
ing on their pedestals along the sides of the Ponte
Sant' Angelo with the emblems of the ·Passion in
their arms.

You are in Rome, of course; the *sbirro* said so,
the *doganiere* bowed it, and the postilion swore it;
but it is a Rome of modern houses, muddy streets,
dingy *caffès*, cigar-smokers, and French soldiers,
the manifest junior of Florence.   And yet full of
anachronisms, for in a little while you pass the column of Antoninus, find the *Dogana* in an ancient
temple whose furrowed pillars show through the
recent plaster, and feel as if you saw the statue of
Minerva in a Paris bonnet.   You are driven to a
hotel where all the barbarian languages are spoken
in one wild conglomerate by the *Commissionnaire*,
have your dinner wholly in French, and wake the
next morning dreaming of the Tenth Legion, to see
a regiment of *Chasseurs de Vincennes* trotting by.

For a few days one undergoes a tremendous recoil.   Other places have a distinct meaning.   Lon-

don is the visible throne of King Stock; Versailles is the apotheosis of one of Louis XIV.'s cast periwigs; Florence and Pisa are cities of the Middle Ages; but Rome seems to be a parody upon itself. The ticket that admits you to see the starting of the horses at carnival has S. P. Q. R. at the top of it, and you give the *custode* a paul for showing you the wolf that suckled Romulus and Remus. The *Senatus* seems to be a score or so of elderly gentlemen in scarlet, and the *Populusque Romanus* a swarm of nasty friars.

But there is something more than mere earth in the spot where great deeds have been done. The surveyor cannot give the true dimensions of Marathon or Lexington, for they are not reducible to square acres. Dead glory and greatness leave ghosts behind them, and departed empire has a metempsychosis, if nothing else has. Its spirit haunts the grave, and waits, and waits till at last it finds a body to its mind, slips into it, and historians moralize on the fluctuation of human affairs. By and by, perhaps, enough observations will have been recorded to assure us that these recurrences are firmamental, and historionomers will have measured accurately the sidereal years of races. When that is once done, events will move with the quiet of an orrery, and nations will consent to their peridynamis and apodynamis with planetary composure.

Be this as it may, you become gradually aware of the presence of this imperial ghost among the Roman ruins. You receive hints and startles of it

through the senses first, as the horse always shies
at the apparition before the rider can see it. Then,
little by little, you become assured of it, and seem
to hear the brush of its mantle through some hall
of Caracalla's baths, or one of those other solitudes
of Rome. And those solitudes are without a parallel; for it is not the mere absence of man, but
the sense of his departure, that makes a profound
loneliness. Musing upon them, you cannot but
feel the shadow of that disembodied empire, and,
remembering how the foundations of the Capitol
were laid where a human head was turned up, you
are impelled to prophesy that the Idea of Rome
will incarnate itself again as soon as an Italian
brain is found large enough to hold it, and to give
unity to those discordant members.

But, though I intend to observe no regular pattern in my Roman mosaic, which will resemble
more what one finds in his pockets after a walk, —
a pagan cube or two from the palaces of the Cæ-
sars, a few Byzantine bits, given with many shrugs
of secrecy by a lay-brother at San Paolo *fuori le
mura*, and a few more (quite as ancient) from the
manufactory at the Vatican, — it seems natural to
begin what one has to say of Rome with something
about St. Peter's; for the saint sits at the gate
here as well as in Paradise.

It is very common for people to say that they
are disappointed in the first sight of St. Peter's;
and one hears much the same about Niagara. I
cannot help thinking that the fault is in themselves; and that if the church and the cataract

were in the habit of giving away their thoughts with that rash generosity which characterizes tourists, they might perhaps say of their visitors, " Well, if *you* are those Men of whom we have heard so much, we are a little disappointed, to tell the truth! " The refined tourist expects somewhat too much when he takes it for granted that St. Peter's will at once decorate him with the order of imagination, just as Victoria knights an alderman when he presents an address. Or perhaps he has been getting up a little architecture on the road from Florence, and is discomfited because he does not know whether he *ought* to be pleased or not, which is very much as if he should wait to be told whether it was fresh water or salt which makes the exhaustless grace of Niagara's emerald curve, before he benignly consented to approve. It would be wiser, perhaps, for him to consider whether, if Michael Angelo had had the building of *him*, his own personal style would not have been more impressive.

It is not to be doubted that minds are of as many different orders as cathedrals, and that the Gothic imagination is vexed and discommoded in the vain endeavor to flatten its pinnacles, and fit itself into the round Roman arches. But if it be impossible for a man to like everything, it is quite possible for him to avoid being driven mad by what does not please him; nay, it is the imperative duty of a wise man to find out what that secret is which makes a thing pleasing to another. In approaching St. Peter's, one must take his Protestant shoes off his feet, and leave them behind him, in the Piazza Rusticucci. Otherwise the great Basilica, with those outstretching colonnades of Bramante, will seem to be a bloated spider lying in wait for him, the poor heretic fly. As he lifts the heavy leathern flapper over the door, and is discharged into the interior by its impetuous recoil, let him disburthen his mind altogether of stone and mortar, and think only that he is standing before the throne of a dynasty which, even in its decay, is the most powerful the world ever saw. Mason-work is all very well in itself, but it has nothing to do with the affair at present in hand.

Suppose that a man in pouring down a glass of claret could drink the South of France, that he could so disintegrate the wine by the force of imagination as to taste in it all the clustered beauty and bloom of the grape, all the dance and song and sun-burnt jollity of the vintage. Or suppose that in eating bread he could transubstantiate it with the tender blade of spring, the gleam-flitted corn-ocean of summer, the royal autumn, with its golden beard, and the merry funerals of harvest. This is what the great poets do for us, we cannot tell how, with their fatally-chosen words, crowding the happy veins of language again with all the life and meaning and music that had been dribbling away from them since Adam. And this is what the Roman Church does for religion, feeding the soul not with the essential religious sentiment, not with a drop or two of the tincture of worship, but making us feel one by one all those original elements of which worship is composed ; not bringing the end to us, but making us pass over and feel beneath our feet all the golden rounds of the ladder by which the climbing generations have reached that end ; not handing us drily a dead and extinguished Q. E. D., but letting it rather declare itself by the glory with which it interfuses the incense-clouds of wonder and aspiration and beauty in which it is veiled. The secret of her power is typified in the mystery of the Real Presence. She is the only church that has been loyal to the heart and soul of man, that has clung to her faith in the imagination, and that would not give over her symbols and images and sacred vessels to the perilous keeping of the iconoclast Understanding. She has never lost sight of the truth, that the product human nature is composed of the sum of flesh and spirit, and has accordingly regarded both this world and the next as the constituents of that other world which we possess by faith. She knows that poor Panza, the body, has his kitchen longings and visions, as well as Quixote, the soul, his ethereal, and has wit enough to supply him with the visible, tangible raw material of imagination. She is the only poet among the churches, and, while Protestantism is unrolling a pocket surveyor's-plan, takes her votary to the pinnacle of her temple, and shows him meadow, upland, and tillage, cloudy heaps of forest clasped with the river's jewelled arm, hillsides white with the perpetual snow of flocks, and, beyond all, the interminable heave of the unknown ocean. Her empire may be traced upon the map by the boun-

daries of races ; the understanding is her great
foe ; and it is the people whose vocabulary was in-
complete till they had invented the archword Hum-
bug that defies her. With that leaden bullet John
Bull can bring down Sentiment when she flies her
highest. And the more the pity for John Bull.
One of these days some one whose eyes are sharp
enough will read in the Times a standing advertisement, " Lost, strayed, or stolen from the farm-
yard of the subscriber the valuable horse Pegasus. Probably has on him part of a new plough-
harness, as that is also missing. A suitable reward,
etc.   J. BULL."
Protestantism reverses the poetical process I
have spoken of above, and gives not even the bread
of life, but instead of it the alcohol, or distilled
intellectual result. This was very well so long as
Protestantism continued to protest ; for enthusiasm
sublimates the understanding into imagination.
But now that she also has become an establishment, she begins to perceive that she made a
blunder in trusting herself to the intellect alone.
She is beginning to feel her way back again, as
one notices in Puseyism, and other such hints.
One is put upon reflection when one sees burly
Englishmen, who dine on beef and porter every
day, marching proudly through St. Peter's on
Palm Sunday, with those frightfully artificial palm-
branches in their hands. Romanism wisely pro-
vides for the childish in men.
Therefore I say again, that one must lay aside
his Protestantism in order to have a true feeling

of St. Peter's. Here in Rome is the laboratory of that mysterious enchantress, who has known so well how to adapt herself to all the wants, or, if you will, the weaknesses of human nature, making the retirement of the convent-cell a merit to the solitary, the scourge or the fast a piety to the ascetic, the enjoyment of pomp and music and incense a religious act in the sensual, and furnishing for the very soul itself a *confidante* in that ear of the dumb confessional, where it may securely disburthen itself of its sins and sorrows. And the dome of St. Peter's is the magic circle within which she works her most potent incantations. I confess that I could not enter it alone without a kind of awe.

But, setting entirely aside the effect of this church upon the imagination, it is wonderful, if one consider it only materially. Michael Angelo created a new world in which everything was colossal, and it might seem that he built this as a fit temple for those gigantic figures with which he peopled it to worship in. Here his Moses should be high-priest, the service should be chanted by his prophets and sibyls, and those great pagans should be brought hither from San Lorenzo in Florence, to receive baptism.

However unsatisfactory in other matters, statistics are of service here. I have seen a refined tourist who entered, Murray in hand, sternly resolved to have St. Peter's look small, brought to terms at once by being told that the canopy over the high altar (looking very like a four-post bedstead) was ninety-eight feet high. If he still obstinates himself, he is finished by being made to measure one of the marble *putti*, which look like rather stoutish babies, and are found to be six feet, every sculptor's son of them. This ceremony is the more interesting, as it enables him to satisfy the guide of his proficiency in the Italian tongue by calling them *putty* at every convenient opportunity. Otherwise both he and his assistant terrify each other into mutual unintelligibility with that *lingua franca* of the English-speaking traveller, which is supposed to bear some remote affinity to the French language, of which both parties are as ignorant as an American Ambassador.

Murray gives all these little statistical nudges to the Anglo-Saxon imagination; but he knows that its finest nerves are in the pocket, and accordingly ends by telling you how much the church cost. I forget how much it is; but it cannot be more, I fancy, than the English national debt multiplied into itself three hundred and sixty-five times. If the pilgrim, honestly anxious for a sensation, will work out this little sum, he will be sure to receive all that enlargement of the imaginative faculty which arithmetic can give him. Perhaps the most dilating fact, after all, is that this architectural world has also a separate atmosphere, distinct from that of Rome by some ten degrees, and unvarying through the year.

I think that, on the whole, Jonathan gets ready to be pleased with St. Peter's sooner than Bull. Accustomed to our lath and plaster expedients for churches, the portable sentry-boxes of Zion, mere solidity and permanence are pleasurable in themselves; and if he get grandeur also, he has Gospel measure. Besides, it is easy for Jonathan to travel. He is one drop of a fluid mass, who knows where his home is to-day, but can make no guess of where it may be to-morrow. Even in a form of government he only takes lodgings for the night, and is ready to pay his bill and be off in the morning. He should take his motto from Bishop Golias's " *Mihi est propositum in tabernâ mori,*" though not in the sufistic sense of that misunderstood Churchman. But Bull can seldom be said to travel at all, since the first step of a true traveller is out of himself. He plays cricket and hunts foxes on the Campagna, makes entries in his betting-book while the Pope is giving his benediction, and points out Lord Calico to you awfully during the Sistine *Miserere.* If he let his beard grow, it always has a startled air, as if it suddenly remembered its treason to Sheffield, and only makes him look more English than ever. A masquerade is impossible to him, and his fancy balls are the solemnest facts in the world. Accordingly, he enters St. Peter's with the dome of St. Paul's drawn tight over his eyes, like a criminal's cap, and ready for instant execution rather than confess that the English Wren had not a stronger wing than the Italian Angel. I like this in Bull, and it renders him the pleasantest of travelling-companions; for he makes you take England along with you, and thus you have two countries at once. And one must not forget in an Italian inn that it is to Bull he owes the clean napkins and sheets, and the privilege of his morning bath. Nor should Bull himself fail to remember that he ate with his fingers till the Italian gave him a fork.

Browning has given the best picture of St. Peter's on a festival-day, sketching it with a few verses in his large style. And doubtless it is the scene of the grandest spectacles which the world can see in these latter days. Those Easter pomps, where the antique world marches visibly before you in gilded mail and crimson doubtlet, refresh the eyes, and are good so long as they continue to be merely spectacle. But if one think for a moment of the servant of the servants of the Lord in cloth of gold, borne on men's shoulders, or of the children receiving the blessing of their Holy Father, with a regiment of French soldiers to protect the father from the children, it becomes a little sad. If one would feel the full meaning of those ceremonials, however, let him consider the coincidences between the Romish and the Buddhist forms of worship, and remembering that the Pope is the direct heir, through the Pontifex Maximus, of rites that were ancient when the Etruscans were modern, he will look with a feeling deeper than curiosity upon forms which record the earliest conquests of the Invisible, the first triumphs of mind over muscle.

To me the noon silence and solitude of St. Peter's were most impressive, when the sunlight, made visible by the mist of the ever-burning lamps in which it was entangled, hovered under the dome like the holy dove goldenly descending. Very grand also is the twilight, when all outlines melt into mysterious vastness, and the arches expand and lose themselves in the deepening shadow. Then, standing in the desert transept, you hear the far-off vespers swell and die like low breathings of the sea on some conjectured shore.

As the sky is supposed to scatter its golden star-pollen once every year in meteoric showers, so the dome of St. Peter's has its annual efflorescence of fire. This illumination is the great show of Papal Rome. Just after sunset, I stood upon the Trinità dei Monti and saw the little drops of pale light creeping downward from the cross and trickling over the dome. Then, as the sky darkened behind, it seemed as if the setting sun had lodged upon the horizon and there burned out, the fire still clinging to his massy ribs. And when the change from the silver to the golden illumination came, it was as if the breeze had fanned the embers into flame again.

Bitten with the Anglo-Saxon gadfly that drives us all to disenchant artifice, and see the springs that fix it on, I walked down to get a nearer look. My next glimpse was from the bridge of Sant' Angelo; but there was no time nor space for pause. Foot-passengers crowding hither and thither, as they heard the shout of *Avanti!* from the mile of coachmen behind, dragoon-horses curtsying backward just where there were most women and children to be flattened, and the dome drawing all eyes and thoughts the wrong way,

made a hubbub to be got out of at any desperate
hazard.   Besides, one could not help feeling ner-
vously hurried; for it seemed quite plain to everybody that this starry apparition must be as momentary as it was wonderful, and that we should
find it vanished when we reached the piazza.   But
suddenly you stand in front of it, and see the soft
travertine of the front suffused with a tremulous,
glooming glow, a mildened glory, as if the building
breathed, and so transmuted its shadow into soft
pulses of light.

After wondering long enough, I went back to
the Pincio, and watched it for an hour longer.
But I did not wish to see it go out.   It seemed
better to go home and leave it still trembling, so
that I could fancy a kind of permanence in it, and
half believe I should find it there again some lucky
evening.   Before leaving it altogether, I went
away to cool my eyes with darkness, and came
back several times;   and every time it was a new
miracle, the more so that it was a human piece of
faëry-work.   Beautiful as fire is in itself, I suspect
that part of the pleasure is metaphysical, and that
the sense of playing with an element which can be
so terrible adds to the zest of the spectacle.   And
then fire is not the least degraded by it, because it
is not utilized.   If beauty were in use, the factory
would add a grace to the river, and we should turn
from the fire-writing on the wall of heaven to look
at a message printed by the magnetic telegraph.
There may be a beauty in the use itself; but utilization is always downward, and it is this feeling

that makes Schiller's Pegasus in yoke so universally pleasing. So long as the curse of work clings to man, he will see beauty only in play. The capital of the most frugal commonwealth in the world burns up five thousand dollars a year in gunpowder, and nobody murmurs. Provident Judas wished to utilize the ointment, but the Teacher would rather that it should be wasted in poem.

The best lesson in æsthetics I ever got (and, like most good lessons, it fell from the lips of no regular professor) was from an Irishman on the day the Nymph Cochituate was formally introduced to the people of Boston. I made one with other rustics in the streets, admiring the dignitaries in coaches with as much Christian charity as is consistent with an elbow in the pit of one's stomach and a heel on that toe which is your only inheritance from two excellent grandfathers. Among other allegorical phenomena, there came along what I should have called a hay-cart, if I had not known it was a triumphal car, filled with that fairest variety of mortal grass which with us is apt to spindle so soon into a somewhat sapless womanhood. Thirty-odd young maidens in white gowns, with blue sashes and pink wreaths of French crape, represented the United States. (How shall we limit our number, by the way, if ever Utah be admitted?) The ship, the printing-press, even the wondrous train of express-wagons, and other solid bits of civic fantasy, had left my Hibernian neighbor unmoved. But this brought him down. Turning to me, as the most appreciative public for the moment, with face of as much delight as if his head had been broken, he cried, "Now this is *raly* beautiful!   Tothally regyardless uv expinse!" Methought my shirt-sleeved lecturer on the Beautiful had hit at least one nail full on the head. Voltaire but epigrammatized the same thought when he said, *Le superflu, chose très-nécessaire.*

As for the ceremonies of the Church, one need not waste time in seeing many of them.   There is a dreary sameness in them, and one can take an hour here and an hour there, as it pleases him, just as sure of finding the same pattern as he would be in the first or last yard of a roll of printed cotton. For myself, I do not like to go and look with mere curiosity at what is sacred and solemn to others.   To how many these Roman shows are sacred, I cannot guess; but certainly the Romans do not value them much.   I walked out to the grotto of Egeria on Easter Sunday, that I might not be tempted down to St. Peter's to see the mockery of Pio Nono's benediction.   It is certainly Christian, for he blesses them that curse him, and does all the good which the waving of his fingers can do to people who would use him despitefully if they had the chance.   I told an Italian servant she might have the day; but she said she did not care for it.

"But," urged I, "will you not go to receive the blessing of the Holy Father?"

"No, sir."

"Do you not wish it?"

"Not in the least: *his* blessing would do me no good. If I get the blessing of Heaven, it will serve my turn."

There were three families of foreigners in our house, and I believe none of the Italian servants went to St. Peter's that day. Yet they commonly speak kindly of Pius. I have heard the same phrase from several Italians of the working-class. "He is a good man," they said, "but ill-led."

What one sees in the streets of Rome is worth more than what one sees in the churches. The churches themselves are generally ugly. St. Peter's has crushed all the life out of architectural genius, and all the modern churches look as if they were swelling themselves in imitation of the great Basil-ica. There is a clumsy magnificence about them, and their heaviness oppresses. Their marble in-crustations look like a kind of architectural ele-phantiasis, and the parts are puffy with a dropsical want of proportion. There is none of the spring and soar which one may see even in the Lombard churches, and a Roman column standing near one of them, slim and gentlemanlike, satirizes silently their tawdry *parvenu*ism. Attempts at mere big-ness are ridiculous in a city where the Colosseum still yawns in crater-like ruin, and where Michael Angelo made a noble church out of a single room in Diocletian's baths.

Shall I confess it? Michael Angelo seems to me, in his angry reaction against sentimental beauty, to have mistaken bulk and brawn for the antithesis of feebleness. He is the apostle of the exaggerated, the Victor Hugo of painting and sculpture. I have a feeling that rivalry was a more powerful motive with him than love of art, that he had the conscious intention to be original, which seldom leads to anything better than being extravagant. The show of muscle proves strength, not power; and force for mere force's sake in art makes one think of Milo caught in his own log. This is my second thought, and strikes me as perhaps somewhat niggardly toward one in whom you cannot help feeling there was so vast a possibility. And then his Eve, his David, his Sibyls, his Prophets, his Sonnets! Well, I take it all back, and come round to St. Peter's again just to hint that I doubt about domes. In Rome they are so much the fashion that I felt as if they were the *goitre* of architecture. Generally they look heavy. Those on St. Mark's in Venice are the only light ones I ever saw, and they look almost airy, like tents puffed out with wind. I suppose one must be satisfied with the interior effect, which is certainly noble in St. Peter's. But for impressiveness both within and without there is nothing like a Gothic cathedral for me, nothing that crowns a city so nobly, or makes such an island of twilight silence in the midst of its noonday clamors.

Now as to what one sees in the streets, the beggars are certainly the first things that draw the eye. Beggary is an institution here. The Church has sanctified it by the establishment of mendicant orders, and indeed it is the natural result of a social system where the non-producing class makes

not only the laws, but the ideas. The beggars of
Rome go far toward proving the diversity of origin
in mankind, for on them surely the curse of Adam
never fell. It is easier to fancy that Adam *Vau-
rien*, the first tenant of the Fool's Paradise, after
sucking his thumbs for a thousand years, took to
wife Eve *Faniente*, and became the progenitor of
this race, to whom also he left a calendar in which
three hundred and sixty-five days in the year were
made feasts, sacred from all secular labor. Accordingly, they not merely do nothing, but they do
it assiduously and almost with religious fervor. I
have seen ancient members of this sect as constant
at their accustomed street-corner as the bit of
broken column on which they sat; and when a man
does this in rainy weather, as rainy weather is in
Rome, he has the spirit of a fanatic and martyr.

It is not that the Italians are a lazy people. On
the contrary, I am satisfied that they are industri-
ous so far as they are allowed to be. But, as I
said before, when a Roman does nothing, he does
it in the high Roman fashion. A friend of mine
was having one of his rooms arranged for a private
theatre, and sent for a person who was said to be
an expert in the business to do it for him. After
a day's trial, he was satisfied that his lieutenant
was rather a hindrance than a help, and resolved
to dismiss him.

" What is your charge for your day's services ? "

" Two scudi, sir."

" Two scudi ! Five pauls would be too much.
You have done nothing but stand with your hands

in your pockets and get in the way of other
people."

"Lordship is perfectly right; but *that* is my
way of working."

It is impossible for a stranger to say who may
not beg in Rome. It seems to be a sudden madness that may seize any one at the sight of a foreigner. You see a very respectable-looking person in the street, and it is odds but, as you pass
him, his hat comes off, his whole figure suddenly
dilapidates itself, assuming a tremble of professional weakness, and you hear the everlasting
qualche cosa per carità! You are in doubt whether
to drop a bajoccho into the next cardinal's hat
which offers you its sacred cavity in answer to your
salute. You·begin to believe that the hat was invented for the sole purpose of ingulfing coppers,
and that its highest type is the great *Triregno* itself, into which the pence of Peter rattle.

But you soon learn to distinguish the established
beggars, and to the three professions elsewhere considered liberal you add a fourth for this latitude,—
mendicancy. Its professors look upon themselves
as a kind of guild which ought to be protected by
the government. I fell into talk with a woman
who begged of me in the Colosseum. Among
other things she complained that the government
did not at all consider the poor.

"Where is the government that does?" I said.

"*Eh già!* Excellency; but this government lets
beggars from the country come into Rome, which
is a great injury to the trade of us born Romans.

There is Beppo, for example; he is a man of property in his own town, and has a dinner of three courses every day. He has portioned two daughters with three thousand scudi each, and left Rome during the time of the Republic with the rest of the nobility."

At first, one is shocked and pained at the exhibition of deformities in the street. But by and by he comes to look upon them with little more emotion than is excited by seeing the tools of any other trade. The melancholy of the beggars is purely a matter of business; and they look upon their maims as Fortunatus purses, which will always give them money. A withered arm they present to you as a highwayman would his pistol; a *goitre* is a life-annuity; a St. Vitus dance is as good as an engagement as *prima ballerina* at the Apollo; and to have no legs at all is to stand on the best footing with fortune. They are a merry race, on the whole, and quick-witted, like the rest of their countrymen. I believe the regular fee for a beggar is a *quattrino*, about a quarter of a cent; but they expect more of foreigners. A friend of mine once gave one of these tiny coins to an old woman; she delicately expressed her resentment by exclaiming, " Thanks, *signoria*. God will reward *even* you! "

A begging friar came to me one day with a subscription for repairing his convent. " Ah, but I am a heretic," said I. " Undoubtedly," with a shrug, implying a respectful acknowledgment of a foreigner's right to choose warm and dry lodgings in the other world as well as in this, "but your money is perfectly orthodox."

Another favorite way of doing nothing is to excavate the Forum. I think the *Fanientes* like this all the better, because it seems a kind of satire upon work, as the witches parody the Christian offices of devotion at their Sabbath. A score or so of old men in voluminous cloaks shift the earth from one side of a large pit to the other, in a manner so leisurely that it is positive repose to look at them. The most bigoted anti-Fourierist might acknowledge this to be attractive industry.

One conscript father trails a small barrow up to another, who stands leaning on a long spade. Arriving, he fumbles for his snuff-box, and offers it deliberately to his friend. Each takes an ample pinch, and both seat themselves to await the result. If one should sneeze, he receives the *Felicità!* of the other ; and, after allowing the titillation to subside, he replies, *Grazia!* Then follows a little conversation, and then they prepare to load. But it occurs to the barrow-driver that this is a good opportunity to fill and light his pipe ; and to do so conveniently he needs his barrow to sit upon. He draws a few whiffs, and a little more conversation takes place. The barrow is now ready ; but first the wielder of the spade will fill *his* pipe also. This done, more whiffs and more conversation. Then a spoonful of earth is thrown into the barrow, and it starts on its return. But midway it meets an empty barrow, and both stop to go through the snuff-box ceremonial once more, and to discuss whatever new thing has occurred in the excavation since their last encounter. And so it goes on all day.

As I see more of material antiquity, I begin to suspect that my interest in it is mostly factitious. The relations of races to the physical world (only to be studied fruitfully on the spot) do not excite in me an interest at all proportionate to that I feel in their influence on the moral advance of mankind, which one may as easily trace in his own library as on the spot. The only useful remark I remember to have made here is, that, the situation of Rome being far less strong than that of any city of the Etruscan league, it must have been built where it is for purposes of commerce. It is the most defensible point near the mouth of the Tiber. It is only as rival trades-folk that Rome and Carthage had any comprehensible cause of quarrel. It is only as a commercial people that we can understand the early tendency of the Romans towards democracy. As for antiquity, after reading history, one is haunted by a discomforting suspicion that the names so painfully deciphered in hieroglyphic or arrow-head inscriptions are only so many more Smiths and Browns masking it in unknown tongues. Moreover, if we Yankees are twitted with not knowing the difference between *big* and *great*, may not those of us who have learned it turn round on many a monument over here with the same reproach ? I confess I am beginning to sympathize with a countryman of ours from Michigan, who asked our Minister to direct him to a specimen ruin and a specimen gallery, that he might see and be rid of them once for all. I saw three young Englishmen going through the Vatican by catalogue and number, the other day, in a fashion which John Bull is apt to consider exclusively American. " Number 300!" says the one with catalogue and pencil, " have you seen it?" "Yes," answer his two comrades, and, checking it off, he goes on with Number 301. Having witnessed the unavailing agonies of many Anglo-Saxons from both sides of the Atlantic in their effort to have the correct sensation before many hideous examples of antique bad taste, my heart warmed toward my business-like British cousins, who were doing their æsthetics in this thrifty auctioneer fashion. Our cart-before-horse education, which makes us more familiar with the history and literature of Greeks and Romans than with those of our own ancestry, (though there is nothing in ancient art to match Shakespeare or a Gothic minster,) makes us the gulls of what we call classical antiquity. Europe were worth visiting, if only to be rid of this one old man of the sea. In sculpture, to be sure, they have us on the hip.

I am not ashamed to confess a singular sympathy with what are known as the Middle Ages. I cannot help thinking that few periods have left behind them such traces of inventiveness and power. Nothing is more tiresome than the sameness of modern cities; and it has often struck me that this must also have been true of those ancient ones in which Greek architecture or its derivatives prevailed, — true at least as respects public buildings. But mediæval towns, especially in Italy, even when only fifty miles asunder, have an individuality of character as marked as that of trees. Nor is it merely this originality that attracts me, but likewise the sense that, however old, they are nearer to me in being modern and Christian. Far enough away in the past to be picturesque, they are still so near through sympathies of thought and belief as to be more companionable. I find it harder to bridge over the gulf of Paganism than of centuries. Apart from any difference in the men, I had a far deeper emotion when I stood on the *Sasso di Dante*, than at Horace's Sabine farm or by the tomb of Virgil. The latter, indeed, interested me chiefly by its association with comparatively modern legend; and one of the buildings I am most glad to have seen in Rome is the Bear Inn, where Montaigne lodged on his arrival.

I think it must have been for some such reason that I liked my Florentine better than my Roman walks, though I am vastly more contented with merely being in Rome. Florence is more noisy; indeed, I think it the noisiest town I was ever in. What with the continual jangling of its bells, the rattle of Austrian drums, and the street-cries, *Ancora mi raccapriccia.* The Italians are a vociferous people, and most so among them the Florentines. Walking through a back street one day, I saw an old woman higgling with a peripatetic dealer, who, at every interval afforded him by the remarks of his veteran antagonist, would tip his head on one side, and shout, with a kind of wondering enthusiasm, as if he could hardly trust the evidence of his own senses to such loveliness, *O, che bellezza! che belle-e-ezza!* The two had been contending as obstinately as the Greeks and Trojans over the body of Patroclus, and I was curious to know what was the object of so much desire on the one side and admiration on the other. It was a half-dozen of weazeny baked pears, beggarly remnant of the day's traffic. Another time I stopped before a stall, debating whether to buy some fine-looking peaches. Before I had made up my mind, the vender, a stout fellow, with a voice like a prize-bull of Bashan, opened a mouth round and large as the muzzle of a blunderbuss, and let fly into my ear the following pertinent observation: " *Belle pesche! belle pe-e-esche!* " (*crescendo.*) I stared at him in stunned bewilderment; but, seeing that he had reloaded and was about to fire again, took to my heels, the exploded syllables rattling after me like so many buckshot. A single turnip is argument enough with them till midnight; nay, I have heard a ruffian yelling over a covered basket, which, I am convinced, was empty, and only carried as an excuse for his stupendous vocalism. It never struck me before what a quiet people Americans are.

Of the pleasant places within easy walk of Rome, I prefer the garden of the Villa Albani, as being most Italian. One does not go to Italy for examples of Price on the Picturesque. Compared with landscape-gardening, it is Racine to Shakespeare, I grant; but it has its own charm, nevertheless. I like the balustraded terraces, the sun-proof laurel walks, the vases and statues. It is only in such a climate that it does not seem inhuman to thrust a naked statue out of doors. Not to speak of their incongruity, how dreary do those white figures look at Fountains Abbey in that shrewd Yorkshire atmosphere! To put them there shows the same bad taste that led Prince Polonia, as Thackeray calls him, to build an artificial ruin within a mile of Rome. But I doubt if the Italian garden will bear transplantation. Farther north, or under a less constant sunshine, it is but half-hardy at the best. Within the city, the garden of the French Academy is my favorite retreat, because little frequented; and there is an arbor there in which I have read comfortably (sitting where the sun could reach me) in January. By the way, there is something very agreeable in the way these people have of making a kind of fireside of the sunshine. With us it is either too hot or too cool, or we are too busy. But, on the other hand, they have no such thing as a chimney-corner.

Of course I haunt the collections of art faithfully; but my favorite gallery, after all, is the street. There I always find something entertaining, at least. The other day, on my way to the Colonna Palace, I passed the Fountain of Trevi, from which the water is now shut off on account of repairs to the aqueduct. A scanty rill of soap-sudsy liquid still trickled from one of the conduits, and, seeing a crowd, I stopped to find out what nothing or other had gathered it. One charm of Rome is that nobody has anything in particular to do, or, if he has, can always stop doing it on the slightest pretext. I found that some eels had been discovered, and a very vivacious hunt was going on, the chief Nimrods being boys. I happened to be the first to see a huge eel wriggling from the mouth of a pipe, and pointed him out. Two lads at once rushed upon him. One essayed the capture with his naked hands, the other, more provident, had armed himself with a rag of woollen cloth with which to maintain his grip more securely. Hardly had this latter arrested his slippery prize, when a ragged rascal, watching his opportunity, snatched it away, and instantly secured it by thrusting the head into his mouth, and closing on it a set of teeth like an ivory vice. But alas for ill-got gain! Rob Roy's

> " Good old plan,
> That he should take who has the power,
> And he should keep who can,"

did not serve here. There is scarce a square rood in Rome without one or more stately cocked hats in it, emblems of authority and police. I saw the flash of the snow-white cross-belts, gleaming through that dingy crowd like the *panache* of Henri Quatre at Ivry, I saw the mad plunge of the canvas-shielded head-piece, sacred and terrible as that of Gessler; and while the greedy throng were dancing about the anguilliceps, each taking his chance twitch at the undulating object of all wishes, the captor dodging his head hither and thither, (vulnerable, like Achilles, only in his 'eel, as a Cockney tourist would say,) a pair of broad blue shoulders parted the assailants as a ship's bows part a wave, a pair of blue arms, terminating in gloves of Berlin thread, were stretched forth, not in benediction, one hand grasped the slippery Briseis by the waist, the other bestowed a cuff on the jaw-bone of Achilles, which loosened (rather by its authority than its physical force) the hitherto refractory incisors, a snuffy bandanna was produced, the prisoner was deposited in this temporary watch-house, and the cocked hat sailed majestically away with the property thus sequestered for the benefit of the state.

> " Gaudeant anguillæ si mortuus sit homo ille,
>   Qui, quasi morte reas, excruciabat eas! "

If you have got through that last sentence without stopping for breath, you are fit to begin on the Homer of Chapman, who, both as translator and author, has the longest wind, (especially for a comparison,) without being long-winded, of all writers I know anything of, not excepting Jeremy Taylor.

KEATS

1854

THERE are few poets whose works contain slighter
hints of their personal history than those of Keats;
yet there are, perhaps, even fewer whose real lives,
or rather the conditions upon which they lived, are
more clearly traceable in what they have written.
To write the life of a man was formerly understood
to mean the cataloguing and placing of circumstances, of those things which stood about the life
and were more or less related to it, but were not
the life itself.   But Biography from day to day
holds dates cheaper and facts dearer.   A man's
life, so far as its outward events are concerned,
may be made for him, as his clothes are by the
tailor, of this cut or that, of finer or coarser material; but the gait and gesture show through, and
give to trappings, in themselves characterless, an
individuality that belongs to the man himself.   It
is those essential facts which underlie the life and
make the individual man that are of importance,
and it is the cropping out of these upon the surface that gives us indications by which to judge of
the true nature hidden below.   Every man has his
block given him, and the figure he cuts will depend
very much upon the shape of that, — upon the

knots and twists which existed in it from the beginning. We were designed in the cradle, perhaps earlier, and it is in finding out this design, and shaping ourselves to it, that our years are spent wisely. It is the vain endeavor to make ourselves what we are not that has strewn history with so many broken purposes and lives left in the rough.

Keats hardly lived long enough to develop a well-outlined character, for that results commonly from the resistance made by temperament to the many influences by which the world, as it may happen then to be, endeavors to mould every one in its own image. What his temperament was we can see clearly, and also that it subordinated itself more and more to the discipline of art.

John Keats, the second of four children, like Chaucer and Spenser, was a Londoner, but, unlike them, he was certainly not of gentle blood. Lord Houghton, who seems to have had a kindly wish to create him gentleman by brevet, says that he was " born in the upper ranks of the middle class." This shows a commendable tenderness for the nerves of English society, and reminds one of Northcote's story of the violin-player who, wishing to compliment his pupil, George III., divided all fiddlers into three classes, — those who could not play at all, those who played very badly, and those who played very well, — assuring his Majesty that he had made such commendable progress as to have already reached the second rank. We shall not be too greatly shocked by knowing that the

father of Keats (as Lord Houghton had told us in
an earlier biography) "was employed in the establishment of Mr. Jennings, the proprietor of large
livery-stables on the Pavement in Moorfields, nearly
opposite the entrance into Finsbury Circus." So
that, after all, it was not so bad; for, first, Mr.
Jennings was a *proprietor;* second, he was the
proprietor of an *establishment;* third, he was the
proprietor of a *large* establishment; and fourth,
this large establishment was *nearly* opposite Finsbury Circus, — a name which vaguely dilates the
imagination with all sorts of potential grandeurs.
It is true Leigh Hunt asserts that Keats "was a
little too sensitive on the score of his origin,"[1] but
we can find no trace of such a feeling either in his
poetry or in such of his letters as have been printed.
We suspect the fact to have been that he resented
with becoming pride the vulgar Blackwood and
Quarterly standard, which measured genius by
genealogies. It is enough that his poetical pedi-
gree is of the best, tracing through Spenser to
Chaucer, and that Pegasus does not stand at livery
even in the largest establishments in Moorfields.

As well as we can make out, then, the father of
Keats was a groom in the service of Mr. Jennings,
and married the daughter of his master. Thus, on
the mother's side, at least, we find a grandfather;
on the father's there is no hint of such an ancestor,
and we must charitably take him for granted. It
is of more importance that the elder Keats was a
man of sense and energy, and that his wife was a

---

[1] Hunt's *Autobiography* (Am. ed.), vol. ii. p. 36.

" lively and intelligent woman, who hastened the birth of the poet by her passionate love of amusement," bringing him into the world, a seven-months' child, on the 29th October, 1795, instead of the 29th of December, as would have been conventionally proper. Lord Houghton describes her as " tall, with a large oval face, and a somewhat saturnine demeanour." This last circumstance does not agree very well with what he had just before told us of her liveliness, but he consoles us by adding that " she succeeded, *however*, in inspiring her children with the profoundest affection." This was particularly true of John, who once, when between four and five years old, mounted guard at her chamber door with an old sword, when she was ill and the doctor had ordered her not to be disturbed.[1]

In 1804, Keats being in his ninth year, his father was killed by a fall from his horse. His mother seems to have been ambitious for her children, and there was some talk of sending John to Harrow. Fortunately this plan was thought too expensive, and he was sent instead to the school of Mr. Clarke at Enfield with his brothers. A maternal uncle, who had distinguished himself by his courage under Duncan at Camperdown, was the hero of his nephews, and they went to school resolved to maintain the family reputation for courage. John was always fighting, and was chiefly noted among his school-fellows as a strange compound of pluck and

---

[1] Haydon tells the story differently, but I think Lord Houghton's version the best.

sensibility.　He attacked an usher who had boxed his brother's ears; and when his mother died, in 1810, was moodily inconsolable, hiding himself for several days in a nook under the master's desk, and refusing all comfort from teacher or friend.

He was popular at school, as boys of spirit always are, and impressed his companions with a sense of his power.　They thought he would one day be a famous soldier.　This may have been owing to the stories he told them of the heroic uncle, whose deeds, we may be sure, were properly famoused by the boy Homer, and whom they probably took for an admiral at the least, as it would have been well for Keats's literary prosperity if he had been.　At any rate, they thought John would be a great man, which is the main thing, for the public opinion of the playground is truer and more discerning than that of the world, and if you tell us what the boy was, we will tell you what the man longs to be, however he may be repressed by necessity or fear of the police reports.

Lord Houghton has failed to discover anything else especially worthy of record in the school-life of Keats.　He translated the twelve books of the Æneid, read Robinson Crusoe and the Incas of Peru, and looked into Shakespeare.　He left school in 1810, with little Latin and no Greek, but he had studied Spence's Polymetis, Tooke's Pantheon, and Lemprière's Dictionary, and knew gods, nymphs, and heroes, which were quite as good company perhaps for him as aorists and aspirates.　It is pleasant to fancy the horror of those respectable writers if their pages could suddenly have become alive under their pens with all that the young poet saw in them.[1]

On leaving school he was apprenticed for five years to a surgeon at Edmonton. His master was a Mr. Hammond, " of some eminence " in his profession, as Lord Houghton takes care to assure us. The place was of more importance than the master, for its neighborhood to Enfield enabled him to keep up his intimacy with the family of his former teacher, Mr. Clarke, and to borrow books of them. In 1812, when he was in his seventeenth year, Mr. Charles Cowden Clarke lent him the " Faerie Queene." Nothing that is told of Orpheus or Amphion is more wonderful than this miracle of Spenser's, transforming a surgeon's apprentice into a great poet. Keats learned at once the secret of

---

[1] There is always some one willing to make himself a sort of accessary after the fact in any success; always an old woman or two, ready to remember omens of all quantities and qualities in the childhood of persons who have become distinguished. Accordingly, a certain "Mrs. Grafty, of Craven Street, Finsbury," assures Mr. George Keats, when he tells her that John is determined to be a poet, "that this was very odd, because when he could just speak, instead of answering questions put to him, he would always make a rhyme to the last word people said, and then laugh." The early histories of heroes, like those of nations, are always more or less mythical, and I give the story for what it is worth. Doubtless there is a gleam of intelligence in it, for the old lady pronounces it odd that any one should *determine* to be a poet, and seems to have wished to hint that the matter was determined earlier and by a higher disposing power. There are few children who do not soon discover the charm of rhyme, and perhaps fewer who can resist making fun of the Mrs. Graftys of Craven Street, Finsbury, when they have the chance. See Haydon's *Autobiography*, vol. i. p. 301.

his birth, and henceforward his indentures ran to Apollo instead of Mr. Hammond. Thus could the Muse defend her son. It is the old story, — the lost heir discovered by his aptitude for what is gentle and knightly. Haydon tells us " that he used sometimes to say to his brother he feared he should never be a poet, and if he was not he would destroy himself." This was perhaps a half-conscious reminiscence of Chatterton, with whose genius and fate he had an intense sympathy, it may be from an inward foreboding of the shortness of his own career.[1]

Before long we find him studying Chaucer, then Shakespeare, and afterward Milton. But Chapman's translations had a more abiding influence on his style both for good and evil. That he read wisely, his comments on the " Paradise Lost " are enough to prove. He now also commenced poet himself, but does not appear to have neglected the study of his profession. He was a youth of energy and purpose, and, though he no doubt penned many a stanza when he should have been anatomizing, and walked the hospitals accompanied by the early gods, nevertheless passed a very creditable examination in 1817. In the spring of this year, also, he prepared to take his first degree as poet, and accordingly published a small volume containing a selection of his earlier essays in verse. It attracted

---

[1] "I never saw the poet Keats but once, but he then read some lines from (I think) the 'Bristowe Tragedy' with an enthusiasm of admiration such as could be felt only by a poet, and which true poetry only could have excited." — J. H. C., in *Notes & Queries*, 4th s. x. 157.

little attention, and the rest of this year seems to
have been occupied with a journey on foot in Scot-
land, and the composition of " Endymion," which
was published in 1818. Milton's " Tetrachordon "
was not better abused; but Milton's assailants
were unorganized, and were obliged each to print
and pay for his own dingy little quarto, trusting to
the natural laws of demand and supply to furnish
him with readers. Keats was arraigned by the
constituted authorities of literary justice. They
might be, nay, they were Jeffrieses and Scroggses,
but the sentence was published, and the penalty
inflicted before all England. The difference between his fortune and Milton's was that between
being pelted by a mob of personal enemies and
being set in the pillory. In the first case, the an-
noyance brushes off mostly with the mud; in the
last, there is no solace but the consciousness of
suffering in a great cause. This solace, to a certain extent, Keats had; for his ambition was
noble, and he hoped not to make a great reputation, but to be a great poet. Haydon says that
Wordsworth and Keats were the only men he had
ever seen who looked conscious of a lofty purpose.

It is curious that men should resent more fiercely
what they suspect to be good verses than what
they know to be bad morals. Is it because they
feel themselves incapable of the one and not of the
other? Probably a certain amount of honest loyalty
to old idols in danger of dethronement is to be
taken into account, and quite as much of the cruelty of criticism is due to want of thought as to

deliberate injustice. However it be, the best poetry has been the most savagely attacked, and men who scrupulously practised the Ten Commandments as if there were never a *not* in any of them, felt every sentiment of their better nature outraged by the " Lyrical Ballads." It is idle to attempt to show that Keats did not suffer keenly from the vulgarities of Blackwood and the Quarterly. He suffered in proportion as his ideal was high, and he was conscious of falling below it. In England, especially, it is not pleasant to be ridiculous, even if you are a lord ; but to be ridiculous and an apothecary at the same time is almost as bad as it was formerly to be excommunicated. *A priori*, there was something absurd in poetry written by the son of an assistant in the livery-stables of Mr. Jennings, even though they were an establishment, and a large establishment, and nearly opposite Finsbury Circus. Mr. Gifford, the ex-cobbler, thought so in the Quarterly, and Mr. Terry, the actor,[1] thought so even more distinctly in Blackwood, bidding the young apothecary " back to his gallipots! " It is not pleasant to be talked down upon by your inferiors who happen to have the advantage of position, nor to be drenched with ditch-water, though you know it to be thrown by a scullion in a garret.

Keats, as his was a temperament in which sensibility was excessive, could not but be galled by this treatment. He was galled the more that he was

---

[1] Haydon (*Autobiography*, vol. i. p. 379) says that he " strongly suspects " Terry to have written the articles in Blackwood.

also a man of strong sense, and capable of understanding clearly how hard it is to make men acknowledge solid value in a person whom they have
once heartily laughed at. Reputation is in itself
only a farthing-candle, of wavering and uncertain
flame, and easily blown out, but it is the light by
which the world looks for and finds merit. Keats
longed for fame, but longed above all to deserve
it. To his friend Taylor he writes, "There is but
one way for me. The road lies through study, application, and thought." Thrilling with the electric touch of sacred leaves, he saw in vision, like
Dante, that small procession of the elder poets to
which only elect centuries can add another lau-
relled head. Might he, too, deserve from posterity
the love and reverence which he paid to those antique glories? It was no unworthy ambition, but
everything was against him, — birth, health, even
friends, since it was partly on their account that
he was sneered at. His very name stood in his
way, for Fame loves best such syllables as are
sweet and sonorous on the tongue, like Spenserian,
Shakespearian. In spite of Juliet, there is a great
deal in names, and when the fairies come with
their gifts to the cradle of the selected child, let
one, wiser than the rest, choose a name for him
from which well-sounding derivatives can be made,
and, best of all, with a termination in *on.* Men
judge the current coin of opinion by the ring, and
are readier to take without question whatever is
Platonic, Baconian, Newtonian, Johnsonian, Wash-
ingtonian, Jeffersonian, Napoleonic, and all the

rest. You cannot make a good adjective out of Keats, — the more pity, — and to say a thing is *Keatsy* is to contemn it. Fortune likes fine names.

Haydon tells us that Keats was very much depressed by the fortunes of his book. This was natural enough, but he took it all in a manly way, and determined to revenge himself by writing better poetry. He knew that activity, and not despondency, is the true counterpoise to misfortune. Haydon is sure of the change in his spirits, because he would come to the painting-room and sit silent for hours. But we rather think that the conversation, where Mr. Haydon was, resembled that in a young author's first play, where the other interlocutors are only brought in as convenient points for the hero to hitch the interminable web of his monologue upon. Besides, Keats had been continuing his education this year, by a course of Elgin marbles and pictures by the great Italians, and might very naturally have found little to say about Mr. Haydon's extensive works, that he would have cared to hear. Lord Houghton, on the other hand, in his eagerness to prove that Keats was not killed by the article in the Quarterly, is carried too far towards the opposite extreme, and more than hints that he was not even hurt by it. This would have been true of Wordsworth, who, by a constant companionship with mountains, had acquired something of their manners, but was simply impossible to a man of Keats's temperament.

On the whole, perhaps, we need not respect

Keats the less for having been gifted with sensibility, and may even say what we believe to be true, that his health was injured by the failure of his book. A man cannot have a sensuous nature and be pachydermatous at the same time, and if he be imaginative as well as sensuous, he suffers just in proportion to the amount of his imagination. It is perfectly true that what we call the world, in these affairs, is nothing more than a mere Brocken spectre, the projected shadow of ourselves; but so long as we do not know this, it is a very passable giant. We are not without experience of natures so purely intellectual that their bodies had no more concern in their mental doings and sufferings than a house has with the good or ill fortune of its occupant. But poets are not built on this plan, and especially poets like Keats, in whom the moral seems to have so perfectly interfused the physical man, that you might almost say he could feel sorrow with his hands, so truly did his body, like that of Donne's Mistress Boulstred, think and remember and forebode. The healthiest poet of whom our civilization has been capable says that when he beholds

> "desert a beggar born,
> And strength by limping sway disabeled,
> And art made tongue-tied by authority,"

alluding, plainly enough, to the Giffords of his day,

> "And simple truth miscalled simplicity,"

as it was long afterward in Wordsworth's case,

> "And captive Good attending Captain Ill,"

that then even he, the poet to whom, of all others, life seems to have been dearest, as it was also the fullest of enjoyment, " tired of all these," had nothing for it but to cry for " restful Death."

Keats, to all appearance, accepted his ill fortune courageously. He certainly did not overestimate " Endymion," and perhaps a sense of humor which was not wanting in him may have served as a buffer against the too importunate shock of disappointment. " He made Ritchie promise," says Haydon, " he would carry his ' Endymion ' to the great desert of Sahara and fling it in the midst." On the 9th October, 1818, he writes to his publisher, Mr. Hessey, " I cannot but feel indebted to those gentlemen who have taken my part. As for the rest, I begin to get acquainted with my own strength and weakness. Praise or blame has but a momentary effect on the man whose love of beauty in the abstract makes him a severe critic of his own works. My own domestic criticism has given me pain without comparison beyond what Blackwood or the Quarterly could inflict ; and also, when I feel I am right, no external praise can give me such a glow as my own solitary reperception and ratification of what is fine. J. S. is perfectly right in regard to ' the slipshod Endymion.' That it is so is no fault of mine. No ! though it may sound a little paradoxical, it is as good as I had power to make it by myself. Had I been nervous about its being a perfect piece, and with that view asked advice and trembled over every page, it would not have been written ; for it is not in my nature to fumble. I will write independently. I have written independently *without judgment.* I may write independently and *with judgment,* hereafter. The Genius of Poetry must work out its own salvation in a man. It cannot be matured by law and precept, but by sensation and watchfulness in itself. That which is creative must create itself. In 'Endymion' I leaped headlong into the sea, and thereby have become better acquainted with the soundings, the quicksands, and the rocks, than if I had stayed upon the green shore, and piped a silly pipe, and took tea and comfortable advice. I was never afraid of failure; for I would sooner fail than not be among the greatest."

This was undoubtedly true, and it was naturally the side which a large-minded person would display to a friend. This is what he thought, but whether it was what he *felt,* I think doubtful. I look upon it rather as one of the phenomena of that multanimous nature of the poet, which makes him for the moment that of which he has an intellectual perception. Elsewhere he says something which seems to hint at the true state of the case. " I must think that difficulties nerve the spirit of a man: *they make our prime objects a refuge as well as a passion.*" One cannot help contrasting Keats with Wordsworth, — the one altogether poet; the other essentially a Wordsworth, with the poetic faculty added, — the one shifting from form to form, and from style to style, and pouring his hot throbbing life into every mould; the other remaining always the individual, producing works, and not so much living in his poems as memorially recording his life in them. When Wordsworth alludes to the foolish criticisms on his writings, he speaks serenely and generously of Wordsworth the poet, as if he were an unbiassed third person, who takes up the argument merely in the interest of literature. He towers into a bald egotism which is quite above and beyond selfishness. Poesy was his employment; it was Keats's very existence, and he felt the rough treatment of his verses as if it had been the wounding of a limb. To Wordsworth, composing was a healthy exercise; his slow pulse and imperturbable self-trust gave him assurance of a life so long that he could wait; and when we read his poems we should never suspect the existence in him of any sense but that of observation, as if Wordsworth the poet were a half-mad land-surveyor, accompanied by Mr. Wordsworth the distributor of stamps as a kind of keeper. But every one of Keats's poems was a sacrifice of vitality; a virtue went away from him into every one of them; even yet, as we turn the leaves, they seem to warm and thrill our fingers with the flush of his fine senses, and the flutter of his electrical nerves, and we do not wonder he felt that what he did was to be done swiftly.

In the mean time his younger brother languished and died, his elder seems to have been in some way unfortunate and had gone to America, and Keats himself showed symptoms of the hereditary disease which caused his death at last. It is in October, 1818, that we find the first allusion to a passion

which was erelong to consume him. It is plain
enough beforehand that those were not moral or
mental graces that should attract a man like Keats.
His intellect was satisfied and absorbed by his art,
his books, and his friends. He could have companionship and appreciation from men ; what he
craved of woman was only repose. That luxurious
nature, which would have tossed uneasily on a
crumpled rose-leaf, must have something softer to
rest upon than intellect, something less ethereal
than culture. It was his body that needed to have
its equilibrium restored, the waste of his nervous
energy that must be repaired by deep draughts of
the overflowing life and drowsy tropical force of an
abundant and healthily poised womanhood. Writing to his sister-in-law, he says of this nameless
person : "She is not a Cleopatra, but is at least a
Charmian ; she has a rich Eastern look ; she has
fine eyes and fine manners. When she comes into a
room she makes the same impression as the beauty
of a leopardess. She is too fine and too conscious
of herself to repulse any man who may address her.
From habit, she thinks that *nothing particular*. I
always find myself at ease with such a woman ; the
picture before me always gives me a life and ani-
mation which I cannot possibly feel with anything
inferior. I am at such times too much occupied in
admiring to be awkward or in a tremble. I forget
myself entirely, because I live in her. You will by
this time think I am in love with her, so, before I
go any farther, I will tell you that I am not. She
kept me awake one night, as a tune of Mozart's

might do. I speak of the thing as a pastime and an amusement, than which I can feel none deeper than a conversation with an imperial woman, the very *yes* and *no* of whose life [lips] is to me a banquet. . . . I like her and her like, because one has no *sensation;* what we both are is taken for granted. . . . She walks across a room in such a manner that a man is drawn toward her with magnetic power. . . . I believe, though, she has faults, the same as a Cleopatra or a Charmian might have had. Yet she is a fine thing, speaking in a worldly way; for there are two distinct tempers of mind in which we judge of things, — the worldly, theatrical, and pantomimical; and the unearthly, spiritual, and ethereal. In the former, Bonaparte, Lord Byron, and this Charmian hold the first place in our minds; in the latter, John Howard, Bishop Hooker rocking his child's cradle, and you, my dear sister, are the conquering feelings. As a man of the world, I love the rich talk of a Charmian; as an eternal being, I love the thought of you. I should like her to ruin me, and I should like you to save me."

It is pleasant always to see Love hiding his head with such pains, while his whole body is so clearly visible, as in this extract. This lady, it seems, is not a Cleopatra, only a Charmian; but presently we find that she is imperial. He does not love her, but he would just like to be ruined by her, nothing more. This glimpse of her, with her leopardess beauty, crossing the room and drawing men after her magnetically, is all we have. She seems to have been still living in 1848, and, as Lord Houghton tells us, kept the memory of the poet sacred. "She is an East-Indian," Keats says, "and ought to be her grandfather's heir." Her name we do not know. It appears from Dilke's "Papers of a Critic" that they were betrothed: "It is quite a settled thing between John Keats and Miss ——. God help them. It is a bad thing for them. The mother says she cannot prevent it, and that her only hope is that it will go off. He don't like any one to look at her or to speak to her." Alas, the tropical warmth became a consuming fire!

> "His passion cruel grown took on a hue
> Fierce and sanguineous."

Between this time and the spring of 1820 he seems to have worked assiduously. Of course, worldly success was of more importance than ever. He began "Hyperion," but had given it up in September, 1819, because, as he said, "there were too many Miltonic inversions in it." He wrote "Lamia" after an attentive study of Dryden's versification. This period also produced the "Eve of St. Agnes," "Isabella," and the odes to the "Nightingale" and to the "Grecian Urn." He studied Italian, read Ariosto, and wrote part of a humorous poem, "The Cap and Bells." He tried his hand at tragedy, and Lord Houghton has published among his "Remains," "Otho the Great," and all that was ever written of "King Stephen." We think he did unwisely, for a biographer is hardly called upon to show how ill his *biographee* could do anything.

In the winter of 1820 he was chilled in riding on

the top of a stage-coach, and came home in a state
of feverish excitement. He was persuaded to go
to bed, and in getting between the cold sheets,
coughed slightly. "That is blood in my mouth,"
he said; "bring me the candle; let me see this
blood." It was of a brilliant red, and his medical
knowledge enabled him to interpret the augury.
Those narcotic odors that seem to breathe seaward,
and steep in repose the senses of the voyager who
is drifting toward the shore of the mysterious Other
World, appeared to envelop him, and, looking up
with sudden calmness, he said, "I know the color
of that blood; it is arterial blood; I cannot be de-
ceived in that color. That drop is my death-war-
rant; I must die."

There was a slight rally during the summer of
that year, but toward autumn he grew worse again,
and it was decided that he should go to Italy. He
was accompanied thither by his friend, Mr. Severn,
an artist. After embarking, he wrote to his friend,
Mr. Brown. We give a part of this letter, which is
so deeply tragic that the sentences we take almost
seem to break away from the rest with a cry of
anguish, like the branches of Dante's lamentable
wood.

"I wish to write on subjects that will not agitate
me much. There is one I must mention and have
done with it. Even if my body would recover of
itself, this would prevent it. The very thing which
I want to live most for will be a great occasion of
my death. I cannot help it. Who can help it?
Were I in health it would make me ill, and how

can I bear it in my state? I dare say you will be
able to guess on what subject I am harping, — you
know what was my greatest pain during the first
part of my illness at your house. I wish for death
every day and night to deliver me from these pains,
and then I wish death away, for death would destroy even those pains, which are better than nothing. Land and sea, weakness and decline, are
great separators, but Death is the great divorcer
forever. When the pang of this thought has
passed through my mind, I may say the bitterness
of death is passed. I often wish for you, that you
might flatter me with the best. I think, without
my mentioning it, for my sake, you would be a
friend to Miss —— when I am dead. You think
she has many faults, but for my sake think she has
not one. If there is anything you can do for her
by word or deed I know you will do it. I am in a
state at present in which woman, merely as woman,
can have no more power over me than stocks and
stones, and yet the difference of my sensations with
respect to Miss —— and my sister is amazing, —
the one seems to absorb the other to a degree incredible. I seldom think of my brother and sister
in America; the thought of leaving Miss —— is
beyond everything horrible, — the sense of darkness coming over me, — I eternally see her figure
eternally vanishing; some of the phrases she was in
the habit of using during my last nursing at Went-
worth Place ring in my ears. Is there another
life? Shall I awake and find all this a dream?
There must be; we cannot be created for this sort
of suffering."

To the same friend he writes again from Naples, 1st November, 1820 : —

"The persuasion that I shall see her no more will kill me. My dear Brown, I should have had her when I was in health, and I should have remained well. I can bear to die, — I cannot bear to leave her. O God! God! God! Everything I have in my trunks that reminds me of her goes through me like a spear. The silk lining she put in my travelling-cap scalds my head. My imagination is horribly vivid about her, — I see her, I hear her. There is nothing in the world of sufficient interest to divert me from her a moment. This was the case when I was in England; I cannot recollect, without shuddering, the time that I was a prisoner at Hunt's, and used to keep my eyes fixed on Hampstead all day. Then there was a good hope of seeing her again, — now! — O that I could be buried near where she lives! I am afraid to write to her, to receive a letter from her, — to see her handwriting would break my heart. Even to hear of her anyhow, to see her name written, would be more than I can bear. My dear Brown, what am I to do? Where can I look for consolation or ease? If I had any chance of recovery, this passion would kill me. Indeed, through the whole of my illness, both at your house and at Kentish Town, this fever has never ceased wearing me out."

The two friends went almost immediately from Naples to Rome, where Keats was treated with great kindness by the distinguished physician, Dr.

(afterward Sir James) Clark.[1] But there was no hope from the first. His disease was beyond remedy, as his heart was beyond comfort. The very fact that life might be happy deepened his despair. He might not have sunk so soon, but the waves in which he was struggling looked only the blacker that they were shone upon by the signal-torch that promised safety and love and rest.

It is good to know that one of Keats's last pleasures was in hearing Severn read aloud from a volume of Jeremy Taylor. On first coming to Rome, he had bought a copy of Alfieri, but, finding on the second page these lines,

> "Misera me! sollievo a me non resta
> Altro che il pianto, ed il pianto è delitto,"

he laid down the book and opened it no more. On the 14th February, 1821, Severn speaks of a change that had taken place in him toward greater quietness and peace. He talked much, and fell at last into a sweet sleep, in which he seemed to have happy dreams. Perhaps he heard the soft footfall of the angel of Death, pacing to and fro under his window, to be his Valentine. That night he asked to have this epitaph inscribed upon his gravestone : —

> "HERE LIES ONE WHOSE NAME WAS WRIT IN WATER."

On the 23d he died, without pain and as if falling asleep. His last words were, "I am dying; I shall

---

[1] The lodging of Keats was on the Piazza di Spagna, in the first house on the right hand in going up the Scalinata. Mr. Severn's Studio is said to have been in the Cancello over the garden gate of the Villa Negroni, pleasantly familiar to all Americans as the Roman home of their countryman Crawford.

die easy; don't be frightened, be firm and thank God it has come!"

He was buried in the Protestant burial-ground at Rome, in that part of it which is now disused and secluded from the rest. A short time before his death he told Severn that he thought his intensest pleasure in life had been to watch the growth of flowers; and once, after lying peacefully awhile, he said, "I feel the flowers growing over me." His grave is marked by a little headstone on which are carved somewhat rudely his name and age, and the epitaph dictated by himself. No tree or shrub has been planted near it, but the daisies, faithful to their buried lover, crowd his small mound with a galaxy of their innocent stars, more prosperous than those under which he lived.[1]

In person, Keats was below the middle height, with a head small in proportion to the breadth of his shoulders. His hair was brown and fine, falling in natural ringlets about a face in which energy and sensibility were remarkably mixed. Every feature was delicately cut; the chin was bold, and about the mouth something of a pugnacious expression. His eyes were mellow and glowing, large, dark, and sensitive. At the recital of a noble action or a beautiful thought they would suffuse

---

[1] Written in 1854. O irony of Time! Ten years after the poet's death the woman he had so loved wrote to his friend Mr. Dilke, that "the kindest act would be to let him rest forever in the obscurity to which circumstances had condemned him"! (*Papers of a Critic*, i. 11.) O Time the atoner! In 1874 I found the grave planted with shrubs and flowers, the pious homage of the daughter of our most eminent American sculptor.

with tears, and his mouth trembled.[1] Haydon says that his eyes had an inward Delphian look that was perfectly divine.

The faults of Keats's poetry are obvious enough, but it should be remembered that he died at twenty-five, and that he offends by superabundance and not poverty. That he was overlanguaged at first there can be no doubt, and in this was implied the possibility of falling back to the perfect mean of diction. It is only by the rich that the costly plainness, which at once satisfies the taste and the imagination, is attainable.

Whether Keats was original or not, I do not think it useful to discuss until it has been settled what originality is. Lord Houghton tells us that this merit (whatever it be) has been denied to Keats, because his poems take the color of the authors he happened to be reading at the time he wrote them. But men have their intellectual ancestry, and the likeness of some one of them is forever unexpectedly flashing out in the features of a descendant, it may be after a gap of several generations. In the parliament of the present every man represents a constituency of the past. It is true that Keats has the accent of the men from whom he learned to speak, but this is to make originality a mere question of externals, and in this sense the author of a dictionary might bring an action of trover against every author who used his words. It is the man behind the words that gives them value, and if Shakespeare help himself to a

---

[1] Leigh Hunt's *Autobiography*, ii. 43.

verse or a phrase, it is with ears that have learned
of him to listen that we feel the harmony of the
one, and it is the mass of his intellect that makes
the other weighty with meaning. Enough that we
recognize in Keats that indefinable newness and
unexpectedness which we call genius. The sunset
is original every evening, though for thousands of
years it has built out of the same light and vapor
its visionary cities with domes and pinnacles, and
its delectable mountains which night shall utterly
abase and destroy.

Three men, almost contemporaneous with each
other, — Wordsworth, Keats, and Byron, — were
the great means of bringing back English poetry
from the sandy deserts of rhetoric, and recovering
for her her triple inheritance of simplicity, sensuousness, and passion. Of these, Wordsworth was
the only conscious reformer, and his hostility to the
existing formalism injured his earlier poems by
tingeing them with something of iconoclastic extravagance. He was the deepest thinker, Keats
the most essentially a poet, and Byron the most
keenly intellectual of the three. Keats had the
broadest mind, or at least his mind was open on
more sides, and he was able to understand Wordsworth and judge Byron, equally conscious, through
his artistic sense, of the greatnesses of the one and
the many littlenesses of the other, while Wordsworth was isolated in a feeling of his prophetic
character, and Byron had only an uneasy and jea-
lous instinct of contemporary merit. The poems of
Wordsworth, as he was the most individual, accord-

ingly reflect the moods of his own nature; those of Keats, from sensitiveness of organization, the moods of his own taste and feeling; and those of Byron, who was impressible chiefly through the understanding, the intellectual and moral wants of the time in which he lived. Wordsworth has influenced most the ideas of succeeding poets; Keats, their forms; and Byron, interesting to men of imagination less for his writings than for what his writings indicate, reappears no more in poetry, but presents an ideal to youth made restless with vague desires not yet regulated by experience nor supplied with motives by the duties of life.

Keats certainly had more of the penetrative and sympathetic imagination which belongs to the poet, of that imagination which identifies itself with the momentary object of its contemplation, than any man of these later days. It is not merely that he has studied the Elizabethans and caught their turn of thought, but that he really sees things with their sovereign eye, and feels them with their electrified senses. His imagination was his bliss and bane. Was he cheerful, he "hops about the gravel with the sparrows"; was he morbid, he "would reject a Petrarcal coronation, — on account of my dying day, and because women have cancers." So impressible was he as to say that he "had no nature," meaning character. But he knew what the faculty was worth, and says finely, "The imagination may be compared to Adam's dream: he awoke and found it truth." He had an unerring instinct for the poetic uses of things, and for him they had no other use. We are apt to talk of the classic *re-naissance* as of a phenomenon long past, nor ever to be renewed, and to think the Greeks and Romans alone had the mighty magic to work such a miracle. To me one of the most interesting aspects of Keats is that in him we have an example of the *renaissance* going on almost under our own eyes, and that the intellectual ferment was in him kindled by a purely English leaven. He had properly no scholarship, any more than Shakespeare had, but like him he assimilated at a touch whatever could serve his purpose. His delicate senses absorbed culture at every pore. Of the self-denial to which he trained himself (unexampled in one so young) the second draft of Hyperion as compared with the first is a conclusive proof. And far indeed is his " Lamia " from the lavish indiscrimination of " Endymion." In his Odes he showed a sense of form and proportion which we seek vainly in almost any other English poet, and some of his sonnets (taking all qualities into consideration) are the most perfect in our language. No doubt there is something tropical and of strange overgrowth in his sudden maturity, but it *was* maturity nevertheless. Happy the young poet who has the saving fault of exuberance, if he have also the shaping faculty that sooner or later will amend it !

As every young person goes through all the world-old experiences, fancying them something peculiar and personal to himself, so it is with every new generation, whose youth always finds its representatives in its poets. Keats rediscovered the de-

light and wonder that lay enchanted in the dictionary. Wordsworth revolted at the poetic diction
which he found in vogue, but his own language
rarely rises above it, except when it is upborne by
the thought. Keats had an instinct for fine words,
which are in themselves pictures and ideas, and
had more of the power of poetic expression than
any modern English poet. And by poetic expression I do not mean merely a vividness in particulars, but the right feeling which heightens or sub-
dues a passage or a whole poem to the proper tone,
and gives entireness to the effect. There is a great
deal more than is commonly supposed in this choice
of words. Men's thoughts and opinions are in a
great degree vassals of him who invents a new
phrase or reapplies an old epithet. The thought
or feeling a thousand times repeated becomes his
at last who utters it best. This power of language
is veiled in the old legends which make the invisible powers the servants of some word. As soon
as we have discovered the word for our joy or
sorrow we are no longer its serfs, but its lords.
We reward the discoverer of an anæsthetic for the
body and make him member of all the societies,
but him who finds a nepenthe for the soul we elect
into the small academy of the immortals.

The poems of Keats mark an epoch in English
poetry; for, however often we may find traces of
it in others, in them found its most unconscious
expression that reaction against the barrel-organ
style which had been reigning by a kind of sleepy
divine right for half a century. The lowest point

was indicated when there was such an utter con-
founding of the common and the uncommon sense
that Dr. Johnson wrote verse and Burke prose.
The most profound gospel of criticism was, that
nothing was good poetry that could not be translated into good prose, as if one should say that the
test of sufficient moonlight was that tallow-candles
could be made of it. We find Keats at first going
to the other extreme, and endeavoring to extract
green cucumbers from the rays of tallow; but we
see also incontestable proof of the greatness and
purity of his poetic gift in the constant return
toward equilibrium and repose in his later poems.
And it is a repose always lofty and clear-aired, like
that of the eagle balanced in incommunicable sunshine. In him a vigorous understanding developed
itself in equal measure with the divine faculty;
thought emancipated itself from expression without
becoming in turn its tyrant; and music and meaning
floated together, accordant as swan and shadow, on
the smooth element of his verse. Without losing
its sensuousness, his poetry refined itself and grew
more inward, and the sensational was elevated into
the typical by the control of that finer sense which
underlies the senses and is the spirit of them.

LIBRARY OF OLD AUTHORS [1]

1858–1864

MANY of our older readers can remember the anticipation with which they looked for each successive volume of the late Dr. Young's excellent series of old English prose-writers, and the delight with which they carried it home, fresh from the press and the bindery in its appropriate livery of evergreen. To most of us it was our first introduction to the highest society of letters, and we still feel grateful to the departed scholar who gave us to share the conversation of such men as Latimer, More, Sidney, Taylor, Browne, Fuller, and Walton. What a sense of security in an old book which Time has criticised for us! What a precious feeling of seclusion in having a double wall of centuries between us and the heats and clamors of contemporary literature! How limpid seems the thought, how pure the old wine of scholarship that has been settling for so many generations in those silent crypts and Falernian *amphoræ* of the Past! No other writers speak to us with the authority of those whose ordinary speech was that of our translation of the Scriptures; to no modern is that frank unconsciousness possible which was natural

[1] London: John Russell Smith. 1856–64.

to a period when yet reviews were not ; and no later style breathes that country charm characteristic of days ere the metropolis had drawn all literary activity to itself, and the trampling feet of the multitude had banished the lark and the daisy from the fresh privacies of language. Truly, as compared with the present, these old voices seem to come from the morning fields and not the paved thoroughfares of thought.

Even the " Retrospective Review " continues to be good reading, in virtue of the antique aroma (for wine only acquires its *bouquet* by age) which pervades its pages. Its sixteen volumes are so many tickets of admission to the vast and devious vaults of the sixteenth and seventeenth centuries, through which we wander, tasting a thimbleful of rich Canary, honeyed Cyprus, or subacidulous Hock, from what dusty butt or keg our fancy chooses. The years during which this review was published were altogether the most fruitful in genuine appreciation of old English literature. Books were prized for their imaginative and not their antiquarian value by young writers who sate at the feet of Lamb and Coleridge. Rarities of style, of thought, of fancy, were sought, rather than the barren scarcities of typography. But another race of men seems to have sprung up, in whom the futile enthusiasm of the collector predominates, who substitute archæologic perversity for fine-nerved scholarship, and the worthless profusion of the curiosity-shop for the sifted exclusiveness of the cabinet of Art. They forget, in their fanaticism for antiquity, that the dust of never so many centuries is impotent to transform a curiosity into a gem, that only good books absorb mellowness of tone from age, and that a baptismal register which proves a patriarchal longevity (if existence be life) cannot make mediocrity anything but a bore, or garrulous commonplace entertaining.   There are volumes which have the old age of Plato, rich with gathering experience, meditation, and wisdom, which seem to have sucked color and ripeness from the genial autumns of all the select intelligences that have steeped them in the sunshine of their love and appreciation;—these quaint freaks of russet tell of Montaigne; these stripes of crimson fire, of Shakespeare; this sober gold, of Sir Thomas Browne; this purpling bloom, of Lamb; in such fruits we taste the legendary gardens of Alcinoüs and the orchards of Atlas; and there are volumes again which can claim only the inglorious senility of Old Parr or older Jenkins, which have outlived their half-dozen of kings to be the prize of showmen and treasuries of the born-to-be-forgotten trifles of a hundred years ago.

We confess a bibliothecarian avarice that gives all books a value in our eyes; there is for us a recondite wisdom in the phrase, "A book is a book"; from the time when we made the first catalogue of our library, in which "Bible, large, 1 vol.," and "Bible, small, 1 vol.," asserted their alphabetic individuality and were the sole *B*s in our little hive, we have had a weakness even for those checker-board volumes that only fill up. We can-

not breathe the thin air of that Pepysian self-
denial, that Himalayan selectness, which, content
with one bookcase, would have no tomes in it but
porphyrogeniti, books of the bluest blood, making
room for choicer new-comers by a continuous ostra-
cism to the garret of present incumbents. There
is to us a sacredness in a volume, however dull ;
we live over again the author's lonely labors and
tremulous hopes ; we see him, on his first appearance after parturition, " as well as could be expected," a nervous sympathy yet surviving between
the late-severed umbilical cord and the wondrous
offspring, as he doubtfully enters the Mermaid, or
the Devil Tavern, or the Coffee-house of Will or
Button, blushing under the eye of Ben or Dryden
or Addison, as if they must needs know him for
the author of the " Modest Enquiry into the Present State of Dramatique Poetry," or of the " Uni-
ties briefly considered by Philomusus," of which
they have never heard and never will hear so much
as the names ; we see the country-gentlemen (sole
cause of its surviving to our day) who buy it as a
book no gentleman's library can be complete without ; we see the spendthrift heir, whose horses and
hounds and Pharaonic troops of friends, drowned
in a Red Sea of claret, bring it to the hammer, the
tall octavo in tree-calf following the ancestral oaks
of the park. Such a volume is sacred to us. But
it must be the original foundling of the book-stall,
the engraved blazon of some extinct baronetcy
within its cover, its leaves enshrining memorial-
flowers of some passion which the churchyard

smothered ere the Stuarts were yet discrowned,
suggestive of the trail of laced ruffles, burnt here
and there with ashes from the pipe of some dozing
poet, its binding worn and weather-stained, that
has felt the inquisitive finger, perhaps, of Malone,
or thrilled to the touch of Lamb, doubtful between
desire and the odd sixpence. When it comes to a
question of reprinting, we are more choice. The
new duodecimo is bald and bare, indeed, compared
with its battered prototype that could draw us with
a single hair of association.

It is not easy to divine the rule which has governed Mr. Smith in making the selections for his
series. A choice of old authors should be a *florilegium*, and not a botanist's *hortus siccus*, to which
grasses are as important as the single shy blossom
of a summer. The old-maidenly genius of anti-
quarianism seems to have presided over the editing
of the "Library." We should be inclined to surmise that the works to be reprinted had been commonly suggested by gentlemen with whom they
were especial favorites, or who were ambitious that
their own names should be signalized on the title-
pages with the suffix of EDITOR. The volumes already published are: Increase Mather's "Remarkable Providences"; the poems of Drummond of
Hawthornden; the "Visions of Piers Ploughman";
the works in prose and verse of Sir Thomas Overbury; the "Hymns and Songs" and the "Hallelujah" of George Wither; the poems of Southwell;
Selden's "Table-Talk"; the "Enchiridion" of
Quarles; the dramatic works of Marston, Webster,

and Lilly; Chapman's translation of Homer; Lovelace, and four volumes of "Early English Poetry." The volume of Mather is curious and entertaining, and fit to stand on the same shelf with the "Magnalia" of his book-suffocated son. Cunningham's comparatively recent edition, we should think, might satisfy for a long time to come the demand for Drummond, whose chief value to posterity is as the Boswell of Ben Jonson. Sir Thomas Overbury's "Characters" are interesting illustrations of contemporary manners, and a mine of footnotes to the works of better men, — but, with the exception of "The Fair and Happy Milkmaid," they are dull enough to have pleased James the First; his "Wife" is a *cento* of far-fetched conceits, — here a tomtit, and there a hen mistaken for a pheasant, like the contents of a cockney's game-bag, and his chief interest for us lies in his having been mixed up with an inexplicable tragedy and poisoned in the Tower, not without suspicion of royal complicity. The "Piers Ploughman" is a reprint, with very little improvement that we can discover, of Mr. Wright's former edition. It would have been very well to have republished the "Fair Virtue," and "Shepherd's Hunting" of George Wither, which contain all the true poetry he ever wrote; but we can imagine nothing more dreary than the seven hundred pages of his "Hymns and Songs," whose only use, that we can conceive of, would be as penal reading for incorrigible poetasters. If a steady course of these did not bring them out of their nonsenses, nothing short of hanging

would. Take this as a sample, hit on by opening
at random : —

> " Rottenness my bones possest ;
> Trembling fear possessèd me ;
> I that troublous day might rest :
> For, when his approaches be
> Onward to the people made,
> His strong troops will them invade."

Southwell is, if possible, worse. He paraphrases
David, putting into his mouth such punning conceits as "fears are my feres," and in his "Saint
Peter's Complaint" makes that rashest and
shortest-spoken of the Apostles drawl through
thirty pages of maudlin repentance, in which the
distinctions between the north and northeast sides
of a sentimentality are worthy of Duns Scotus. It
does not follow, that, because a man is hanged for
his faith, he is able to write good verses. We
would almost match the fortitude that quails not at
the good Jesuit's poems with his own which carried
him serenely to the fatal tree. The stuff of which
poets are made, whether finer or not, is of a very
different fibre from that which is used in the tough
fabric of martyrs. It is time that an earnest protest should be uttered against the wrong done to
the religious sentiment by the greater part of what
is called religious poetry, but which is commonly a
painful something misnamed by the noun and mis-
qualified by the adjective. To dilute David, and
make doggerel of that majestic prose of the Prophets which has the glow and wide - orbited metre
of constellations, may be a useful occupation to
keep country-gentlemen out of litigation or retired

clergymen from polemics; but to regard these metrical mechanics as sacred because nobody wishes to touch them, as meritorious because no one can be merry in their company, — to rank them in the same class with those ancient songs of the Church, sweet with the breath of saints, sparkling with the tears of forgiven penitents, and warm with the fervor of martyrs, — nay, to set them up beside such poems as those of Herbert, composed in the upper chambers of the soul that open toward the sun's rising, is to confound piety with dulness, and the manna of heaven with its sickening namesake from the apothecary's drawer. The "Enchiridion" of Quarles is hardly worthy of the author of the "Emblems," and is by no means an unattainable book in other editions, — nor a matter of heartbreak, if it were. Of the dramatic works of Marston and Lilly it is enough to say that they are truly *works* to the reader, but in no sense dramatic, nor, as literature, worth the paper they blot. They seem to have been deemed worthy of republication because they were the contemporaries of true poets; and if all the Tuppers of the nineteenth century will buy their plays on the same principle, the sale will be a remunerative one. It was worth while, perhaps, to reprint Lovelace, if only to show what dull verses may be written by a man who has made one lucky hit. Of the "Early English Poetry," nine tenths had better never have been printed at all, and the other tenth reprinted by an editor who had some vague suspicion, at least, of what they meant. The Homer of Chapman is so precious a gift, that we are ready to forgive all Mr. Smith's shortcomings in consideration of it. It is a vast *placer*, full of nuggets for the philologist and the lover of poetry.

Having now run cursorily through the series of Mr. Smith's reprints, we come to the closer question of *How are they edited?* Whatever the merit of the original works, the editors, whether self-elected or chosen by the publisher, should be accurate and scholarly. The editing of the Homer we can heartily commend; and Dr. Rimbault, who carried the works of Overbury through the press, has done his work well; but the other volumes of the Library are very creditable neither to English scholarship nor to English typography. The Introductions to some of them are enough to make us think that we are fallen to the necessity of reprinting our old authors because the art of writing correct and graceful English has been lost. William B. Turnbull, Esq., of Lincoln's Inn, Barrister at Law, says, for instance, in his Introduction to Southwell: "There was resident at Uxendon, near Harrow on the Hill, in Middlesex, a Catholic family of the name of Bellamy whom [which] Southwell was in the habit of visiting and providing with religious instruction when he exchanged his ordinary [ordinarily] close confinement for a purer atmosphere" (p. xxii.) Again, (p. xxii,) " He had, in this manner, for six years, pursued, with very great success, the objects of his mission, when these were abruptly terminated by his foul betrayal into the hands of his enemies in 1592."

We should like to have Mr. Turnbull explain how
the *objects* of a mission could be terminated by a
betrayal, however it might be with the mission itself.   From the many similar flowers in the Introduction to Mather's " Providences," by Mr. George
Offor, (in whom, we fear, we recognize a countryman,) we select the following : " It was at this
period when, [that,] oppressed by the ruthless hand
of persecution, our Pilgrim Fathers, threatened
with torture and death, succumbed not to man, but
trusting on [in] an almighty arm, braved the dangers of an almost unknown ocean, and threw themselves into the arms of men called savages, who
proved more beneficent than national Christians."
To whom or what our Pilgrim Fathers *did* succumb,
and what " national Christians " are, we leave, with
the song of the Sirens, to conjecture.   Speaking of
the " Providences," Mr. Offor says, that " they
faithfully delineate the state of public opinion two
hundred years ago, the most striking feature being
an implicit faith in the power of the [in-]visible
world to hold visible intercourse with man : — not
the angels to bless poor erring mortals, but of de-
mons imparting power to witches and warlocks to
injure, terrify and destroy," — a sentence which we
defy any witch or warlock, though he were Michael
Scott himself, to parse with the astutest demonic
aid.   On another page, he says of Dr. Mather, that
" he was one of the first divines who discovered
that very many strange events, which were considered preternatural, had occurred in the course
of nature or by deceitful juggling ; that the Devil

could not speak English, nor prevail with Protestants; the smell of herbs alarms the Devil; that medicine drives out Satan!" We do not wonder that Mr. Offor put a mark of exclamation at the end of this surprising sentence, but we do confess our astonishment that the vermilion pencil of the proof-reader suffered it to pass unchallenged. Leaving its bad English out of the question, we find, on referring to Mather's text, that he was never guilty of the absurdity of believing that Satan was less eloquent in English than in any other language; that it was the British (Welsh) tongue which a certain demon whose education had been neglected (not *the* Devil) could not speak; that Mather is not fool enough to say that the Fiend cannot prevail with Protestants, nor that the smell of herbs alarms him, nor that medicine drives him out. Anything more helplessly inadequate than Mr. Offor's preliminary dissertation on Witchcraft we never read; but we could hardly expect much from an editor whose citations from the book he is editing show that he had either not read or not understood it.

Mr. Offor is superbly Protestant and iconoclastic, — not sparing, as we have seen, even Priscian's head among the rest; but, *en revanche*, Mr. Turnbull is ultramontane beyond the editors of the *Civiltà Cattolica*. He allows himself to say, that, "after Southwell's death, one of his sisters, a Catholic in heart, but timidly and blamably simulating heresy, wrought, with some relics of the martyr, several cures on persons afflicted with desperate and deadly diseases, which had baffled the skill of all physicians." Mr. Turnbull is, we suspect, a recent convert, or it would occur to him that doctors are still secure of a lucrative practice in countries full of the relics of greater saints than even Southwell. That father was hanged (according to Protestants) for treason, and the relic which put the whole pharmacopœia to shame was, if we mistake not, his neckerchief. But whatever the merits of the Jesuit himself, and however it may gratify Mr. Turnbull's catechumenical enthusiasm to exalt the curative properties of this integument of his, even at the expense of Jesuits' bark, we cannot but think that he has shown a credulity that unfits him for writing a fair narrative of his hero's life, or making a tolerably just estimate of his verses. It is possible, however, that these last seem prosaic as a necktie only to heretical readers.

We have singled out the Introductions of Messrs. Turnbull and Offor for special animadversion because they are on the whole the worst, both of them being offensively sectarian, while that of Mr. Offor in particular gives us almost no information whatever. Some of the others are not without grave faults, chief among which is a vague declamation, especially out of place in critical essays, where it serves only to weary the reader and awaken his distrust. In his Introduction to Wither's "Hallelujah," for instance, Mr. Farr informs us that "nearly all the best poets of the latter half of the sixteenth century — for that was the period when the Reformation was fully established — and the whole of the seventeenth century were sacred poets," and that " even Shakespeare and the contemporary dramatists of his age sometimes attuned their well-strung harps to the songs of Zion." Comment on statements like these would be as useless as the assertions themselves are absurd.

We have quoted these examples only to justify us in saying that Mr. Smith must select his editors with more care if he wishes that his " Library of Old Authors " should deserve the confidence and thereby gain the good word of intelligent readers, — without which such a series can neither win nor keep the patronage of the public. It is impossible that men who cannot construct an English sentence correctly, and who do not know the value of clearness in writing, should be able to disentangle the knots which slovenly printers have tied in the thread of an old author's meaning; and it is more than doubtful whether they who assert carelessly, cite inaccurately, and write loosely are not by nature disqualified for doing thoroughly what they undertake to do. If it were unreasonable to demand of every one who assumes to edit one of our early poets the critical acumen, the genial sense, the illimitable reading, the philological scholarship, which in combination would alone make the ideal editor, it is not presumptuous to expect some one of these qualifications singly, and we have the right to insist upon patience and accuracy, which are within the reach of every one, and without which all the others are wellnigh

vain. Now to this virtue of accuracy Mr. Offor
specifically lays claim in one of his remarkable
sentences. "We are bound to admire," he says,
" the accuracy and beauty of this specimen of
typography. Following in the path of my late
friend William Pickering, our publisher rivals
the Aldine and Elzevir presses, which have been
so universally admired." We should think that
it was the product of those presses which had
been admired, and that Mr. Smith presents a
still worthier object of admiration when he contrives to follow a path and rival a press at the
same time. But let that pass ; — it is the claim
to accuracy which we dispute ; and we deliberately
affirm, that, so far as we are able to judge by
the volumes we have examined, no claim more
unfounded was ever set up. In some cases, as
we shall show presently, the blunders of the original work have been followed with painful accuracy in the reprint ; but many others have been
added by the carelessness of Mr. Smith's printers
or editors. In the thirteen pages of Mr. Offor's
own Introduction we have found as many as seven
typographical errors, — unless some of them are
to be excused on the ground that Mr. Offor's stud-
ies have not yet led him into those arcana where
we are taught such recondite mysteries of language as that verbs agree with their nominatives.
In Mr. Farr's Introduction to the " Hymns and
Songs " nine short extracts from other poems of
Wither are quoted, and in these we have found
no less than seven misprints or false readings

which materially affect the sense. Textual inaccuracy is a grave fault in the new edition of an old poet; and Mr. Farr is not only liable to this charge, but also to that of making blundering misstatements which are calculated to mislead the careless or uncritical reader. Infected by the absurd cant which has been prevalent for the last dozen years among literary sciolists, he says, — "The language used by Wither in all his various works — whether secular or sacred — is pure Saxon." Taken literally, this assertion is manifestly ridiculous, and, allowing it every possible limitation, it is not only untrue of Wither, but of every English poet, from Chaucer down. The translators of our Bible made use of the German version, and a poet versifying the English Scriptures would therefore be likely to use more words of Teutonic origin than in his original compositions. But no English poet can write English poetry except in English, — that is, in that compound of Teutonic and Romanic which derives its heartiness and strength from the one and its canorous elegance from the other. The Saxon language does not sing, and, though its tough mortar serve to hold together the less compact Latin words, porous with vowels, it is to the Latin that our verse owes majesty, harmony, variety, and the capacity for rhyme. A quotation of six lines from Wither ends at the top of the very page on which Mr. Farr lays down his extraordinary *dictum*, and we will let this answer him, Italicizing the words of Romance derivation : —

> " Her true *beauty* leaves behind
> *Apprehensions* in the mind,
> Of more sweetness than all *art*
> Or *inventions* can *impart ;*
> Thoughts too deep to be *expressed*,
> And too strong to be *suppressed*."

Mr. Halliwell, at the close of his Preface to the Works of Marston, (vol. i. p. xxii,) says, " The dramas now collected together are reprinted absolutely from the early editions, which were placed in the hands of our printers, who thus had the advantage of following them without the intervention of a transcriber. They are given as nearly as possible in their original state, the only modernizations attempted consisting in the alternations of the letters *i* and *j*, and *u* and *v*, the retention of which " (does Mr. Halliwell mean the letters or the " alternations " ?) " would have answered no useful purpose, while it would have unnecessarily perplexed the modern reader."

This is not very clear ; but as Mr. Halliwell is a member of several learned foreign societies, and especially of the Royal *Irish* Academy, perhaps it would be unfair to demand that he should write clear English. As one of Mr. Smith's editors, it was to be expected that he should not write it idiomatically. Some malign constellation (Taurus, perhaps, whose infaust aspect may be supposed to preside over the makers of bulls and blunders) seems to have been in conjunction with heavy Saturn when the Library was projected. At the top of the same page from which we have made our quotation, Mr. Halliwell speaks of " conveying a favorable impression *on* modern readers." It was surely to no such phrase as this that Ensign Pistol alluded when he said, "*Convey* the *wise* it call."

A literal reprint of an old author may be of value in two ways : the orthography may in certain cases indicate the ancient pronunciation, or it may put us on a scent which shall lead us to the burrow of a word among the roots of language. But in order to this, it surely is not needful to undertake the reproduction of all the original errors of the press ; and even were it so, the proofs of carelessness in the editorial department are so glaring, that we are left in doubt, after all, if we may congratulate ourselves on possessing all these sacred blunders of the Elizabethan type-setters in their integrity, and without any debasement of modern alloy. If it be gratifying to know that there lived stupid men before our contemporary Agamemnons in that kind, yet we demand absolute accuracy in the report of the phenomena in order to arrive at anything like safe statistics. For instance, we find (vol. i. p. 89) "ACTUS SECUNDUS, SCENA PRIMUS," and (vol. iii. p. 174) "*exit ambo*," and we are interested to know that in a London printing-house, two centuries and a half ago, there was a philanthropist who wished to simplify the study of the Latin language by reducing all the nouns to one gender and all the verbs to one number. Had his emancipated theories of grammar prevailed, how much easier would that part of boys which cherubs want have found the school-room benches ! How would birchen bark, as an educational tonic, have fallen in repute! How white would have been the (now black-and-blue) memories of Dr. Busby and so many other educational *lictors*, who, with their bundles of rods, heralded not alone the consuls, but all other Roman antiquities to us! We dare not, however, indulge in the grateful vision, since there are circumstances which lead us to infer that Mr. Halliwell himself (member though he be of so many learned societies) has those vague notions of the speech of ancient Rome which are apt to prevail in regions which count not the *betula* in their *Flora*. On page xv of his Preface, he makes Drummond say that Ben Jonson "was dilated" (*delated*, — Gifford gives it in English, *accused*) "to the king by Sir James Murray," — Ben, whose corpulent person stood in so little need of that malicious increment!

What is Mr. Halliwell's conception of editorial duty? As we read along, and the once fair complexion of the margin grew more and more pitted with pencil-marks, like that of a bad proof-sheet, we began to think that he was acting on the principle of every man his own washerwoman, — that he was making blunders of set purpose, (as teachers of languages do in their exercises,) in order that we might correct them for ourselves, and so fit us in time to be editors also, and members of various learned societies, even as Mr. Halliwell himself is. We fancied, that, magnanimously waving aside the laurel with which a grateful posterity crowned General Wade, he wished us "to see these roads *before* they were made," and develop our intellectual muscles in getting over them. But no ; Mr. Halliwell has appended notes to his edition, and among them are some which correct misprints, and therefore seem to imply that he considers that service as belonging properly to the editorial function. We are obliged, then, to give up our theory that his intention was to make every reader an editor, and to suppose that he wished rather to show how disgracefully a book might be edited and yet receive the commendation of professional critics who read with the ends of their fingers. If this were his intention, Marston himself never published so biting a satire.

Let us look at a few of the intricate passages, to help us through which Mr. Halliwell lends us the light of his editorial lantern. In the Induction to "What you Will" occurs the striking and unusual phrase, "Now out up-pont," and Mr. Halliwell favors us with the following note: "Page 221, line 10. *Up-pont.* — That is, upon 't." Again in the same play we find, —

> " Let twattling fame cheatd others rest,
> I um no dish for rumors feast."

Of course, it should read, —

> "Let twattling [twaddling] Fame cheate others' rest,
> I am no dish for Rumor's feast."

Mr. Halliwell comes to our assistance thus: "Page 244, line 21, [22 it should be,] *I um*, — a printer's error for *I am.*" *Dignus vindice nodus!* Five lines above, we have "whole" for "who 'll," and four lines below, "helmeth" for "whelmeth"; but

Mr. Halliwell vouchsafes no note. In the "Fawn"
we read, "Wise *neads* use few words," and the
editor says in a note, "a misprint for *heads*"!
Kind Mr. Halliwell!

Having given a few examples of our "Editor's"
corrections, we proceed to quote a passage or two
which, it is to be presumed, he thought perfectly
clear.

> "A man can skarce put on a tuckt-up cap,
>   A button'd frizado sute, skarce eate good meate,
>   *Anchoves, caviare,* but hee's satyred
>   And term'd phantasticall.   By the muddy spawne
>   Of slymie neughtes, when troth, phantasticknesse
>   That which the naturall sophysters tearme
>   *Phantusia incomplexa* — is a function
>   Even of the bright immortal part of man.
>   It is the common passe, the sacred dore,
>   Unto the prive chamber of the soule;
>   That bar'd, nought passeth past the baser court
>   Of outward scence by it th' inamorate
>   Most lively thinkes he sees the absent beauties
>   Of his lov'd mistres."   (Vol. i. p. 241.)

In this case, also, the true readings are clear
enough : —

> "And termed fantastical by the muddy spawn
>   Of slimy newts ";

and

> " . . . past the baser court
> Of outward sense "; —

but, if anything was to be explained, why are we
here deserted by our *fida compagna?*   Again,
(vol. ii. pp. 55, 56,) we read, "This Granuffo is
a right wise good lord, a man of excellent discourse,
and never speakes his signes to me, and men of

profound reach instruct aboundantly; hee begges suites with signes, gives thanks with signes," etc. This Granuffo is qualified among the "Interlocutors" as "a silent lord," and what fun there is in the character (which, it must be confessed, is rather of a lenten kind) consists in his genius for saying nothing. It is plain enough that the passage should read, "a man of excellent discourse, and never speaks; his signs to me and men of profound reach instruct abundantly," etc.

In both the passages we have quoted, it is not difficult for the reader to set the text right. But if not difficult for the reader, it should certainly not have been so for the editor, who should have done what Broome was said to have done for Pope in his Homer, — "gone before and swept the way." An edition of an English author ought to be intelligible to English readers, and, if the editor do not make it so, he wrongs the old poet, for two centuries lapt in lead, to whose works he undertakes to play the gentleman-usher. A play written in our own tongue should not be as tough to us as Æschylus to a ten years' graduate, nor do we wish to be reduced to the level of a chimpanzee, and forced to gnaw our way through a thick shell of misprints and mispointings only to find (as is generally the case with Marston) a rancid kernel of meaning after all. But even Marston sometimes deviates into poetry, as a man who wrote in that age could hardly help doing, and one of the few instances of it is in a speech of *Erichtho*, in the first scene of the fourth act of "Sophonisba," (vol. i. p. 197,) which Mr. Halliwell presents to us in this shape: —

> " hardby the reverent (!) ruines
> Of a once glorious temple rear'd to Jove
> Whose very rubbish .   .   .   .
> .   .   .   .   .   yet beares
> A deathlesse majesty, though now quite rac'd, [razed,]
> Hurl'd down by wrath and lust of impious kings,
> So that where holy Flamins [Flamens] wont to sing
> Sweet hymnes to Heaven, there the daw and crow,
> The ill-voyc'd raven, and still chattering pye,
> Send out ungratefull sounds and loathsome filth ;
> Where statues and Joves acts were vively limbs,
> .   .   .   .
> Where tombs and beautious urnes of well dead men
> Stood in assured rest," etc.

The last verse and a half are worthy of Chapman ; but why did not Mr. Halliwell, who explains *uppont* and *I um*, change " Joves acts were vively limbs " to " Jove's acts were lively limned," which was unquestionably what Marston wrote ?

In the " Scourge of Villanie," (vol. iii. p. 252,) there is a passage which till lately had a modern application in America, though happily archaic in England, which Mr. Halliwell suffers to stand thus : —

> "Once Albion lived in such a cruel age
> Than man did hold by servile vilenage :
> Poore brats were slaves of boudmen that were borne,
> And marted, sold : but that rude law is torne
> And disannuld, as too too inhumane."

This should read —

> " *Man* man did hold in servile villanage ;
> Poor brats were slaves (of bondmen that were born) " ;

and perhaps some American poet will one day write
in the past tense similar verses of the barbarity of
his forefathers.

We will give one more scrap of Mr. Halliwell's
text : —

> " Yfaith, why then, caprichious mirth,
> Skip, light moriscoes, in our frolick blond,
> Flagg'd veines, sweete, plump with fresh-infused joyes! "

which Marston, doubtless, wrote thus : —

> " I'faith, why then, capricious Mirth,
> Skip light moriscoes in our frolic blood !
> Flagg'd veins, swell plump with fresh-infused joys ! "

We have quoted only a few examples from
among the scores that we had marked, and against
such a style of " editing " we invoke the shade of
Marston himself. In the Preface to the Second
Edition of the " Fawn," he says, " Reader, know I
have perused this coppy, *to make some satisfaction
for the first faulty impression ; yet so urgent hath
been my business that some errors have styll passed,
which thy discretion may amend.*"

Literally, to be sure, Mr. Halliwell has availed
himself of the permission of the poet, in leaving all
emendation to the reader ; but certainly he has
been false to the spirit of it in his self-assumed
office of editor. The notes to explain *up-pont* and
I um give us a kind of standard of the highest
intelligence which Mr. Halliwell dares to take for
granted in the ordinary reader. Supposing this
nousometer of his to be a centigrade, in what hitherto unconceived depths of cold obstruction can he
find his zero-point of entire idiocy? The expansive

force of average wits cannot be reckoned upon, as we see, to drive them up as far as the temperate degree of misprints in one syllable, and those, too, in their native tongue. *A fortiori*, then, Mr. Halliwell is bound to lend us the aid of his great learning wherever his author has introduced foreign words and the old printers have made *pie* of them. In a single case he has accepted his responsibility as dragoman, and the amount of his success is not such as to give us any poignant regret that he has everywhere else left us to our own devices. On p. 119, vol. ii., *Francischina*, a Dutchwoman, exclaims, "O, mine aderliver love." Here is Mr. Halliwell's note : "*Aderliver.* — This is the speaker's error for *alder-liever*, the best beloved by all." Certainly not "the *speaker's* error," for Marston was no such fool as intentionally to make a Dutchwoman blunder in her own language. But is it an error for *alderliever?* No, but for *alderliefster.* Mr. Halliwell might have found it in many an old Dutch song. For example, No. 96 of Hoffmann von Fallersleben's "Niederländische Volkslieder" begins thus : —

"Mijn hert altijt heeft verlanghen
Naer u, die *alderliefste* mijn."

But does the word mean "best beloved by all"? No such thing, of course ; but "best beloved of all," — that is, by the speaker.

In "Antonio and Mellida" (vol. i. pp. 50, 51) occur some Italian verses, and here we hoped to fare better ; for Mr. Halliwell (as we learn from the title-page of his Dictionary) is a member of the "*Reale Academia di Firenze.*" This is the *Accademia della Crusca,* founded for the conservation of the Italian language in its purity, and it is rather a fatal symptom that Mr. Halliwell should indulge in the heresy of spelling *Accademia* with only one *c.* But let us see what our Della Cruscan's notions of conserving are. Here is a specimen : —

> " Bassiammi, coglier l' aura odorata
> Che in sua neggia in quello dolce labra.
> Dammi pimpero del tuo gradit' amore."

It is clear enough that we ought to read, —

"Lasciami coglier, . . . Che ha sua seggia, . . . Dammi l' impero."

A Della Cruscan academician might at least have corrected by his dictionary the spelling and number of *labra.*

We think that we have sustained our indictment of Mr. Halliwell's text with ample proof. The title of the book should have been, "The Works of John Marston, containing all the Misprints of the original Copies, together with a few added for the first Time in this Edition, the whole carefully let alone by James Orchard Halliwell, F. R. S., F. S. A." It occurs to us that Mr. Halliwell may be also a Fellow of the Geological Society, and may have caught from its members the enthusiasm which leads him to attach so extraordinary a value to every goose-track of the Elizabethan formation. It is bad enough to be, as Marston was, one of those middling poets whom neither gods nor men nor columns (Horace had never seen a newspaper) tolerate; but, really, even they do not deserve the frightful retribution of being reprinted by a Halliwell.

We have said that we could not feel even the dubious satisfaction of knowing that the blunders of the old copies had been faithfully followed in the reprinting. We see reason for doubting whether Mr. Halliwell ever read the proof-sheets. In his own notes we have found several mistakes. For instance, he refers to p. 159 when he means p. 153; he cites "I, but her *life*," instead of "*lip*"; and he makes Spenser speak of "old Pithonus." Marston is not an author of enough importance to make it desirable that we should be put in possession of all the corrupted readings of his text, were such a thing possible even with the most minute painstaking, and Mr. Halliwell's edition loses its only claim to value the moment a doubt is cast upon the accuracy of its inaccuracies. It is a matter of special import to us (whose means of access to originals are exceedingly limited) that the English editors of our old authors should be faithful and trustworthy, and we have singled out Mr. Halliwell's Marston for particular animadversion only because we think it on the whole the worst edition we ever saw of any author.

Having exposed the condition in which our editor has left the text, we proceed to test his competency in another respect, by examining some of the emendations and explanations of doubtful passages which he proposes. These are very few; but had they been even fewer, they had been too many.

Among the *dramatis personæ* of the " Fawn,"
as we said before, occurs "Granuffo, *a silent lord.*"
He speaks only once during the play, and that in
the last scene.   In Act I. Scene 2, *Gonzago* says,
speaking to *Granuffo*,—

> " Now, sure, thou art a man
> Of a most learned *scilence,* and oue whose words
> Have bin most pretious to me."

This seems quite plain, but Mr. Halliwell annotates thus : " *Scilence.*—Query, *science?* The common reading, *silence,* may, however, be what is intended."   That the spelling should have troubled
Mr. Halliwell is remarkable; for elsewhere we find
" god-boy " for " good-bye," " seace " for " cease,"
" bodies " for " boddice," " pollice " for " policy,"
" pitittying " for " pitying," " scence " for "sense,"
" Misenzius " for " Mezentius," " Ferazes " for
" Ferrarese,"—and plenty beside, equally odd.
That he should have doubted the meaning is no
less strange; for on p. 41 of the same play we
read, " My Lord Granuffo, you may likewise stay,
for I know *you'l say nothing,*"—on pp. 55, 56,
" This Granuffo is a right wise good lord, *a man of*
excellent discourse and never speaks,"—and on
p. 94, we find the following dialogue :—

> " *Gon.* My Lord Granuffo, this Fawne is an excellent fellow.
> " *Don.* Silence.
> " *Gon. I warrant you for my lord here.*"

In the same play (p. 44) are these lines :—

> " I apt for love ?
> Let lazy idlenes fild full of wine
> Heated with meates, high fedde with lustfull ense
> Goe dote on culler [color].   As for me, why, death a sence,
> I court the ladie ? "

This is Mr. Halliwell's note : "*Death a sence.*—
'Earth a sense,' ed. 1633. Mr. Dilke suggests :
'For me, why, earth's as sensible.' The original
is not necessarily corrupt. It may mean, — why,
you might as well think Death was a sense, one of
the senses. See a like phrase at p. 77." What
help we should get by thinking Death one of the
senses, it would demand another Œdipus to un-
riddle. Mr. Halliwell can astonish us no longer,
but we are surprised at Mr. Dilke, the very competent editor of the " Old English Plays," 1815.
From him we might have hoped for better things.
" Death o' sense ! " is an exclamation. Throughout these volumes we find *a* for *o'*, — as, "a clock "
for " o'clock," "a the side " for " o' the side." A
similar exclamation is to be found in three other
places in the same play, where the sense is obvious.
Mr. Halliwell refers to one of them on p. 77, —
" Death a man ! is she delivered ? " The others
are, — " Death a justice ! are we in Normandy ? "
(p. 98) ; and " Death a discretion ! if I should
prove a foole now," or, as given by Mr. Halliwell,
" Death, a discretion ! " Now let us apply Mr.
Halliwell's explanation. " Death a man ! " you
might as well think Death was a man, that is, one
of the men ! — or a discretion, that is, one of the
discretions ! — or a justice, that is, one of the quorum ! We trust Mr. Halliwell may never have the
editing of Bob Acres's imprecations. " Odd's triggers ! " he would say, " that is, as odd as, or as
strange as, triggers."

Vol. iii. p. 77, " the vote-killing mandrake."

Mr. Halliwell's note is, " *Vote-killing. —* ' Voice-killing,' ed. 1613. It may well be doubted whether either be the correct reading." He then gives a familiar citation from Browne's " Vulgar Errors." " Vote-killing " may be a mere misprint for " note-killing; " but " voice-killing " is certainly the better reading. Either, however, makes sense. Although Sir Thomas Browne does not allude to the deadly property of the mandrake's shriek, yet Mr. Halliwell, who has edited Shakespeare, might have remembered the

> " Would curses kill, *as doth the mandrake's groan,* "
> (Second Part of Henry VI., Act III. Scene 2,)

and the notes thereon in the *variorum* edition. In Jacob Grimm's " Deutsche Mythologie," (Vol. II. p. 1154,) under the word *Alraun*, may be found a full account of the superstitions concerning the mandrake. " When it is dug up, it groans and shrieks so dreadfully that the digger will surely die. One must, therefore, before sunrise on a Friday, having first stopped one's ears with wax or cotton-wool, take with him an entirely black dog without a white hair on him, make the sign of the cross three times over the *alraun*, and dig about it till the root holds only by thin fibres. Then tie these by a string to the tail of the dog, show him a piece of bread, and run away as fast as possible. The dog runs eagerly after the bread, pulls up the root, and falls stricken dead by its groan of pain."

These, we believe, are the only instances in which Mr. Halliwell has ventured to give any opinion upon the text, except as to a palpable misprint, here and there. Two of these we have already cited. There is one other, — "p. 46, line 10. *Iu-constant. —* An error for *inconstant.*" Wherever there is a real difficulty, he leaves us in the lurch. For example, in "What you Will," he prints without comment, —

"Ha! he mount Chirall on the wings of fame!"

(Vol. I. p. 239.)

which should be "mount cheval,"[1] as it is given in Mr. Dilke's edition (Old English Plays, vol. ii. p. 222). We cite this, not as the worst, but the shortest, example at hand.

Some of Mr. Halliwell's notes are useful and interesting, — as that on "keeling the pot," and a few others, — but the greater part are utterly useless. He thinks it necessary, for instance, to explain that "*to speak pure foole* is in sense equivalent to 'I will speak like a pure fool,'" — that "belkt up" means "belched up," — that "aprecocks" means "apricots." He has notes also upon "meal-mouthed," "luxuriousnesse," "termagant," "fico," "estro," "a nest of goblets," which indicate either that the "general reader" is a less intelligent person in England than in America, or that Mr. Halliwell's standard of scholarship is very low. We ourselves, from our limited reading, can supply him with a reference which will explain the allusion to the "Scotch barnacle" much better than his citations from Sir John Maundeville and Giraldus Cambrensis, — namely, note 8, on page 179

---

[1] "Mount our Chevalls." Dekker's Northward Ho! *Works.* iii. 50.

of a Treatise on Worms, by Dr. Ramesey, court physician to Charles II.

We turn now to Mr. Hazlitt's edition of Webster. We wish he had chosen Chapman; for Mr. Dyce's Webster is hardly out of print, and, we believe, has just gone through a second and revised edition. Webster was a far more considerable man than Marston, and infinitely above him in genius. Without the poetic nature of Marlowe, or Chapman's somewhat unwieldy vigor of thought, he had that inflammability of mind which, untempered by a solid understanding, made his plays a strange mixture of vivid expression, incoherent declamation, dramatic intensity, and extravagant conception of character. He was not, in the highest sense of the word, a great dramatist. Shakespeare is the only one of that age. Marlowe had a rare imagination, a delicacy of sense that made him the teacher of Shakespeare and Milton in versification, and was, perhaps, as purely a poet as any that England has produced; but his mind had no balance-wheel. Chapman abounds in splendid enthusiasms of diction, and now and then dilates our imaginations with suggestions of profound poetic depth. Ben Jonson was a conscientious and intelligent workman, whose plays glow, here and there, with the golden pollen of that poetic feeling with which his age impregnated all thought and expression; but his leading characteristic, like that of his great namesake, Samuel, was a hearty common sense, which fitted him rather to be a great critic than a great poet. He had a keen and ready eye for the comic in situation, but no humor. Fletcher was as much a poet as fancy and sentiment can make any man. Only Shakespeare wrote comedy and tragedy with truly ideal elevation and breadth. Only Shakespeare had that true sense of humor which, like the universal solvent sought by the alchemists, so fuses together all the elements of a character, (as in Falstaff,) that any question of good or evil, of dignified or ridiculous, is silenced by the apprehension of its thorough humanity. Rabelais shows gleams of it in Panurge; but, in our opinion, no man ever possessed it in an equal degree with Shakespeare, except Cervantes; no man has since shown anything like an approach to it, (for Molière's quality was comic power rather than humor,) except Sterne, Fielding, and perhaps Richter. Only Shakespeare was endowed with that healthy equilibrium of nature whose point of rest was midway between the imagination and the understanding, — that perfectly unruffled brain which reflected all objects with almost inhuman impartiality, — that outlook whose range was ecliptical, dominating all zones of human thought and action, — that power of veri-similar conception which could take away Richard III. from History, and Ulysses from Homer, — and that creative faculty whose equal touch is alike vivifying in Shallow and in Lear. He alone never seeks in abnormal and monstrous characters to evade the risks and responsibilities of absolute truthfulness, nor to stimulate a jaded imagination by Caligulan horrors of plot. He is never, like many of his fellow-dramatists, confronted with unnatural Frankensteins of his own making, whom he must get off his hands as best he may. Given a human foible, he can incarnate it in the nothingness of Slender, or make it loom gigantic through the tragic twilight of Hamlet. We are tired of the vagueness which classes all the Elizabethan playwrights together as " great dramatists,"— as if Shakespeare did not differ from them in kind as well as in degree. Fine poets some of them were ; but though imagination and the power of poetic expression are, singly, not uncommon gifts, and even in combination not without secular examples, yet it is the rarest of earthly phenomena to find them joined with those faculties of perception, arrangement, and plastic instinct in the loving union which alone makes a great dramatic poet possible. We suspect that Shakespeare will long continue the only specimen of the genus. His contemporaries, in their comedies, either force what they call " a humor " till it becomes fantastical, or hunt for jokes, like rat-catchers, in the sewers of human nature and of language. In their tragedies they become heavy without grandeur, like Jonson, or mistake the stilts for the cothurnus, as Chapman and Webster too often do. Every new edition of an Elizabethan dramatist is but the putting of another witness into the box to prove the inaccessibility of Shakespeare's stand-point as poet and artist.

Webster's most famous works are " The Duchess of Malfy " and " Vittoria Corombona," but we are strongly inclined to call "The Devil's Law-Case" his best play. The two former are in a great measure answerable for the "spasmodic" school of poets, since the extravagances of a man of genius are as sure of imitation as the equable self-possession of his higher moments is incapable of it. Webster had, no doubt, the primal requisite of a poet, imagination, but in him it was truly untamed, and Aristotle's admirable distinction between the *Horrible* and the *Terrible* in tragedy was never better illustrated and confirmed than in the "Duchess" and "Vittoria." His nature had something of the sleuth-hound quality in it, and a plot, to keep his mind eager on the trail, must be sprinkled with fresh blood at every turn. We do not forget all the fine things that Lamb has said of Webster, but, when Lamb wrote, the Elizabethan drama was an El Dorado, whose micaceous sand, even, was treasured as auriferous, — and no wonder, in a generation which admired the "Botanic Garden." Webster is the Gherardo della Notte of his day, and himself calls his "Vittoria Corombona" a "night-piece." Though he had no conception of Nature in its large sense, as something pervading a whole character and making it consistent with itself, nor of Art, as that which dominates an entire tragedy and makes all the characters foils to each other and tributaries to the catastrophe, yet there are flashes of Nature in his plays, struck out by the collisions of passion, and dramatic intensities of phrase for which it would be hard to find the match. The "prithee, undo this button" of

Lear, by which Shakespeare makes us feel the swelling of the old king's heart, and that the bodily results of mental anguish have gone so far as to deaden for the moment all intellectual consciousness and forbid all expression of grief, is hardly finer than the broken verse which Webster puts into the mouth of Ferdinand when he sees the body of his sister, murdered by his own procurement : —

"Cover her face : mine eyes dazzle : she died young."

He has not the condensing power of Shakespeare, who squeezed meaning into a phrase with an hydraulic press, but he could carve a cherry-stone with any of the *concettisti*, and abounds in imaginative quaintnesses that are worthy of Donne, and epigrammatic tersenesses that remind us of Fuller. Nor is he wanting in poetic phrases of the purest crystallization.   Here are a few examples : —

"Oh, if there be another world i' th' moon,
  As some fantastics dream, I could wish all *men*,
  The whole race of them, for their inconstancy,
  Sent thither to people that ! "

(Old Chaucer was yet slier. After saying that Lamech was the first faithless lover, he adds, —

"And he invented *tents*, unless men lie," —

implying that he was the prototype of nomadic men.)

"Virtue is ever sowing of her seeds:
  In the trenches, for the soldier; in the wakeful study,
  For the scholar; in the furrows of the sea,
  For men of our profession [merchants]; all of which
  Arise and spring up honor."

("Of all which," Mr. Hazlitt prints it.)

> "Poor Jolenta ! should she hear of this,
> She would not after the report keep fresh
> So long as flowers on graves."

> "For sin and shame are ever tied together
> With Gordian knots of such a strong thread spun,
> They cannot without violence be undone."

> "One whose mind
> Appears more like a ceremonious chapel
> Full of sweet music, than a thronging presence."

> "What is death ?
> The safest trench i' th' world to keep man free
> From Fortune's gunshot."

> "It has ever been my opinion
> That there are none love perfectly indeed,
> But those that hang or drown themselves for love,"

says Julio, anticipating Butler's

> "But he that drowns, or blows out 's brains,
> The Devil 's in him, if he feigns."

He also anticipated La Rochefoucauld and Byron
in their apophthegm concerning woman's last love.
In "The Devil's Law-Case," Leonora says, —

> "For, as we love our youngest children best,
>   So the last fruit of our affection,
>   Wherever we bestow it, is most strong,
>   Most violent, most unresistible ;
>   Since 't is, indeed, our latest harvest-home,
>   Last merriment 'fore winter."

It is worth remark that there are a greater number of reminiscences, conscious or unconscious, of
Shakespeare in Webster's plays than in those of
any other Elizabethan dramatist.

In editing Webster, Mr. Hazlitt had the advantage (except in a single doubtful play) of a pre-

decessor in the Rev. Alexander Dyce, beyond all question the best living scholar of the literature of the times of Elizabeth and James I. If he give no proof of remarkable fitness for his task, he seems, at least, to have been diligent and painstaking. His notes are short and to the point, and — which we consider a great merit — at the foot of the page. If he had added a glossarial index, we should have been still better pleased. Mr. Hazlitt seems to have read over the text with some care, and he has had the good sense to modernize the orthography, or, as he says, has "observed the existing standard of spelling throughout." Yet — for what reason we cannot imagine — he prints " I " for " ay," taking the pains to explain it every time in a note, and retains " banquerout " and " coram " apparently for the sake of telling us that they mean " bankrupt " and " quorum." He does not seem to have a quick ear for scansion, which would sometimes have assisted him to the true reading. We give an example or two : —

> " The obligation wherein we all stood bound
>   Cannot be concealed [*cancelled*] without great reproach."

> " The realm, not they,
>   Must be regarded.   Be [we] strong and bold,
>   We are the people's factors."

> " Shall not be o'erburdened [*overburdened*] in our reign."

> " A merry heart
>   And a good stomach to [a] feast are all."

> " Have her meat serv'd up by bawds and ruffians." [*dele* " up."]

> " Brother or father
>   In [a] dishonest suit, shall be to me."

> " What 's she in Rome your greatness cannot awe,
>   Or your rich purse purchase ?   Promises and threats."   [*dele*
>   the second " your."]

> " Through clouds of envy and disast [rous] change."

> " The Devil drives; 'tis [it is] full time to go."

He has overlooked some strange blunders.   What
is the meaning of

> " Laugh at your misery, as foredeeming you
>   An idle meteor, which drawn forth, the earth
>   Would soon be lost i' the air " ?

We hardly need say that it should be

> " An idle meteor, which, drawn forth the earth,
>   Would," &c.

" *For*wardness " for " *fro*wardness," (vol. ii. p.
87,) " tennis-balls struck and ban*ded* " for " ban-
died," (Ib. p. 275,) may be errors of the press;
but

> " Come, I 'll love you wisely :
>   That 's jealousy,"

has crept in by editorial oversight for " wisely,
that 's jealously."   So have

> " Ay, the great emperor of [*or*] the mighty Cham ";

and

> " This wit [*with*] taking long journeys ";

and

> " Virginius. thou dost but supply my place,
>   I thine : Fortune hath lift me [*thee*] to my chair,
>   And thrown me headlong to thy pleading bar ";

and

> " I 'll pour my soul into my daughter's belly, [*body,*]
>   And with my soldier's tears embalm her wounds."

We suggest that the change of an *a* to an *r* would

make sense of the following: "Come, my little punk, with thy two compositors, to this unlawful painting-house," [printing-house,] which Mr. Hazlitt awkwardly endeavors to explain by this note on the word *compositors*, — " i. e. (conjecturally), making up the composition of the picture "! Our readers can decide for themselves; — the passage occurs vol. i. p. 214.

We think Mr. Hazlitt's notes are, in the main, good; but we should like to know his authority for saying that *pench* means "the hole in a bench by which it was taken up," — that "descant" means "look askant on," — and that " I wis " is equivalent to " I surmise, imagine," which it surely is not in the passage to which his note is appended.   On page 9, vol. i., we read in the text,

"To whom, my lord, bends thus your awe,"

and in the note, i. e. submission. The original has *aue*, which, if it mean *ave*, is unmeaning here." Did Mr. Hazlitt never see a picture of the Annunciation with *ave* written on the scroll proceeding from the bending angel's mouth? We find the same word in vol. iii. p. 217 : —

" Whose station's built on avees and applause."

Vol. iii. pp. 47, 48 : —

" And then rest, gentle bones ; yet pray
That when by the precise you are view'd,
A supersedeas be not sued
To remove you to a place more airy,
That in your stead they may keep chary
Stockfish or seacoal, for the abuses
Of sacrilege have turned graves to viler uses."

To the last verse Mr. Hazlitt appends this note, " Than that of burning men's bones for fuel." There is no allusion here to burning men's bones, but simply to the desecration of graveyards by building warehouses upon them, in digging the foundations for which the bones would be thrown out.   The allusion is, perhaps, to the " Churchyard of the Holy Trinity " ; — see Stow's *Survey*, ed. 1603, p. 126.   Elsewhere, in the same play, Web-'ster alludes bitterly to " begging church-land."

Vol. i. p. 73, " And if he walk through the street, he ducks at the penthouses, like an ancient that dares not flourish at the oathtaking of the prætor for fear of the signposts."   Mr. Hazlitt's note is, " *Ancient* was a standard or flag ; also an *ensign*, of which Skinner says it is a corruption. What the meaning of the simile is the present editor cannot suggest."   We confess we find no difficulty.   The meaning plainly is, that he ducks for fear of hitting the penthouses, as an ensign on the Lord Mayor's day dares not flourish his standard for fear of hitting the signposts.   We suggest the query, whether *ancient*, in this sense, be not a corruption of the Italian word *anziano*.

Want of space compels us to leave many other passages, which we had marked for comment, un-noticed.   We are surprised that Mr. Hazlitt, (see his Introduction to " Vittoria Corombona,") in un-dertaking to give us some information concerning the Dukedom and Castle of Bracciano, should uni-formly spell it *Brachiano*.   Shakespeare's *Petru-chio* might have put him on his guard.   We should be glad also to know in what part of Italy he places *Malfi*.

Mr. Hazlitt's General Introduction supplies us with no new information, but this was hardly to be expected where Mr. Dyce had already gone over the field. We wish that he had been able to give us better means of distinguishing the three almost contemporary John Websters one from the other, for we think the internal evidence is enough to show that all the plays attributed to the author of the " Duchess " and " Vittoria " could not have been written by the same person. On the whole, he has given us a very respectable, and certainly a very pretty, edition of an eminent poet.

We could almost forgive all other shortcomings of Mr. Smith's *library* for the great gift it brings us in the five volumes of Chapman's translations. Coleridge, sending Chapman's Homer to Wordsworth, writes, " What is stupidly said of Shakespeare is really true and appropriate of Chapman ; mighty faults counterpoised by mighty beauties. . . . It is as truly an original poem as the Faery Queene ; — it will give you small idea of Homer, though a far truer one than Pope's epigrams, or Cowper's cumbersome most anti-Homeric Miltonism. For Chapman writes and feels as a poet, — as Homer might have written had he lived in England in the reign of Queen Elizabeth. In short, it is an exquisite poem, in spite of its frequent and perverse quaintnesses and harshnesses, which are, however, amply repaid by almost unexampled sweetness and beauty of language, all over spirit and feeling." [1] From a passage of his Preface it would appear that Chapman had been criticised pretty sharply in his own day for amplifying his author. " And this one example I thought necessary to insert here to show my detractors that they have no reason to vilify my circumlocution sometimes, when their most approved Grecians, Homer's interpreters generally, hold him fit to be so converted. Yet how much I differ, and with what authority, let my impartial and judicial reader judge. Always conceiving how pedantical and absurd an affectation it is in the interpretation of any author (much more of Homer) to turn him word for word, when (according to Horace and other best lawgivers to translators) it is the part of every knowing and judicial interpreter not to follow the number and order of words, but the material things themselves, and sentences to weigh diligently, and to clothe and adorn them with words and such a style and form of oration as are most apt for the language in which they are converted." Again in his verses *To the Reader*, he speaks of

> " The *ample transmigration* to be shown
>   By nature-loving Poesy,"

and defends his own use of " needful periphrases," and says that " word for word " translation is to

> " Make fish with fowl, camels with whales, engender."

> " For even as different a production
>   Ask Greek and English : since, as they in sounds
>   And letters shun one form and unison,

[1] *Literary Remains*,   vol. i. pp. 259, 260.

> So have their sense and elegancy bounds
> In their distinguished natures, and require
> Only a judgment to make both consent
> In sense and elocution.''

There are two theories of translation, — literal paraphrase and free reproduction. At best, the translation of poetry is but an imitation of natural flowers in cambric or wax ; and however much of likeness there may be, the aroma, whose charm of indefinable suggestion in the association of ideas is so powerful, is precisely what is lost irretrievably.

> '' The parting genius is with sighing sent ''

from where it lurked in the immortal verse, a presence divined rather than ascertained, baffling the ear which it enchanted, escaping the grasp which yet it thrilled, airy, evanescent, imperishable, beckoning the imagination with promises better than any fulfilment. The paraphrase is a plaster-cast of the Grecian urn ; the reproduction, if by a man of genius, such as the late Mr. Fitzgerald, is like Keats's ode, which makes the figures move and the leaves tremble again, if not with the old life, with a sorcery which deceives the fancy. Of all English poets, Keats was the one to have translated Homer.

In any other than a mere prose version of a great poem, we have a right to demand that it give us at least an adequate impression of force and originality. We have a right to ask, If this poem were published now for the first time, as the work of a contemporary, should we read it, not with the same, but with anything like the same conviction of its freshness, vigor, and originality, its high level of style and its witchery of verse, that Homer, if now for the first time discovered, would infallibly beget in us? Perhaps this looks like asking for a new Homer to translate the old one; but if this be too much, it is certainly not unfair to insist that the feeling given us should be that of life, and not artifice.

The Homer of Chapman, whatever its defects, alone of all English versions has this crowning merit of being, where it is most successful, thoroughly alive. He has made for us the best poem that has yet been Englished out of Homer, and in so far gives us a truer idea of him. Of all translators he is farthest removed from the fault with which he charges others, when he says that " our divine master's most ingenious imitating the life of things (which is the soul of a poem) is never respected nor perceived by his interpreters only standing pedantically on the grammar and words, utterly ignorant of the sense and grace of him." His mastery of English is something wonderful even in an age of masters, when the language was still a mother-tongue, and not a contrivance of pedants and grammarians. He had a reverential sense of " our divine Homer's depth and gravity, which will not open itself to the curious austerity of belaboring art, but only to the natural and most ingenious soul of our thrice-sacred Poesy." His task was as holy to him as a version of Scripture; he justifies the tears of Achilles by those of Jesus, and the eloquence of his horse by that of Balaam's

less noble animal. He does not always keep close
to his original, but he sins no more, even in this,
than any of his rivals. He is especially great in
the similes. Here he rouses himself always, and
if his enthusiasm sometimes lead him to heighten a
little, or even to add outright, he gives us a picture
full of life and action, or of the grandeur and
beauty of nature, as stirring to the fancy as his
original. Of all who have attempted Homer, he
has the topping merit of being inspired by him.

In the recent discussions of Homeric translation
in England, it has always been taken for granted
that we had or could have some adequate conception of Homer's metre. Lord Derby, in his Preface, plainly assumes this. But there can be no
greater fallacy. No human ears, much less Greek
ones, could have endured what, with our mechanical knowledge of the verse, ignorance of the accent, and English pronunciation, we blandly accept for such music as Homer chanted. We have
utterly lost the tune and cannot reproduce it. Mr.
Newman conjectures it to have been something
like Yankee Doodle; Mr. Arnold is sure it was
the English hexameter; and they are both partly
right so far as we may trust our reasonable impressions; for, after all, an impression is all that we
have. Cowper attempts to give the ring of the
ἀργυρέοιο βιοῖο by

" Dread-sounding, bounding on the silver bow,"

which only too fatally recalls the old Scottish dan·
cing-tune, —

> " Amaisit I gaisit
> To see, led at command,
> A strampant and rampant
> Ferss lyon in his hand."

The attempt was in the right direction, however, for Homer, like Dante and Shakespeare, like all who really command language, seems fond of playing with assonances. No doubt the Homeric verse consented at will to an eager rapidity, and no doubt also its general character is that of prolonged but unmonotonous roll. Everybody says it is like the long ridges of the sea, some overtopping their neighbors a little, each with an independent undulation of its crest, yet all driven by a common impulse, and breaking, not with the sudden snap of an unyielding material, but one after the other, with a stately curve, to slide back and mingle with those that follow. Chapman's measure (in the Iliad) has the disadvantage of an association with Sternhold and Hopkins, but it has the merit of length, and, where he is in the right mood, is free, spirited, and sonorous. Above all, there is everywhere the movement of life and passion in it. Chapman was a master of verse, making it hurry, linger, or stop short, to suit the meaning. Like all great versifiers he must be read with study, for the slightest change of accent loses the expression of an entire passage. His great fault as a translator is that he takes fire too easily and runs beyond his author. Perhaps he *intensifies* too much, though this be a fault on the right side; he certainly sometimes weakens the force of passages by crowding in particulars which Homer had wisely omitted, for Homer's simplicity is by no means mere simplicity of thought, nor, as it is often foolishly called, of nature. It is the simplicity of consummate art, the last achievement of poets and the invariable characteristic of the greatest among them. To Chapman's mind once warmed to its work, the words are only a mist, suggesting, while it hides, the divine form of the original image or thought; and his imagination strives to body forth that, as he conceives it, in all its celestial proportions. Let us compare with Lord Derby's version, as the latest, a passage where Chapman merely intensifies, (Book XIII., beginning at the 86th verse in Lord Derby, the 73d of Chapman, and the 76th of Homer) : —

> " Whom answered thus the son of Telamon:
> ' My hands, too, grasp with firmer hold the spear,
> My spirit, like thine, is stirred ; I feel my feet
> Instinct with fiery life ; nor should I fear
> With Hector, son of Priam, in his might
> Alone to meet, and grapple to the death.' "

Thus Lord Derby. Chapman renders : —

> " This Telamonius thus received : ' So, to my thoughts, my hands
> Burn with desire to toss my lance ; *each foot beneath me stands
> Bare on bright fire to use his speed ;* my heart is raised so high,
> That to encounter Hector's self I long insatiately.' "

There is no question which version is the more energetic. Is Lord Derby's nearer the original in being tamer? He has taken the " instinct with fiery life " from Chapman's hint. The original has simply " restless," or more familiarly " in a fidget." There is nothing about " grappling to the

death," and "nor should I fear" is feeble where
Chapman with his "long insatiately" is literal.
We will give an example where Chapman has am-
plified his original (Book XVI. v. 426 ; Derby,
494 ; Chapman, 405) : —

"Down jumped he from his chariot ; down leapt his foe as light ;
And as, on some far-looking rock, a cast of vultures fight,
Fly on each other, strike and truss, part, meet, and then stick by,
Tug both with crooked beaks and seres, cry, fight, and fight and
    cry,
So fiercely fought these angry kings." [1]

Lord Derby's version is nearer : —

> "He said, and from his car, accoutred, sprang ;
> Patroclus saw and he too leaped to earth.
> As on a lofty rock, with angry screams,
> Hook-beaked, with talons curved, two vultures fight,
> So with loud shouts these two to battle rushed."

Chapman has made his first line out of two in
Homer, but, granting the license, how rapid and
springy is the verse ! Lord Derby's " withs " are
not agreeable, his " shouts " is an ill-chosen word
for a comparison with vultures, " talons curved " is
feeble, and his verse is, as usual, mainly built up
of little blocks of four syllables each. "To battle "
also is vague. With whom ? Homer says that
they rushed each at other. We shall not discuss
how much license is loyal in a translator, but, as
we think his chief aim should be to give a feeling
of that life and spirit which makes the immortality
of his original, and is the very breath in the nos-
trils of all poetry, he has a right to adapt himself
to the genius of his own language. If he would

---

[1] Chapman himself was evidently pleased with this, for he cites
it as a sample of his version.

do justice to his author, he must make up in one passage for his unavoidable shortcomings in another. He may here and there take for granted certain exigencies of verse in his original which he feels in his own case. Even Dante, who boasted that no word had ever made him say what he did not wish, should have made an exception of rhyming ones, for these sometimes, even in so abundant a language as the Italian, have driven the most straightforward of poets into an awkward *détour*.

We give one more passage from Chapman : —

" And all in golden weeds

He clothed himself ; the golden scourge most elegantly done
He took and mounted to his seat; and then the god begun
To drive his chariot through the waves. From whirl-pits every
    way
The whales exulted under him, and knew their king; the sea
For joy did open, and his horse so swift and lightly flew
The under axle-tree of brass no drop of water drew."

Here the first half is sluggish and inadequate, but what surging vigor, what tumult of the sea, what swiftness, in the last! Here is Lord Derby's attempt : —

" All clad in gold, the golden lash he grasped
   Of curious work, and, mounting on his car,
   Skimmed o'er the waves ; from all the depths below
   Gambolled around the monsters of the deep,
   Acknowledging their king ; the joyous sea
   Parted her waves ; swift flew the bounding steeds,
   Nor was the brazen axle wet with spray."

Chapman here is truer to his master, and the motion is in the verse itself. Lord Derby's is description, and not picture. " Monsters of the deep " is an example of the hackneyed periphrases in

which he abounds, like all men to whom language
is a literary tradition, and not a living gift of the
Muses. " *Lash* " is precisely the wrong word.
Chapman is always great at sea. Here is another
example from the Fourteenth Book : —

" And as, when with unwieldy waves *the great sea forefeels winds*
That both ways murmur, and no way her certain current finds,
But pants and swells confusedly, here goes, and there will stay,
Till on it air casts one firm wind, and then it rolls away."

Observe how the somewhat ponderous movement of
the first verse assists the meaning of the words.

He is great, too, in single phrases and lines : —

" And as, from top of some steep hill, the Lightener strips a cloud
And lets a great sky out of Heaven, in whose delightsome light
All prominent foreheads, forests, towers, and temples cheer the
       sight."   (Book XVI. v. 286.)

The lion " lets his rough brows down so low they
hide his eyes " ; the flames " wrastle " in the
woods; " rude feet dim the day with a fog of
dust ; " and so in a hundred other instances.

For an example of his more restrained vigor,
take the speech of Sarpedon in the Twelfth Book
of the Iliad, and for poetic beauty, the whole story
of Ulysses and Nausikaa in the Odyssey. It was
here that Keats made himself Grecian and learned
to versify.

Mr. Hooper has done his work of editing well.
But he has sometimes misapprehended his author,
and distorted his meaning by faulty punctuation.
In one of the passages already cited, Mr. Hooper's text stands thus : " Lest I be prejudiced with
opinion, to dissent, of ignorance, or singularity."

All the commas which darken the sense should be removed. Chapman meant to say, " Lest I be condemned beforehand by people thinking I dissent out of ignorance or singularity." (Iliad, vol. i. p. 23.) So on the next page the want of a hyphen makes nonsense : " And saw the round coming [round-coming] of this silver bow of our Phoebus," that is, the crescent coming to the full circle. In the translations, too, the pointing needs reformation now and then, but shows, on the whole, a praiseworthy fidelity. We will give a few examples of what we believe to be errors on the part of Mr. Hooper, who, by the way, is weakest on points which concern the language of Chapman's day. We follow the order of the text as most convenient.

" Bid " (Il. i.) is explained to mean " threaten, challenge," where " offer " would be the right word.

" And cast
The offal of all to the deep." (Il. i. 309.)

Surely a slip of Chapman's pen. He must have intended to write " Of all the offal," a transversion common with him and needed here to avoid a punning jingle.

"So much I must affirm our power exceeds th' inhabitant."
(Il. ii. 110.)

Mr. Hooper's note is " inhabiters, viz. of Troy." " Inhabitant " is an adjective agreeing with " power." Our power without exceeds that within.

" Yet all this time to stay,
Out of our judgments, for our end, and now to take our way
Without it were absurd and vile." (Il. ii. 257.)

A note on this passage tells us that " out of judg-

ments " means " against our inclinations." It
means simply " in accordance with our good judgment," just as we still say " out of his wisdom."
Compare Il. iii. 63,

"Hector, because thy sharp reproof is *out of justice* given,
  I take it well."

" And as Jove, brandishing a star which men a comet call,
  Hurls out his curlëd hair abroad, that from his brand exhals
  A thousand sparks." (Il. iv. 85.)

Mr. Hooper's note is " ' *Which men a comet call* '
— so both the folios. Dr. Taylor has printed
' *which man a comet calls.*' This certainly suits
the rhyme, but I adhere to Chapman's text."
Both editors have misunderstood the passage.
The fault is not in "call" but in " exhals," a clear
misprint for "exhall," the spelling, as was common, being conformed to the visible rhyme.
"That" means " so that" (a frequent Elizabethan
construction) and " exhall " is governed by
" sparks." The meaning is, " As when Jove,
brandishing a comet, hurls out its curled hair so
that a thousand sparks exhale from its burning."

" The *evicke* skipping from the rock."

Mr. Hooper tell us, " It is doubtful what this word
really is. Dr. Taylor suggests that it may probably mean the *evict*, or doomed one — but? It is
possible Chapman meant to Anglicize the Greek
αἴξ ; or should we read Ibex, as the αἴξ ἴξαλος was
such ? " The word means the *chamois*, and is
merely the English form of the French *ibiche*. Dr.
Taylor's reading would amaze us were we not familiar with the commentators on Shakespeare.

" And now they *out-ray* to your fleet."   (Il. v. 793.)

" *Out-ray* — spread out in array; abbreviated from array. Dr. Taylor says 'rush out,' from the Anglo-Saxon '*rean*,' to flow; but there seems no necessity for such an etymology." We should think not! Chapman, like Pope, made his first sketch from the French, and corrected it by the Greek. Those who would understand Chapman's English must allow for traces of his French guide here and there. This is one of them, perhaps. The word is etymologically unrelated to *array*. It is merely the old French *oultréer*, a derivative of *ultra*. It means " they pass beyond their gates even to your fleet." He had said just before that formerly " your foes durst not a foot address *without their ports*." The word occurs again, Il. xxiii. 413.

" When none, though many kings put on, could make his vaunt,
    he led
Tydides to renewed assault or issued first the dike."
(Il. viii. 217.)

" *Tydides*. — He led Tydides, i. e. Tydides he led. An unusual construction." Not in the least. The old printers or authors sometimes put a comma where some connecting particle was left out. We had just now an instance where one took the place of *so*. Here it supplies *that*. " None could make his vaunt that he led (that is, was before) Tydides." We still use the word in the same sense, as the " leading " horse in a race.

" And all did wilfully expect the silver-throned morn."
(Il. viii. 497.)

"*Wilfully* — willingly, anxiously."   *Wishfully*, as elsewhere in Chapman.

"And as, upon a rich man's crop of barley or of wheat,
  Opposed for swiftness at their work, a sort of reapers sweat."

" *Opposed* — standing opposite to one another for expedition's sake."   We hope Mr. Hooper understood his own note, for it baffles us utterly.   The meaning is simply "pitted against each other to see which will reap most swiftly."   In a note (Il. xi. 417) we are told that "the etymology [of *lucern*] seems uncertain."   It is nothing more than a corruption of the old French *leucerve* (*loup-cervier*).

"I would then make-in in deed and steep
  My income in their bloods."   (Il. xvii. 481.)

" *Income* — communication, or infusion, of courage from the Gods.   The word in this sense Todd says was a favorite in Cromwell's time."   A surprising note!   *Income* here means nothing more than "onfall," as the context shows.

"To put the best in *ure*."   (Il. xvii. 545.)

"*Ure* — use.   Skinner thinks it a contraction of *usura*.   It is frequent in Chaucer.   Todd gives examples from Hooker and L'Estrange."   The word is common enough, but how Mr. Hooper could seriously quote good old Skinner for such an etymology we cannot conceive.   It does not mean " in use," but "to work," being merely the English form of *en œuvre*, as " manure " is of *manœuvrer*.

"So troop-meal Troy pursued a while."   (Il. xvii. 634.)

" *Troop-meal* — in troops, troop by troop.   So

piece-meal. To *meal* was to mingle, mix together; from the French *mêler*. . . . The reader would do well to consult Dr. Jamieson's excellent 'Dictionary of the Scottish Language' in voce '*mell*.'" No doubt the reader might profit by consulting it under any other word beginning with M, and any of them would be as much to the purpose as *mell*. *Troop-meal*, like *inch-meal*, *piece-meal*, implies separation, not mingling, and is from a Teutonic root. Mr. Hooper is always weak in his linguistic. In a note on Il. xviii. 144, he informs us that "To *sterve* is to *die;* and the sense of *starve*, with cold or hunger originated in the 17th century." We would it had! But we suspect that men had died of both these diseases earlier. What he should have said was that the restriction of meaning to that of dying with hunger was modern.

Il. xx. 239 we have " the God's " for " the Gods'," and a few lines below " Anchisiades' " for " Anchisiades's "; Il. xxi. 407, " press'd " for " prest."

We had noted a considerable number of other slips, but we will mention only two more. " Treen broches " is explained to mean " branches of trees." (Hymn to Hermes, 227.) It means " wooden spits." In the Bacchus (28, 29) Mr. Hooper restores a corrupt reading which Mr. Singer (for a wonder) had set right He prints, —

> " Nay, which of all the Pow'r fully-divined
> Esteem ye him ? "

Of course it should be powerfully - divined, for otherwise we must read " Pow'rs." The five volumes need a very careful revision in their punctu-

ation, and in another edition we should advise Mr.
Hooper to strike out every note in which he has
been tempted into etymology.

We come next to Mr. W. C. Hazlitt's edition of
Lovelace. Three short pieces of Lovelace's have
lived, and deserved to live: "To Lucasta from
Prison," "To Lucasta on going to the Wars," and
"The Grasshopper." They are graceful, airy, and
nicely finished. The last especially is a charming
poem, delicate in expression, and full of quaint
fancy, which only in the latter half is strained to
conceit. As the verses of a gentleman they are
among the best, though not of a very high order as
poetry. He is to be classed with the *lucky* authors
who, without great powers, have written one or two
pieces so facile in thought and fortunate in phrase
as to be carried lightly in the memory, poems in
which analysis finds little, but which are charming
in their frail completeness. This faculty of hitting
on the precise *lilt* of thought and measure that shall
catch the universal ear, and make them sing themselves in everybody's memory, is a rare gift. We
have heard many ingenious persons try to explain
the *cling* of such a poem as "The Burial of Sir
John Moore," and the result of all seemed to be,
that there were certain verses that were good, not
because of their goodness, but because one could not
forget them. They have the great merit of being
portable, and we have to carry so much luggage
through life that we should be thankful for what
will pack easily and take up no room.

All that Lovelace wrote beside these three poems is utterly worthless, mere chaff from the threshing of his wits. Take out the four pages on which they are printed, and we have two hundred and eighty-nine left of the sorriest stuff that ever spoiled paper. The poems are obscure, without anything in them to reward perseverance, dull without being moral, and full of conceits so far-fetched that we could wish the author no worse fate than to carry them back to where they came from. We are no enemies to what are commonly called conceits, but authors bear them, as heralds say, with a difference. And a terrible difference it is! With men like Earle, Donne, Fuller, Butler, Marvell, and even Quarles, conceit means wit; they would carve the merest cherry-stone of thought in the quaintest and delicatest fashion. But with duller and more painful writers, such as Gascoigne, Marston, Felltham, and a score of others, even with cleverer ones like Waller, Crashawe, and Suckling, where they insisted on being fine, their wit is conceit. Difficulty without success is perhaps the least tolerable kind of writing. Mere stupidity is a natural failing; we skip and pardon. But the other is Dulness in a domino, that travesties its familiar figure, and lures us only to disappoint. These unhappy verses of Lovelace's had been dead and lapt in congenial lead these two hundred years; — what harm had they done Mr. Hazlitt that he should disinter them? There is no such disenchanter of peaceable reputations as one of these resurrection-men of literature, who will not let mediocrities rest in the grave, where the kind sexton, Oblivion, had buried them, but dig them up to make a profit on their lead.

Of all Mr. Smith's editors, Mr. W. Carew Hazlitt is the worst.   He is at times positively incredible, worse even than Mr. Halliwell, and that is saying a good deal. Worthless as Lovelace's poems were, they should have been edited correctly, if edited at all.   Even dulness and dirtiness have a right to fair play and to be dull and dirty in their own fashion.   Mr. Hazlitt has allowed all the misprints of the original (or by far the greater part of them) to stand, but he has ventured on many emendations of the text, and in every important instance has blundered, and that, too, even where the habitual practice of his author in the use of words might have led him right.   The misapprehension shown in some of his notes is beyond the belief of any not familiar with the way in which old books are edited in England by the job.   We have brought a heavy indictment, and we proceed to our proof, choosing only cases where there can be no dispute.   We should premise that Mr. Hazlitt professes to have corrected the punctuation.

> " And though he sees it full of wounds,
>   Cruel one, still he wounds it.   (p. 34.)

Here the original reads, "Cruel still on," and the only correction needed was a comma after "cruel."

> " And by the glorious light
>   Of both those stars, which of their spheres bereft,
>   Only the jelly 's left."   (p. 41.)

The original has "of which," and rightly, for

" their spheres bereft " is parenthetic, and the sense is " of which only the jelly 's left." Lovelace is speaking of the eyes of a mistress who has grown old, and his image, confused as it is, is based on the belief that stars shooting from their spheres fell to the earth as jellies, — a belief, by the way, still to be met with in New England.

Lovelace, describing a cow (and it is one of the few pretty passages in the volume), says, —

> " She was the largest, goodliest beast
> That ever mead or altar blest,
> Round as her udder, and more white
> Than is the Milky-Way in night." (p. 64.)

Mr. Hazlitt changes to " Round was her udder," thus making that white instead of the cow, as Lovelace intended. On the next page we read, —

> "She takes her leave o' th' mournful neat,
> Who. by her toucht. now prizeth her life,
> Worthy alone the hollowed knife."

Compare Chapman (Iliads, xviii. 480) : —

> "Slew all their white fleec'd sheep and *neat*."

The original was " prize their life," and the use of " neat " as a singular in this way is so uncommon, if not unprecedented, and the verse as corrected so halting, that we have no doubt Lovelace so wrote it. Of course " hollowed " should be " hallowed," though the broader pronunciation still lingers in our country pulpits.

> " What need she other bait or charm
> But look ? or angle but her arm ? " (p. 65.)

So the original, which Mr. Hazlitt, missing the sense, has changed to " what hook or angle."

> " Fly Joy on wings of Popinjays
>   To courts of fools *where* as your plays
>   Die laught at and forgot."   (p. 67.)

The original has " there."   Read,—

> " Fly, Joy, on wings of popinjays
>   To courts of fools ; there, as your plays,
>   Die," &c.

" Where as," as then used, would make it the " plays " that were to die.

> " As he Lucasta nam'd, a groan
>   Strangles the fainting passing tone ;
>   But as she heard, Lucasta smiles,
>   Posses her round ; she 's slipt meanwhiles
>   Behind the blind of a thick bush."   (p. 68.)

Mr. Hazlitt's note on " posses " could hardly be matched by any member of the *posse comitatus* taken at random : —

" This word does not appear to have any very exact meaning. See Halliwell's *Dictionary of Archaic Words*, art. *Posse*, and Worcester's Dict., *ibid.*, &c. The context here requires *to turn sharply or quickly*."

The " *ibid.*, &c." is delightful ; in other words, " find out the meaning of *posse* for yourself." Though dark to Mr. Hazlitt, the word has not the least obscurity in it. It is only another form of *push*, nearer the French *pousser*, from Latin *pul-sare*, and " the context here requires " nothing more than that an editor should read a poem if he wish to understand it. The plain meaning is, —

> " But, as she heard *Lucasta*, smiles
>   Possess her round."

That is, when she heard the name *Lucasta*,— for thus far in the poem she has passed under the

pseudonyme of *Amarantha*. " Possess her round "
is awkward, but mildly so for Lovelace, who also
spells " commandress " in the same way with a
single *s*.   *Process* is spelt *prosses* in the report of
those who absented themselves from Church in
Stratford.

> " O thou, that swing'st upon the waving eare,
>   Of some well-filled oaten beard."   (p. 94.)

Mr. Hazlitt, for some inscrutable reason, has
changed " haire " to " eare " in the first line, preferring the ear of a *beard* to its hair !
   Mr. Hazlitt prints, —

> " Poor verdant foole ! and now green ice, thy joys
>   Large and as lasting as thy peirch of grass,
>   Bid us lay in 'gainst winter raine and poize
>   Their flouds with an o'erflowing glasse."   (p. 95.)

Surely we should read : —

> " Poor verdant foole and now green ice, thy joys,
>   Large and as lasting as thy perch of grass,
>   Bid," &c.

i. e. " Poor fool now frozen, the shortness of thy
joys, who mad'st no provision against winter, warns
us to do otherwise."

> " The radiant gemme was brightly set
>   In as divine a carkanet ;
>   Of which the clearer was not knowne
>   Her minde or her complexion."   (p. 101.)

The original reads rightly " for which," &c., and,
the passage being rightly pointed, we have, —

> " For which the clearer was not known,
>   Her mind or her complexion."

Of course " complexion " had not its present limited meaning.

> ". . . my future daring bayes
> Shall bow itself." (p. 107.)

"We should read *themselves*," says Mr. Hazlitt's note authoritatively. Of course a noun ending in *s* is plural! Not so fast. In spite of the dictionaries, *bays* was often used in the singular.

> "Do plant a sprig of cypress, not of bays,"

says Robert Randolph in verses prefixed to his brother's poems; and Felltham in "Jonsonus Virbius,"

> "A greener bays shall crown Ben Jonson's name."

But we will cite Mr. Bayes himself : —

> "And, where he took *it* up, resigns the *bays*."

> "But we (defend us!) are divine,
> [Not] female, but madam born, and come
> From a right-honorable wombe." (p. 115.)

Here Mr. Hazlitt has ruined both sense and metre by his unhappy "not." We should read "Female, but madam-born," meaning clearly enough "we are women, it is true, but of another race."

> "In every hand [let] a cup be found
> That from all hearts a health may sound." (p. 121.)

Wrong again, and the inserted "let" ruinous to the measure. Is it possible that Mr. Hazlitt does not understand so common an English construction as this?

> "First told thee into th' ayre, then to the ground." (p. 141.)

Mr. Hazlitt inserts the "to," which is not in the original, from another version. Lovelace wrote

"aÿer." We have noted two other cases (pp. 203
and 248) where he makes the word a dissyllable.
On the same page we have "shewe's " changed to
"shew " because Mr. Hazlitt did not know it
meant "show us" and not "shows." On page 170,
"their " is substituted for " her," which refers to
Lucasta, and could refer to nothing else.

Mr. Hazlitt changes "quarrels *the* student Mercury" to "quarrels *with*," not knowing that *quarrels* was once used as a transitive verb (p. 189).

Wherever he chances to notice it, Mr. Hazlitt
changes the verb following two or more nouns connected by an "and " from singular to plural. For
instance : —

> "You, sir, alone, fame, and all conquering rhyme
> File the set teeth," &c., (p. 224)

for "files." Lovelace commonly writes so ; — on
p. 181, where it escaped Mr. Hazlitt's grammatical
eye, we find, —

> "But broken faith, and th' canse of it,
> All damning gold, *was* damned to the pit."

Indeed, it was usual with writers of that day.
Milton in one of his sonnets has —

> "Thy worth and skill *exempts* thee from the throng," —

and Leigh Hunt, for the sake of the archaism, in
one of his, " Patience and Gentleness *is* power."

Weariness, and not want of matter, compels us
to desist from further examples of Mr. Hazlitt's
emendations. But we must also give a few specimens of his notes, and of the care with which he
has corrected the punctuation.

In a note on " flutes of canary" (p. 76) too long
to quote, Mr. Hazlitt, after citing the glossary of
Nares (edition of 1859, by Wright and Halliwell,
a very careless book, to speak mildly), in which
flute is conjectured to mean *cask*, says that he is
not satisfied, but adds, " I suspect that a flute *of
canary* was so called from the cask having several
vent-holes." But flute means simply a tall glass.
Lassel, describing the glass-making at Murano,
says, " For the High Dutch they have high glasses
called *Flutes*, a full yard long." So in Dryden's
Sir Martin Mar-all, " bring two flute-*glasses* and
some stools, ho! We'll have the ladies' health."
The origin of the word, though doubtful, is probably nearer to *flood* than *flute*. But conceive of
two gentlemen, members of one knows not how
many learned societies, like Messrs. Wright and
Halliwell, pretending to edit Nares, when they
query a word which they could have found in any
French or German Dictionary!

On page 93 we have, —

> " Hayle, holy cold! chaste temper, hayle! the fire
> Raved o'er my purer thoughts I feel t' expire."

Mr. Hazlitt annotates thus : " *Rav'd* seems here to
be equivalent to *reav'd* or *bereav'd*. Perhaps the
correct reading may be ' reav'd.' See Worcester's
Dictionary, art. RAVE, where Menage's supposition
of affinity between *rave* and *bereave* is perhaps a
little too slightingly treated."

The meaning of Lovelace was, " the fire *that*
raved." But what Mr. Hazlitt would make with

"reaved o'er my purer thoughts," we cannot conceive. On the whole, we think he must have written the note merely to make his surprising glossological suggestion. All that Worcester does for the etymology, by the way, is to cite Richardson, no safe guide.

"Where now one *so so* spatters, t'other: no!" (p. 112..)

The comma in this verse has, of course, no right there, but Mr. Hazlitt leaves the whole passage so corrupt that we cannot spend time in disinfecting it. We quote it only for the sake of his note on "*so so*." It is marvellous.

"An exclamation of approval when an actor made a hit. The corruption seems to be somewhat akin to the Italian, '*si, si*,' a corruption of '*sia, sia*.'"

That the editor of an English poet need not understand Italian we may grant, but that he should not know the meaning of a phrase so common in his own language as *so-so* is intolerable. Lovelace has been saying that a certain play might have gained applause under certain circumstances, but that everybody calls it *so-so*, — something very different from "an exclamation of approval," one should say. The phrase answers exactly to the Italian *così così*, while *sì* (not *si*) is derived from *sic*, and is analogous with the affirmative use of the German *so* and the Yankee *jes' so*.

"Oh, how he hast'ned death, burnt to be fryed!" (p. 141.)

The note on *fryed* is, —

"I. e. freed. *Free* and *freed* were sometimes pronounced like *fry* and *fryed;* for Lord North, in his *Forest of Varieties*, 1645, has these lines : —

> ' Birds that long have lived free,
>   Caught and cag'd, but pine and die.'

Here evidently *free* is intended to rhyme with *die.*"

"Evidently!" An instance of the unsafeness of rhyme as a guide to pronunciation. It was *die* that had the sound of *dee*, as everybody (but Mr. Hazlitt) knows. Lovelace himself rhymes *die* and *she* on p. 269. But what shall we say to our editor's not knowing that *fry* was used formerly where we should say *burn?* Lovers used to *fry* with love, whereas now they have got out of the frying-pan into the fire. In this case a martyr is represented as burning (i. e. longing) to be fried (i. e. burned).

"Her beams ne'er shed or change like th' hair of day." (p. 224.)

Mr. Hazlitt's note is, —

"*Hair* is here used in what has become quite an obsolete sense. The meaning is outward form, nature, or character. The word used to be by no means uncommon; but it is now, as was before remarked, out of fashion ; and indeed I do not think that it is found even in any old writer used exactly in the way in which Lovelace has employed it."

We should think not, as Mr. Hazlitt understands it ! Did he never hear of the golden hair of Apollo, —of the *intonsum Cynthium?* Don Quixote was a better scholar where he speaks of *las doradas hebras de sus hermosos cabellos.* But *hair* never meant what Mr. Hazlitt says it does, even when used as he supposes it to be here. It had nothing to do with " outward form, nature, or character," but had a meaning much nearer what we express by temperament, which its color was and is thought to indicate.

On p. 232 " *wild* ink " is explained to mean " *unrefined.*"   It is a mere misprint for " *vild.*"

Page 237, Mr. Hazlitt, explaining an allusion of Lovelace to the " east and west " in speaking of George Sandys, mentions Sandys's Oriental travels, but seems not to know that he translated Ovid in Virginia.

Pages 251, 252 : —

> " And as that soldier conquest doubted not,
>   Who but one splinter had of Castriot,
>   But would assault ev'n death, so strongly charmed,
>   And naked oppose rocks, with this bone armed."

Mr. Hazlitt reads *his* for *this* in the last verse, and his note on " bone " is : —

> " And he found a new jawbone of an ass, and put forth his hand and took it, and slew a thousand men therewith.   (Judges xv. 15.)"

Could the farce of " editing " go further?   To make a " splinter of Castriot " an ass's jawbone is a little too bad.   We refer Mr. Hazlitt to " The Life of George Castriot, King of Epirus and Albania," &c., &c., (Edinburgh, 1753,) p. 32, for an explanation of this profound difficulty.   He will there find that the Turkish soldiers wore relics of Scanderbeg as charms.

Perhaps Mr. Hazlitt's most astounding note is on the word *pickear* (p. 203).

> "So within shot she doth pickear,
>   Now gall's [galls] the flank and now the rear."

"In the sense in which it is here used this word seems to be peculiar to Lovelace. *To pickear*, or *pickeer*, means *to skirmish*." And, pray, what other possible meaning can it have here?

Of his corrections of the press we will correct a few samples.

Page 34, for "Love *nee're* his standard," read "*neere*." Page 82, for "fall *too*," read "fall *to*" (or, as we ought to print such words, "fall-to"). Page 83, for "star-made firmament," read "star, made firmament." Page 161, for "To look their enemies *in* their hearse," read, both for sense and metre, *into*. Page 176, for "the gods *have* kneeled," read *had*. Page 182, for "In beds they tumbled *off* their own," read *of*. Page 184, for "in mine one monument I lie," read *owne*. Page 212, for "Deucalion's *black*flung stone," read "backflung." Of the punctuation we shall give but one specimen, and that a fair average one : —

> "Naso to his Tibullus flung the wreath,
>   He to Catullus thus did each bequeath.
>   This glorious circle, to another round,
>   At last the temples of a god it bound."

Our readers over ten years of age will easily correct this for themselves.

Time brings to obscure authors [1] an odd kind of reparation, an immortality, not of love and interest and admiration, but of curiosity merely. In pro-

---

[1] *Early Popular Poetry.* Edited by W. Carew Hazlitt.

portion as their language was uncouth, provincial, or even barbarous, their value becomes the greater. A book of which only a single copy escaped its natural enemies, the pastry-cook and trunk-maker, may contain one word that makes daylight in some dark passage of a great author, and its name shall accordingly live forever in a note. Is not, then, a scholiastic athanasy better than none? And if literary vanity survive death, or even worse, as Brunetto Latini's made him insensible for a moment to the rain of fire and the burning sand, the authors of such books as are not properly literature may still comfort themselves with a *non omnis moriar*, laying a mournful emphasis on the adjective, and feeling that they have not lived wholly in vain while they share with the dodo a fragmentary continuance on earth. To be sure, the immortality, such as it is, belongs less to themselves than to the famous men they help to illustrate. If they escape oblivion, it is by a back door, as it were, and they survive only in fine print at the page's foot. At the banquet of fame they sit below the salt. After all, perhaps, the next best thing to being famous or infamous is to be utterly forgotten, for this also is to achieve a kind of definite result by living. To hang on the perilous edge of immortality by the nails, liable at any moment to drop into the fathomless ooze of oblivion, is at best a questionable beatitude. And yet sometimes the merest barnacles that have attached themselves to the stately keels of Dante or Shakespeare or Milton have an interest of their own by letting us know in what remote waters those hardy navigators went a pearl-fishing. Has not Mr. Dyce traced Shakespeare's "dusty death" to Anthony Copley, and Milton's "back resounded Death!" to Abraham Fraunce? Nay, is it not Bernard de Ventadour's lark that sings forever in the diviner air of Dante's Paradise?

> "Quan vey laudeta mover
>   De joi sas alas contra'l rai,
>   Que s'oblida e s laissa cazer
>   Per la doussor qu 'al cor li 'n vai."

> "Qual lodoletta che in aere si spazia,
>   Prima cantando, e poi tace contenta
>   Dell' ultima dolcezza che la sazia."

We are not sure that Bernard's "Que s'oblida e s laissa cazer" is not sweeter than Dante's "tace contenta," but it was plainly the *doussor* that gave its cue to the greater poet's memory, and he has improved on it with that exquisite *ultima*, as his master Virgil sometimes did on Homer.

But authors whose interest for us is mainly bibliographic belong rather in such collections as Mr. Allibone's. As literature they are oppressive; as items of literary history they find their place in that vast list which records not only those named for promotion, but also the killed, wounded, and missing in the Battle of the Books. There our hearts are touched with something of the same vague pathos that dims the eye in some deserted graveyard. The brief span of our earthly immortalities is brought home to us as nowhere else. What a necrology of notability! How many a controversialist, terrible in his day, how many a rising genius that somehow stuck on the horizon, how many a withering satirist, lies here shrunk all away to the tombstone brevity of a name and date! Think of the aspirations, the dreams, the hopes, the toil, the confidence (of himself and wife) in an impartial and generous posterity, — and then read "Smith J. [ohn?] 1713 – 1784 (?). The Vision of Immortality, an Epique Poem in twelve books, 1740, 4to. See *Lowndes*." The time of his own death less certain than that of his poem, (which we may fix pretty safely in 1740,) and the only posterity that took any interest in him the indefatigable compiler to whom a name was valuable in proportion as it was obscure. Well, to have even so much as your title-page read after it has rounded the corner of its first century, and to enjoy a posthumous public of one is better than nothing. This is the true Valhalla of Mediocrity, the *Libro d' oro* of the *onymi-anonymi*, of the never-named authors who exist only in name. Parson Adams would be here had he found a printer for his sermons, and Mr. Primrose, if a copy existed of his tracts on monogamy. Papyrorcetes junior will turn here with justifiable pride to the name of his respectable progenitor. Here we are secure of perpetuity at least, if of nothing better, and are sons, though we may not be heirs, of fame. Here is a handy and inexpensive substitute for the waxen *imagines* of the Roman patriciate, for those must have been inconvenient to pack on a change of lodgings, liable to melt in warm weather (even the elder Brutus himself might soften in the dog-days) and not readily

salable unless to some *novus homo* willing to buy a
set of ancestors ready-made, as some of our own
enthusiasts in genealogy are said to order a family-
tree from the heraldic nurseryman, skilled to imp a
slip of Scroggins on a stock of De Vere or Mont-
morenci. Fame, it should seem, like electricity, is
both positive and negative, and if a writer must be
Somebody to make himself of permanent interest to
the world at large, he must not less be Nobody to
have his namelessness embalmed by M. Guérard.
The benignity of Providence is nowhere more
clearly to be seen than in its compensations. As
there is a large class of men madly desirous to
decipher cuneiform and other inscriptions, simply
because of their illegibility, so there is another
class driven by a like irresistible instinct to the
reprinting of unreadable books. Whether these
have even a philologic value for us depends on the
accuracy and learning bestowed upon them by the
editor.

For there is scarcely any rubbish-heap of literature out of which something precious may not be
raked by the diligent explorer, and the late Mr.
Dyce (since Gifford, the best editor of our literature of the Tudor and Jacobean periods) might
well be called the Golden Dustman, so many were
the precious trifles sifted out by his intelligent industry. It would not be easy to name any work
more thoroughly done than his edition of Skelton.
He was not a philologist in the stricter sense, but
no man had such a commonplace-book as he, or
knew so exactly the meaning with which words

were used during the period he did so much to illustrate. Elegant scholarship is not often, as in him, patient of drudgery and conscientious in pains-taking. Between such a man and Mr. Carew Hazlitt the contrast is by no means agreeable. The one was not more distinguished by modest accuracy than the other is by the rash conceit of that half-knowledge which is more mischievous in an editor than downright ignorance. This language is strong because it is true, though we should not have felt called upon to use it but for the vulgar flippancy with which Mr. Hazlitt alludes depreciatingly to the labors of his predecessors, — to such men as Ritson, Utterson, Wright, and Sir Frederick Madden, his superiors in everything that goes to the making of a good editor. Most of them are now dead and nailed in their chests, and it is not for us to forget the great debt we owe to them, and others like them, who first opened paths for us through the tangled wilderness of our early literature. A modern editor, with his ready-made helps of glossary, annotation, and comment, should think rather of the difficulties than the defects of these pioneers.

How different is Mr. Hazlitt's spirit from that of the thorough and therefore modest scholar! In the Preface to his *Altenglische Sprachproben*, Mätzner says of an editor, *das Beste was er ist verdankt er Andern*, an accidental pentameter that might seem to have dropped out of *Nathan der Weise*. Mr. Hazlitt would profit much by getting some friend to translate for him the whole paragraph in which it occurs.

We see it announced that Mr. Hazlitt is to
superintend a new edition of Warton's History of
English Poetry, and are pained to think of the
treatment that robust scholar and genial poet is
likely to receive at the hands of an editor without
taste, discrimination, or learning. Of his taste a
single specimen may suffice. He tells us that "in
an artistic and constructive point of view, the
Mylner of Abington is superior to its predecessor," that predecessor being Chaucer's *Reve's Tale*,
which, with his usual inaccuracy, he assigns to the
Miller! Of his discrimination we have a sufficient
test in the verses he has fathered upon Herrick in a
late edition of the most graceful of our lyric poets.
Perhaps discrimination is not, after all, the right
word, for we have sometimes seen cause to doubt
whether Mr. Hazlitt ever reads carefully the very
documents he prints. For example, in the Biographical Notice prefixed to the Herrick he says
(p. xvii): "Mr. W. Perry Herrick has plausibly
suggested that the payments made by Sir William
to his nephew were simply on account of the fortune which belonged to Robert in right of his father,
and which his uncle held in trust; this was about
£400; and I think from allusions in the letters
printed elsewhere that this view may be the correct
one." *May* be! The poet says expressly, "I en-
treat you out of *my little possession* to deliver to
this bearer the *customarye* £10, without which I
cannot meate [?] my ioyrney." The words we
have italicized are conclusive. By the way, Mr.
Hazlitt's wise-looking query after "meate" is con-

clusive also as to his fitness for editorship. Did he never hear of the familiar phrase "to *meet* the expense"? If so trifling a misspelling can mystify him, what must be the condition of his mind in face of the more than Protean travesties which words underwent before they were uniformed by Johnson and Walker? Mr. Hazlitt's mind, to be sure, like the wind Cecias, always finds its own fog. In another of Herrick's letters we find, "For what her monie can be effected (*sic*) when there is diuision 'twixt the hart and hand?" "Her monie" of course means *harmonie*, and *effected* is therefore right. What Mr. Hazlitt may have meant by his "(*sic*)" it were idle to inquire.

We have already had occasion to examine some of Mr. Hazlitt's work, and we are sorry to say that in the four volumes before us we find no reason for changing our opinion of his utter disqualification for the duties of editorship. He seldom clears up a real difficulty (never, we might say, with lights of his own), he frequently creates a darkness where none was before, and the peculiar *bumptiousness* of his incapacity makes it particularly offensive. We shall bring a few instances in proof of what we assert, our only embarrassment being in the superabundance of our material. In the Introduction to the second volume of his collection, Mr. Hazlitt speaks of "the utter want of common care on the part of previous editors of our old poetry." Such oversights as he has remarked upon in his notes are commonly errors of the press, a point on which Mr. Hazlitt, of all men, should have been charitable, for his own volumes are full of them. We call his attention to one such which is rather amusing. In his "additional notes" we find "line 77, *wylle.* Strike out the note upon this word; but the explanation is correct. *Be wroght* was a misprint, however, for *he wroght.*" The error occurs in a citation of three lines in which *lother* is still left for *tother.* The original note affords us so good an example of Mr. Hazlitt's style of editing as to be worth preserving. In the "Kyng and the Hermit" we read, —

> " He ne wyst w[h]ere that he was
> Ne out of the forest for to passe,
> And thus he rode all wylle."

And here is Mr. Hazlitt's annotation on the word *wylle* : —

" *i. e.* evil. In a MS. of the *Tale of the Basyn,* supposed by Mr. Wright, who edited it in 1836, to be written in the Salopian dialect, are the following lines : —

> ' The lother hade litull thoght,
> Off husbandry cowth he noght,
> But alle his wyves *will* be wroght.' "   (Vol. i. p. 16.)

It is plain that he supposed *will,* in this very simple passage, to mean *evil !* This he would seem to rectify, but at the same time takes care to tell us that " the explanation [of *wylle*] is correct." He is willing to give up one blunder, if only he may have one left to comfort himself withal! *Wylle* is simply a rhyming fetch for *wild,* and the passage means that the king rode at random. The use of *wild* with this meaning is still common in such phrases as "he struck wild." In "Havelok" we find it in the nearly related sense of *being at a loss, knowing not what to do:*—

> "To lincolne barfot he yede
>   Hwan he kam ther he was ful *wil*,
>   Ne hauede he no frend to gangen til."

All wylle, in short, means the kind of editing that is likely to be done by a gentleman who picks up his misinformation as he goes along. We would hint that a person must know *something* before he can use even a glossary with safety.

In the "King and the Barker," when the tanner finds out that it is the king whom he has been treating so familiarly, and falls upon his knees, Mr. Hazlitt prints,

> "He had no meynde of hes hode, nor cape, ne radell,"

and subjoins the following note: "Radell, or raddle, signifies a side of a cart; but here, apparently, stands for the cart itself. Ritson printed *ner adell*." Mr. Hazlitt's explanation of *raddle*, which he got from Halliwell, is incorrect. The word, as its derivation (from O. F. *rastel*) implies, means the side or end of a *hay*-cart, in which the uprights are set like the teeth of a rake. But what has a cart to do here? There is perhaps a touch of what an editor of old doggerel would benignantly call humor, in the tanner's forgetfulness of his raiment, but the cart is as little to the purpose as one of Mr. Hazlitt's own notes. The tanner was on horseback, as the roads of the period required that he

should be, and good old Ritson was plainly on the
right track in his reading, though his text was
muddled by a misprint. As it was, he got *one*
word right, and so far has the advantage of Mr.
Hazlitt. The true reading is, of course, *ner a dell*,
never a deal, not a whit. The very phrase occurs
in another poem which Mr. Hazlitt has reprinted
in his collection, —

> "For *never a dell*
> He wyll me love agayne."   (Vol. iii. p. 2.)

That *adell* was a misprint in Ritson is proved by
the fact that the word does not appear in his glossary. If we were to bring Mr. Hazlitt to book for
his misprints! In the poem we have just quoted
he gravely prints, —

> "Matter in dede,
> My sides did blede,"

for " mother, indede," " through ryght wysenes "
for " though ryghtwisenes," " with man vnkynde "
for " sith man vnkynde," " ye knowe a parte " for
" ye knowe aperte," " here in " for " herein," all of
which make nonsense, and all come within the first
one hundred and fifty lines, and those of the shortest, mostly of four syllables each. Perhaps they
rather prove ignorance than want of care. One
blunder falling within the same limits we have reserved for special comment, because it affords a
good example of Mr. Hazlitt's style of editing : —

> "Your herte souerayne
> Clouen in twayne
> By longes the blynde."   (Vol. iii. p. 7.)

Here the uninstructed reader would be as completely in the dark as to what *longes* meant as the editor plainly was himself. The old rhymer no doubt wrote Longis, meaning thereby Longinus, a personage familiar enough, one should think, to any reader of mediæval poetry. Mr. Hazlitt absolves himself for not having supplied a glossary by the plea that none is needed by the class of readers for whom his volumes are intended. But this will hardly seem a valid excuse for a gentleman who often goes out of his way to explain in his notes such simple matters as that "shape" means "form," and that "Johan of the golden mouthe" means "St. Chrysostom," which, indeed, it does not, any more than Johannes Baptista means St. Baptist. We will supply Mr. Hazlitt with an illustration of the passage from Bekker's *Ferabras*, the more willingly as it may direct his attention to a shining example of how an old poem should be edited : —

> " en la crotz vos pendero li fals Iuzieu trnan,
> can Longis vos feric de sa lansa trencan :
> el non avia vist en trastot son vivan ;
> lo sanc li venc per l'asta entro al punh colan ;
> e [el] toquet ne sos huelhs si vic el mantenan."

Mr. Hazlitt, to be sure (who prints *sang parlez* for *sanz parler*) (vol. i. p. 265), will not be able to form any notion of what these verses mean, but perhaps he will be able to draw an inference from the capital L that *longes* is a proper name. The word *truan* at the end of the first verse of our citation may also suggest to him that *truant* is not

quite so satisfactory an explanation of the word
trewāt as he seems to think.   (Vol. iv. p. 24, *note.*)
In deference to Mr. Hazlitt's presumed familiarity
with an author sometimes quoted by him in his
notes, we will point him to another illustration : —

> " Ac ther cam forth a knyght,
>   With a kene spere y-grounde
>   Highte Longeus, as the lettre telleth,
>   And longe hadde lore his sighte."
>
> *Piers Ploughman*, Wright, p. 374.

Mr. Hazlitt shows to peculiar advantage where
Old French is in question.   Upon the word *Osyll*
he favors us with the following note : " The blackbird.   In East Cornwall *ozell* is used to signify the
windpipe, and thence the bird may have had its
name, as Mr. Couch has suggested to me."   (Vol.
ii. p. 25.)   Of course the blackbird, alone among
fowls, is distinguished by a windpipe!   The name
is merely another form of O. F. *oisil*, and was
usurped naturally enough by one of the commonest
birds, just as *pajaro* (L. *passer*) in Spanish, by a
similar process in the opposite direction, came to
mean bird in general.   On the very next page he
speaks of " the Romance which is vulgarly entitled
Lybeaus Disconus, i. e. *Le Beau Disconnu.*"   If
he had corrected *Disconus* to *Desconus,* all had
been well ; but *Disconnu* neither is nor ever was
French at all.   Where there is blundering to be
done, one stone often serves Mr. Hazlitt for two
birds.   *Ly beaus Disconus* is perfectly correct old
French, and another form of the adjective (*bius*)
perhaps explains the sound we give to the first syl-

lable of *beauty* and *Beaufort*.   A barrister at law,
as Mr. Hazlitt is, may not be called on to know
anything about old English or modern French, but
we might fairly expect him to have at least a smat-
tering of Law French!   In volume fourth, page
129, a goodman trying his wife,

> " Bad her take the pot that sod ouer the fire
> And set it abooue vpon the astire."

Mr. Hazlitt's note upon *astire* is " hearth, i. q.
astre."   Knowing that the modern French was
âtre, he too rashly inferred a form which never existed except in Italian.   The old French word is
aistre or *estre*, but Mr. Hazlitt, as usual, prefers
something that is neither old French nor new.   We
do not pretend to know what *astire* means, but a
hearth that should be *abooue* the pot seething over
the fire would be uuusual, to say the least, in our
semi-civilized country.

In the " Lyfe of Roberte the Deuill " (vol. i. p.
232), Mr. Hazlitt twice makes a knight *sentre* his
lance, and tells us in a note that the " Ed. 1798
has *fentered*," a very easy misprint for the right
word *feutered*.   What Mr. Hazlitt supposed to be
the meaning of *sentre* he has not vouchsafed to tell
us.   *Fautre* (sometimes *faltre* or *feutre*) means in
old French the *rest* of a lance.   Thus in the *Roman
du Renart* (26517),

> " Et mist sa lance sor le *fautre*."

But it also meant a peculiar *kind* of rest.   In Sir
F. Madden's edition of *Gawayne* (to which Mr.
Hazlitt refers occasionally) we read,

> " They *feutred* their lances, these knyghtes good " ;

and in the same editor's " William and the Wer-
wolf,"

> " With sper festened in *feuter*, him for to spille."

In a note on the latter passage Sir F. Madden says,
" There seems no reason, however, why it [feuter]
should not mean the rest attached to the armour."
But Roquefort was certainly right in calling it a
" garniture d'une selle pour tenir la lance."   A
spear fastened to the saddle gave more deadly
weight to the blow.   The " *him for to spille* " implies this.   So in " Merlin " (E. E. Text Soc., p.
488) : " Than thei toke speres grete and rude, and
putte hem in fewtre, and that is the grettest crew-
elte that oon may do, ffor turnement oweth to be
with-oute felonye, and they meved to smyte hem as
in mortall werre."   The context shows that the
fewtre turned sport into earnest.   A citation in
Raynouard's *Lexique Roman* (though wrongly explained by him) directed us to a passage which
proves that this particular kind of rest for the
lance was attached to the saddle, in order to ren-
der the blow heavier : —

> " Lances à [lege *as*] arçons afeutrées
>   *Pour plus de dures colées rendre.*"
>   *Branche des Royaux Lignages*, 4514, 4515.

Mr. Hazlitt, as we have said, lets no occasion slip
to insinuate the inaccuracy and carelessness of his
predecessors.   The long and useful career of Mr.
Wright, who, if he had given us nothing more than
his excellent edition of " Piers Ploughman " and
the volume of " Ancient Vocabularies," would

have deserved the gratitude of all lovers of our literature or students of our language, does not save him from the severe justice of Mr. Hazlitt, nor is the name of Warton too venerable to be coupled with a derogatory innuendo. Mr. Wright needs no plea in abatement from us, and a mischance of Mr. Hazlitt's own has comically avenged Warton. The word *prayer*, it seems, had somehow substituted itself for *prayse* in a citation by Warton of the title of the " Schole-House of Women." Mr. Hazlitt thereupon takes occasion to charge him with often " speaking at random," and after suggesting that it might have been the blunder of a copyist, adds, " or it is by no means impossible that Warton himself, having been allowed to inspect the production, was guilty of this oversight." (Vol. iv. p. 98.) Now, on the three hundred and eighteenth page of the same volume, Mr. Hazlitt has allowed the following couplet to escape his conscientious attention :

> " Next, that no gallant should not ought suppose
>   That *prayers* and glory doth consist in cloathes."

Lege, nostro periculo, PRAYSE ! Were dear old Tom still on earth, he might light his pipe cheerfully with any one of Mr. Hazlitt's pages, secure that in so doing he was consuming a brace of blunders at the least. The word *prayer* is an unlucky one for Mr. Hazlitt. In the " Knyght and his Wyfe " (vol. ii. p. 18) he prints : —

> " And sayd, Syre, I rede we make
>   In this chapel oure prayers,
>   That God us kepe both in ferrus."

Why did not Mr. Hazlitt, who explains so many

things that everybody knows, give us a note upon *in ferrus?* It would have matched his admirable elucidation of *waygose,* which we shall notice presently. Is it not barely possible that the MS. may have read *prayere* and *in fere? Prayere* occurs two verses further on, and not as a rhyme.

Mr. Hazlitt even sets Sir Frederick Madden right on a question of Old English grammar, telling him superciliously that *can,* with an infinitive, in such phrases as *he can go,* is used not " to denote a *past* tense, but an *imperfect* tense." By *past* we suppose him to mean *perfect.* But even if an imperfect tense were not a past one, we can show by a passage in one of the poems in this very collection that *can,* in the phrases referred to, sometimes not only denotes a past but a perfect tense : —

> " And thorow that worde y felle in pryde;
> As the aungelle can of hevyn glyde,
> And with the tywnkling [1] of an eye
> God for-dud alle that maystrye
> And so hath he done for my gylte."

Now the angel here is Lucifer, and *can of hevyn glyde* means simply *fell from heaven,* not *was falling.* It is in the same tense as *for-dud* in the next line. The fall of the angels is surely a *fait accompli.* In the last line, by the way, Mr. Hazlitt changes " my for " to " for my," and wrongly, the *my* agreeing with *maystrye* understood. In modern English we should use *mine* in the same way. But Sir Frederick Madden can take care of himself.

[1] The careless Ritson would have printed this *twynkling.*

We have less patience with Mr. Hazlitt's impertinence to Ritson, a man of ample reading and excellent taste in selection, and who, real scholar as he was, always drew from original sources. We have a *foible* for Ritson with his oddities of spelling, his acerb humor, his unconsciously depreciatory mister Tyrwhitts and mister Bryants, and his obstinate disbelief in Doctor Percy's folio manuscript. Above all, he was a most conscientious editor, and an accurate one so far as was possible with the lights of that day. Mr. Hazlitt has reprinted two poems, " The Squyr of Low Degre " and " The Knight of Curtesy," which had already been edited by Ritson. The former of these has passages that are unsurpassed in simple beauty by anything in our earlier poetry. The author of it was a good versifier, and Ritson, though he corrected some glaring errors, did not deal so trenchantly with verses manifestly lamed by the copyist as perhaps an editor should.[1] Mr. Hazlitt says of Ritson's text, that " it offers more than *an hundred* departures from the original," and of the " Knight of Courtesy," that " Ritson's text is by no means accurate." Now Mr. Hazlitt has adopted nearly all of Ritson's emendations, without giving the least hint of it. On the contrary, in some five or six instances, he gives the original reading in a foot-note with an " old ed. has " so and so, thus leaving the reader to

---

[1] For example : —

> " And in the arber was a tre
> A fairer in the world might none be,"

should certainly read,

> " None fairer in the world might be."

infer that the corrections were his own. Where
he has not followed Ritson, he has almost uniformly
blundered, and that through sheer ignorance. For
example, he prints,

> " Alas ! it tourned to *wroth her heyle*,"

where Ritson had substituted *wrotherheyle*. The
measure shows that Ritson was right. *Wroth her
heyle*, moreover, is nonsense. It should have been
wrother her heyle at any rate, but the text is far
too modern to admit of that archaic form. In the
" Debate of the Body and the Soul " (Mätzner's
A. E. Sprachproben, 103) we have,

> " Why schope thou me to wrother-hele,"

and in " Dame Siris " (Ibid., 110),

> " To goder hele ever came thou hider."

Mr. Hazlitt prints,

> " For yf it may be found in thee
> That thou them [de] fame for enuyte."

The emendation [de] is Ritson's, and is probably
right, though it would require, for the metre's sake,
the elision of *that* at the beginning of the verse.
But what is *enuyte?* Ritson reads *enmyte*, which
is, of course, the true reading. Mr. Hazlitt prints
(as usual either without apprehending or without
regarding the sense),

> " With browes *bent* and eyes full mery,"

where Ritson has *brent*, and gives parallel passages
in his note on the word. Mr. Hazlitt gives us

> " To here the bugles there yblow,
> With their *bugles* in that place,"

though Ritson had made the proper correction to *begles*. Mr. Hazlitt, with ludicrous *nonchalance*, allows the Squire to press into the throng

"With a bastard large and longe,"

and that with the right word (*baslarde*) staring him in the face from Ritson's text. We wonder he did not give us an illustrative quotation from Falconbridge! Both editors have allowed some gross errors to escape, such as "come *not*" for "come" (v. 425); "so leue *he* be" for "ye be" (v. 593); "vnto *her* chambre" for "vnto your" (v. 993); but in general Ritson's is the better and more intelligent text of the two. In the "Knight of Curtesy," Mr. Hazlitt has followed Ritson's text almost *literatim*. Indeed, it is demonstrable that he gave it to his printers as *copy* to set up from. The proof is this: Ritson has accented a few words ending in *tè*. Generally he uses the grave accent, but now and then the acute. Mr. Hazlitt's text follows all these variations exactly. The main difference between the two is that Ritson prints the first personal pronoun *i*, and Mr. Hazlitt, I. Ritson is probably right; for in the "Schole-House of Women" (vv. 537, 538) where the text no doubt was

"i [i. e. one] deuil a woman to speak may constrain,
But all that in hel be cannot let it again,"

Mr. Hazlitt changes "i" to "A," and says in a note, "Old ed. has *I*." That by his correction he should miss the point was only natural; for he evidently conceives that the *sense* of a passage does not in the least concern an editor. An instance or

two will suffice.   In the " Knyght and his Wyfe "
(vol. ii. p. 17) we read,

> " The fynd tyl hure hade myche tene
> As hit was a sterfull we seme ! "

Mr. Hazlitt in a note explains *tene* to mean " trouble or sorrow " ; but if that were its meaning here,
we should read *made*, and not *hade*, which would
give to the word its other sense of *attention*.   The
last verse of the couplet Mr. Hazlitt seems to
think perfectly intelligible as it stands.   We should
not be surprised to learn that he looked upon it as
the one gem that gave lustre to a poem otherwise
of the dreariest.   We fear we shall rob it of all
its charm for him by putting it into modern English : —

> " As it was after full well seen."

So in the "Smyth and his Dame" (vol. iii. p.
204) we read,

> " It were a lytele maystry
> To make a blynde man to se,"

instead of " *as* lytell."   It might, indeed, be as
easy to perform the miracle on a blind man as on
Mr. Hazlitt.   Again, in the same poem, a little
further on,

> " For I tell the now trevely,
> Is none so wyse ne *to* sle,
> But ever *ye* may som what lere,"

which, of course, should be,

> " ne *so* sle
> But ever *he* may som what lere."

Worse than all, Mr. Hazlitt tells us (vol. i. p. 158)

that when they bury the great Khan, they lay his body in a tabernacle,

> "With sheld and spere and other wede
> With a whit mere to gyf him in ylke."

We will let Sir John Maundeville correct the last verse : "And they seyn that when he shale come into another World . . . the mare schalle *gheven him mylk.*" Mr. Hazlitt gives us some wretched doggerel by "Piers of Fulham," and gives it swarming with blunders. We take at random a couple of specimens : —

> "And loveship goith ay to warke
> Where that presence is put a bake,"
>
> (Vol. ii. pp. 13, 14,)

where we should read "love's ship," "wrake," and "abake." Again, just below,

> "Ffor men haue seyn here to foryn,
> That love laugbet when men be forsworn."

Love should be "Iove." Ovid is the obscure person alluded to in the "men here to foryn" :

> "Jupiter e cœlo perjuria ridet amantum."

We dare say Mr. Hazlitt, if he ever read the passage, took it for granted that "to foryn" meant *too foreign*, and gave it up in despair. But surely Shakespeare's

> "At lovers' perjuries,
> They say, Jove laughs,"

is not too foreign to have put him on the right scent.

Mr. Hazlitt is so particular in giving us *v* for *u*

and *vice versa*, that such oversights are a little annoying. Every man his own editor seems to be his theory of the way in which old poetry should be reprinted. On this plan, the more riddles you leave (or make) for the reader to solve, the more pleasure you give him. To correct the blunders in any book edited by Mr. Hazlitt would give the young student a pretty thorough training in archaic English. In this sense the volumes before us might be safely recommended to colleges and schools. When Mr. Hazlitt undertakes to correct, he is pretty sure to go wrong. For example, in "Doctour Doubble Ale" (vol. iii. p. 309) he amends thus : —

> "And sometyme mikle strife is
> Among the ale wyfes, [y-wis] ; "

where the original is right as it stands. Just before, in the same poem, we have a parallel instance : —

> "And doctours dulpatis
> That falsely to them pratis,
> And bring them to the gates."

The original probably reads (or should read) *wyfis* and *gatis*. But it is too much to expect of Mr. Hazlitt that he should remember the very poems he is editing from one page to another, nay, as we shall presently show, that he should even read them. He will change *be* into *ben* where he should have let it alone (though his own volumes might have furnished him with such examples as "were go," "have se," "is do," and fifty more), but he will sternly retain *bene* where the rhyme requires *be*, and Ritson had so printed. In "Adam Bel" the word *pryme* occurs (vol. ii. p. 140), and he vouchsafes us the following note: "i. e. noon. It is commonly used by early writers in this sense. In the *Four* P. P., by John Heywood, circa 1540, the apothecary says,

> 'If he taste this boxe nye aboute the pryme
> By the masse, he is in heven or even songe tyme.' "

Let our readers admire with us the easy "it is commonly used" of Mr. Hazlitt, as if he had store of other examples in his note-book. He could an if he would! But unhappily he borrowed this single quotation from Nares, and, as usual, it throws no scintilla of light upon the point in question, for his habit in annotation is to find by means of a glossary some passage (or passages if possible) in which the word to be explained occurs, and then — why, then to give the word as an explanation of itself. But in this instance, Mr Hazlitt, by the time he had reached the middle of his next volume (vol. iii. p. 281) had wholly forgotten that *pryme* was "commonly used by early writers" for *noon*, and in a note on the following passage,

> "I know not whates a clocke
> But by the countre cocke,
> The mone nor yet the pryme,
> Vntyll the sonne do shyne,"

he informs us that it means "six o'clock in the morning"! Here again this editor, who taxes Ritson with want of care, prints *mone* for *none* in the very verse he is annotating, and which we may therefore presume that he had read.   A man who did not know the moon till the sun showed it him is a match even for Mr. Hazlitt himself. We wish it were as easy as he seems to think it to settle exactly what *pryme* means when used by our " early writers," but it is at least absolutely certain that it did not mean *noon*.

But Mr. Hazlitt, if these volumes are competent witnesses, knows nothing whatever about English, old or new.   In the " Mery Jest of Dane Hew " he finds the following verses,

> " Dame he said what shall we now doo
> Sir she said so mote go
> The munk in a corner ye shall lay "

which we print purposely without punctuation.   Mr. Hazlitt prints them thus,

> " Dame, he said, what shall we now doo ?
> Sir, she said, so mote [it] go.
> The munk," &c.,

and gives us a note on the locution he has invented to this effect, "? so might it be managed." And the Chancellor said, *I doubt!*   Mr. Hazlitt's query makes such a singular exception to his more natural mood of immediate inspiration that it is almost pathetic.   The amended verse, as everybody (not confused by too great familiarity with our " early writers ") knows, should read,

> " Sir, she said, so might I go,"

and should be followed only by a comma, to show its connection with the next.   The phrase "so mote I go," is as common as a weed in the

works of the elder poets, both French and English; it occurs several times in Mr. Hazlitt's own
collection, and its other form, "so mote I fare,"
which may also be found there, explains its meaning. On the phrase *point-device* (vol. iii. p. 117)
Mr. Hazlitt has a positively incredible note, of
which we copy only a part: " This term, which is
commonly used in early poems " [mark once more
his intimacy with our earlier literature] "to signify extreme exactitude, originated in the points
which were marked on the astrolabe, as one of the
means which the astrologers and dabblers in the
black art adopted to enable them (as they pre-
tended) to read the fortunes of those by whom they
were consulted in the stars and planetary orbs.
The excessive precision which was held to be requisite in the delineation of these points " [the
delineation of a *point* is good!] " &c. on the astrolabe, led to *point-device*, or points-device (as it is
sometimes found spelled), being used as a proverbial expression for minute accuracy of any kind."
Then follows a quotation from Gower, in which an
astrolabe is spoken of " with points and cercles
merveilous," and the note proceeds thus: " Shakespeare makes use of a similar figure of speech in
the *Tempest*, I. 2, where the following dialogue
takes place between Prospero and Ariel: —

<blockquote>
' *Prosp.* Hast thou, spirit,
Performed *to point* the tempest that I bade thee ?
Ar. In every article.' "
</blockquote>

Neither the proposed etymology nor the illustration requires any remark from us. We will only

say that *point-device* is excellently explained and illustrated by Wedgwood.

We will give a few more examples out of many to show Mr. Hazlitt's utter unfitness for the task he has undertaken. In the " Kyng and the Hermyt " are the following verses,

> " A wyld wey, I hold, it were
>   The wey to wend, I you swere,
>   Bot ye the dey may se,"

meaning simply, " I think it would be a wild thing (in you) to go on your way unless you wait for daylight." Mr. Hazlitt punctuates and amends thus : —

> " A wyld wey I hold it were,
>   The wey to wend, I you swere,
>   Ye bot [by] the dey may se."   (Vol. i. p. 19.)

The word *bot* seems a stumbling-block to Mr. Hazlitt. On page 54 of the same volume we have,

> " Herd I neuere bi no leuedi
>   *Hote* hendinesse and curteysi."

The use of the word *by* as in this passage should seem familiar enough, and yet in the " Hye Way to the Spittel Hous " Mr. Hazlitt explains it as meaning *be.* Any boy knows that *without* sometimes means *unless* (Fielding uses it often in that sense), but Mr. Hazlitt seems unaware of the fact. In his first volume (p. 224) he gravely prints : —

> " They trowed verelye that she shoulde dye ;
>   *With that* our ladye wold her helpe and spede."

The semicolon after *dye* shows that this is not a misprint, but that the editor saw no connection between the first verse and the second. In the same volume (p. 133) we have the verse,

" He was a grete tenement man, and ryche of londe and lede,"

and to *lede* Mr. Hazlitt appends this note : " *Lede*, in early English, is found in various significations, but here stands as the plural of *lad*, a servant." In what conceivable sense is it the plural of *lad ?* And does *lad* necessarily mean a servant? The *Promptorium* has *ladde* glossed by *garcio*, but the meaning *servant*, as in the parallel cases of παῖς, *puer*, *garçon*, and *boy*, was a derivative one, and of later origin. The word means simply *man* (in the generic sense) and in the plural *people*. So in the " Squyr of Low Degre,"

" I will forsake both land and *lede*,"

and in the " Smyth and his Dame,"

" That hath both land and *lyth*."

The word was *not* " used in various significations." Even so lately as " Flodden Ffeild " we find,

" He was a noble *leed* of high degree."

Connected with *land* it was a commonplace in German as well as in English. So in the *Tristan* of Godfrey of Strasburg,

„Er bevalch sin liut unde sin lant
Un sines marscalles hant."

Mr. Hazlitt is more nearly right than usual when he says that in the particular case cited above *lede* means *servants*. But were these of only one sex? Does he not know that even in the middle of the last century when an English nobleman spoke of " my people," he meant simply his domestics ?

Encountering the familiar phrase *No do!* (vol.
iv. p. 64), Mr. Hazlitt changes it to *Not do!* He
informs us that *Goddes are* (vol. i. p. 197) means
"God's heir"! He says (vol. ii. p. 146): "*To borrow* in the sense of *to take, to guard,* or *to protect,*
is so common in early English that it is unnecessary to bring forward any illustration of its use in
this way." But he relents, and presently gives us
two from *Ralph Roister Doister,* each containing
the phrase "Saint George to borrow!" That *borrow* means *take,* no owner of books need be told,
and Mr. Hazlitt has shown great skill in *borrow-
ing* other people's illustrations for his notes, but
the phrase he quotes has no such meaning as he
gives it. Mr. Dyce in a note on Skelton explains
it rightly, "St. George being my pledge or surety."

We gather a few more of these flowers of expo-
sition and etymology : —

"The while thou sittest in chirche, thi bedys schalt thou bidde."
(Vol. i. p. 181.)

i. e. thou shalt offer thy prayers. Mr. Hazlitt's
note on *bidde* is, "i. e. *bead.* So in *The Kyng and
the Hermit,* line 111 : —

'That herd an hermyte there within
Unto the gate he gan to wyn
Bedying his prayer.' "

Precisely what Mr. Hazlitt understands by *beading*
(or indeed by anything else) we shall not presume
to divine, but we *should* like to hear him translate
"if any man bidde the worshyp," which comes a
few lines further on. Now let us turn to page 191
of the same volume. "Maydenys ben loncliche and

no thing sekir." Mr. Hazlitt tells us in a note that "sekir or sicker" is a very common form of *secure*, and quotes in illustration from the prose *Morte Arthure*, " A ! said Sir Launcelot, comfort your-selfe, for it shall bee unto us as a great honour, and much more then if we died in any other places : for of death wee be *sicker*." Now in the text the word means *safe*, and in the note it means *sure*. Indeed *sure*, which is only a shorter form of *secure*, is its ordinary meaning. " I mak sicker," said Kirkpatrick, a not unfitting motto for certain editors, if they explained it in their usual phonetic way.

In the " Frere and the Boye," when the old man has given the boy a bow, he says : —

> " Shote therin, whan thou good thynke ;
> For yf thou shote and wynke,
> The prycke thow shalte hytte."

Mr. Hazlitt's explanation of *wynke* is " to close one eye in taking aim," and he quotes a passage from Gascoigne in support of it. Whatever Gascoigne meant by the word (which is very doubt-ful), it means nothing of the kind here, and is another proof that Mr. Hazlitt does not think it so important to understand what he reads as St. Philip did. What the old man said was, " even if you shut both your eyes, you can't help hitting the mark." So in " Piers Ploughman " (Whitaker's text),

> " Wynkyng, as it were, wytterly ich saw hyt."

Again, for our editor's blunders are as endless as

the heads of an old-fashioned sermon, in the
"Schole-House of Women" (vol. iv. p. 130), Mr.
Hazlitt has a note on the phrase "make it nice,"

> ("And yet alwaies they bible bable
> Of euery matter and make it nice,")

which reads thus: "To make it pleasant or *snug*.
I do not remember to have seen the word used in
this sense very frequently. But Gascoigne has it
in a precisely similar way : —

> 'The glosse of gorgeous Courtes by thee did please mine eye,
>   A stately sight me thought it was to see the braue go by,
>   To see their feathers flaunte, to make [marke!] their straunge
>   deuise,
>   To lie along in ladies lappes, to lispe, and make it nice.'"

To *make it nice* means nothing more nor less
than to *play the fool*, or rather, to *make a fool of
yourself, faire le niais*. In old English the French
niais and *nice*, from similarity of form and analogy
of meaning, naturally fused together in the word
nice, which, by an unusual luck, has been promoted
from a derogatory to a respectful sense. Gascoigne's *lispe* might have put Mr. Hazlitt on his
guard, if he ever considered the sense of what he
quotes. But he never does, nor of what he edits
either. For example, in the "Smyth and his
Dame" we find the following note : "*Prowe*, or
proffe, is not at all uncommon as a form of *profit*.
In the 'Seven Names of a Prison,' a poem printed
in *Reliquiæ Antiquæ*, we have, —

> 'Quintum nomen istius foveæ ita probatum,
>   A place of *proff* for man to know bothe frend and foo.'"

Now *proff* and *prow* are radically different words. *Proff* here means *proof*, and if Mr. Hazlitt had read the stanza which he quotes, he would have found (as in all the others of the same poem) the meaning repeated in Latin in the last line, *proba-cio amicorum.*

But we wish to leave our readers (if not Mr. Hazlitt) in good humor, and accordingly we have reserved two of his notes as *bonnes bouches.* In " Adam Bel," when the outlaws ask pardon of the king,

> " They kneeled downe without lettyng
> And each helde vp his hande."

To this passage (tolerably plain to those not *too* familiar with " our early literature ") Mr. Hazlitt appends this solemn note : "*To hold up the hand* was formerly a sign of respect or concurrence, or a mode of taking an oath ; and thirdly as a signal for mercy. In all these senses it has been employed from the most ancient times ; nor is it yet out of practice, as many savage nations still testify their respect to a superior by holding their hand [either *their hands* or *the hand*, Mr. Hazlitt!] over their head. *Touching the hat* appears to be a vestige of the same custom. In the present passage the three outlaws may be understood to kneel on approaching the throne, and to hold up each a hand as a token that they desire to ask the royal clemency or favour. In the lines which are subjoined it [what?] implies a solemn assent to an oath :

> ' This swore the duke and all his men,
>   And all the lordes that with him lend,
>   And tharto to[1] held they up thaire hand.' "
>
> Minot's Poems, ed. 1825, p. 9.

The admirable Tupper could not have done better than this, even so far as the mere English of it is concerned. Where all is so fine, we hesitate to declare a preference, but, on the whole, must give in to the passage about *touching the hat*, which is as good as " mobbled queen." The Americans are still among the " savage nations " who " imply a solemn assent to an oath " by holding up the hand. Mr. Hazlitt does not seem to know that the question whether to kiss the book or hold up the hand was once a serious one in English politics.

But Mr. Hazlitt can do better even than this! Our readers may be incredulous; but we shall proceed to show that he can. In the " Schole-House of Women," among much other equally delicate satire of the other sex, (if we may venture still to call them so,) the satirist undertakes to prove that woman was made, not of the rib of a man, but of a dog : —

> " And yet the rib, as I suppose,
>   That God did take out of the man
>   A dog vp caught, and a way gose
>   Eat it clene; so that as than
>   The woork to finish that God began
>   Could not be, as we haue said,
>   Because the dog the rib conuaid.

---

[1] The *to* is, we need not say, an addition of Mr. Hazlitt's. What faith can we put in the text of a man who so often copies even his quotations inaccurately ?

> A remedy God found as yet;
> Out of the dog he took a rib."

Mr. Hazlitt has a long note on *way gose*, of which the first sentence shall suffice us: " The origin of the term way-goose is involved in some obscurity." We should think so, to be sure! Let us modernize the spelling and grammar, and correct the punctuation, and then see how it looks : —

> " A dog up caught and away goes,
> Eats it up."

We will ask Mr. Hazlitt to compare the text, as he prints it, with

> "Into the hall he gose."   (Vol. iii. p. 67.)

We should have expected a note here on the " hall he-goose." Not to speak of the point of the joke, such as it is, a goose that could eat up a man's rib could only be matched by one that could swallow such a note, — or write it!

We have made but a small florilegium from Mr. Hazlitt's remarkable volumes. His editorial method seems to have been to print as the Lord would, till his eye was caught by some word he did not understand, and then to make the reader comfortable by a note showing that the editor is as much in the dark as he. We are profoundly thankful for the omission of a glossary. It would have been a nursery and seminary of blunder. To expose pretentious charlatanry is sometimes the unpleasant duty of a reviewer. It is a duty we never seek, and should not have assumed in this case but for the impertinence with which Mr. Hazlitt has treated dead and living scholars, the latchets of whose shoes he is not worthy to unloose, and to express their gratitude to whom is, or ought to be, a pleasure to all honest lovers of their mother-tongue. If he who has most to learn be the happiest man, Mr. Hazlitt is indeed to be envied; but we hope he will learn a great deal before he lays his prentice hands on Warton's "History of English Poetry," a classic in its own way. If he does not learn before, he will be likely to learn after, and in no agreeable fashion.

EMERSON THE LECTURER

1861–68

It is a singular fact, that Mr. Emerson is the most steadily attractive lecturer in America. Into that somewhat cold-waterish region adventurers of the sensational kind come down now and then with a splash, to become disregarded King Logs before the next season. But Mr. Emerson always draws. A lecturer now for something like a third of a century, one of the pioneers of the lecturing system, the charm of his voice, his manner, and his matter has never lost its power over his earlier hearers, and continually winds new ones in its enchanting meshes. What they do not fully understand they take on trust, and listen, saying to themselves, as the old poet of Sir Philip Sidney, —

> "A sweet, attractive, kind of grace,
>   A full assurance given by looks,
>   Continual comfort in a face,
>   The lineaments of gospel books."

We call it a singular fact, because we Yankees are thought to be fond of the spread-eagle style, and nothing can be more remote from that than his. We are reckoned a practical folk, who would rather hear about a new air-tight stove than about Plato; yet our favorite teacher's practicality is not

in the least of the Poor Richard variety. If he
have any Buncombe constituency, it is that unreal-
ized commonwealth of philosophers which Plotinus
proposed to establish; and if he were to make an
almanac, his directions to farmers would be something like this: "October: *Indian Summer;*
now is the time to get in your early Vedas."
What, then, is his secret? Is it not that he out-
Yankees us all? that his range includes us all?
that he is equally at home with the potato-disease
and original sin, with pegging shoes and the Over-
soul? that, as we try all trades, so has he tried all
cultures? and above all, that his mysticism gives
us a counterpoise to our super-practicality?

There is no man living to whom, as a writer,
so many of us feel and thankfully acknowledge
so great an indebtedness for ennobling impulses,
— none whom so many cannot abide. What does
he mean? ask these last. Where is his system?
What is the use of it all? What the deuse have
we to do with Brahma? I do not propose to write
an essay on Emerson at this time. I will only say
that one may find grandeur and consolation in a
starlit night without caring to ask what it means,
save grandeur and consolation; one may like Montaigne, as some ten generations before us have
done, without thinking him so systematic as some
more eminently tedious (or shall we say tediously
eminent?) authors; one may think roses as good
in their way as cabbages, though the latter would
make a better show in the witness-box, if cross-
examined as to their usefulness; and as for Brahma,

why, he can take care of himself, and won't bite us at any rate.

The bother with Mr. Emerson is, that, though he writes in prose, he is essentially a poet. If you undertake to paraphrase what he says, and to reduce it to words of one syllable for infant minds, you will make as sad work of it as the good monk with his analysis of Homer in the " Epistolæ Obscurorum Virorum." We look upon him as one of the few men of genius whom our age has pro duced, and there needs no better proof of it than his masculine faculty of fecundating other minds. Search for his eloquence in his books and you will perchance miss it, but meanwhile you will find that it has kindled all your thoughts. For choice and pith of language he belongs to a better age than ours, and might rub shoulders with Fuller and Browne, — though he does use that abominable word *reliable*. His eye for a fine, telling phrase that will carry true is like that of a backwoodsman for a rifle; and he will dredge you up a choice word from the mud of Cotton Mather himself. A diction at once so rich and so homely as his I know not where to match in these days of writing by the page; it is like homespun cloth-of-gold. The many cannot miss his meaning, and only the few can find it. It is the open secret of all true genius. It is wholesome to angle in those profound pools, though one be rewarded with nothing more than the leap of a fish that flashes his freckled side in the sun and as suddenly absconds in the dark and dreamy waters again. There is keen excitement, though there be no ponderable acquisition. If we carry nothing home in our baskets, there is ample gain in dilated lungs and stimulated blood. What does he mean, quotha? He means inspiring hints, a divining-rod to your deeper nature. No doubt, Emerson, like all original men, has his peculiar audience, and yet I know none that can hold a promiscuous crowd in pleased attention so long as he. As in all original men, there is something for every palate. "Would you know," says Goethe, "the ripest cherries? Ask the boys and the blackbirds."

The announcement that such a pleasure as a new course of lectures by him is coming, to people as old as I am, is something like those forebodings of spring that prepare us every year for a familiar novelty, none the less novel, when it arrives, because it is familiar. We know perfectly well what we are to expect from Mr. Emerson, and yet what he says always penetrates and stirs us, as is apt to be the case with genius, in a very unlooked-for fashion. Perhaps genius is one of the few things which we gladly allow to repeat itself, — one of the few that multiply rather than weaken the force of their impression by iteration? Perhaps some of us hear more than the mere words, are moved by something deeper than the thoughts? If it be so, we are quite right, for it is thirty years and more of "plain living and high thinking" that speak to us in this altogether unique lay-preacher. We have shared in the beneficence of this varied culture, this fearless impartiality in criticism and speculation, this masculine sincerity, this sweetness of nature which rather stimulates than cloys, for a generation long. If ever there was a standing testimonial to the cumulative power and value of Character, (and we need it sadly in these days,) we have it in this gracious and dignified presence. What an antiseptic is a pure life! At sixty-five (or two years beyond his grand climacteric, as he would prefer to call it) he has that privilege of soul which abolishes the calendar, and presents him to us always the unwasted contemporary of his own prime. I do not know if he seem old to his younger hearers, but we who have known him so long wonder at the tenacity with which he maintains himself even in the outposts of youth. I suppose it is not the Emerson of 1868 to whom we listen. For us the whole life of the man is distilled in the clear drop of every sentence, and behind each word we divine the force of a noble character, the weight of a large capital of thinking and being. We do not go to hear what Emerson says so much as to hear Emerson. Not that we perceive any falling-off in anything that ever was essential to the charm of Mr. Emerson's peculiar style of thought or phrase. The first lecture, to be sure, was more disjointed even than common. It was as if, after vainly trying to get his paragraphs into sequence and order, he had at last tried the desperate expedient of *shuffling* them. It was chaos come again, but it was a chaos full of shooting-stars, a jumble of creative forces. The second lecture, on " Criticism and Poetry," was quite up to the level of old times, full of that power of strangely-subtle association whose indirect approaches startle the mind into almost painful attention, of those flashes of mutual understanding between speaker and hearer that are gone ere one can say it lightens. The vice of Emerson's criticism seems to be, that while no man is so sensitive to what is poetical, few men are less sensible than he of what makes a poem. He values the solid meaning of thought above the subtler meaning of style. He would prefer Donne, I suspect, to Spenser, and sometimes mistakes the queer for the original.

To be young is surely the best, if the most precarious, gift of life; yet there are some of us who would hardly consent to be young again, if it were at the cost of our recollection of Mr. Emerson's first lectures during the consulate of Van Buren. We used to walk in from the country to the Masonic Temple (I think it was), through the crisp winter night, and listen to that thrilling voice of his, so charged with subtle meaning and subtle music, as shipwrecked men on a raft to the hail of a ship that came with unhoped-for food and rescue. Cynics might say what they liked. Did our own imaginations transfigure dry remainder-biscuit into ambrosia? At any rate, he brought us *life*, which, on the whole, is no bad thing. Was it all transcendentalism? magic-lantern pictures on mist? As you will. Those, then, were just what we wanted. But it was not so. The delight and the benefit were that he put us in communication with a larger style of thought, sharpened our wits with a more

pungent phrase, gave us ravishing glimpses of an
ideal under the dry husk of our New England;
made us conscious of the supreme and everlasting
originality of whatever bit of soul might be in any
of us; freed us, in short, from the stocks of prose
in which we had sat so long that we had grown
wellnigh contented in our cramps. And who that
saw the audience will ever forget it, where every
one still capable of fire, or longing to renew in himself the half-forgotten sense of it, was gathered?
Those faces, young and old, agleam with pale intellectual light, eager with pleased attention, flash
upon me once more from the deep recesses of the
years with an exquisite pathos. Ah, beautiful
young eyes, brimming with love and hope, wholly
vanished now in that other world we call the Past,
or peering doubtfully through the pensive gloam-
ing of memory, your light impoverishes these
cheaper days! I hear again that rustle of sensation, as they turned to exchange glances over some
pithier thought, some keener flash of that humor
which always played about the horizon of his mind
like heat-lightning, and it seems now like the sad
whisper of the autumn leaves that are whirling
around me. But would my picture be complete if
I forgot that ample and vegete countenance of
Mr. R—— of W——, — how, from its regular
post at the corner of the front bench, it turned in
ruddy triumph to the profaner audience as if he
were the inexplicably appointed fugleman of appreciation? I was reminded of him by those hearty
cherubs in Titian's Assumption that look at you as

who should say, " Did you ever see a Madonna like
that?   Did you ever behold one hundred and fifty
pounds of womanhood mount heavenward before
like a rocket ? "

To some of us that long-past experience remains
as the most marvellous and fruitful we have ever
had.   Emerson awakened us, saved us from the
body of this death.   It is the sound of the trumpet
that the young soul longs for, careless what breath
may fill it.   Sidney heard it in the ballad of
" Chevy Chase," and we in Emerson.   Nor did it
blow retreat, but called to us with assurance of victory.   Did they say he was disconnected ? So were
the stars, that seemed larger to our eyes, still keen
with that excitement, as we walked homeward with
prouder stride over the creaking snow.   And were
they not knit together by a higher logic than our
mere sense could master?   Were we enthusiasts?
I hope and believe we were, and am thankful to the
man who made us worth something for once in our
lives.   If asked what was left? what we carried
home? we should not have been careful for an
answer.   It would have been enough if we had said
that something beautiful had passed that way.   Or
we might have asked in return what one brought
away from a symphony of Beethoven?   Enough
that he had set that ferment of wholesome discon-
tent at work in us.   There is one, at least, of those
old hearers, so many of whom are now in the frui-
tion of that intellectual beauty of which Emerson
gave them both the desire and the foretaste, who
will always love to repeat : —

> "Che in la mente m'è fitta, ed or m'accuora
> La cara e buona immagine paterna
> Di voi, quando nel mondo ad ora ad ora
> M'insegnavaste come l'uom s'eterna."

I am unconsciously thinking, as I write, of the third lecture of the present course, in which Mr. Emerson gave some delightful reminiscences of the intellectual influences in whose movement he had shared. It was like hearing Goethe read some passages of the " Wahrheit aus seinem Leben." Not that there was not a little *Dichtung*, too, here and there, as the lecturer built up so lofty a pedestal under certain figures as to lift them into a prominence of obscurity, and seem to masthead them there. Everybody was asking his neighbor who this or that recondite great man was, in the faint hope that somebody might once have heard of him. There are those who call Mr. Emerson cold. Let them revise their judgment in presence of this loyalty of his that can keep warm for half a century, that never forgets a friendship, or fails to pay even a fancied obligation to the uttermost farthing. This substantiation of shadows was but incidental, and pleasantly characteristic of the man to those who know and love him. The greater part of the lecture was devoted to reminiscences of things substantial in themselves. He spoke of Everett, fresh from Greece and Germany ; of Channing ; of the translations of Margaret Fuller, Ripley, and Dwight ; of the Dial and Brook Farm. To what he said of the latter an undertone of good-humored irony gave special zest. But what every one of his hearers felt was that the protagonist in the drama was left out. The lecturer was no Æneas to babble the *quorum magna pars fui*, and, as one of his listeners, I cannot help wishing to say how each of them was commenting the story as it went along, and filling up the necessary gaps in it from his own private store of memories. His younger hearers could not know how much they owed to the benign impersonality, the quiet scorn of everything ignoble, the never-sated hunger of self-culture, that were personified in the man before them. But the older knew how much the country's intellectual emancipation was due to the stimulus of his teaching and example, how constantly he had kept burning the beacon of an ideal life above our lower region of turmoil. To him more than to all other causes together did the young martyrs of our civil war owe the sustaining strength of thoughtful heroism that is so touching in every record of their lives. Those who are grateful to Mr. Emerson, as many of us are, for what they feel to be most valuable in their culture, or perhaps I should say their impulse, are grateful not so much for any direct teachings of his as for that inspiring lift which only genius can give, and without which all doctrine is chaff.

This was something like the *caret* which some of us older boys wished to fill up on the margin of the master's lecture. Few men have been so much to so many, and through so large a range of aptitudes and temperaments, and this simply because all of us value manhood beyond any or all other qualities

of character. We may suspect in him, here and
there, a certain thinness and vagueness of quality,
but let the waters go over him as they list, this
masculine fibre of his will keep its lively color and
its toughness of texture. I have heard some great
speakers and some accomplished orators, but never
any that so moved and persuaded men as he. There
is a kind of undertow in that rich baritone of his
that sweeps our minds from their foothold into
deeper waters with a drift we cannot and would not
resist. And how artfully (for Emerson is a long-
studied artist in these things) does the deliberate ut-
terance, that seems waiting for the fit word, appear
to admit us partners in the labor of thought and
make us feel as if the glance of humor were a sudden suggestion, as if the perfect phrase lying written
there on the desk were as unexpected to him as to
us ! In that closely-filed speech of his at the Burns
centenary dinner, every word seemed to have just
dropped down to him from the clouds. He looked
far away over the heads of his hearers, with a
vague kind of expectation, as into some private
heaven of invention, and the winged period came
at last obedient to his spell. " My dainty Ariel ! "
he seemed murmuring to himself as he cast down
his eyes as if in deprecation of the frenzy of approval and caught another sentence from the Sibyl-
line leaves that lay before him, ambushed behind a
dish of fruit and seen only by nearest neighbors.
Every sentence brought down the house, as I never
saw one brought down before, — and it is not so
easy to hit Scotsmen with a sentiment that has no

hint of native brogue in it. I watched, for it was an interesting study, how the quick sympathy ran flashing from face to face down the long tables, like an electric spark thrilling as it went, and then exploded in a thunder of plaudits. I watched till tables and faces vanished, for I, too, found myself caught up in the common enthusiasm, and my excited fancy set me under the *bema* listening to him who fulmined over Greece. I can never help applying to him what Ben Jonson said of Bacon: "There happened in my time one noble speaker, who was full of gravity in his speaking. His language was nobly censorious. No man ever spake more neatly, more pressly, more weightily, or suffered less emptiness, less idleness, in what he uttered. No member of his speech but consisted of his own graces. His hearers could not cough, or look aside from him, without loss. He commanded where he spoke." Those who heard him while their natures were yet plastic, and their mental nerves trembled under the slightest breath of divine air, will never cease to feel and say : —

> " Was never eye did see that face,
>   Was never ear did hear that tongue,
>   Was never mind did mind his grace,
>   That ever thought the travail long ;
>   But eyes, and ears, and every thought,
>   Were with his sweet perfections caught."

THOREAU

1865

W HAT contemporary, if he was in the fighting
period of his life, (since Nature sets limits about
her conscription for spiritual fields, as the state
does in physical warfare,) will ever forget what
was somewhat vaguely called the " Transcendental
Movement " of thirty years ago? Apparently set
astir by Carlyle's essays on the " Signs of the
Times," and on " History," the final and more immediate impulse seemed to be given by " Sartor
Resartus."   At least the republication in Boston of
that wonderful Abraham à Sancta Clara sermon on
Falstaff's text of the miserable forked radish gave
the signal for a sudden mental and moral mutiny.
Ecce nunc tempus acceptabile! was shouted on all
hands with every variety of emphasis, and by
voices of every conceivable pitch, representing the
three sexes of men, women, and Lady Mary Wort-
ley Montagues. The nameless eagle of the tree
Ygdrasil was about to sit at last, and wild-eyed enthusiasts rushed from all sides, each eager to thrust
under the mystic bird that chalk egg from which
the new and fairer Creation was to be hatched in
due time. *Redeunt Saturnia regna,* — so far was
certain, though in what shape, or by what meth-

ods, was still a matter of debate. Every possible form of intellectual and physical dyspepsia brought forth its gospel. Bran had its prophets, and the presartorial simplicity of Adam its martyrs, tailored impromptu from the tar-pot by incensed neighbors, and sent forth to illustrate the " feathered Mercury," as defined by Webster and Worcester. Plainness of speech was carried to a pitch that would have taken away the breath of George Fox; and even swearing had its evangelists, who answered a simple inquiry after their health with an elaborate ingenuity of imprecation that might have been honorably mentioned by Marlborough in general orders. Everybody had a mission (with a capital M) to attend to everybody-else's business. No brain but had its private maggot, which must have found pitiably short commons sometimes. Not a few impecunious zealots abjured the use of money (unless earned by other people), professing to live on the internal revenues of the spirit. Some had an assurance of instant millennium so soon as hooks and eyes should be substituted for buttons. Communities were established where everything was to be common but common-sense. Men renounced their old gods, and hesitated only whether to bestow their furloughed allegiance on Thor or Budh. Conventions were held for every hitherto inconceivable purpose. The belated gift of tongues, as among the Fifth Monarchy men, spread like a contagion, rendering its victims incomprehensible to all Christian men ; whether equally so to the most distant possible heathen or not was unexperi-

mented, though many would have subscribed liberally that a fair trial might be made. It was the
pentecost of Shinar. The day of utterances repro-
duced the day of rebuses and anagrams, and there
was nothing so simple that uncial letters and the
style of Diphilus the Labyrinth could not turn it
into a riddle. Many foreign revolutionists out of
work added to the general misunderstanding their
contribution of broken English in every most ingenious form of fracture. All stood ready at a
moment's notice to reform everything but themselves. The general motto was : —

> " And we 'll *talk* with them, too,
> And take upon 's the mystery of things
> As if we were God's spies."

Nature is always kind enough to give even her
clouds a humorous lining. I have barely hinted
at the comic side of the affair, for the material was
endless. This was the whistle and trailing fuse
of the shell, but there was a very solid and serious
kernel, full of the most deadly explosiveness.
Thoughtful men divined it, but the generality suspected nothing. The word " transcendental " then
was the maid of all work for those who could not
think, as " Pre-Raphaelite " has been more recently
for people of the same limited housekeeping. The
truth is, that there was a much nearer metaphysical relation and a much more distant æsthetic and
literary relation between Carlyle and the Apostles
of the Newness, as they were called in New England, than has commonly been supposed. Both
represented the reaction and revolt against *Philis-*

terei, a renewal of the old battle begun in modern times by Erasmus and Reuchlin, and continued by Lessing, Goethe, and, in a far narrower sense, by Heine in Germany, and of which Fielding, Sterne, and Wordsworth in different ways have been the leaders in England. It was simply a struggle for fresh air, in which, if the windows could not be opened, there was danger that panes would be broken, though painted with images of saints and martyrs. Light, colored by these reverend effigies, was none the more respirable for being picturesque. There is only one thing better than tradition, and that is the original and eternal life out of which all tradition takes its rise. It was this life which the reformers demanded, with more or less clearness of consciousness and expression, life in politics, life in literature, life in religion. Of what use to import a gospel from Judæa, if we leave behind the soul that made it possible, the God who keeps it forever real and present? Surely Abana and Pharpar *are* better than Jordan, if a living faith be mixed with those waters and none with these.

Scotch Presbyterianism as a motive of spiritual progress was dead; New England Puritanism was in like manner dead; in other words, Protestantism had made its fortune and no longer protested ; but till Carlyle spoke out in the Old World and Emerson in the New, no one had dared to proclaim, *Le roi est mort : vive le roi !* The meaning of which proclamation was essentially this : the vital spirit has long since departed out of this form once so kingly, and the great seal has been in commission long enough; but meanwhile the soul of man, from which all power emanates and to which it reverts, still survives in undiminished royalty; God still survives, little as you gentlemen of the Commission seem to be aware of it, — nay, will possibly outlive the whole of you, incredible as it may appear. The truth is, that both Scotch Presbyterianism and New England Puritanism made their new avatar in Carlyle and Emerson, the heralds of their formal decease, and the tendency of the one toward Authority and of the other toward Independency might have been prophesied by whoever had studied history. The necessity was not so much in the men as in the principles they represented and the traditions which overruled them. The Puritanism of the past found its unwilling poet in Hawthorne, the rarest creative imagination of the century, the rarest in some ideal respects since Shakespeare; but the Puritanism that cannot die, the Puritanism that made New England what it is, and is destined to make America what it should be, found its voice in Emerson. Though holding himself aloof from all active partnership in movements of reform, he has been the sleeping partner who has supplied a great part of their capital.

The artistic range of Emerson is narrow, as every well-read critic must feel at once; and so is that of Æschylus, so is that of Dante, so is that of Montaigne, so is that of Schiller, so is that of nearly every one except Shakespeare; but there is a gauge of height no less than of breadth, of

individuality as well as of comprehensiveness, and,
above all, there is the standard of genetic power,
the test of the masculine as distinguished from
the receptive minds. There are staminate plants
in literature, that make no fine show of fruit, but
without whose pollen, quintessence of fructifying
gold, the garden had been barren. Emerson's
mind is emphatically one of these, and there is
no man to whom our æsthetic culture owes so
much. The Puritan revolt had made us ecclesi-
astically and the Revolution politically independent, but we were still socially and intellectually
moored to English thought, till Emerson cut the
cable and gave us a chance at the dangers and
the glories of blue water. No man young enough
to have felt it can forget or cease to be grateful for the mental and moral *nudge* which he
received from the writings of his high-minded and
brave-spirited countryman. That we agree with
him, or that he always agrees with himself, is
aside from the question; but that he arouses in
us something that we are the better for having
awakened, whether that something be of opposi-
tion or assent, that he speaks always to what is
highest and least selfish in us, few Americans of
the generation younger than his own would be
disposed to deny. His oration before the Phi
Beta Kappa Society at Cambridge, some thirty
years ago, was an event without any former parallel in our literary annals, a scene to be always
treasured in the memory for its picturesqueness
and its inspiration. What crowded and breathless

aisles, what windows clustering with eager heads, what enthusiasm of approval, what grim silence of foregone dissent! It was our Yankee version of a lecture by Abelard, our Harvard parallel to the last public appearances of Schelling.

I said that the Transcendental Movement was the protestant spirit of Puritanism seeking a new outlet and an escape from forms and creeds which compressed rather than expressed it. In its motives, its preaching, and its results, it differed radically from the doctrine of Carlyle. The Scotchman, with all his genius, and his humor gigantesque as that of Rabelais, has grown shriller and shriller with years, degenerating sometimes into a common scold, and emptying very unsavory vials of wrath on the head of the sturdy British Socrates of worldly common-sense. The teaching of Emerson tended much more exclusively to self-culture and the independent development of the individual man. It seemed to many almost Pythagorean in its voluntary seclusion from commonwealth affairs. Both Carlyle and Emerson were disciples of Goethe, but Emerson in a far truer sense; and while the one, from his bias toward the eccentric, has degenerated more and more into mannerism, the other has clarified steadily toward perfection of style, — exquisite fineness of material, unobtrusive lowness of tone and simplicity of fashion, the most high-bred garb of expression. Whatever may be said of his thought, nothing can be finer than the delicious limpidness of his phrase. If it was ever questionable whether de-

mocracy could develop a gentleman, the problem
has been affirmatively solved at last. Carlyle, in
his cynicism and his admiration of force in and
for itself, has become at last positively inhuman;
·Emerson, reverencing strength, seeking the highest
outcome of the individual, has found that society
and politics are also main elements in the attain-
ment of the desired end, and has drawn steadily
manward and worldward. The two men represent
respectively those grand personifications in the
drama of Æschylus, Βία and Κράτος.

Among the pistillate plants kindled to fruitage
by the Emersonian pollen, Thoreau is thus far
the most remarkable; and it is something eminently fitting that his posthumous works should
be offered us by Emerson, for they are straw-
berries from his own garden. A singular mixture of varieties, indeed, there is; — alpine, some
of them, with the flavor of rare mountain air;
others wood, tasting of sunny roadside banks or
shy openings in the forest; and not a few seed-
lings swollen hugely by culture, but lacking the
fine natural aroma of the more modest kinds.
Strange books these are of his, and interesting
in many ways, — instructive chiefly as showing
how considerable a crop may be raised on a comparatively narrow close of mind, and how much
a man may make of his life if he will assiduously
follow it, though perhaps never truly finding it
at last.

I have just been renewing my recollection of
Mr. Thoreau's writings, and have read through his

six volumes in the order of their production. I
shall try to give an adequate report of their impression upon me both as critic and as mere reader.
He seems to me to have been a man with so high
a conceit of himself that he accepted without ques-
tioning, and insisted on our accepting, his defects
and weaknesses of character as virtues and powers
peculiar to himself. Was he indolent, he finds
none of the activities which attract or employ
the rest of mankind worthy of him. Was he
wanting in the qualities that make success, it is
success that is contemptible, and not himself that
lacks persistency and purpose. Was he poor,
money was an unmixed evil. Did his life seem a
selfish one, he condemns doing good as one of the
weakest of superstitions. To be of use was with
him the most killing bait of the wily tempter Uselessness. He had no faculty of generalization from
outside of himself, or at least no experience which
would supply the material of such, and he makes
his own whim the law, his own range the horizon of the universe. He condemns a world, the
hollowness of whose satisfactions he had never
had the means of testing, and we recognize Ape-
mantus behind the mask of Timon. He had little
active imagination ; of the receptive he had much.
His appreciation is of the highest quality ; his critical power, from want of continuity of mind, very
limited and inadequate. He somewhere cites a
simile from Ossian, as an example of the superiority of the old poetry to the new, though, even
were the historic evidence less convincing, the sen-

timental melancholy of those poems should be conclusive of their modernness. He had none' of the
artistic mastery which controls a great work to
the serene balance of completeness, but exquisite
mechanical skill in the shaping of sentences and
paragraphs, or (more rarely) short bits of verse
for the expression of a detached thought, sentiment, or image. His works give one the feeling of
a sky full of stars, — something impressive and
exhilarating certainly, something high overhead
and freckled thickly with spots of isolated bright-
ness ; but whether these have any mutual relation with each other, or have any concern with
our mundane matters, is for the most part matter of conjecture, — astrology as yet, and not as-
tronomy.

It is curious, considering what Thoreau afterwards became, that he was not by nature an ob-
server. He only saw the things he looked for,
and was less poet than naturalist. Till he built
his Walden shanty, he did not know that the hick-
ory grew in Concord. Till he went to Maine, he
had never seen phosphorescent wood, a phenomenon
early familiar to most country boys. At forty he
speaks of the seeding of the pine as a new discovery, though one should have thought that its gold-
dust of blowing pollen might have earlier drawn
his eye. Neither his attention nor his genius was
of the spontaneous kind. He discovered nothing.
He thought everything a discovery of his own,
from moonlight to the planting of acorns and nuts
by squirrels. This is a defect in his character,

but one of his chief charms as a writer. Everything grows fresh under his hand. He delved in his mind and nature; he planted them with all manner of native and foreign seeds, and reaped assiduously. He was not merely solitary, he would be isolated, and succeeded at last in almost persuading himself that he was autochthonous. He valued everything in proportion as he fancied it to be exclusively his own. He complains in " Walden " that there is no one in Concord with whom he could talk of Oriental literature, though the man was living within two miles of his hut who had introduced him to it. This intellectual selfishness becomes sometimes almost painful in reading him. He lacked that generosity of " communication " which Johnson admired in Burke. De Quincey tells us that Wordsworth was impatient when any one else spoke of mountains, as if he had a peculiar property in them. And we can readily understand why it should be so: no one is satisfied with another's appreciation of his mistress. But Thoreau seems to have prized a lofty way of thinking (often we should be inclined to call it a remote one) not so much because it was good in itself as because he wished few to share it with him. It seems now and then as if he did not seek to lure others up " above our lower region of turmoil," but to leave his own name cut on the mountain peak as the first climber. This itch of originality infects his thought and style. To be misty is not to be mystic. He turns commonplaces end for end, and fancies it makes something new of them.

As we walk down Park Street, our eye is caught by Dr. Winship's dumb-bells, one of which bears an inscription testifying that it is the heaviest ever put up at arm's length by any athlete; and in reading Mr. Thoreau's books we cannot help feeling as if he sometimes invited our attention to a particular sophism or parodox as the biggest yet maintained by any single writer. He seeks, at all risks, for perversity of thought, and revives the age of *concetti* while he fancies himself going back to a pre-classical nature. "A day," he says, "passed in the society of those Greek sages, such as described in the Banquet of Xenophon, would not be comparable with the dry wit of decayed cranberry-vines and the fresh Attic salt of the moss-beds." It is not so much the True that he loves as the Out-of-the-Way. As the Brazen Age shows itself in other men by exaggeration of phrase, so in him by extravagance of statement. He wishes always to trump your suit and to *ruff* when you least expect it. Do you love Nature because she is beautiful? He will find a better argument in her ugliness. Are you tired of the artificial man? He instantly dresses you up an ideal in a Penobscot Indian, and attributes to this creature of his otherwise-mindedness as peculiarities things that are common to all woodsmen, white or red, and this simply because he has not studied the pale-faced variety.

This notion of an absolute originality, as if one could have a patent-right in it, is an absurdity. A man cannot escape in thought, any more than he can in language, from the past and the present. As no one ever invents a word, and yet language somehow grows by general contribution and necessity, so it is with thought. Mr. Thoreau seems to me to insist in public on going back to flint and steel, when there is a match-box in his pocket which he knows very well how to use at a pinch. Originality consists in power of digesting and assimilating thoughts, so that they become part of our life and substance. Montaigne, for example, is one of the most original of authors, though he helped himself to ideas in every direction. But they turn to blood and coloring in his style, and give a freshness of complexion that is forever charming. In Thoreau much seems yet to be foreign and unassimilated, showing itself in symptoms of indigestion. A preacher-up of Nature, we now and then detect under the surly and stoic garb something of the sophist and the sentimentalizer. I am far from implying that this was conscious on his part. But it is much easier for a man to impose on himself when he measures only with himself. A greater familiarity with ordinary men would have done Thoreau good, by showing him how many fine qualities are common to the race. The radical vice of his theory of life was that he confounded physical with spiritual remoteness from men. A man is far enough withdrawn from his fellows if he keep himself clear of their weaknesses. He is not so truly withdrawn as exiled, if he refuse to share in their strength. "Solitude," says Cowley, "can be well fitted and set right but upon a very few persons. They must have enough knowledge of the world to see the vanity of it, and enough virtue to despise all vanity." It is a morbid self-consciousness that pronounces the world of men empty and worthless before trying it, the instinctive evasion of one who is sensible of some innate weakness, and retorts the accusation of it before any has made it but himself. To a healthy mind, the world is a constant challenge of opportunity. Mr. Thoreau had not a healthy mind, or he would not have been so fond of prescribing. His whole life was a search for the doctor. The old mystics had a wiser sense of what the world was worth. They ordained a severe apprenticeship to law, and even ceremonial, in order to the gaining of freedom and mastery over these. Seven years of service for Rachel were to be rewarded at last with Leah. Seven other years of faithfulness with her were to win them at last the true bride of their souls. Active Life was with them the only path to the Contemplative.

Thoreau had no humor, and this implies that he was a sorry logician. Himself an artist in rhetoric, he confounds thought with style when he undertakes to speak of the latter. He was forever talking of getting away from the world, but he must be always near enough to it, nay, to the Concord corner of it, to feel the impression he makes there. He verifies the shrewd remark of Sainte-Beuve, "On touche encore à son temps et très-fort, même quand on le repousse." This egotism of his is a Stylites pillar after all, a seclusion which keeps him in the public eye. The dignity of man is an excellent thing, but therefore to hold one's self too sacred and precious is the reverse of excellent. There is something delightfully absurd in six volumes addressed to a world of such " vulgar fellows " as Thoreau affirmed his fellowmen to be. I once had a glimpse of a genuine solitary who spent his winters one hundred and fifty miles beyond all human communication, and there dwelt with his rifle as his only confidant. Compared with this, the shanty on Walden Pond has something the air, it must be confessed, of the Hermitage of La Chevrette. I do not believe that the way to a true cosmopolitanism carries one into the woods or the society of musquashes. Perhaps the narrowest provincialism is that of Self ; that of Kleinwinkel is nothing to it. The natural man, like the singing birds, comes out of the forest as inevitably as the natural bear and the wildcat stick there. To seek to be natural implies a consciousness that forbids all naturalness forever. It is as easy — and no easier — to be natural in a *salon* as in a swamp, if one do not aim at it, for what we call unnaturalness always has its spring in a man's thinking too much about himself. " It is impossible," said Turgot, "for a vulgar man to be simple."

I look upon a great deal of the modern sentimentalism about Nature as a mark of disease. It is one more symptom of the general liver-complaint. To a man of wholesome constitution the wilderness is well enough for a mood er a vacation, but not

for a habit of life. Those who have most loudly
advertised their passion for seclusion and their
intimacy with nature, from Petrarch down, have
been mostly sentimentalists, unreal men, misan-
thropes on the spindle side, solacing an uneasy suspicion of themselves by professing contempt for
their kind. They make demands on the world in
advance proportioned to their inward measure of
their own merit, and are angry that the world pays
only by the visible measure of performance. It is
true of Rousseau, the modern founder of the sect,
true of Saint Pierre, his intellectual child, and of
Châteaubriand, his grandchild, the inventor, we
might almost say, of the primitive forest, and who
first was touched by the solemn falling of a tree
from natural decay in the windless silence of the
woods. It is a very shallow view that affirms trees
and rocks to be healthy, and cannot see that men
in communities are just as true to the laws of their
organization and destiny; that can tolerate the
puffin and the fox, but not the fool and the knave;
that would shun politics because of its dema-
gogues, and snuff up the stench of the obscene fun-
gus. The divine life of Nature is more wonderful,
more various, more sublime in man than in any
other of her works, and the wisdom that is gained
by commerce with men, as Montaigne and Shakespeare gained it, or with one's own soul among men,
as Dante, is the most delightful, as it is the most
precious, of all. In outward nature it is still man
that interests us, and we care far less for the things
seen than the way in which they are seen by poetic

eyes like Wordsworth's or Thoreau's, and the reflections they cast there. To hear the to-do that
is often made over the simple fact that a man sees
the image of himself in the outward world, one is
reminded of a savage when he for the first time
catches a glimpse of himself in a looking-glass.
" Venerable child of Nature," we are tempted to
say, " to whose science in the invention of the
tobacco-pipe, to whose art in the tattooing of thine
undegenerate hide not yet enslaved by tailors, we
are slowly striving to climb back, the miracle thou
beholdest is sold in my unhappy country for a
shilling ! " If matters go on as they have done,
and everybody must needs blab of all the favors
that have been done him by roadside and river-
brink and woodland walk, as if to kiss and tell
were no longer treachery, it will be a positive re-
freshment to meet a man who is as superbly indifferent to Nature as she is to him. By and by we
shall have John Smith, of No. –12 –12th Street,
advertising that he is not the J. S. who saw a cow-
lily on Thursday last, as he never saw one in his
life, would not see one if he could, and is prepared
to prove an alibi on the day in question.

Solitary communion with Nature does not seem
to have been sanitary or sweetening in its influence
on Thoreau's character. On the contrary, his letters show him more cynical as he grew older.
While he studied with respectful attention the
minks and woodchucks, his neighbors, he looked
with utter contempt on the august drama of destiny
of which his country was the scene, and on which

the curtain had already risen. He was converting
us back to a state of nature " so eloquently," as
Voltaire said of Rousseau, " that he almost persuaded us to go on all fours," while the wiser fates
were making it possible for us to walk erect for the
first time. Had he conversed more with his fellows, his sympathies would have widened with the
assurance that his peculiar genius had more appreciation, and his writings a larger circle of readers,
or at least a warmer one, than he dreamed of.
We have the highest testimony[1] to the natural
sweetness, sincerity, and nobleness of his temper,
and in his books an equally irrefragable one to the
rare quality of his mind. He was not a strong
thinker, but a sensitive feeler. Yet his mind
strikes us as cold and wintry in its purity. A light
snow has fallen everywhere in which he seems to
come on the track of the shier sensations that
would elsewhere leave no trace. We think greater
compression would have done more for his fame.
A feeling of sameness comes over us as we read so
much. Trifles are recorded with an over-minute
punctuality and conscientiousness of detail.   He
registers the state of his personal thermometer thirteen times a day. We cannot help thinking sometimes of the man who

> "Watches, starves, freezes, and sweats
> To learn but catechisms and alphabets
> Of unconcerning things, matters of fact,"

and sometimes of the saying of the Persian poet,

---

[1] Mr. Emerson, in the Biographical Sketch prefixed to the
Excursions.

that "when the owl would boast, he boasts of catching mice at the edge of a hole." We could readily part with some of his affectations. It was well enough for Pythagoras to say, once for all, "When I was Euphorbus at the siege of Troy"; not so well for Thoreau to travesty it into "When I was a shepherd on the plains of Assyria." A naïve thing said over again is anything but naïve. But with every exception, there is no writing comparable with Thoreau's in kind, that is comparable with it in degree where it is best; where it disengages itself, that is, from the tangled roots and dead leaves of a second-hand Orientalism, and runs limpid and smooth and broadening as it runs, a mirror for whatever is grand and lovely in both worlds.

George Sand says neatly, that "Art is not a study of positive reality," (*actuality* were the fitter word,) "but a seeking after ideal truth." It would be doing very inadequate justice to Thoreau if we left it to be inferred that this ideal element did not exist in him, and that too in larger proportion, if less obtrusive, than his nature-worship. He took nature as the mountain-path to an ideal world. If the path wind a good deal, if he record too faithfully every trip over a root, if he botanize somewhat wearisomely, he gives us now and then superb outlooks from some jutting crag, and brings us out at last into an illimitable ether, where the breathing is not difficult for those who have any true touch of the climbing spirit. His shanty-life was a mere impossibility, so far as his own conception of it goes, as an entire independency of mankind. The tub of Diogenes had a sounder bottom. Thoreau's experiment actually presupposed all that complicated civilization which it theoretically abjured. He squatted on another man's land; he borrows an axe; his boards, his nails, his bricks, his mortar, his books, his lamp, his fish-hooks, his plough, his hoe, all turn state's evidence against him as an accomplice in the sin of that artificial civilization which rendered it possible that such a person as Henry D. Thoreau should exist at all. *Magnis tamen excidit ausis.* His aim was a noble and a useful one, in the direction of " plain living and high thinking." It was a practical sermon on Emerson's text that " things are in the saddle and ride mankind," an attempt to solve Carlyle's problem (condensed from Johnson) of " lessening your denominator." His whole life was a rebuke of the waste and aimlessness of our American luxury, which is an abject enslavement to tawdry upholstery. He had " fine translunary things " in him. His better style as a writer is in keeping with the simplicity and purity of his life. We have said that his range was narrow, but to be a master is to be a master. He had caught his English at its living source, among the poets and prose-writers of its best days; his literature was extensive and recondite; his quotations are always nuggets of the purest ore: there are sentences of his as perfect as anything in the language, and thoughts as clearly crystallized; his metaphors and images are always fresh from the soil; he had watched Nature

like a detective who is to go upon the stand; as
we read him, it seems as if all-out-of-doors had
kept a diary and become its own Montaigne; we
look at the landscape as in a Claude Lorraine
glass; compared with his, all other books of similar aim, even White's "Selborne," seem dry as a
country clergyman's meteorological journal in an
old almanac.   He belongs with Donne and Browne
and Novalis; if not with the originally creative
men, with the scarcely smaller class who are peculiar, and whose leaves shed their invisible thought-
seed like ferns.